MW01439019

Hot

This book is
Bethesda Sa
and statistic
real and ba
public figure
circumstanc
All other ch
described ir
enjoyment.

Copyright© 2
ISBN: 978-1-08
eBook ISBN:

For my cousin Joe and my friend Taylor.

PART I: THE PLAYER

Chapter 1

The prospect of a 105-degree day in July was already simmering the black tar on Highway Nine in Northwest Missouri, as the sun was just beginning to peek over the horizon. Alex Santucci was returning to downtown Kansas City from Riss Lake after a rare Monday off in the middle of the baseball season.

Always an early riser, Alex awoke before five thirty on this Tuesday morning, July 10, hoping to sneak out without awaking his girlfriend, Sally Keegan. She inhabited a nice house in the well-maintained Riss Lake section just a mile north of Park University's main campus, where she was now an associate professor in the school of Public Affairs. They met five years ago during a fund-raiser at the president's home on the Park University campus.

Alex started taking graduate courses five years ago, when he turned thirty, at the downtown campus of Park University. The "campus" was actually a building at 911 Main Street, a couple of blocks from his twenty-fifth-floor condo at the famous 909 Walnut Street structure, a thirty-story high-rise built in downtown Kansas City in 1931. A local bank backed the project as the Depression hit the country in 1930. The bank went bankrupt in 1932, so the brand-new building sat empty for three years until the federal government took it over as an office building until 1994, when they moved elsewhere. It stayed vacant until 2000, when some rich Texans bought it and spent sixty million to turn it into a luxury condo building. Now it attracted young professionals, including athletes like Alex, looking to stay in downtown Kansas City.

As his first semester of graduate school was ending, his professor finally realized he had a rich baseball player in his class, so he invited him to a fund-raiser for the Hauptmann School for Public Affairs at Park University.

Then assistant professor Sally Keegan was a greeter at the door when the blond-haired, six-foot, four-inch, 225-pound, Kansas City Crowns third baseman came up the steps at the school president's home. Alex, half-Swedish and half-Italian, was immediately drawn to Dr. Keegan's jet-black hair and blue eyes. Her Catholic schoolgirl looks and radiant smile had Alex's knees buckling like facing a Nolan Ryan curveball.

They were both overwhelmingly drawn to each other and had to limit their time together because they might run off and get married. Both had careers to consider before studying the subject of matrimony. Now, after five years of love and passion, final exams were coming up.

• • •

Alex sped through the quiet streets of north Kansas City, crossing the Heart of America Bridge over the Missouri River as he entered downtown Kansas City. He loved being alone in silence with the streets before sunrise. After a couple of turns, he continued south on Grand Boulevard and then west on Eleventh Street and north on Walnut Street, bringing him to his garage next to his condo building. The roof of the six-story garage also doubled as a beautiful tree-lined green space for boccie ball or games of catch, with a long trellis- covered area for lounging or afternoon naps.

The Kansas City Crowns were opening a six-game home stand heading into the All-Star break. Starting in a week, he would have four days off, for his soon-to-be thirty-six-year-old body, to enjoy some rest. Unfortunately, his mom at home in Bethesda, Maryland, and the rest of his extended family had different expectations for those four days.

Entering his modest, two-thousand square-foot condo, he picked up the paper in front of his door and started his favorite morning ritual, reading the *Washington Daily's* final- edition sports page, which he had specially delivered each day by 5:45 am CDT. Growing up in the suburbs of the nation's capital, devouring the *Daily* was a better stimulant than a cup of coffee. His dad said being an early riser was in his DNA. Even before he could read, Alex, in his pajamas, would grab the morning paper off the front porch and run to his parents' bed so his dad could read the sports page to him.

His first memories were stories about the Washington Redskins in 1981 under then first-year coach, Joe Gibbs. His dad, Gene Santucci, taught him to study the statistics on quarterbacks, running backs, and wide receivers. His father's favorite football player growing up was Charley Taylor.

Alex's preferred stories were about the 1967 NFL season when the great Sonny Jurgensen was the quarterback and the Redskins had the first, second, and fourth leading receivers in the league. Hall of Fame wide receiver Bobby Mitchell and tight end Jerry Smith joined Taylor to make up that great trio of receivers. Alex chose Art Monk as his favorite player in 1981 because his dad said he was the second coming of Charley Taylor!

The Redskins ended that season eight and eight after starting with a zero and five record. They were dominating teams by the end of the season with a young offensive line. Gene predicted they would be very tough to beat in the 1982 season. Of course, the Redskins proved Gene right by winning the Super Bowl at the end of that season. Alex trusted his dad to be exact because Gene was brilliant and seemed to be always right about everything, even sometimes predicting the future. But he was wrong about one thing: being his real dad!

Chapter 2

The condo was nicely furnished with mainly IKEA furniture, a style between the DC suburbs and living in the Midwest. It was very Scandinavian, like half of his bloodline, and very similar to the home he grew up in the 1980s. The DC suburbs were invaded in the 1970s by Scan Furniture and other similar stores. It was solid and efficient furniture made mostly out of teak wood. Then imagine if Wal-Mart developed the Scandinavian furniture idea into a low-cost, efficient enterprise. That would be the present-day IKEA.

When he signed his six-year, fifty five million dollar contract with the Kansas City Crowns before the 2007 season, Alex decided that a downtown Kansas City condo would be a comfortable spot to call home. He had a wonderful northern view of the Missouri River as it traveled east across the State of Missouri, flowing eventually into the Mississippi.

He enjoyed being able to walk to restaurants, shops, and markets north of the downtown Business District toward the Missouri or the recently finished Power and Light District just a few blocks to the south. His condo was large enough for some of his family to visit but small enough to take care of by himself.

He liked playing in the Midwest since he was drafted out of Princeton University by the Minnesota Gemini. They had been the original Washington baseball franchise but moved to the Twin Cities in 1961. They were replaced in DC by an expansion franchise named the Washington Senators. In his family, Minnesota was less hated than the Texas franchise because baseball continued in DC in the 1960s until the Senators were moved to Texas after the 1971 season

Clark Griffith was the long-time, loyal owner of the original Washington Franchise from 1912 to 1955. He left the team to his nephew, Calvin Griffith, who started running the club in the early fifties. Clark had been a manager and Hall of Fame pitcher for over twenty years combined when he took over the struggling Washington franchise. He loved DC and would have likely integrated the team if he had been healthy through the 1950s. It would be kind to say that his nephew Calvin was not a baseball man and even kinder to say he was not comfortable with the demographic makeup of Washington, DC, in the 1950s. He took the money and moved his team to the American heartland of the Twin Cities.

    Bob Short was the owner that bought the Senators in 1969 and moved them to Texas after the 1971 season. He also moved the NBA Lakers from his hometown, Minnesota, to Los Angeles in 1960. After hiring Ted Williams to manage the Senators in 1969, they went eighty-six and seventy-six as attendance doubled at RFK Stadium. After the 1970 season, Short traded four young, talented players to Detroit for the washed-up Denny McLain. With the help of those players, Detroit won the AL East in 1972. McLain went on to lose twenty-two games in 1971 as the team nosedived to a last place finish. Attendance fell as ticket prices became the highest in the American League to pay for McLain's salary. By August of 1971, Bob Short made a deal for ten million dollars to move the team to Texas with approval from Major League Baseball and Commissioner Bowie Kuhn, a DC native. In less than two seasons, Washington had gone from great excitement about a winning baseball team and a future pennant to bad baseball and then absolutely no baseball. Losing the Senators to Texas left Washington without a baseball team for thirty-three seasons.

Chapter 3

Alex's birth mother, Leah Raines, was a devout Seventh-Day Adventist of Swedish descent. She was a beautiful- blonde singer-songwriter who married at age nineteen. Phillip Finelli, the birth father, was twenty-two and had just graduated Princeton.

Phillip and Leah had been dating for a year and were madly in love, but the relationship was doomed to failure because their heritage and religions did not have a chance to grow together. After breaking up in June 1975, Leah found comfort from a former college boyfriend and married the fellow Adventist in the fall of 1975. After three months of marriage in Tennessee, she became miserable and depressed. She was away from her family, while her husband drove a truck and was gone for days at a time. Her passion for music had been disrupted, and there was no love in the relationship.

Leah came home to Potomac, Maryland, for Thanksgiving and never went back. She saw Phillip in early December and through the Christmas holiday of 1975. Their passion for each other finally had a chance to be consummated. They spent a very intimate month together, which became a very special memory, but soon their cultural differences were too much to overcome. Leah decided to leave both her marriage and Phillip by going to Denver to pursue a Christian singing career. She wrote a song, "Torn between Two Lovers," and discovered she was pregnant a month later.

After much discussion during the following months, Leah and Phillip agreed that family friends, the Santucci's, were a wonderful option for adoption. They were very close friends with Phillip's parents and lived in Bethesda. In addition, Gene was Italian, and Laura was Swedish. They had five older children that were all over ten.

Gene was a successful practicing doctor and researcher in Bethesda, and Laura was a stay-at-home mom. They were very excited and thrilled to have a newborn baby. Phillip and Leah were relieved. They knew they were not ready to be parents, but

Leah was comforted by the fact that Phillip would always know their son was well taken care of and maybe someday be a part of his life.

When Leah came to terms with giving up her son for adoption, after carrying him for nine months and giving birth to him on August 8, 1976, she also accepted that she might never see her son again.

Phillip was thirty-eight, married five years, and a new father when he met his son, Alex, in December 1991. Four months after his adoptive father, Gene died, Alex and his adoptive mom, Laura, were invited to the Finelli house for a small get-together with the family to meet their new baby, Grace.

Alex's half-sister was a month old, born during an incredible few days in November when Hurricane Grace ripped up the Chesapeake Bay. Even though they were named separately, the storm almost deposited the named infant into the Patuxent River. Phillip had come out of a courthouse in Upper Marlboro, Maryland, running toward his wife, Carol, who was carrying their newly born infant across a small bridge. The wind, blowing veraciously, gusted to hurricane strength and knocked Carol over with the baby into the air, twirling like a spinning top and then slowly toward the river below. After an amazing broad jump onto the bridge and a miraculous dive into the river, Phillip caught the baby safely. Pummeling into the water, Phillip's massive paws covered the baby's face as they both received a good baptism. Great hands ran through the Finelli family and in Alex's DNA!

Alex and Phillip immediately became enamored of each other. Their first meeting was like joining the same team, after living apart in parallel universes. They fit perfectly together. They knew each other's questions and most of the answers. Alex wanted to hear every story about his birth father's childhood, especially in his love for baseball.

Phillip was eight when he went to his first baseball game. It was at Griffith Stadium in Washington, DC, on August 11 against the greatest team of all time, the 1961 New York Yankees. He told the story of how Roger Maris hit his forty- third homerun to tie the game at one. The big crowd of mostly Yankee fans was silenced in the eighth inning by Nats catcher Gene Green's grand slam to win the game 5-1.

His birth father had tears in his eyes as he related the story, recalling the ride in his Uncle Ernesto's 1947 Nash, passing the smells of the Wonder Bread Bakery on Seventh Street, eating the hot dogs, seeing the beautiful emerald- green grass as he entered the stadium. These were memories that become a part of Alex's life.

He told other stories about Frank Howard's monster homeruns at RFK, Mickey Mantle hitting homeruns with one healthy leg, Frank Robinson hitting two grand slams off the upper deck at RFK, meeting Ted Williams as a ball boy in 1971, and fetching peanuts for a washed-up thirty-one- game winner Denny McLain.

His father Philip knew everything about Walter Johnson, the player, the person, the high school, and how he won the 1924 World Series, pitching four scoreless innings in relief. A famous ground ball hit a tiny rock in the third base line and jumped over third base into the left field corner as the winning run scored in extra innings.

Those memories reinforced everything Alex wanted to do and feel forever-play baseball, hit homeruns, win the World Series in and for DC. All in the memory of Johnson, "The Big Train"!

• • •

Despite being drafted by professional baseball out of high school, Alex always knew he would go to college. He was a good student, a strong reader, and loved to keep up with current events. When he was in high school, he spent a lot of Sundays at his Grandma and Grandpa Finelli's house in Parkwood, watching shows like *Meet The Press* and *The*

McLaughlin Group with family members. His father and grandfather would love to argue politics at lunch and watch football or golf in the afternoon.

He learned that his grandfather had to forgo playing football for Princeton in the fall of 1930 because the Depression made it impossible to afford. Alex became obsessed with the idea of going to Princeton. He loved the campus and that area of New Jersey, just twenty minutes from his grandfather's hometown of Raritan.

Alex was a star at Princeton while getting his degree in business and economics in three years. He was drafted in the first round by the Minnesota Gemini. Alex signed immediately and played almost a full year in the minors after graduating from Princeton in 1998. He went from A to AA baseball by the end of the season. After a fabulous spring training to start the 1999 season, he became the starting third baseman on Opening Day at the age of twenty-two. He signed an extension during his first year of arbitration that kept him in Minnesota for eight seasons. Those last two seasons he really found his power stroke and hit 70 Hrs with 220 RBIs in the friendly confines of the Twin Cities Dome.

At the end of the 2006 season, Minnesota did not extend a contract offer. They offered arbitration but mainly to get draft choices if Alex became a free agent. He hoped that the new Washington Presidents (nicknamed POTUS after President of the United States) would sign him, but the timing was not right. They had already drafted Bruce Hammersly out of the University of Virginia to be their centerpiece player. Building from the draft and not free agency was the right direction for the new ownership in 2006.

Kansas City Crown's owner, Larry Garson, had contacted Alex immediately after the season and made him an offer he could not refuse. Alex had played there many times since they were in the same division. It was a comfortable fit with a future great friend, so he agreed to a contract with the Crowns during his first visit there.

Chapter 4

He opened the curtains in the living room to let the sunrise gently flow onto the white-stained, maple floors. His northern view of the Missouri River from the twenty-fifth floor was very calming in the morning. The smell of coffee emanating from his IKEA-furnished kitchen alerted his senses as he carried in the *Daily* and laid out the sports page on the counter. He poured a cup of coffee with his right hand as he unfolded the paper with his left. Tilting the coffee cup ever so slowly into his mouth to taste that first sip of fever rich flavor, he scanned the headlines.

Bruce Hammersly Injured, POTUS Drop sixth In a Row!

A freak injury on a back-handed stop in the hole at shortstop would put the POTUS All-Star shortstop on the disabled list for four to eight weeks. It was a play incumbent to all infielders. Usually a quick, full-out dive was instinctively taken to the right, getting full extension, but sometimes the ball would spin back toward the infielder. In the middle of the dive, an adjustment would be made by the glove hand to follow the ball coming into the body. Unfortunately, the right hand was forgotten about, and the wrist would land not fully extended. It would impact the smooth, compacted, clay dirt facing down, carrying the full weight of the ballplayer.

The replay on *ESPN* was played over and over again on the morning highlights as Alex turned on the television. The video looked devastating, but miraculously the wrist was not broken. MRIs would determine the extent of the damage.

Veteran Jerry Gonzalez would take over at shortstop. He had been currently playing third base. A great fielder and a solid hitter, Gonzales could play fulltime at shortstop without a loss defensively. The big hole would be created at third base, both offensively and defensively. Hammersly was having an MVP season, voted as the starter at shortstop for the All-Star game. He was hitting .308 with 24 Hrs and 62 RBIs. The POTUS owners knew they would be big numbers to replace.

The Presidents had dropped out of first place in the NL East during the losing streak. Their young and talented pitching staff, along with the slugging of Hammersly, had created an excitement in DC about baseball not witnessed since the return of baseball in 2005 and their last winning season as the Senators in 1969. Their last pennant race was in 1945 when they ended up in second place, and their last pennant win was in 1933.

Pitcher Walter Johnson was the last great Washington baseball player, who led them to their only World Series Win in 1924. The next great player discovered by the Presidents would be Bruce Hammersly. Would he lead them to their next World Series win? It did not appear likely this season.

Alex quickly turned off the television and returned to his *Washington Daily* newspaper to read about the upcoming professional football league season.

• • •

The Washington professional football team was renamed the Potomacs (pronounced Po-to-MACS), a decade after owner Burton Parker bought the team in the late nineties. Besides being the river that borders the western side of Washington, DC, the name Potomacs refers to a tribe of Indians called the Patawomecks that resided in the area before John Smith first roamed up the unnamed river in 1608. Parker felt the name change was more respectful to the Indian heritage in the area. Besides, he figured the famous helmet logo would not have to change.

The Potomacs, referred to as "The Macs," still received a great deal of coverage even during the off-season. With training camp approaching, there were stories all over the front page about the new rookie class and the best free agents signed. Their new African American rookie quarterback Marcus McNeil III was the number one pick in the entire draft and was being hailed as the new messiah for DC. His new nickname was "Big Mac III."

On the bottom of the sports front page, Ron Roswell had a headline in his article that shouted, "POTUS Needs a Power Bat." The veteran sportswriter was in his fifth decade of covering DC sports. His true love was baseball, and like many DC natives, he had survived thirty-three seasons without a team and was short on patience for a winning season. "Ownership has to loosen up the purse strings and get a power hitting replacement for Hammersly. Relying on the POTUS bench will not do the job to stay in the pennant race!"

Alex then felt a tingle that shocked the bottom of his spine as he read the next line.

"A veteran like Alex Santucci would fit like a glove in the POTUS lineup."

Roswell went on to the fill in details about the salary hit this year and free agency, but he finished the article with a plea from a youngster sounding like he wanted his dad to come home. "Santucci is a hometown boy ready for a Cinderella story. Of course, that means it will never happen! Well, it's fun to dream every once in a while."

Alex put down the paper and knew it was time for some breakfast. He needed something in his stomach to help digest what he had just read. Then he had a game to get ready for at home in front of the Crowns fans. He was a professional ballplayer and a well-paid one. Batting .262 with 8 Hrs and 38 RBIs was not good enough for him.

The last year of his contract was paying him fifteen million dollars with a no-trade clause. He wanted to finish the year playing his best. Reading about something that was never going to happen would not put some power back in his swing.

Chapter 5

Alex grew up on Johnson Avenue in Bethesda in a house on the same block and down the street from the Walter Johnson House, a community landmark on Old Georgetown Road across from the National Institutes of Health (NIH). Basically Alex grew up in The Big Train's Backyard, because the Santucci house was on Johnson's original property. Johnson lived at that house from 1925 to 1936.

The 8.5-acre farm had chickens, fox hounds, an apple orchard, and, most importantly, a baseball diamond where the local kids played baseball, with some supervision from The Big Train, no doubt. The property was subdivided into forty-three lots in 1937 when Johnson moved to another farm in Germantown, about twenty miles north of Bethesda.

Walter Johnson was the greatest Washington baseball player of all time. Arguably the greatest Major League pitcher of all time, he pitched for twenty-one seasons for the Washington Nationals franchise, from 1907 to 1927. He won 417 games along with 110 shutouts and a lifetime 2.17 ERA for a team that was near last place for the first decade of his career.

His achievements were a statistical dream, as he won over 20 games, ten years in a row, including back-to-back years of 33 and 36 wins. His ERA was under 2.00 for seven straight years. He went 38 and 26 in 1-0 games. On September 4, 5, and 7 in 1908, he shut out the New York Highlanders in all three games. He batted .283 and .433 for the two pennant-winning years of 1924 and 1925 in 210 at bats. He was tied for ninth as a pitcher in career homeruns with twenty-three, along with a .235 career batting average.

His great athleticism was matched by his character. He

was friends with hated players like Ty Cobb and respected players like Babe Ruth. The press referred to him as "The Big Swede" even though his ancestors were from the British Isles.

Along with owner Clark Griffith, Johnson made DC into a winning franchise, finally going to the World Series in 1924 and 1925, beating out the great New York Yankee teams with Babe Ruth and Lou Gehrig for the American League pennant. He managed the Nationals for four years, 1929 to 1932, served as a Montgomery County Commissioner and a Bethesda community leader until his death in 1946.

When Walter Johnson High School was opened in 1958, about a mile north of his former Bethesda farm on Old Georgetown Road, it became the first school in the country named after a baseball player. It continues today to be one of the top public high schools in the country in SAT scores and Merit Scholars.

Alex Santucci went to Walter Johnson High School 1n Bethesda wanting to emulate The Big Train. Johnson received this nickname during his playing days because the players complained that the ball he threw was too hard to see but could be heard whistling by the plate like a big train. A bronze plaque honoring Walter Johnson in his throwing motion found a home at the high school after having been transferred from Griffith Stadium after it closed in 1961.

Alex liked to watch football but loved to play baseball. He played in the backyards of houses up and the down the block that were a part of Johnson's original land. When he was a kid, he would cross the backyards of the few properties between his yard and the old Walter Johnson house with his glove and ball in hand. He learned to scale, then jump, and eventually hurdle these fences with ease.

When he entered Big Train's Backyard, he would look up to the house and envision Walter Johnson himself appearing at the back door, waving him on up to the house. Alex would find his favorite spot in the backyard, believing it was a pitching mound, and start throwing fastballs like Walter Johnson or, other times, play the infield behind the make-believe Big Train pitching. In reality, the house was unoccupied for years during his youth, making the backyard an oasis for his fantasies.

When he was ten years old, he went to a one hundredth birthday celebration at Walter Johnson High School with his adopted dad. They showed a film of The Big Train pitching, and it was a style he never forgot. Alex would throw his fastball, whipping his arm around in a three-quarter fashion similar to The Big Train's delivery. Sometimes he would imagine striking out a dozen batters in a row or other times just field the ball coming off the wall like a grounder in the infield. He would smoothly pick up the ball and make the throw back off the brick part of the house, beating the runner in his mind by a step. He could simulate throwing a whole game off the bricks if he had time. He loved to pitch, but sometimes fielding, and certainly hitting was even more fun.

He learned to hit homeruns during the summers of his youth at the recreation center down the street at Ayrlawn Elementary School. The school had a stretch of fields surrounded by trees that seem to go forever. The summer heat in July would become so intolerable that playing ball on the dusty fields was filthy torture. Instead, kids adopted the shaded big blacktop as their homerun park for softball.

The rectangular-shaped, asphalt top had some basketball courts and markings for games on it. It was encircled by a ten-foot fence to keep balls from going in to the ditch in front of the woods. With shade from the trees in the morning this asphalt playing surface was ideal for softball games until the sun starting baking it before lunchtime.

The left field line to the fence was 110 feet, center field was 130 feet, and the short right field fence was only 80 feet and just a double. Kids received ridicule for hitting it to right field. Only lefties were given a reprieve, but no credits were given for homeruns to fight field.

Games would start as early as 7:00 a.m., two hours before the official opening of the recreation center. Only three kids a side were needed to play; four a side was the maximum. As the morning went on, foursomes would challenge the winning side after three innings of play. The only individual statistic that was kept was homeruns.

The chalk board inside the kindergarten room, which was used as the Ping-Pong room for the Recreation Center, was updated daily with the top ten homerun leaders. You had to be fourteen to touch the chalkboard. Usually, sixteen was the oldest age for a kid to play homerun softball.

During the week, regular softball games were played on the ball fields with full teams and coaches against other recreation centers. Kids ten and under were on the Pee Wee team, ages eleven to twelve were Midgets, thirteen to fourteen were Juniors, and fifteen to seventeen were Seniors.

Generally, juniors dominated homerun softball, but occasionally a Senior would show up to pound out a few bell ringers to just keep his name on the board. Alex started to watch homerun softball during the summer when he turned seven. He would tail one of the Junior age kids in the neighborhood going to the black-top early in the morning and started to bring his mitt with him. A twenty-year-old, Maury Wills signature glove fit him like an oversized first baseman's mitt. It was donated by his birth father, Phillip, unknown to him at the time. After a few weeks of watching, he finally convinced the big kids to let him be the permanent catcher behind home plate. His first experience playing catcher landed him in the emergency room. The story was told that Alex, not knowing where to stand behind the plate but wanting to impress the older boys, crouched a little too close behind the first batter. Unfortunately, he stood up as the batter took his swing, which extended his stomach upward and caught the back end of a homerun swing. He received thirty stitches for the wound and a stomachache for the next few weeks, but it did not keep him from becoming the permanent catcher at age seven.

Apparently, he learned quickly to avoid a batter's swing. As the catcher behind the plate, he spent hours examining the strokes of the hitters trying to yank it over the fence. The pull hitters were the most successful, as they seemed to magically snag any ball on the inside half of the plate with their bat and, with a snap of their wrists, deposit the ball over the fence. Line drive hitters never seemed to produce enough height for the ball. They would smash the ball into the fence or on a bounce. Alex noticed that snapping or turning your wrists at the time of impact with the ball could make a huge difference in whether the ball was hit on the ground, lined into the fence, or lofted deep for a homerun. He would think of a spinning top on a desk keeping its plane: eventually before the top slowed, it would tilt to the side like it was taking off. That was the angle and the timing of the swing he developed.

Homerun hitting was an art with techniques as varied as the difference between watercolor and oil painting. Some strokes caused high arcing fly balls that landed a few feet over the fence. Other swings were like hitting a bad two-iron golf shot that quickly hooked into the woods. The most majestic strokes were the sweet sounds of hitting the bull's-eye of the bat that fired the ball like a liner to short, but then the ball would have a second stage like a rocket and would launch, cascading skyward, long gone over the fence.

Alex would learn to envision every type of swing. Sometimes after catching, he would head up to Big Train's backyard with just his bat and practice his homerun swing. He could close his eyes and visualize The Big Train's windup and bring his hands down, leading his stroke into an uppercut position, and snap his wrist at the exact moment of impact. After thousands of swings, he imagined hearing the sweet sound of the bull's-eye of the bat hitting the ball, launching it into orbit. Like watching a spinning top in his fantasy world slowing to the right angle, Alex was shaping his homerun stroke!

Chapter 6

Alex was first told about being adopted when he entered kindergarten at age five. His parents wanted the news to come first from them. His adoption was not a secret in the neighborhood and was celebrated by friends and neighbors.

His adoptive dad, Dr. Gene Sanucci, was getting notoriety for his blood research work at NIH. He made his first presentation in November 1982 and traveled quite a few times over the next year. His father's traveling and the news about his adoption seemed not to make much difference in his life until he got to the asphalt jungle during the summer of 1983. Kids would call him Dopter, a hybrid of adopted and doctor. For the younger kids it was sign of affection to be nicknamed. By the middle of the summer of 1983, he was accepted as an intern in the school of homerun hitting. On his seventh birthday on August 8, the last day of the summer recreation center, he hit his first homerun. He remembered telling his dad on the phone, because he was away at a conference, how it barely cleared the fence down the left field line.

At age ten, Alex was playing in the Midget League and leading the chalkboard in the homerun league race. His Little League baseball coach told him to stop playing homerun softball, but there was no chance of that. Baseball seemed fairly easy to him. The ball came in straighter and went out farther. The softball they played was fast pitch without a windup. Sometimes the ball came in straight like a fastball, other times it came in slow like a hanging curveball. His last season of homerun softball was at age thirteen. At midseason, he had so many homeruns they limited his at bats to once a week because they had lost so many balls into the woods.

The WJ High School coach had known about Alex for

four years when he came out his freshmen year for the first fall practices in 1990. Alex had scholarship offers from every private school in the area to play baseball. As much as he liked hitting homeruns, Alex was inspired to play by the legend of Walter Johnson and his mastery as a pitcher. He always remembered throwing a fastball as hard as he could against the bricks of the Johnson house. In his mind, playing for Walter Johnson High School was part of his destiny!

Gene made time in his schedule to come to the three weeks of fall practices in 1990. His three older sons, Kenneth, Franklin, and John, then in their early thirties, were outdoorsmen, not ballplayers. All three were practicing medical doctors scattered across the country. At that time only one of his two daughters, Nina, lived within thirty miles. She was twenty-eight and newly married, while his youngest daughter, Linda, at twenty-four, was in law school in Boston. All of his children had gone to private Catholic school. He was enjoying the new experience of being a parent of a public school kid, especially at Walter Johnson High School.

At fourteen, Alex was six-feet, two-inches, 180 pounds. The football coach was in agony that Alex found no interest in playing football on Friday nights. He loved to watch football practice and ended up throwing passes with the receivers to help out with the passing game. The coach was all for it, hoping it would entice him to play. Soon the word was out in the halls of WJ that fall baseball practice was the place to be. Usually, the coach would have to beg for full participation of his players, much less having classmates out to watch. First it would be watching Alex throw batting practice. Alex could never throw easy; even his warm-up throws were hard. He could be ready to throw in a game in eight to ten pitches. The coach soon learned that he had to limit Alex's pitches to fifty or less because no one was making contact other than fouling it off. Then there would be the fireworks caused by Alex and his bat. By the end of the three-week fall practice, over two hundred kids were watching Alex taking batting practice. He would bat with the last group, with ten of his teammates over the fence, mitts ready, to catch the homeruns.

Gene enjoyed the high school baseball season in the spring of 1991 like a fine wine. The pitching, the hitting, the fielding, the umpire calls, were all very intoxicating. He watched Alex pitch, hit, and field his position at third base like a future professional. He was a natural at the hot corner, making all the plays with precision and grace. As a freshman, he made the All-County team, slugging homeruns in half of the games. By the end of the playoffs, college and professional scouts were sprinkled in the jammed bleachers.

The sixty-two year old doctor marveled at the strength of the forearms and hands of his adopted son. He knew that a great deal of it came from his best friend, Guy Finelli, a first generation Italian soon to be eighty. He was Alex's real grandfather and Phillip's father. Gene and Guy had met in the early 1970s as members of the Italian Club in Bethesda. Gene, an only child, had finally met a mentor, or more like an older brother. Guy Finelli's athletic career was almost mythical. He had become the only player in New Jersey high school history to play only one season of football and make the All-State team. At five-feet, five-inches, 135 pounds, and with very poor eyesight, he played guard and led his team to an undefeated, unscored upon state title in 1929. Guy used his enormous upper body strength in his shoulders, forearms, and hands to fend off much bigger players to make tackle after tackle. Working labor every day after school until his senior year made him into a football player with tiger-like quickness and lion-type strength.

Gene kept Guy informed of his grandson's progress, relaying the play-by-play of Alex's at bats and defensive plays in the field. Guy never asked to watch or meet his grandson because he felt it was in appropriate. He hoped some day they would meet with a powerful handshake before he passed from this world. His hands would pass along the values of his immigrant parents, Geraldo and Philomena, both gentle and loving people who had been pillars of strength in his life.

• • •

Near the end of the summer season of baseball in the August heat of 1991, Gene watched his adopted son play for the last time. Alex, who just had turned fifteen, slugged a three-run, eighth-inning homerun that won the game. Gene hugged his son as the game ended and drove him home, discussing all the aspects of the game, especially the homerun.

Feeling sluggish from being in the heat, Gene was also too excited to go to sleep. He sat at the kitchen table while Alex ate like a teenager in from the wild. They were watching the local sports station reporting on the Redskins training camp. Alex worried the Redskins season would be full of disappointment but Gene assured him that it would be their best ever. "They might go undefeated." Gene said, "They have all the talent to go to the Super Bowl."

Alex looked puzzled but felt assured by his father's confidence. Gene walked behind his son, hugged him, and said in his ear, "Who knows, next year the Redskins win the Super Bowl and WJ wins the state championship!" His dad as usual was right!

Gene went to bed smiling. As he closed his eyes, he saw a beautiful night with Alex running, throwing, and hitting on the emerald-green grass of the baseball diamond. He fell into a dream about the power and happiness of his son's future. As he followed the ball explode off Alex's bat, he was suddenly above the field watching this line drive become a rocket toward the heavens. Along with it went his glorious soul from a great life on Earth.

Chapter 7

It was still early enough in the morning for a run even though the heat was just starting to simmer the city like a pan getting ready to fry a steak. After some oatmeal and an apple, Alex headed out north on Walnut, then east on Ninth Street to north on Grand Boulevard, which took him under Interstate 70 toward the Missouri River.

As the sweat was already pouring out of his body, he went along Route 9, the bridge he had crossed over just an hour ago. He finally got to Richard L. Barkley Park, which had open the bridge he had crossed over just an hour ago. He finally got to Richard L. Barkley Park, which had open boiling morning.

Alex loved to run. As a kid, most of his life involved running or sprinting. Whether it was in block tag during summertime before dusk, invading the enemy in capture the flag, or evading tacklers in maul ball during recess at school -flying above the ground, over the hills, around the trees, jumping the fences, feeling the wind in your face was life at its best. He developed sprinter calves, running back thighs, and a backside with its own ledge.

After running for almost an hour, Alex finally found a shady spot in the park with a view of the river. During his run he had visualized a thousand times his batting swing. It was better for him to visualize it after watching film of his at-bats. Visualizing the pitch and meeting the ball was his key to his power stroke, a technique he started as a kid playing in Big Train's backyard.

In the past few years, he had tried to open his stroke by hitting the ball to right field. He had been a dead pull-hitter for years but had been having less success in the past two seasons hitting homeruns. He had averaged 32 Hrs for the first four years of his contract but dropped to 24 last year and only 8 so far this year. His career mark was 368 homeruns, 14 short of the great Washington Senator, Frank

Howard (Hondo) at 382. The calmness of the river in the distance helped him focus as he closed his eyes. His first thought was of the gentle giant and his ferocious homerun swing.

Hondo was a hero to his birth Dad, Phillip. In the sixties, Hondo woke up the baseball fans in DC with his seven years of upper deck blasts at RFK Stadium. He averaged 34 Hrs and 96 RBIs in DC during a pitching-dominated era. 1968 was the year of the pitcher. They changed the height of the mound and the strike zone in 1969 because pitching was so dominate. Denny McLain won thirty-one games, and Bob Gibson had an ERA of 1.12, breaking the record of 1.14 set by Johnson in 1913. The American League as a whole batted a combined, all-time low of .231 and had only one player, Carl Yastrzemski, crack the .300 mark, hitting .301 for the 1968 batting title, the lowest winning average in the history of baseball.

It was under those pitching-dominated circumstances that Frank Howard put on a power display that rivals DC's fireworks display on the Fourth of July. For a special week in May 1968, baseball witnessed "The Streak" that gave the nation hope that things would return to normal again. After weeks of riots in cities across the country in April, Federal troops lined the streets of DC to keep riots from spreading after the great African American leader, Martin Luther King, had been slain. In a city that was over 70 percent African American, which gave false incentive for one baseball owner to leave with his team in 1960, and home to a football team that was the last to be integrated in the NFL, a giant of a man gave pause to the pain.

At six-foot, eight-inches and 295 pounds, Frank Howard would today still look like a monster at the plate. "The Streak" started on a Sunday, May 12, in Detroit against Mickey Lolich, the hero of the 1968 World Series who won three games in the fall classic, including the last win coming against Bob Gibson in a seventh-game showdown on two days' rest. The first homerun came in the sixth inning, followed by another in the seventh inning. After an off day on May 13, Hondo hit two more homeruns on May 14 and another on May 15. After another off day, he hit two more homeruns on May 16, then another one on May 17. The final two homeruns on May 18 were again against Mickey Lolich. Finally Tiger pitcher Earl Wilson stopped the bludgeoning of the baseball on May 19. Hondo went on the hit three more homeruns in the next ten games for a total of thirteen homeruns in sixteen games, also a record.

"The Streak" blasted through in six games and took only twenty at bats. Ten homeruns were launched during the power display, never accomplished before or since during the 137 years of professional baseball. The final casualties were 13 hits in twenty at bats for a .650 average, with 17 RBIs and 44 total bases.

Howard ended the 1968 season with a league-leading 44Hrs, a .552 slugging percentage, 330 total bases, 106 RBIs and a respectable .274 average. The 1969 season was even better with 48Hrs, 111 RBIs and a .296 average.

Phillip had given Alex all the details of that time period: the war in Vietnam, the years of protests, LBJ bowing out of the presidential race, the terrible shock of the assassinations of Martin Luther King and Robert Kennedy. He remembered as a teenager driving through DC with armed military on the corners throughout the city. Listening to "The Streak" on the radio every day and night lifted his spirits and gave hope and pause to a city enduring desperation.

Alex awoke from the visualization and memories. As the blood returned to his brain while resting under the tree, Alex could now see the swing change he would make. He practiced using his hands extending down, bringing down his right shoulder to make his swing plane almost like a slightly tilted Ferris wheel instead of a horizontal carousel ride. Only men of steel, like Hondo and Babe Ruth, could hit homeruns consistently with horizontal swings. That is why Hondo hit line shots that grazed an infielder's head and still banged against the mezzanine at RFK for a homerun.

Occasionally Alex could get the entire sweet spot of the bat on the entire fat part of the baseball and rocket it out to center or right field for a homerun, but it was not his strength as a power hitter. Alex concluded that they were paying him to be a power hitter, not a spray hitter. Soon he would unlock that swing and find power to all parts of a ballpark.

• • •

Alex ran home, showered, finished reading the paper, and called his mom about his plans for next week. She was thrilled to hear he would be flying on Monday to spend three or four days in Bethesda. Oddly enough the Mid-Atlantic area was being spared this triple-digit heat suffocating the Midwest. He hoped that would last through next week.

He also called his father, Phillip, to plan out a visit. They caught up on news about his half-sister, Grace, and his half-brother, Guy, named after their grandfather. Grace was working during the summer at NASA as an aerospace engineer student. She was entering her senior year at North Carolina State in Raleigh. Grace was very petite at barely five-foot, two-inches, just short of her mother, Carol. She had that dark Italian skin and black hair with movie star looks like a Gina Lollobrigida, but she was surrounded most of the time by engineering nerds who had no idea how to approach her for a date. Grace was always busy, so silly things like that did not concern her. She was excited to see Alex whenever he visited DC. In the spring, she quietly started dating a special guy in Raleigh and was hopeful that Alex would meet him soon.

Guy was getting ready for college football practice in August and the season in the fall. He was just as big as Alex, with similar skills. After a great senior year at Walter Johnson, he chose the University of Maryland for his playing career. He was a star quarterback and safety in high school but was ready to start at safety as a freshman. He had gigantic hands, great speed, and could throw the ball a mile.

Last summer, Alex flew Grace and Guy out to Kansas City for a long weekend to visit. They met Sally and came to a weekend of games. They both put on uniforms for batting practice before a Friday night game and met all the players. Grace drew the most attention, as she consistently smoked line drives through the infield. She had been a varsity third baseman for the Girls high school softball team and knew how to swing a bat and field grounders. Many of the younger ballplayers gave her lots of tips on how to hit a fastball. She seemed to have no trouble with curve-balls either.

Guy never played high school baseball but had spent enough time in batting cages with Alex to perfect a swing. The bat looked tiny in his hands, as he easily roped line drives to right center. Alex was throwing batting practice and told Guy to turn on the next two inside pitches. He fired down and in, and Guy got his hands through, propelling two monster drives down the line over the bleachers out of the stadium. "That was enough showing off!" Alex thought.

Chapter 8

The Acura TL easily accelerated to merge onto Interstate 70 for the ten-minute ride to the Harry S. Truman Sports Complex. Alex cruised in his sporty vehicle while still feeling a buzz from his long run. His mind was envisioning his swing propelling toward the incoming spinning baseball on the inner half of the plate. He had been getting jammed lately because the advance scouts were reporting, "likes to extend his arms, can't get hands through on inside pitch, out in front on breaking pitches." He was ready to make the adjustments. It might take a few games, but he now figured out the game plan.

Alex was meeting with the team physician at two o'clock to go over tests taken last week on his liver and kidney function. These were routine tests taken every three months to judge the effect, if any, on his anti-inflammatory and pain medication. For pain relief he had tried ice treatments, various NSAIDs including; ibuprofen, aspirin and naproxen, as well as acetaminophen, and shots of ketorolac. All had some level of effectiveness for Alex over the years.

Though Alex had avoided major injury in his career, playing through minor injuries were commonplace for him. He worked lightly with weights throughout his career, relying on isometrics, stretching through yoga, swimming, and running to keep up his endurance, strength, and flexibility.

At their last appointment, the team physician introduced the idea of a new medication to limit his intake of anti-inflammatory drugs. His last lab tests after spring training in April showed some stress on his liver, kidneys, and pancreas. A substance called blood urea nitrogen, or BUN, a waste product formed in the liver and filtered out of the blood by the kidneys, had been pushing the upper limit of twenty milligrams.

A consistent higher mark would indicate liver or kidney disease. In addition, his calcium levels were running near the high mark of eleven milligrams, meaning the possibility of the onset of pancreatitis or a neurological disorder.

Alex walked into the doctor's office near the locker room in the baseball stadium at the sports complex. Dr. Henry Walton handed him the test results and then explained the tests associated with kidney, liver, and pancreatic function. He explained they were probably elevated due to his ibuprofen and acetaminophen use and his continued long- distance running.

Dr. Walton was a Harvard-educated physician with the Center for Sports Medicine located in Kansas City. He had started the center over twenty years ago before centers throughout the country became the place to treat athletic injuries. He was a blood specialist as well, who had done a fellowship at NIH in the early eighties. While there, he served under Dr. Santucci, who had been a leader in blood disorders research at that time. He was thrilled to work with Alex and had formed a close bond with him during his time in Kansas City.

Henry took the results from Alex's hands. "I want you to start on Duloxetine and try it for three weeks." He explained the origins of the drug and its encouraging results for arthritis and general pain. It was originally developed as a depression medication for elderly patients. The research showed it lower pain in patients by raising serotonin and norepinephrine levels in the brain.

Alex looked up, a bit startled, and joked about getting old. "So will I need a walker any time soon?"

Henry, seeking a soothing tone but wanting to clarify, said, "I am impressed with the results on the elderly, but you, on the other hand, are too active!" He paused for effect and continued. "It wouldn't hurt to cut back on the running as well."

Alex smiled at the advice. He listened to further instructions, which included stopping the ibuprofen and acetaminophen. Dr. Walton wanted him to start with ten milligrams of Duloxetine for ten days and then increase to twenty milligrams for another ten days. If it was effective, the pain would subside, with little or no side effects. Dr. Walton entered into his electronic medical records (EMR) to check with Alex after ten days. At the least, he thought it would give his kidney and liver a little time off from flushing the NSAIDs and acetaminophen out of his system. He gave him sample doses for the next three weeks

Duloxetine was a medication being advertised on television as the new answer for pain relief. Elsa Lilac was urging people to ask their doctors for information. It was introduced in 2004 as a medication to treat major-depressive-disorder. Somewhere along the line, a researcher noticed patients complained of less pain as well while on the drug. It worked chemically by changing levels of serotonin and norepinephrine in the brain. Norepinephrine, along with other hormones, is released by the adrenal gland in the body. It is located on the top of both kidneys under the pancreas.

Everyone is familiar with the term adrenaline rush. For teenagers through college age kids, it means a good party or the use of drugs. Otherwise, it is usually associated with getting excited, angry, or being scared. There are tall tales about people being able to pick up a car or breaking down a door to save a life.

But some-times these hormones are at levels too low for the body to function properly, usually causing depression. This medication was intended to lower pain by raising those hormones in the brain without taxing the liver, kidneys or pancreas. Alex was interested in something that worked and not so much in the details.

Dr. Walton prescribed a sonogram test for Alex's internal organs, including his liver, kidneys, and pancreas, to get a picture to go along with his medical tests. Rare as it was, he wanted to rule out a tumor sitting on an organ, causing dysfunction as well as other issues involving how blood flowed from organ to organ. He was not concerned, just being thorough. Getting the results by Monday along with a week on a new medicine would make it clear if they were going in the right direction. He could not be careful enough for his prized patient. Looking for something that should not be there was what he go the paid to do.

• • •

Sally Keegan pulled into the Crowns player's parking lot at 4:05 hoping to catch Alex before batting practice. She loved to watch baseball and knew her way around the stadium. She caught the eye of a security man as she leaned out the window of her Honda CRV entering the player's lot. She smiled at him as he got on the radio to tell the locker room attendant that "a prized package had arrived for Mr. Santucci."

Professor Keegan was escorted to the visitor's lounge to wait. Alex walked in wearing a T-shirt and shorts. His wavy blond locks hung on his muscular neck and broad shoulders; his large paws carried a bat in one hand and some flowers in the other. He sat next to Sally in her pretty dress, nestling up to her with his massive thighs and large backside. Surrounding her neck with his left arm, he presented the red roses with his left hand. She held back a gasp but smelled the roses as she clutched them with both hands. Alex whispered in her ear. "I'm working on my swing right now, so I can show it off to you later, maybe by the seventh inning!" He kissed her neck and bolted up from her side. "See you after the game at my place?

Sally looked up from the roses and answered. "If you get lucky and show me something with that swing by the seventh. I don't want to wait around all night!"

Getting ready for a 7:05 p.m. game meant starting around 4:00 with swings in the underground batting cages, medical attention, and getting dressed. Batting practice for the home team started around 5:00. Most players had already hit for a half hour with the inside batting machines. Hitting outdoors, comparatively, was like being on the playground. There was lots of joking, hanging out, catching up with friends, and visiting friends from the opposing team. Alex hit with the last crew. He liked to get his fielding work done first. It was pure joy taking grounders at third base. The grass was perfect; even the heat and humidity did little to ebb his delight. He liked no more than fifteen swings in the outdoor batting cage. Getting used to batting practice fastballs was not his favorite thing. He did his catching up with teammates in the locker room and did not believe in fraternizing with the opponent until after the game. Spending at least thirty minutes before each game signing autographs gave him the right feel for the game. He relished smelling the popcorn and the hot dogs, seeing the smiles and T-shirts of the fans, hearing the stories and names for the autographs, listening to the names of towns where fans were from and how far they traveled to watch the game. This tradition went back 112 years for the Junior Circuit, 137 years for the Senior Circuit and before that in small towns across America before, during, and after the Civil War.

This night on the diamond, he sensed the baseball heroes of the game as they had traveled across the country from town to town. One of those heroes was born across the Kansas River in Humbelt, Kansas, and traveled with his family in the 1890s to California to work on a farm. In 1902 as the American League was starting its second year, Walter Johnson went on the road at age fourteen to play minor

league baseball in small towns up and down the California coast. Five years later he was pitching in Idaho, when a Washington Nationals scout came to see him and was so impressed he sent a telegram to then Manager Joe Cantillon to take a cross-country train to see him. What he saw was the smoke of a legendary 105-mph fastball coming from The Big Train! The Nats manager was unsuccessful convincing the eighteen-year-old to come to an eastern city. The next year Nats catcher Cliff Blankenship was sent to Idaho and successfully convinced Walter Johnson that DC would not corrupt him. Blankenship and nineteen-year-old Walter Johnson rode a train across the country to the nation's capital to pitch in the major leagues. In the summer of 1907, Walter Johnson himself stood in Griffith Stadium before his first game, perhaps feeling the same emotion Alex was feeling now as he walked across a similar infield over a century later, ready for another night of baseball. Maybe Johnson even though what Alex was thinking,
"What a wonderful dream I have achieved!"

• • •

Kansas City was six games under 500 entering this home stand. They were facing three games against the Seattle Shoreman and three games against the Oakland Bays. The Crowns were a young team with young pitching- usually not a good combination. Lately though, their pitching had kept them in games, while their hitting was not up to par.

Alex had been dropped to sixth in the lineup because his power numbers were down. Additionally, their three young power-hitting outfielders, Marty Miller in left, Felix Mantilla in center, and the best of the young studs, Homer Watson in Right, were developing some chemistry at the power spots of three, four, and five in the lineup.

Alex enjoyed mentoring this young trio full of energy and great fan appeal. It was his idea to drop himself down in the lineup and put those three back-to-back-to-back. Manager Pete Bowers had been Alex's third manager in the majors and second at Kansas City. He arrived three years ago to make Kansas City a competitive ball club with a great future. Santucci had been a part of the last big free agent splash in 2007 that the Crowns had taken, which included a big contract for a veteran pitcher who lasted three years before retiring with arm trouble. They were now committed to drafting young talent and developing them through the minor league system. Tonight they were facing the young ace of the Seattle staff, Rolando Lamas, nicknamed "Marvelous." He was a Cy Young winner in 2010 and threw high heat.

Alex came up in the second inning against him with one out and nobody on. His game plan was simple: look for a fastball inside, otherwise foul it off or let it go by. On a 2-2 count, he saw the spin on the baseball was downward and heading outside, an unhittable pitch, but also strike three. Alex headed to the dugout, pleased he did not swing, but noticed the crowd was not happy with the outcome.

In the fourth and fifth innings, Alex got pitches he wanted and doubled each time down the third base line, scoring in the fourth inning and knocking in two in the fifth. He caught each pitch up in the strike zone, with his hands snapping quickly over top. He hooked the baseball over the third base bag in the fourth inning and then on a line into the corner in the fifth.

The game was tied at three in the eighth inning, when he was kneeling in the on deck circle watching Mantilla take a four-pitch walk to lead off the inning. He recognized the relief pitcher as an old teammate of his from his Minnesota days, Wayne Cauley, a pure sinker ball pitcher. Just what he was looking for tonight!

Alex caught sight of Sally leaning forward in her seat about ten rows back across the way behind the Seattle dugout. With her hair pulled back in a ponytail and glasses on because of her near-sightedness, she was in professor mode. She liked some-times to be away from other players' girlfriends or wives when she wanted to focus on Alex and his swing. Her serious look while clapping and cheering Alex's name brought a smile to his face. Sometimes he just knew when he had all the cards in the poker game.

The crowd of 21,257 was quietly awaking to the thought of a winning rally. His previous two at-bats had brought back the crowd from their earlier displeasure. Clapping and responding to the announced rally calls, the volume was rising. Cauley worked from the stretch and threw over to first twice, making the crowd antsy and louder. His first two pitches to Alex were down and away for balls. Alex stepped out of the batter's box and visualized the left field line. He knew he needed his hands out in front of the ball to ride it deep. He was ready for down and in. Like an Amtrak Train on time, the ball came whistling down the tracks, spinning down but not enough for Wayne Cauley to be happy!

It was a matter of fair or foul, not how far. Alex held the bat, took a step toward first, and listened as the quiet of the crowd become loud, then louder and soon deafening as he rounded first and the fireworks went off. As he touched home plate, he winked at Professor Keegan in her glasses, knowing he was already lucky tonight.

• • •

He stayed on the field after the game for over an hour doing interviews and then signing autographs with fans. The night was cooling down and so was his racing mind that seemed to be in overdrive all night. Finally the usher thinned out the crowd and Alex went to the dugout where most of his teammates were still waiting for him. He soaked in all of the "old man jokes" and "getting detention from the professor" jabs.

He made his way over to Seattle's dressing room and found Wayne Cauley, who was getting treatment for his arm, and thanked him for the stinking sinker he left up for him.

Wayne responded after sipping from at least his fifth beer. "It looked like you needed a present, considering the year you're having!" Cauley took another long gulp and threw a perfect strike with the finished beer can into the recycle trash bin a good twenty feet away. "I hope you're not making that young schoolgirl who was in the stands yelling for Alex to hit a homer, wait for you!" Wayne was laughing and smiling the whole time. Alex waved on his way out and said, "No, she's back at the condo. Still cheering for me and making dinner!"

As he headed to the parking lot, he thought this night was the best of baseball, and he was sure proud and thrilled to be a part of it. When he got home that night and got on the elevator, he felt like he was going to the top of the world.

Sally had done some shopping and was starting dinner as advertised at the condo when Alex arrived. She was aroused with energy and looked happy taking care of her baseball hero! "That was something! You must feel great and pleased with yourself, even though you were an inning late!"

"I guess I missed my chance, darn it!" As Alex laid down his bag, he moved quickly to surround Sally as she attended to the chicken in the pan, hoping she would reconsider.

"Well, maybe I can make an exception to the deadline in this case since you did try your hardest," she replied as she turned just in time throw her arms around his neck. She kissed him gently several times, looking at his brown Italian eyes and that Swedish blond hair. She thought to herself, "I am deeply in love with this guy, boy, am I in trouble."

During dinner and throughout the rest of the night, they talked like never before. Sally was a night owl, so staying up until 2:00 a.m. was nothing unusual. Alex was usually in bed by midnight on game nights but otherwise earlier, usually by ten. But tonight something was special; he wanted her to travel east with him next week to see his family. She had met his family several times but never stayed there. She felt awkward at first talking about it, but Alex had such vigor describing how fun it would be that she became comfortable about it. Her schedule was clear: no lectures to give, no tests or papers to grade. She toasted,

"DC, here we come!"

• • •

The rest of the home stand was full of wins: six in a row to get to .500 at the All-Star break for the first time in five years. Kansas City was only three games out of a wild card spot and five and half out of the division lead. The crowds averaged thirty thousand fans for the Oakland Series, usually a tough draw in July. Alex had found his power stroke. He was twelve for twenty-one with 4 doubles, 2 Hrs and 7 RBIs in the two, three-game series.

Manager Pete Bowers came into the dressing room on Sunday afternoon after the last game of the home stand against Oakland and called the team together. He was a man of few words in meetings with the whole team. His strength was connecting with players on an individual basis. He cleared his voiced like he was going to do his best Nick Nolte imitation. "You kids and even the old men like Santucci played some real baseball this past week. It's been a pleasure to watch." He found a cup near where he was standing and spit out some juice from the chew he was still working on. "Now stay out of trouble, get some rest, see your families-that doesn't mean the strippers in Vegas, Miller and Mantilla!" Staring at two of his young out field, he paused to let the laughing calm down. "Now let's hear it for Homer Watson. He's going to the All-Star game, and I'll be there to keep an eye on him!"

Ironically, the eighty-third All-Star game was being held

in Kansas City, while Alex was fleeing the town and would miss the festivities. He had been six times in his career: the last three years with Minnesota and the first three years with Kansas City. Before the season started, he thought how special it might be to get back to the All-Star game before the home fans. His hot week of hitting had gotten his average up to .285 with 10 HR's and 45 RBI's but too late to be noticed by Texas All-Star Manager Joe Jefferson.

After a few more spits into the cup, Manager Pete Bowers finished his talk to his team with some reminders of when to return on Thursday for the upcoming road trip to the East Coast for nine games. When he finished, Pete slowly worked his way over to Alex's stall and told him to come by his office on his way out.

Alex got his stuff and walked into the manager's office.

Pete said to sit down next to his desk. "Alex, you are best third basemen I ever coached! You should be on that All-Star team! I tried to convince Joe, but I think the politics from the league office pushed the young kid on him. I feel...very bad about it. You deserve that chance before the home crowd." Pete held back his voice for a moment as his throat closed up with emotion.

Alex was clearly touched by the gesture and put his hand on Pete's shoulder and then shook his hand. "Those kids are the future of this franchise. I'm excited for Homer. Besides, I'm bringing Sally east for a visit with the family."

Relieved, Pete wiped his nose and stood up and nodded his head in agreement. Still having trouble finding his voice, finally he cleared it. "Well, look... Alex, enjoy yourself with that sweet gal and just meet us Friday in Baltimore. No reason to come back here.

Alex appreciated the accommodation and the gesture. He nodded and left for his car to meet his "gal" for a week off.

• • •

It had been a magical week in Kansas City. With such wonderful energy in downtown, Sally and Alex went out to dinner Sunday night in the city. They walked out from the condo and walked the streets, hand in hand, to the local Italian eatery, Anthony's Restaurant and Lounge at 701 Grand Boulevard.

A nice crowd was inside as his favorite waitress, Rosemary, led them to a table in the back corner. They enjoyed seeing the happy faces and waves as they walked through the room. Rosemary was about to turn eighty-one but looked sixty-five. She was a lifetime Kansas City gal and half Italian. She loved to dote on Alex and his gal, Sally. In her twenty-seven years at Anthony's, she had never seen such a handsome couple, she would say.

All night they were interrupted by fans for autographs. With pleasure, Alex obliged and later mingled with the crowd at the bar. Sally normally felt uneasy being around all this attention given to a baseball star, but this felt different. It was real. She felt a part of it, and a real part of his life.

• • •

They headed to DC on Monday morning and landed at National Airport just across the Potomac from the capital city at 10:03 a.m. Alex drove the rental car on the familiar drive up George Washington Parkway, past Arlington Cemetery and the Lincoln Memorial, under the Kennedy Center and beside the Watergate. Eventually they headed out of the city following the Potomac to the Capital Beltway east to Old Georgetown Road, then south a mile to Johnson Avenue. Then it was just a right turn, with a wave to the WJ house, and four houses to his real home

Chapter 9

Alex's mom, Laura, was getting the house ready for a special lunch for the three of them. She was now seventy-two, looking as elegant as an elderly Princess Grace or as motherly as the pearl wearing actress Barbara Billingsly playing the mom on *Leave it to Beaver.* The smell of French onion soup, Alex's favorite, was tantalizing their senses as the handsome couple walked into the dining room to view the table set with the Santucci china. Laura had been a widow for almost twenty-one years but never missed a beat in taking care of her six children and now a dozen grandchildren.

The trio spent several hours catching up on stories about the family and on Sally's new associate professorship appointment at Park University. Alex tried hard not to be the spotlight of conversation. He was thrilled to hear all the news about his adoptive family. Not answering questions about his career was a great relief.

He felt safe in this comfortable and now grand house on Johnson Avenue. When Alex was young, the Santucci added a huge addition in the back that took up half of the backyard. There were now six bedrooms and six baths for family to visit at any time. Alex and Sally would stay there tonight in separate bedrooms to see Mom through the morning on Tuesday. He had a three-night surprise planned for Sally at the Westin Hotel in the west end of DC next to Georgetown. Alex was looking forward to exploring Georgetown with Sally and maybe a nice drive into the Shenandoah Valley for an afternoon.

After a wonderful and warm lunch with Laura, Alex took Sally for a ride to his birth father's neighborhood in Kensington. Phillip Pinelli grew up in Parkwood across from Rock Creek Park. He had just finished a remodeling of his parent's house and moved Carol and the kids in the previous summer. Phillip's mom, Rose, who was Alex's birth grandmother, had died a couple of years ago at the wonderful age of ninety-six, surviving her husband by seventeen years. Phillip bought the house from his older brothers to move back into the neighborhood. His oldest brother, Anthony, lived only a few blocks away on Brookfield Drive.

    Alex and Sally drove up Parkwood drive to check out his grandparents' former house. It was quite a little complex considering its roots as a three-bedroom rambler on a 7,500-square-foot lot. An impressive five-foot stone wall surrounded the corner property on a hill for almost fifty years. With some recent maintenance, the two hundred tons of stone looked perfect. Grandfather Guy Pinelli had hired some Italian stone masons who were in this country working on the National Shrine and National Cathedral projects in DC in the sixties. They had been recommended by his friend Tony Campitelli, who had built a large number of Parkwood houses, including the Pinelli house. The masons also worked on two stone fireplaces in the house and a stone-and-brick mini-house used as a shed in the backyard. Guy Pinelli wanted his home to be remembered for a couple of hundred years!

    They had paid a whopping thirteen-thousand dollars in 1951 to move from their apartment in Anacostia, just across the Anacostia River from the future RPK Stadium. He put three-quarter-inch solid wood paneling on almost every wall in the house, from simple pine in the basement to walnut, cherry, oak, ash, and mahogany on the main floor. He was committed to wood on the walls and the floors, except for the flagstone in the basement and family room extension. After the kids grew, he made a patio of the entire backyard using brick and flagstone. He then used more stone for the back retaining wall, the fountain, and the garden area. It cut down on the lawn mowing.

    Alex walked up the side steps from Parkwood Drive into the backyard and then onto the patio to the side-door entrance. He saw a note from Phillip saying he went down to Anthony's house for a walk with his brother in the park through the Puller Road entrance and for them to come find them. Alex smiled and headed back to the car. To his left he saw the beautiful garden area surrounded by a two-foot stone wall sectioned off into four perfect rectangles. A glossy white St. Francis of Assisi statue stood in the middle holding a small dish of water for the birds. He paused for a moment to look closely at the garden he visited, often as a teenager. A rush of emotions came upon him as he pictured his two short grandparents with wide-brimmed hats working in the dirt of the garden, planting and weeding. They both turned and paused, shaking dirt off their gloves, opening their arms with wide smiles, inviting him to come for a hug. Unexpectedly tears came rushing out. He looked down hoping to calm himself while still remembering and feeling the comfort of being at Phillip's home. He continued back to the car, glanced back over for another vision of the garden, and this time he saw a lovely variety of peppers-red, yellow, green, small and large. Wiping away the tears as he walked down the steps, he felt comfort in knowing that the soil in the garden contained his roots.

• • •

Sally noticed that Alex had wet cheeks as he returned to the car. She waited until he clicked his seat belt, gently touching his arm.

"Alex, are you okay? Is there something wrong?"

"No, nothing is wrong just a happy memory or two."

She had known Alex for five years. It was unlike him to show emotion in such a flash. He never got too high or too low. Even during his grandmother's funeral two years ago, he never cried. He was comfortable around emotion, but it was usually her that was crying or crazy over things. He was wonderful about keeping her grounded during her peaks and valleys. There was something in the past week or so that was different about Alex. He was more loving and happier toward her, while playing baseball with a different verve. His intensity about life in general had picked up, and she was noticing.

Alex shared with Sally his garden vision. He talked about knowing his grandfather for only two years but the gift of knowing his grandmother for nineteen years. He remembered that she was so consistent in her love of life and family. He spoke softly about her lasting presence in his life, wondering if that would last forever.

They pulled into the dead end of Puller Road that led into Puller Park. As they walked down the field, he saw his father and uncle on the path near the creek. He waved and they turned to meet them near some benches facing back toward the entrance. Sally and Alex, hand in hand, strolled through this hallowed ground that was so much a part of his baseball talent.

His uncle Anthony was the greatest homerun hitter ever to come through these parts. Only horrible knee injuries in high school curtailed his baseball career, a career started in Puller Park hitting a softball.

Before Beach Drive was put through this part of Rock Creek in the mid-1960s, Puller Park attracted all the kids from the newly built Kensington neighborhoods of the 1950s. It was a natural ballpark for the kids even before the County Parks Department realized it could use a backstop and an infield cut out. With the creek behind home plate and running along the right field line, Puller was also a homerun park for pull hitters to left field. Trees and boulders lined right and center fields, with fences in left and left-center from the backyards of the houses that had the misfortune of backing up to Puller Park.

The left field line was about 225 feet with a Crosley Field-type hill and a white cross wood fence on top, making it about fifteen feet high for a ball to clear it. The roof of the house in the yard beyond the fence was about 300 feet away. The fence line headed farther away from the left field foul line as it headed to center field like in Yankee Stadium.

It was at least 350 feet to hit the boulders in center field, an improbable poke with a softball and a wooden bat. The center field boulders were called "The Monuments" because they reminded everyone of Yankee Stadium with Mickey Mantle roaming in center field.

Anthony learned to pull homeruns down the line in the late 1950s and early 1960s through his high school years. There was always a game after school during the spring and summer. Even a young priest from nearby Holy Redeemer Catholic Church would come and play with the kids. Everyone wanted a chance to hit the house in left field.

Sometimes with only a handful of kids, they would play games like "work up" and "line ball". With as few as four kids you could have a game. Learning to hit the ball to the left field or left center was very important because in most games you were out after a few foul balls if you hit to center or right fields. When the rarity of a left-handed batter showed up, the pitcher would walk over to the third base line to pitch so the batter could hit to left field.

When Phillip was in a stroller to about twelve years old, he would come to watch and then play in Puller Park. His big brother had Henry Aaron-type wrists that would just whip the bat and lash the ball down the line. On the right pitch, he would get the ball in the air enough to hook it into the backyard in left field. As he got to the end of high school, he started to hit Titanic high drives that would land on the house's roof in left field. He even put a couple in the monument section of center field; unfortunately in line-ball they were foul balls!

In the mid-1960s, after Puller Park was cut in half because of Beach Drive, Phillip and his friends brought these games to the blacktop during the summers at the Parkwood Elementary. Eventually the popularity of this summer game made its way into the 1970s, to Ayrlawn Elementary in Bethesda. The adopted Alex Santucci learned his craft from a game played thirty years earlier by his family that he would not meet until 1991!

•••

    Alex and his thoughts were swimming in memories as he listened to the stories his father and uncle traded about Puller Park. Sally sat between Phillip and Uncle Anthony as they heaped attention on Alex's favorite lady and made fun of Alex. Alex sat across from them with his legs propped up, enjoying the roasting he was getting from three of his favorite people. The tales of the games played in the park were getting taller as Alex laughed with tears. Characters from the past, almost mythical in nature, were woven into great neighborhood lore.

    Sally was holding her stomach and bent over in laughter, when she suddenly straightened up and noticed a black limousine pull in next to their rental car. Two large men stepped out and opened the door for a shorter man in a suit. The man quickly headed down toward the benches, waving in the distance.

    As they got closer, Phillip noticed the well-dressed gentleman in a blue suit with cufflinks. He pointed him out to Alex as he stared with amazement.

    "Oh my God is that Burton Parker, the owner of the Potomacs?"

    "I hear Alex was out here hanging out with family." Burton Parker quickly shouted as he got within thirty feet. He went to Anthony and Phillip Pinelli and shook their hands and bowed to Sally as she reached out her hand to shake. "I am so sorry for interrupting your family time. It is great to meet you."

    Alex pulled his six-foot, four-inch frame off of the bench and stood to meet the celebrity. They had met several times before at Super Bowls, All-Stars games, and fund-raisers. Burton Parker had traveled to Kansas City for a fund-raiser that Sally hosted at the university for tornado victims several years ago. Alex suggested she call him, and without hesitation he accepted and brought along several high-price donors. The man had endless energy, and he loved the spotlight and sports. Alex was always excited to see Mr. Parker, being a big Potomacs fan even though the last decade had been tough on the burgundy and gold.

"Alex what a pleasure it is to see you and Sally again. This must be your dad and uncle. I can see the resemblance! Listen, Alex, everyone has been trying to get a hold of you. Your phone must be off."

Alex quickly remembered their phones had been quiet since the plane ride. It did seem like a lovely morning without any phone calls!

Before Alex could answer, Burton Parker stepped back and announced, "I got some great news. Alex has been named to the All-Star team! Miguel Estanza woke up with back spasms and can't move, so Joe Jefferson named you as the replacement!"

Alex was confused by the news and was speechless. He looked at Sally, who was smiling with sudden tears of joy, as he tried to clear his throat to say something.

"Sounds crazy, but I know the Kansas City owner, Larry Gar-son. So, when your manager couldn't get a hold of you, he called me because he knew I was coming to KC for the homerun derby tonight and the All-Star game tomorrow. Whew, am I ready to eat some beef in KC or what! Ha, ha, ha! Anyway, I was in DC of course, and with a little detective work, well, it was your lovely mom who gave me the lead to Kensington. She is a special lady. She said you guys had a wonderful lunch and I could catch you in Parkwood. What a great family you have!" He turned and took a couple of steps away and then turned back. "Too bad you all are WJ Alumni! Ha, ha, ha!"

Burton Parker had gone to Woodward High School, built literally less than a mile from Walter Johnson High School in the late 1960s. It closed in the mid 1980s for lack of baby boomer children and money in the Montgomery County budget. Unfortunately, the rich folks at Woodward made the newly merged Walter Johnson change their nickname from the Spartans to the Wildcats, which was the Woodward mascot. Everybody from the county, except for the losing side of the few wealthy Woodward backers, wondered what was so special about Wildcats. It was probably the most used mascot in history. Some suggested Big Train, Senators, or something related to baseball. Everyone ever associated with WJ hated it.

Burton composed himself from his awkward joke and waved his arms toward the car. "Listen, sorry about that. But seriously, they want you there by, oh, four p.m. My plane is at the airpark in Gaithersburg, about twenty minutes away. You can all come! Really, everything is on me."

Sally knew Alex's apprehension about leaving the family, so she jumped in. "Oh, Alex, this would be great. We can come back during the Baltimore series. Everyone will understand. It's in KC, for God's sake!"

Phillip and Anthony jumped in with positive responses and agreed to take the trip to Kansas City. Alex was still overwhelmed and nodded in agreement but then thought of his mother.

Burton Parker read the body language and added, "Listen, we will swing by your mom's house and get your stuff, see if she wants to go. Then we'll meet in Gaithersburg and make it by four o'clock."

Alex nodded and finally spoke, looking at Burton Parker first, then to Sally.

"Wow. Thank you so much. This is...quite a surprise. Thank you for your effort. Sally, this is crazy. Are you all sure you want to do this?"

She nodded in agreement, and off in the limousine they went. His uncle and father would meet them at the airport after a quick dash home. The family was going to be together, flying on *BigMacl* and going to a home crowd in KC!

Chapter 10

Burton Parker had a car service pick up his entourage at the Charles B. Wheeler Downtown Airport just across the Missouri River from downtown Kansas City. He dropped Alex at the sports complex around four thirty and took the rest of the crew out to feast on prime rib at Jess and Jim's Steak House, south of Kansas City. Mr. Parker knew the owner and called ahead for a large table in the back. It was not fancy, but the prime rib was worthy of the Midwest. After the outstanding meal, the limousine traveled up Brooklyn Avenue, just past Eighteenth Street, to pick up barbeque at the world famous Arthur Bryant's to enjoy later in the suite at the stadium.

They then traveled to Eighteenth and Vine to tour the Negro Leagues and American Jazz museums. They spent a great hour there, especially enjoying the Kansas City Monarchs and Homestead Grays teams represented by wonderful memorabilia and great films about the players. All-time greats like Cool "Papa" Bell, Buck Leonard, and Josh Gibson played in Griffith Stadium in Washington for the Grays, winning Negro League pennants for seven consecutive years. They were stunned to learn in 1931 that Homestead Grays star Josh Gibson hit seventy homeruns, and the Grays went 138 and 6 for the season.

Alex was met at the security fence by some workers at the stadium, Crown Field. They were smiling with pride, knowing one of their own would be joining the young kid Homer Watson for the All-Star game. His favorite security worker, Hal Baker, met Alex at the stadium entrance and walked him down the hallways to the press room filled with reporters. Hal was known as "The Dough Man" because of his name and his love of pizza as well as the Michelin-sized tire of weight he carried around his waist. Hal was a nonstop talker and loved Alex because he actually listened to his diatribes and always slipped him twenty bucks. Tonight, it was a C-note!

    Alex believed in tipping. In 1990, when he was fourteen, he saw the movie *My Blue Heaven* and loved the line by Steve Martin's character, "It's not tipping I believe in. It's over-tipping."

• • •

    The adrenaline rush of walking into a room of seventy-five reporters, bright lights, and cameras was something that never unsettled Alex. Usually, his even demeanor allowed him to focus on the task at hand, public relations. He understood the process and found it interesting at times. He was a professional and realized the job of reporters and very rarely took anything they reported personally. He was well liked by the media, including print, radio, and television. He usually made himself available for comments before and after games. But as he sat down, he realized the emotions of the morning, the laughter of the day, and the blur of the afternoon were still swirling in his head like a Midwest tornado looking to touch down somewhere in his brain. An emotional reaction was about to be stirred up by this force; which one was not clear right now to Alex. He stepped up to the microphone like heading into the batting box.

    The first question was a fastball but a little inside.

    "Do you think you deserve to be here?" asked a Saint Louis reporter who covered mostly the National League.

    "It's an honor to be asked to be here. I guess they thought I was asleep in my condo and could just roll out of bed to get here." Laughter swept through the crowd. "I was the closest infielder with a glove available!"

    A Kansas City reporter in the front row jumped up and threw him a slow pitch softball. "Alex, you have played your guts out for six years for this franchise. How does it feel to be here in front of the KC fans?"

Suddenly the Midwest tornado swirling in his head touched down in his soul and to the emotion of the morning, spending time with his mother, sensing his grandparents in the garden, and touching hands so intimately with Sally. He started to talk, but his throat closed up quickly. Stalling for a moment, he pulled on his All-Star cap, hoping to settle his emotions and speak with some eloquence. "This is something very special to me. The fans deserve this game. The ownership has rebuilt this team during my six years here, and my teammate, Homer Watson, represents that young talent." Alex was hoping that would quiet his emotions and those types of questions, but the next question dug deeper, like a hanging curveball ready to be crushed.

Veteran *Washington Daily* baseball reporter Ron Roswell had the information about the entourage that came out to Kansas City with Alex. He wanted to get Alex to tell his story. "Alex, you have your family here, flown out with you on *Big Mac I*. Does that make getting into the game important to you?"

A quiet settled over the room as Alex collected his thoughts. Suddenly he felt tears running down his face. Seconds seemed like minutes as Alex thought of that peaceful garden, he saw this morning. Feeling the presence of those who had worked so hard to put him in this place, he thought of his adopted father, Gene, whom he had never grieved for. In a way he was replaced by his birth father, Phillip, who was dedicated to his son that he gave up for adoption. It was all so powerful and confusing, and for the first time in his life, these feelings were swirling around in his head. He gladly accepted a handkerchief from his favorite "Dough Man," Hal Baker, who had tears in his eyes. Alex wiped his face and felt calm for the first time since this morning.

"I spent this morning with my mom and then saw my grandparent's house, then hung out with my father and uncle. It was like heaven. Then Mr. Parker graciously spent his valuable time hunting me down to get me here. To have all these people care for me is very humbling. Hopefully, I will get a chance tomorrow night to thank the KC fans. It would be an honor to get on the field tomorrow and play for them. Any player would want that, but I understand that I am the last guy named to this team, so winning is the most important thing. Home team advantage for the World Series! I'm almost thirty-six, and this is a young man's game. Manager Jefferson honored me by selecting me to wear a KC uniform in an All-Star game in Kansas City. That is enough for me. Winning the game is more important than me playing!"

Ron Roswell had been standing the whole time, listening to this soulful response by a remarkable man. He had never heard such a real statement from a ballplayer. With the rest of the reporters quiet, Ron responded, "I hope you do get in the game; it would be a pleasure to watch, Alex, thanks for your time." Like the pope giving a blessing, Ron walked up to Alex and shook his hand. All the reporters put away their notes and followed Ron's lead, going up to Alex, wishing him well, asking some background tidbits, especially traveling on *Big MacI*.

The circus was now officially in town, and Alex had been the first act. As he got up to leave the room with many of the reporters trailing him in the hallway, he wondered if he would be in the final act of the KC All-Star Show!

• • •

Dr. Henry Walton was in his office at the stadium, looking over some medical records of his Kansas City Crown players. In addition to his regular duties, today he was heading a staff of medical professionals to oversee the greatest baseball talent on earth. He had just received the sonogram results from last week on Alex Santucci. The results were confusing to him. There seemed to be a spot on his pancreas that was not supposed to be there. It was near his adrenal gland, which bridged both kidneys. Many times, in his experience, these tests showed false positives that were shadows from other organs or vascular growths on tissue around the organs. His instincts told him it would turn out to be normal, but he would order an MRI for Alex Santucci soon after the All-Star break, just to follow up. He reviewed his notes from their last appointment and noticed the dosage on the new pain medication, Duloxetine, was set to increase to 20 mg soon. He would use this as an excuse to contact Alex about his reaction to the medication so far, to remind him about increasing the dosage, and, most importantly, to set up an appointment for an MRI on his pancreas. He would tell Alex the MRI test was a routine follow up to the sonogram and lab results. Nothing unusual, he would say, positive that he was right.

• • •

Alex Santucci escaped the press room and headed down to the inside batting cages for some swings to clear his head. The cages were empty. It gave him solitary time to release some energy. The ball machine could be set to pure fastballs or curves. He would start with fastballs and switch to curves. He loved being able to read the spin of the ball coming out of the pitcher's hand. It was his greatest talent. When he started in the majors at age twenty-two, he had 20/15 vision. When he was tested two years ago, his vision had become 20/20, still excellent but not as special as the previous ten years. Since he started the new medication ten days ago, he wondered if his vision had become more acute. He was definitely more comfortable seeing the spin of the ball.

His batting stroke felt smooth and easy. Alex used a

very heavy thirty-six-ounce bat with a thick handle. It was contrary to what every batting coach would recommend these days, but for Alex it helped him develop great power from his compact swing. His mechanics were quick and simple to the ball with no hitches or leg lifting. He tapped the plate as he set his feet in the batter's box, then settled the bat on his shoulder, standing tall as the pitcher got his sign from the catcher. As the pitcher started his windup or got into the stretch, Alex would extend the bat straight back with his wrists cocked forward, bending at the waist and knees. Alex, at six foot four, had a stature similar to Bob Allison, but his stance was similar to Hall of Fame slugger Harmon "The Killer" Killebrew; both players were Washington Senators before being hijacked to Minnesota in 1961. They led Minnesota along with ex-Senators, Jim Kaat, Camilo Pascual, Earl Battey, Don Mincher, and Zollo Versalles, to the World Series in 1965.

Alex learned to use heavy wood bats to hit softballs when he was seven and was crushing the ball by the time he was ten years old. He hated metal bats but was forced to use them when they became the norm in high school and college baseball. During summers, between years of college, he played in several wooden bat baseball leagues. It reminded him of how much he loved the sound and feel of a wooden bat on a baseball.

Rarely did Alex break a bat during batting practice or a game. His thick-handled bats allowed him to power balls off the handle that would normally shatter most new bats used by players these days. The question was, could an older player keep up bat speed with a heavier bat? For a year and a half, pitchers had been having success keeping his slugging numbers down. This past week things had changed for Alex. He felt reenergized, free of pain, and was seeing the ball better. The medication was working. He knew the dosage change was coming. In another ten days his body should be totally adjusted to the medication.

• • •

The head trainer, Roland Harper, knocked on Dr. Walton's office to remind him of a meeting of medical personnel for the homerun derby at six o'clock. "The Press room was quite a scene, Dr. Walton. Our boy Alex sure had them speechless!" Roland proudly reported.

"You saw Alex?"

"Yes, sir, it was a show worth watching."

"Is he still here?"

"He went down to the batting cages to let off some stress, I think."

Confused, Dr. Walton thanked Roland for the update on Alex and excused himself to find him. "We'll catch up at the meeting. I have to see Alex for a minute. You say there was quite a scene?"

Yes, but Alex, I think, was just feeling some emotion about playing in the All-Star game before the home crowd. It was special to see someone be so honest about his feelings."

Henry Walton had never seen Alex emotional in his long experience of knowing the Santucci's. He was curious to meet with Alex.

• • •

Alex finished up his last swing and closed his eyes to see his mastery of his universe. His hands were feeling alive, his wrists were flexing like he was fifteen and could swing all day, and his forearms had plenty of strength left after 150 swings, which was five times his normal session. As Alex headed to the locker room for a shower and to meet some players, Dr. Walton caught him in the hallway.

"Alex, congratulations, this is so exciting! How are you doing?"

"Thanks Dr. Walton, I feel great. It's been quite a day."

Alex shared with Henry the theatrics of what was supposed to be his first day of a four-day vacation. He described the positive effect of the new medication on his hands and wrists especially, but over all he had felt free of pain for almost a week. He did not mention that his emotions were flowing freely. Alex thought it was a reaction to how he was playing, winning six in a row and the circus atmosphere of the day.

Dr. Walton was curious about the emotional experience he had at the press conference. "Alex, I hear you silenced the press corp! What happened?"

Alex seemed embarrassed by the question but deflected it by again noting the events of the day.

Dr. Walton accepted the answer, reminding him to increase the dose to 20 mg starting tomorrow. "Alex, you seem to be doing so well with medication. Go ahead and increase the dose tonight or tomorrow, and we'll talk next week."

Alex nodded and shook hands with his trusted doctor and friend.

Dr. Walton started to turn away and remembered something. "Alex, can you set up with my staff an MRI before the end of the week? I want to follow up on the sonogram results. It's pretty routine stuff."

Alex was a professional athlete, and MRIs were like a teeth cleaning. Every pulled muscle, every strained hamstring, everything but catching a cold was checked out by an MRI. Organizations wanted to make sure their investments were making them a profit. Missing something obvious could cost a player a month or two on the disabled list, which cost a team extra money paying another player a major league salary.

Dr. Walton would be in Baltimore for weekend series while catching up with some friends in the area. He suggested to Alex that he could arrange the MRI on Friday in Baltimore. Alex agreed and headed to the shower, looking forward to watching the show of the homerun derby.

Ironically, Alex had never participated in the homerun derby. He had never been asked. It seemed like a lot of work but also a lot of fun. His teammate Homer Watson was representing the home team. He had fifteen homeruns at the All-Star break and had power to all fields. He would hopefully put on a show for the home fans.

• • •

Homer flamed out in the second round after crushing a dozen of balls in the first round. The fans were happy, and Alex got to rest in his own bed after an emotional day. He was able to get his mom, Phillip, and Anthony in a condo next door to him. His next-door neighbor and friend was out of town and happy that Alex could use his place for his family. He was a big baseball fan and would do anything for Alex. Sally decided to head home for the night and would get together with him and the family for lunch.

After getting his family settled next door, he slipped into his favorite shorts and T-shirt. He opened some wine and pulled open his blinds that displayed his view of the northern sky. His condo was quiet, the river looked calm, and the heat had broken.

He sipped some wine with the light of the city reaching across his arms. Pondering the past week, he reflected on the wealth of feelings he had discovered. He was deeply in love with Sally. There was no going back to the red light/green light game they had been playing in the relationship. He was ready to leap forward without fear of being caught and thrown out of the game. Suddenly he realized learning about deep emotional feelings was like moving from the minors to the majors in baseball. It was a challenge but a good one with the right tools. His family had given him those tools, and he was starting to use them. He now could settle into love and not be fearful of failure.

Somehow he had gained confidence is the relationship during the past week. They had spent some beautiful moments together. At the same time, his swing was in a groove, and his team was on a winning streak. In the past twenty-four hours, baseball had recognized his talents by naming him to the All-Star team. This gave him the luxury of playing tomorrow in front of a sold-out, Kansas City crowd and national television.

On his coffee table in front of the couch was today's unopened *Washington Daily*. He had forgotten to open it before leaving this morning. What a treat, he thought, to get a chance to read it in such a peaceful setting. He quickly pulled out the sports page and read the lead story about the Presidents finally breaking a ten-game losing streak, but only five games behind the Miami Sugarcanes for the division lead. Next to it was a story about training camp opening for the Potomacs with a rookie quarterback who was about to solve all their problems. "No wonder Burton Park seemed so happy," he said as he turned to CS to read about the Kansas City game and to check out the standings. Finally, he noticed a small headline recognizing the Kansas City six-game win streak and three paragraphs about the game- even a sentence about his 12 for 21 streak.

And then he saw something else at the end. "Amid trade rumors, the veteran third basemen is playing like his All- Star years of past while leading KC to their sixth win in a row!" Under news and notes he scanned for further information about the Presidents game. Again, at the end, he saw something about trade speculation. "Rumors might be put on hold with the Presidents win Sunday, but trading for power hitting third basemen, Alex Santucci, is the talk of the press box."

Alex grabbed his computer and looked up *PBL Rumor Mill,* a website about everything baseball. There it was as the top story. "Hot hitting Alex Santucci, named as replacement to the All-Star game, is in the sights of POTUS to help stop their hitting woes!" The story, well, in Alex's view, really a collection of meandering sentences representative of bloggers these days, went on to speculate that Santucci went to DC to meet secretly with the owners of the Washington Presidents about a trade. Details could be worked out at the All-Star game and almost certainly before the July 31 trade deadline. It also mentioned that Alex represents himself and that his emotional answers today at the press conference may reflect the possibility of a trade to his hometown.

    Alex closed the computer and chugged back the glass of wine. He walked over to the kitchen counter and filled up his glass again. Turning toward his beautiful panel of windows above the ground almost three hundred feet, he slowly paced toward the glass and rested his right ear on a pane as if he were listening to the rumors flying through the atmosphere. He opened his eyes and sipped from the glass and looked west. In the distance were the plains of Kansas where storms popped up like burnt bread out of a toaster. Even though he was standing inside his condo, he thought he could feel some wind stirring in the distance. Maybe a storm was coming toward the city, or maybe the air-conditioning duct was right over top of him! Either way he knew tomorrow would be a circus and great entertainment for the family. He realized it was time to put on a good show for Kansas City!

Chapter 11

Alex slept a little past dawn, his normal wakeup time. He brewed some coffee and went next door to check on his family. All three were dressed and sitting at the kitchen counter. Mom had made some coffee and was updating his dad and uncle on the escapades of her three older sons Kenneth, Franklin, and John. Every year in July, the three of them would take a week off from their medical practices and venture to some far-off place in Canada. This year they were just returning from a fishing and hunting trip in northern Manitoba.

"Ah, my sleepy boy, what a beautiful morning it is! Are you ready for the big game tonight?" Laura hugged her wide-shouldered son and offered him some coffee. "Will Sally be joining us for breakfast, my dear? I hope she got home safely."

Alex knew it was too early to wake the beautiful Irish girl before it was necessary.

"She's fine, I'm sure. We will probably see her around noon time," Alex assured his mom. "Everyone slept well, I hope?" Three heads nodded in unison. "I was thinking... Let's hop in the car. I like to do a run in the morning-when I can- so let's grab some coffee, maybe pick up some bread or pastry, a couple newspapers, and we can drive down to Swope Park. It would be perfect this morning down there."

A quick agreement was reached, and within ten minutes they all got in the Acura TL and headed south on Walnut a couple of blocks into the Kansas City Power and Light District to Constantino's Market for some goodies. The KC

P&L District was a nine-square block of businesses and entertainment, including the new indoor arena, The Sprint Center, constructed in 2007. Like his young KC Crowns ball club, it was still growing.

On the way, Alex received a text from Sally reporting she was awake and ready for duty. Surprised by her morning energy, Alex got his mom to call her back and invite her to their morning picnic. They quickly arrived at Swope Park, beating any morning traffic. Swope Park was a 1,804- acre city park named after Colonel Thomas H. Swope, who donated the land to the city in 1896. It included the Kansas City Zoo, the eight-thousand-seat Starlight outdoor theater, a public golf course, Frisbee golf, tons of baseball and soccer fields, and the Lakeside Nature Center. They quickly found a table under a beautiful large limestone shelter and settled in with their goodies and newspapers. They noticed there were many gorgeous limestone structures throughout the park.

Alex took off for a quick run, giving his mom instructions to text him when Sally arrived. Thirty minutes later, the five of them were together drinking coffee and eating rolls and pastries. The temperature was in the high seventies, and the sun was beaming in the sky. They were enjoying the perfect weather for the middle of July.

Phillip had searched his son's car and found a football in the trunk, just like he would always have in his car. He pulled it out and gave instructions to his son, brother, and Sally to get up and run some pass patterns! Sally was prepared, wearing her best athletic shoes, shorts, a tank top, and her custom-made, royal-blue Crowns hat. Her petite but athletic body with her flowing black hair coming out of her ball cap was a sight for sore eyes. She followed instructions, running a short post and catching the dead-on pass of the pigskin from Phillip. Defensive coverage from Alex was clearly lacking, but he quickly made a solid tackle after the catch, picking her up midstride and depositing her back at the line of scrimmage. She loved the contact but complained to Phillip about the yards lost after the catch. She playfully stuffed the ball in Alex's stomach as she ran away, seeking a spot behind Anthony as he lined up for the next pass!

Anthony grabbed the next low toss with one hand from Phil-lip, who had led him too far for his battered knees to keep up with in stride. Pulling in the football, he then rolled over on the ground and got up with his hands extended over his head, emphasizing the theatrics of the catch. He received a standing ovation from the family crowd!

Alex then snuck in line in front of Sally and took his instructions to run a deep post. Phillip wanted to show off his still-live arm as he approached the age of sixty. Alex glided out the first fifteen yards, then cut at a forty-five degree angle toward the middle and turned for the ball. Phillip had launched it a good fifty-five yards. Instinctively Alex turned on his 4.5-second, forty-yard speed and saw the football heading down toward his hands. The football landed softly in the tips of his fingers. He pulled in the pigskin, then secured it in his elbow and smiled with joy from the memories of the thousands of passes he caught from his dad and uncle.

He returned to his family, getting high fives from his dad and uncle and a big hug from Sally. He settled at the table next to his mom, who handed him some pastry and bottled water. She said something about not catching cold, not aware of his daily athletic sweating.

Laura told stories about first setting her eyes on Alex when he was just a day old. She spoke about the youth and beauty of his birth mother, Leah. How brave she was to make such a selfless decision to have the baby and to give him up for adoption. She prayed for her every day, hoping she accepted her decision and that God would give her strength and happiness. Laura always spoke openly with Alex about his birth mother after they told him that he was adopted. She felt it was important for Alex to understand the circumstances of the situation. He had very few questions about his birth mother, but enjoyed Laura talking about her. Alex assumed he would never meet his birth mother. Now at his age, it rarely entered his mind. Laura was his mom, and

Gene had been his dad. He felt lucky that Phillip had entered his life after Gene died; being his birth father was just a bonus.

Laura was much like Alex's Grandmother Rose, a very spiritual woman. Alex had never met any of his adopted grandparents before Rose and Guy, so accepting them as his real grandparents had never been an issue. Laura and Rose had been close friends. They were both Catholic to their core, including saying the rosary every day. Their greatest qualities were their discipline and dignity. They commanded great respect because they were always gentle and forgiving, even when they were tough in their parenting. Much like a good manager in baseball, they ran a system in their household. If you liked winning, you bought into it, and the system would take care of you.

Alex had always bought into the system. The winning in the Santucci and Finelli families was love and respect. Laura loved her Alex as her son and hoped Leah felt the same way, even from a distance.

The day had just begun with a perfect morning. Sally had volunteered to play tour guide for the day with Laura, Phillip, and Anthony. They were guests tonight along with Burton Parker at the Kansas City owner's suite for the All-Star game. Unaware of the rumors swirling in the air, Sally and the family would enjoy the city and the festivities of the day.

Alex was ready to take on the whirlwind of the All-Star game. With a storm in the air, he knew the rest of the day would not continue to be a picnic!

• • •

Alex had started the new dose of his medication in the morning. He was ecstatic at the effectiveness and the absence of side effects of the medication. Reading the literature of the medication, he knew it had originally been a drug for depression. He knew very little about depression in his family, even though there was a history of it on both sides. Both Phillip and Leah had bouts of depression in their lives. Phillip's father, Guy, had struggled with depression after becoming legally blind in the early 1960s. Leah's mother committed suicide later in her life from depression. That loss in 1980 caused Leah to spend several years in her late twenties in therapy, working through both the loss of her mother and her son for adoption. Fortunately, in the mid-1980s, she found happiness in a marriage and having three children. Success in a singing career in Christian music and later on as fitness trainer followed. She was currently living in Florida, a successful businesswoman guiding her kids through college and graduate school.

After both Phillip and Leah had found partners to marry in the late 1980s, they made contact with each other through writing. It was therapeutic for both to know that each other had found happiness. Leah never asked about Alex, but starting in 1991, Phillip would update her at Christmas time about his life. She was saddened when she learned of Gene's death but relieved that Phillip was now in his life.

Leah knew of his great athletic talent and often read about his career in silence. Her husband was well aware of her past life but supported her choice to keep it quiet in their family. Their three children had no idea they had a half-brother who was so famous in the baseball world. Leah prayed to God every day, thanking him for giving Alex such gift sand watching over him. She also hoped that one day she would see him display his talent.

• • •

The All-Star circus was officially in town. The player's parking lot was surrounded by fans taking pictures and yelling for autographs at four o'clock, three hours before game time.

Alex was familiar with the entrance and knew how to avoid the crowds, but he had never seen anything like this for a Crowns game. He called "The Dough Man," Hal Baker, on his way to the stadium to alert him that he was coming. Professional Baseball League (PBL) security, along with state police, was all over the place, keeping the crowds away.

Hal spotted Alex's Acura and waved him in a side gate. He was escorted by PBL security to the American League locker room, which happened to be the Crowns locker room.

Manager Joe Jefferson walked into the locker room soon after to address all the players. He went over the schedule for the evening and stated his strategy for the game. "Texas has been to the last two World Series, and as you know, we have lost both."

There were no laughs in the locker room. The Lawmen had lost an excruciating World Series last year, and not having the last two games at home did not help. PBL had instituted a policy several years ago that the league that won the All-Star game would get home field advantage in the World Series. The National League had won the last two, so the Texas Lawmen, with the best record in baseball, did not have home field advantage, helping them lose two World Series in a row.

"I know that you all would like to play tonight. Respectfully, I don't care. I will manage the game to win tonight. Now, most of you will get in the game, but some might not. I apologize ahead of time for that, and please don't take it personal." Jefferson sounded like a high school principal speaking to parents of seniors who had asked for extra graduation tickets. "I hope every American League team plans to get into the World Series this year, because they will have home field advantage! Personally, I'm doing it for Texas, because we plan to get back there." He finally cracked a smile. "Now get yourself ready for the game, enjoy the night, and be ready to play if I need you. Now let's get out there and kick the shit out of them!"

Alex felt relieved hearing Jefferson rant about winning. It was smart strategy to play to win. Besides, he thought, it would take the pressure off of him playing. The dressing room thinned out with players exiting to do interviews, get rubdowns, treatments for ailments, or hit in the batting cages. Batting and fielding practice on the field was an hour away.

Jefferson called for Alex to come into his office. "Alex, be ready to play after the third inning. I'm getting Martinez out of there after three innings." Mario Martinez was an aging superstar at third base always voted in by the New York fan base no matter what he was hitting. Alex came in second to him at third base in the voting six years in a row. He had never started an All-Star game but played in all six. "I need someone that is hot, and that is you!" Jefferson pointed at him with his famous toothpick sticking out of his mouth. "I wanted you on this team from the beginning, but the commissioner pushed me in another direction-if you know what I mean. So, when £stanza went down, I called your manager in a heartbeat. I'm glad they tracked you down." Alex smiled and thanked Manager Jefferson.

"I got to win this, Alex. We're going back this year to the Series, and I got to win it." Jefferson's desperation was showing.

Alex stood up and assured Joe. "Hey, I got you covered, I'll be ready to go, whatever you need, Joe." They shook hands, and Alex headed out to the field.

The sun was descending behind the third base upper deck at Crown Field as Alex walked out of the dugout. He headed out to the infield and took some grounders, trading smiles with Mario Martinez at third base. Martinez was the richest player in base-ball. He was two years older than Alex but had four years left on his $275-million contract and was currently making $30 million this year. Alex loved to watch Mario take infield practice and swing the bat. He was the most graceful big man he had ever seen.

After finishing his work in the infield, he asked to speak

to Alex. They had never spoken in the previous six All-Star games other than cordial greetings.

"Alex, I wanted to say, this is your game! The people here deserve to see you. Everybody in the club house thinks the same. I've got to play three innings, but I want Joe to put you in right away. You should have started half those games before." He paused and looked down. Alex grabbed his hand and nodded as Mario turned and headed to the batting cage.

Alex took his turn at third base fielding grounders and making his classic three-quarter arm throw to first. Over the next ten minutes, every player on the American League team came by and tapped gloves with him. It was a sign of respect he could not have imagined during his career. He was a steady ballplayer during his fourteen years, never seeking the spotlight, never promoting his game. He was happy just to be successful in the big leagues. Being noticed by the greatest players in the game was a whole different feeling.

A couple of local stations interviewed him before the game, but none of the national stations had noticed his story. He found his usual spot in the security office of his friend, Hal Baker, to settle down and collect his thoughts. The show would start in a half an hour. It was time to visualize his talents so he could block out the festivities when he was called into the game. In his previous six All-Star games, he was a combined four for ten with two doubles and three RBIs, while errorless in the field. Those were in other major league cities, where he was not the focus of attention in front of the home crowd.

He faded into a daydream, where he quickly found himself playing catcher as a little boy. His mom was whispering in his ear to be careful, but wait, he was watching the perfect swing, his uncle Anthony turning on the ball and crushing it deep into the woods. Going, going, gone! Then he felt a pain coming from his stomach. Suddenly he awoke and found himself curled in a ball, feeling nauseated with an ache penetrating his stomach. He tried to breathe slowly as he straightened out his legs. Finally, he sat up sweating and holding a spot in his stomach that was pulsating pain.

He called Dr. Walton and met him in the training room. The pain had subsided after he vomited. Henry thought it was food poisoning and gave him small dose of Xanax to relax. Alex was relieved the pain had subsided and felt calmer after taking the anti-anxiety medicine. He was familiar with it from all the MRIs he had taken. It made the close quarters of the MRI tunnel easier to handle.

He dressed for the game, wearing his home white Crowns uniform with his familiar number seven, his lucky number. As he headed down the tunnel to the dugout, he thought of his family watching from the owner's suite. He knew the love from his family, the love from the fans, and the respect of the players would make the ache in his stomach go away. At least he hoped it would by the fourth inning!

Chapter 12

The sun had set on a beautiful skyline, and the lights lit up a sold-out Crown Field like a million, quadrillion fireflies hovering over a campsite. The wind was stirring, thinking about bratty ways to bring trouble to the field. The crowd was politely clapping as the National League players were introduced, taking their places on the third base line. They tipped their caps to the small number of National League fans who drove in their RVs from Saint Louis, Milwaukee, and Chicago or other far-away NL towns to see their favorite players perform on this revered stage for baseball royalty.

The All-Star manager, Joe Jefferson, excited the hometown KC crowd as he trotted out to home plate to shake the National League manager's hand and take his place on the first base line. He turned to face the crowd and waved his cap. Peter DeGregorio had come back to manage the National League All-Star game after retiring, following last year's thrilling World Series win. Jefferson was still seething, having to see the nearly canonized DeGregorio soak up the attention in the spotlight. Joe was looking to present Peter with a dose of humility by embarrassing him with an All-Star beating.

The AL nonstarters were introduced by team, with the Crowns coming last before the starting lineup was announced. Alex Santucci was standing in the dugout behind Homer Watson and in front of Erik Peters, the future Hall of Fame New York Icons short-stop, who would lead off for the Junior Circuit. Erik was the same age as Alex and one of a few players on another team he was close to. As famous as Erik was in New York, he always had time for Alex to help with charity causes or host Alex and Sally for a visit in New York City during the off-season. He had a top-floor penthouse in Manhattan that was ten times the size of Alex's condo. Alex was stunned two years ago when Erik showed up for his grandmother's funeral and waited at the grave site for the burial with a rosary in his hand. He told Alex that he would never forget Rose's cooking and had felt honored that she would whip up a meal of homemade manicotti and meatballs at age ninety-two during a drop-in visit years before.

Erik led a "We want Alex" cheer from the dugout that caught on with the crowd behind the dugout as Joe Jefferson had been introduced. The crowd's wave of the cheer began to whip around the first base side, to behind the plate, up the third base side, and then finally to the upper deck. Suddenly the cheer was drowning out the great play-by-play announcer Fred Fielder who was facing the crowd behind home plate.

As the reserve players were finding their place on the first base line, Homer Watson, next to be announced, turned to Alex and shouted, "You're da man!" The home town crowd hardly noticed as Homer was introduced. He sprinted out to his spot, keeping his head down, trying not to catch any attention.

It was a sweet move but unnecessary, as the crowd was now standing, clapping, and chanting like a choir singing a joyous hymn, as Fred Fielder shouted out, "From the Kansas City Crowns, Third Basemen Alex Santucciiiiiiiiiiii..."

Alex felt a push from Erik. Suddenly the pain in his stomach was replaced with exhilaration as he hopped out of the dugout and trotted out to his place on the first base line. A surge of wind seemed to cycle the roar from the crowd onto the baseball diamond. He shook hands with each player of his team, then finally found his place next to Homer Watson and turned to face the crowd.

Erik Peters motioned to Fred Fielder to silence his introduction as the ovation continued. The fans had read the papers reporting the rumors of trading Alex to Washington. Tonight, the fans were weighing in on that trade rumor with a resounding "We want Alex!"

For the next two minutes, the crowd continued their chant. National television was getting nervous over losing some precious advertising minutes. The drama was not lost to the casual fan watching the impressive scene. Alex stood stoically with his head down listening to the chants, thinking of his wonderful years in Kansas City and never once being booed because of his big contract. The fans always appreciated his great hustle and consistency through some tough rebuilding years. Alex was honored to be on this field at this time. It was like all of Missouri was getting a chance to be on the front page, and Alex felt empowered by the recognition. His teammate Homer Watson put his arm around him, telling him to walk forward and recognize the crowd. Before he could look up and walk forward, National League Manager Peter Gregorio walked over and shook hands again with Alex. He congratulated him for the crowd recognition and his great career. Humbled, Alex finally stepped forward, took off his cap, held it over his heart, and blew a kiss to the crowd while tapping his cap over his heart. He then pointed to Fred Fielder to continue the introduction.

Finally, Erik came out clapping his hands to honor his All-Star teammate and friend. The rest of the starting lineup followed suit as the whole team crowded around Alex, congratulating him and getting pumped for the game. This team knew at that moment the National League was going to take a bad whipping from this pumped-up talented crew!

• • •

The first three innings of the game featured two players: B. B. King, a hard-throwing left-hander from the New York Icons, pitching hitless ball, and Kyle Burr, reigning AL MVP from the Texas Lawmen, hitting a three-run homer and a two-run double to go ahead five to zero. Both Erik Peters and Mario Martinez had two hits and two runs scored a piece.

Alex replaced Mario at third base to start the fourth inning, while Homer Watson took over right field for Kyle Burr. Homer made a nice sliding catch of a ball headed for the right field foul line for the first out. The National League followed with their first two hits of the night, putting runners on first and second. The next batter scalded a line drive down the third base line for a double, scoring one and putting runners on second and third with one out.

Next up was the nineteen-year-old Blake Hopson, a rookie from the Washington Presidents, voted to the starting lineup by millions of fans wooed by his youth, hustle, and exciting talent. Most veteran sports writers thought Blake did not deserve to start the All-Star game because of his mediocre statistics since being brought up in April. But most were looking forward to see him perform on this national stage. A left-handed hitter, Blake had struck out on three pitches his first time up against the tough left-hander King.

Rolando Lamas, a Seattle Shoremen flame-thrower, was pitching the top of the fourth inning, giving up three hits to the first four batters. Hopson was born to hit a fastball and feasted on the pitch over the outside corner, drilling a one hopper to Alex at third, who was playing in because Hopson was known to bunt. The ball hopped over his glove, hit him in his stomach, and bounced off his chin, knocking him to the ground as it headed toward the stands. Two runs scored and Blake Hopson stood on second with a two-RBI double.

Alex sat on the infield dirt and saw stars for a few seconds before he realized the crowd and the game going on. Blood was streaming from his chin, and a huge red bruise was left on his stomach. The trainers came out and found the cut, bandaged it up, and did some concussion tests on him. He knew he was fine as he spit out some blood and gingerly put his cap back on. Manager Joe Jefferson meandered around the infield wasting time. He went to the mound and ordered the pitcher to, very slowly, intentionally walk the batter to set up a double play and give Alex some more time to recover.

They would pitch to the right-handed swinging Colorado Mountains shortstop, Adam Achilles. Adam was a second generation, Cal Ripken-type shortstop-big, strong, graceful, and athletic. Alex played him deep while guarding the line. On a two and two count, Fabulous Rolando came to the plate as Blake Hopson took off to steal third. Instinctively Alex broke toward third to cover the base. Achilles turned on the inside slider and topped a medium paced two-hopper toward third. Alex scooped up the ball near the bag as Blake was beginning to slide into third. Converging bodies and a baseball were merging together. Alex caught the ball with his glove hand below his knees. He reached down to tag Hopson, whose cleated shoes led his body. Then in one motion, Alex pulled his mitt up, jumped over Hopson, and landed on his left foot while transferring the ball to his right hand. Then diving sideways, he extended his right arm and flung the ball across his body to first base, like an arrow shot from a bow getting Achilles by a heel!

Alex hit the ground and rolled over. As he lay on the ground, he heard the crowd roar with delight. Blake Hopson stood over him, extending a hand to help pull him up and said,

"The best play I've ever seen, man. I hope I see you soon in DC!" Blake winked at him as he headed to the dugout.

Alex entered the dugout to high fives as the big video board showed the amazing double play from five different angles.

Jefferson was vocal in the dugout about this game becoming a dogfight, which he was not about to lose. Alex was sixth up in the bottom of the fourth inning. The National League pitcher, left-handed Winston "Smokey" Camels, was wild and throwing hard tonight, not usually a good combination. The Philadelphia ace was known to come inside on right-handed hitters. As Alex finally came to the on-deck circle, there were two on from a walk and a hit batsman, with two out. The crowd was delirious from the previous inning and still standing, cheering for Homer

Watson's first All-Star at-bat.

Alex could see that Camels had no control over his cutter, which was usually his bread and butter pitch to right-handed hitters. Homer worked another walk to load the bases. The crowd hushed for a few seconds as if to catch their collective breath. Then the announcer introduced Alex to the home crowd as he strolled to the batter's box. The National League catcher nodded to him as he called time and walked to the mound. The chanting of "We want Alex..." started to increase in decibels.

Alex stepped into the box and felt the dirt at his feet. He tried to settle in inches off the plate. As the catcher returned to his seat behind the plate, the umpire, a thirty-year veteran, Hector Moralles, said to Alex, "Son, you got to step out and tip your cap. It's your time." Moralles walked in front of the plate, slowly pulled out his hand broom from his back pocket, and meticulously swept invisible dirt off an already clean plate.

Forty-five thousand fans standing on their feet were cheering their favorite player. Alex stepped out, overwhelmed by the recognition. He never sought out their attention but always respected that it was their game and their city, and he had the privilege to earn a living. He laid down his bat and turned to the crowd and looked up toward the owner's box to see his mom, dad, uncle, and Sally standing, cheering, and waving toward him. He lifted his helmet as tears started to stream from his eyes. The moment he had dreamed of as a child was here. He was representing his team, his family, his heritage. He was fulfilling his dream of base-ball, the destiny he had known at the age of seven. The heroic actions of his family coming to America over a hundred years ago had made a life so that later generations could have this kind of dream. He thought of his father and his birth mother making the decision to give him life while facing embarrassment and pain in the years to come.

• • •

At that same moment at a Hampton Inn in St. Augustine, Florida, his birth mother, Leah, by herself, was watching her first baseball game in a hotel room. She made an excuse about a business meeting in Orlando to stay overnight and watch her son play for the first time. It was a world that she spent the last thirty-six years avoiding because she promised her God and family that the punishment for her sin was never to try the forbidden fruit of seeing her son. While growing up, it had been taboo to watch television, listen to the radio, dance, swear, drink, eat meat or fish, and of course have sex. Meeting Phillip at age eighteen, while working as a lifeguard at the YMCA, was like entering another world. She was so in love and completely attracted to his Italian looks.

She broke away from him twice over the next three years to keep her promise to God, but she finally sinned at her lowest point in life. He was the greatest love in her life, and he gave her the gift of Alex. Through her prayer, she learned to give him up, but now she could no longer keep her promise. Tears streamed down her face as she felt great joy watching her son on the television. She ached seeing his beauty and gracefulness. Leah asked God to free her from her promise and let her be in his life. At least for tonight she was a part of it.

• • •

Alex, feeling the love from the fans, put on his helmet and wiped his eyes as Winston "Smokey" Camels stepped off the mound to stroll around it to get the rosin bag. He respected Alex but had never faced him in a game. Smokey wanted to get a strike and believed Alex was not ready to hit the first pitch.

Alex was looking for an inside fastball on the first pitch

as Camels came to a set. He stepped into a perfect pitch and got all of it as he watched a titanic shot sail over the stands in left field and out of the stadium like his half-brother Guy had twice done during batting practice. But unfortunately, foul! He slowly walked back to the plate as the fans let out a collective pained hush. He dug into the batter's box, tapped the plate with his bat, and then rested it on his right shoulder. Camels returned to the stretch and threw a cutter to the outside corner. Alex guessed right again, dropped his hands quickly inside the bat barrel, and lined the pitch down the right field line, fair by inches. The bases cleared as he flew around first, barely touched second, and flashed toward third: finishing with a perfect headfirst dive. He was safe by plenty, as the crowd erupted, watching the excitement of a three-run triple.

Alex stood on top of the world at third base while the crowd continued its lovefest with him. The American League continued the beat down of the National League with a 12-5 win. Alex went 3 for 3 with a walk, 3 runs scored, and 5 RBIs. The MVP went to the current league MVP, Kyle Burr, with his five RBIs in two at bats.

Manager Joe Jefferson got his win, which he hoped to use in October for home field advantage in the World Series. In the locker room, he made a point to hug Alex and wished him the best in the future, as long as he was not an opponent. Little did he know that a storm named Alex had already started in the Midwest. It was about to impact baseball as Alex and the Kansas City Crowns headed for a nine game road trip on the East Coast.

• • •

Alex stayed on the field for an extended period time after the game, signing autographs and taking pictures with the fans. Consciously, he was soaking up every last bit of the love that was a part of the evening as the outfield clock moved past midnight and toward one in the morning. Unconsciously, his emotions were stirring and not just focused on the rumors swirling around about a trade to Washington. He tried to stay centered on today and the adoring fans.

At 1:01 a.m., the final fan, a ninety-five-year-old man dressed in a beautiful suit, accompanied by a well-dressed butler or driver, leaned over the railing and handed Alex a thin bag with some sort of magazine in it. "I hear you grew up on Johnson Avenue. Well, here's something that I want you to have. I know you'll take good care of it. God Bless you, Alex." With his mission complete, the man turned and started walking slowly up the steps.

Alex looked in the thin bag and saw a plastic-covered something wrapped in yellowed newspaper. "Sir, wait. What is this? How will I thank you for it?"

The man turned, took off his fedora and placed it over his heart, and replied, "Son, someone great wanted you to have it. I didn't know all my life until I read the papers this morning, and read all about you, and came to see you myself. All the fans tonight, all the love, like him he waited and was always patient like you. Until the last fan was happy, I can still remember his eyes. I have to go now. It is awfully late. Never change, Alex!"

A snowball of chills ran down Alex's back, just like the night air was freezing his hand holding the bag. What could it be? Suddenly the tall lights hovering above the stadium turned silent into darkness, causing his chills to further shake him. Hal Baker took Alex's arm and walked him slowly back to the dugout.

"You don't see an old guy like at the ballpark these days, much less wait for an autograph. What did he want?" Hal inquired, trying to hold together his weary friend.

"He gave me a gift, Hal, something very special. I think I'll wait until I get home to open it. It was very valuable to him-probably from his father, maybe."

Hal chuckled and told him that his equipment would

be in Baltimore Friday and assured him there was nothing to worry about. He then reported that his family had headed back to Washington, DC, with Burton Parker. Sally was at the condo.

'The Dough Man" waited for Alex to shower and dress so that he could walk him to a car service outside the stadium. As Alex went to shake his hand and pass him another C-note, Hal Baker refused both the handshake and the money. Instead he went for a hug. With tears starting to come on to his plump cheeks, he said, "Alex, it was an honor to witness tonight. That is payment many times over."

Alex nodded and was not worried about the rejected money exchange. He had a friend in the payroll department who knew how to transfer money into Hal's account. It was time to sneak in several T-bills that he would not be able to refuse!

• • •

He arrived at his condo at 2:07 a.m. Sally was in a deep sleep on the couch; clearly she had plans to stay awake for her man. Their plans in the morning were to take the ten fifteen flights to DC and check into the Westin at Twenty-Fifth and M Streets near George-town for a couple of days of rest and relaxation. He brushed away her lovely black hair covering her face and kissed her cheek down to her shoulder. The Crowns jersey she was wearing came barely down to her thighs. She fell easily into his arms as he picked her up and carried her to the bedroom. Her eyelids fluttered a sweet dream, perhaps being rescued by her handsome prince! He covered her with a blanket and put on a T-shirt and shorts. As he poured some wine, he noticed the moonless sky above
the lights of the city. He pulled out the single item from the paper bag. It was in a foot long, plastic sealed bag with a thickness used for freezers or for water proofing.

Inside was something eight by eleven inches and covered with newspaper that was very old. He unzipped the plastic and pulled out the item. The newspaper was yellowed with small print from at least a generation ago. He started to un-wrap the paper and noticed the header said *The Washington Star* and dated from the 1940s. The *Star* was an afternoon newspaper in Washington that went out of business in 1981, when Alex was five years old.

He put down the item and sipped some more wine. The emotions he felt from the evening had barely begun to settle within his stomach, which he became aware, was starting to feel very sore. He went to the refrigerator and took out an ice pack and placed it on his bruised stomach. He tried to remember the events of the evening: the cheering, the excitement, the cheering, the tumbles, the cheering, the hitting and the cheering. Thinking about the best part lasted into the night. Suddenly the darkness was gone and the dawn was heading west from Saint Louis. He crawled out of the couch and down the hall into his bed. He slid in behind Sally and wrapped his hand around her ribs and held her tight. Alex knew it would be a glorious time to be together with Sally over the next few days, because the excitement had just begun.

PART II: THE TRADE

Chapter 13

The managing owner of the Washington Presidents was Hank Meyers, a soon-to-be sixty-year-old son of Frederick Meyers, the real estate mogul from Washington, DC. Frederick bought the bankrupt team in 2005 from the National League for $470 million and brought it to DC. Now at eighty-nine, he enjoyed watching Hank and other family members run the team, while he continued deals in real estate, buying up bargain lots and properties. Currently Frederick was focused around the newly constructed Presidents Ballpark. He decided to develop several blocks around the stadium that bordered the Anacostia River to eventually help with attendance. Presidents Ballpark could become the crown jewel of a new, architecturally chic, and ready for jet-set crowd, waterfront development. He lived on the top floor of one of his new buildings, just a block from the stadium. At night he loved to see the lights from the game sparkle under the moonlight that hovered over the Anacostia. The 8.7 mile river, named after the Anacostan Native Indians, starts in Maryland above historic Bladensburg, which was established in 1742 as an inspection port for tobacco. The river winds its way into northeast DC, flowing past the historic RFK Stadium into southeast DC and the Potomac River, just a short distance past the new ballpark. Frederick Meyer was born in 1923, the year before the only Washington World Series triumph and was ten when he saw the last World Series game played in DC at Griffith Stadium in 1933. He was determined to see several more in DC before he left this earth.

Hank walked into his father's penthouse apartment before dawn at 5:37 this Wednesday morning, July 18. He had pressing business and knew from history that if it involved spending money, he needed to see his father early in the morning. Frederick was on the rooftop balcony, his favorite spot in the world, having coffee and reading several papers before the July sun made things too unbearable to be outside. The ball club was on an eighty-million-dollar payroll budget this year. Frederick Meyers made a profit every year with this team and had no intention of deviating from that plan unless it involved something like getting into the playoffs. They had been the most profitable team in baseball since he purchased them in 2005.

"Good morning, Father. I'm guessing you didn't stay up for the All-Star game last night?" Hank kissed his seated father on the check and then sat across from him. "Actually, I saw every second of it. What a performance by the American League. Very exciting... very emotional with that player from Kansas City... Alex Starr something!" Frederick put down his coffee and shuffled for the sports section.

"Santucci, Father! Yes, it was quite something." Hank stirred in his seat a bit, getting ready to ask for ten million dollars. "Actually, that is quite helpful that you saw the game last night, Father, because that is who I want to talk to you about: Alex Santucci!"

• • •

About five hours later, Alex and Sally arrived at the Westin Hotel in DC. The Kansas City Crowns owner, Larry Garson, had called Alex at 5:07 to offer a ride to DC on his private jet. He was attending to some business in New York and wanted Alex to get to spend as much time with his family in DC as possible. Alex and Sally drove the fifteen minutes to the airport and were on the jet by 6:03. Mr. Garson was so excited about the success of the All-Star game, the play of his young star Homer Watson, and his veteran All-Star Alex that he stayed up all night from the adrenaline rush. His team was playing well and back to the .500 mark at 43-43. He cleared his schedule after his business in New York and planned to follow the team on their nine-game East Coast trip as well as planning another adventure.

Alex thanked him for hosting his family at the game and the ride to Washington, but Mr. Garson could not stop talking about Alex's mom, Laura.

"Where have you been hiding her? What a jewel that woman is."

Larry, now in his late seventies, was fit and trim as a Man thirty years younger. Educated as an electrical engineer, he had pioneered various medical diagnostic and imaging devices, making hundreds of millions that helped him buy the Crowns ten years ago. He was Midwest born and raised as well as currently single. His wife of forty-five years died of cancer six years ago.

"I hope she can come to a game in Baltimore or maybe New York. Would you mind if I invited her?"

Alex, who was struggling to stay awake, thought he was dreaming the question. Luckily Sally was paying attention and jumped in with an answer.

"I'm sure that would be wonderful, Mr. Garson. Alex would be pleased to have his mom get to travel to see him play in either city, I'm sure! Can I give you her number?"

He nodded thanks with a smile!

• • •

Alex hit the bed as soon as he entered the hotel room and quickly fell into a deep sleep until 12:13 p.m. Sally spent the time going to the workout room and then took a long shower. She was changing into a lovely medium-blue summer dress as Alex first showed signs of life.

"Time for lunch, sleepy head!" Sally jumped on Alex and nestled her face and hair into his cheek and ear, while kissing him up and down his neck until he opened his eyes.
"Where did you get all this energy?" Alex muttered.
"Happiness, I guess. I'm ready to walk through Georgetown and find the perfect restaurant and have a scrumptious lunch." Sally was ready for a big day of adventure with Alex.

The air smelled delicious and was delightfully cool with temperatures in the low seventies for this mid-July day. Humidity was taking a day off after thunderstorms had blown through the area early in the morning. Alex knew he had missed a great day to run but hoped to rise early in the morning tomorrow to enjoy a long, adventurous run in Rock Creek Park, which was only two blocks from their hotel. They walked straight north up Twenty-Fifth Street toward the eastern border of the park and found an open field with a nice trail to continue north to P Street. As they reached the edge of the Park, they looked down the fifty-to-hundred-foot drop to see Beach Drive and Rock Creek meandering through the city, south toward the Potomac, just west of the Kennedy Center and the Watergate. The happy couple strolled hand in hand, west across the P Street Bridge to enter Georgetown. The historic bridge was a 336-foot long, concrete arch bridge, first construction in 1855 to span Rock Creek.

The lunch crowds were enjoying the view as Alex took Sally onto some side streets to see the grand homes, row houses, and town homes that make up most of Georgetown. A small ball field with basketball courts bordered the western part of Rock Creek Park. It was being used by mostly young people from all over the world: catching, shooting, throwing various balls and Frisbees while jumping, diving, and running into the suddenly clean air.

Alex had a feeling to jump into the synergy of the groups but held back knowing his current status in the world. As a celebrity, especially out with Sally, he had to carve out his time free of that status to try to live a normal life. He missed those times in college when the campus was full of energy and he could be free to mingle with anyone, as well as those times in high school when he roamed Georgetown and other parts of DC with friends to relish the excitement of being downtown.

They headed west on Dumbarton Street between O and N Streets for the six blocks to Wisconsin Avenue. The cobblestone streets were lined by massive houses that sometimes took up a third of a block, along with small row houses no more than fifteen feet wide. The first fifty houses built in Georgetown dated back to 1751, when it was first settled as a port, the most northern point for ships to travel up the Potomac River. Forty years later, George Washington picked the swamps east of it to build the capital of the newly formed United States. It became and still is the oldest section and community of Washington, DC.

After a peaceful fifteen-minute stroll along historic Dumbarton Street, they came out to the active Wisconsin Avenue, the north-south artery of Georgetown. They turned left and headed south a block to eat at Paolo's Restaurant. Alex immediately ordered some mussels in garlic sauce, fresh mozzarella, and tomatoes with basil and olive oil, steamed artichokes, with two sides of pasta in a red sauce. With a bottle of pinot noir to drink, they were set for some much-needed nourishment. They sat at a table just inside a huge open window that looked out onto the narrow street and the steady stream of beautiful people walking up and down the avenue. Alex and Sally were quiet for the next twenty minutes, eating and drinking, realizing how famished they had become. The last three days had been full of amazing experiences with little time to focus on eating. Alex had never seen Sally soak up so much food. She finished off the bread, dipping in it the mussels sauce.

"This is so good. How can you stand it?" she muttered between bites.

Alex inhaled the pasta and artichokes while asking the

waiter for some more bread. He poured another glass of wine for himself while topping off Sally's.

"Are you trying to take advantage of me in the middle of the day? After all of this wining and dining in the last three days!" Sally gleamed with a smile that dove right into Alex's heart.
He took her face in his hand and leaned over the table to kiss her luscious lips.

"Guilty as charged!" Alex announced as he went back to scooping the mussels out of their shells while soaking up the minced pieces of garlic.

After their lunch they walked for hours through Georgetown, then down to the river, back through the Foggy Bottom area, and to the hotel for a short nap and other activities. They changed into some nicer clothes and took the rental car for a journey into Virginia, touring the Shenandoah Valley and finishing with a ride on Skyline Drive. They ended up in Winchester, Virginia, for dinner. The hour-and-a-half drive back began at the edge of dusk and finished with the heart of darkness, which did not put the lights out on an intimate and delightful day.

After returning their car to the hotel, they strolled out south on Twenty-Fifth Street, heading toward Pennsylvania Avenue to seek an outdoor cafe. Sitting at an outdoor table on the Grand Avenue during a magnificent evening, Alex knew it was time. They were alone in a nook of the cafe as he took Sally's hand, bent on one knee, and asked her to marry him. She looked down at Alex. Holding back the sudden onset of tears while feeling surprised and euphoric, she quietly nodded yes. Alex pulled out his mother's engagement ring from his pocket, slid it on her finger, and sealed it with a lovely kiss. The moment was everything that Sally had imagined. She had loved Alex for years but always had to hold back and be careful not to overwhelm him with the waves of her emotions. Alex never imagined this scene until a week ago when he finally realized he loved her. When he told his mom about his feelings in private on Monday, she passed along her ring just in case. He knew his life had changed in a week, and his emotions had been unleashed. Had they always been there, or was he just finding out the depth of them, he wondered. These feelings were making him a better man, and now he had a chance to be a great athlete with history to make!

• • •

Kansas City General Manager Frank Fellows was in his office on Thursday morning, July 19, reading e-mails from his in-box. Most were scouting updates, but some were inquiries about ballplayers on his forty-man roster. One player, Alex Santucci, was getting some attention from some teams, but no GM had called him personally to discuss a trade. The deadline was thirteen days away. He expected to field calls soon about his veteran third baseman.

Washington Presidents General Manager Jim Franco just had a meeting with managing partner Hank Meyers. The main topic was Alex Santucci. Jim had informed Hank soon after the Hammersley injury that Alex would be a nice addition to the ball club. Hank had passed along the good news to Jim that the ten million dollars necessary to acquire Santucci would be available. His salary for the last two months of the season was a little over six million dollars, with a four-million-dollar buyout of his sixteen-million-dollar salary for 2013, which was contingent with five hundred plate appearances this year. Alex was well on his way this season to meet this incentive.

"Hi, Frank, this is Jim Franco from the Presidents. Do you have a minute?"

Frank Fellows had read the rumors for the last week or so about the pending Santucci trade to the Presidents, but now was the first time he had any contact with them.

"Great time Jim, things settling down around here, nice and quiet for now." Frank chuckled.

Jim had not worked with Frank before but respected the veteran GM for rebuilding the Crowns into a young but talented ball club." Well, Frank, let me get to the point. I guess the media has us already as best buddies, but I do want to see what your ball club thinks about Alex Santucci and his availability."

Frank had not been in this position for several years, trading most of his veterans five years ago. It was a nice change to hold an asset that he could trade for some great prospects, but he was always a straight shooter when it came to deals.

"Well, to be honest, Jim, I've got a big problem with holding all the cards with Santucci. You see, this morning Mr. Garson told me in plain words, 'Do not trade Alex Santucci!'"

Jim Franco sat back and sighed. He did not see that coming. "I understand, Frank. Yeah, sometimes it's tough to get an owner on board, but jeez, it would save him ten million dollars this year, not to mention the talent you'd be getting.

Frank did not want to string him along. "I tell ya, Jim, I've been waiting a couple years for this deal. I mean, don't get me wrong. Alex is the best kid ever. This would kill me, but it's like your daughter getting married-got to happen sometime." Then Frank added the bombshell. "Jim, between you and me, I think Mr. Garson is sweet on Alex's mother, Laura. He hosted her here with the Potomacs owner and such. I think he wants to bring her to the New York series."

"An Affair to Remember No shit!"

Jim settled down and thought for a moment. "Well, if they break up, what are you looking for, Frank?"

Frank appreciated the tone from Jim. "I would love two top ten guys, probably pushing for a third to make it work!"

"Frank, I think we're on the same page. Maybe three in the top fifteen or something close. E-mail me some names, and maybe we could get something ready in case the romance goes south!"

Chapter 14

Alex called his mom Thursday morning and told her to invite the whole family to the Pines of Rome restaurant in Bethesda to have a dinner for a special occasion. It had been the favorite location for both the Santucci and the Finelli families for the past thirty-five years. Alex called Marco, the owner, to set up the back room for thirty and to make sure Pepe was there as the waiter.

Alex and Sally were on top of the clouds all day emotionally. They ventured out to Great Falls in Potomac, Maryland, for some climbing of rocks and hiking on the C & O Canal. Great Falls was a powerful area of descending water from the Potomac River about ten miles north of DC. In high school, Alex spent countless hours hanging out with friends in all the nooks and crannies of the huge boulders and rocks around the falls. Getting a tan and watching the falls was spectacular, along with exploring the canal and the locks built back in 1828. The C & OC Canal operated from 1831 to 1924, extending for 184 miles to Cumberland, Maryland. It started in Georgetown where Rock Creek entered into the Potomac. The enormity of the project was something Alex could never comprehend. Now the beauty of it on this special day was overwhelming. Holding Sally's hand, walking up and down the canal, was both peaceful and energizing.

For the first time on his DC trip, someone recognized him. They stopped and chatted for a while. The man was in his mid-eighties and very fit, wearing a POTUS hat. He declared himself a big baseball fan. "I remember the last time there was a World Series in Washington-1933. I just turned six and was in grade school. Really would like to see another one.

I read somewhere you might be coming to DC. Well, good luck, son. I don't want to keep you and your pretty girl on your day off."

Alex thanked him while shaking his hand. He felt a

strange tingle, like the one back in KC at the stadium with the-suddenly he remembered the old man at the stadium after the All-Star game. What did he do with the bag? I must have fallen asleep on the couch and never opened the bag, he thought. The next morning, they left so quickly that he forgot about it. Was it still in his condo? He could not remember; it would drive him crazy this whole trip. Maybe his buddy was home next door and could FedEx it to him or something.

Sally noticed he looked confused as the older man went on his way down the canal path. "What's wrong, Alex? Are you getting tired from your run this morning?"

Alex reacted, shaking his head. "No, no. I'm fine. Just thinking about the condo, I think I left that bag with something in it from the old man at the ballpark."

Sally was excited to have the trump card in this deal. "Don't worry, sweetie. I grabbed it on the way out. I got it in my bag, in the car!"

Relieved and stunned by the clutch decision and decisive action by Sally, Alex suddenly felt an urgency to get back to the car and to the hotel. "I think I need a nap. I guess I forgot my medication with all the excitement of yesterday and this morning."

Sally gazed up at his deep brown eyes and felt a joy in being able to comfort her big guy. She kissed him with a smile and then took his hand to head back to the car. Now, she thought, "What the hell is in that damn bag!"

They sat in the backseat of the car with Sally's carry-on bag for the trip between them. She unzipped it and pulled out the brown paper bag for Alex. He slowly reached inside and pulled out the plastic bag with the newspaper-covered item he never opened the other night.

Sally looked at the yellow-stained newspaper and uttered, *"The Washington* Star...What is that?"

Alex started to un-wrap the newspaper and told her some background about the old and since closed newspaper company from DC. He finally got to the item underneath. He placed it on his lap and looked at the cover.

Sally inched closer, leaned on his chest, and looked at the print on the cover. "World Series 1924. Washington versus New York. Are you kidding me? It's a scorebook from 1924!" She read a little farther down the cover. "Seventh game... October 10, 1924. Wow!"

Alex had his eyes wide open and let out a deep breath. He noticed something in the bottom right corner. It was upside down and little hard to read. He turned the scorebook, tilted it, and brought it closer.

Sally examined it with her professor eyes like she was reading bad handwriting from a final exam answer. Except this was neat and classic handwriting, just a little faded because it was in pencil. She made out the first line to herself and gasped.

Alex was clueless and looked at Sally with anticipation. "Sally, what does it say?"

She turned with tears filling her eyes and answered, "It says, 'To Alex, A Great Fan and future Star Player."

Puzzled, Alex squinted at the line below it, wondering how she could read such handwriting. "Can you read the last line?"

Sally wiped her eyes and focused again on it to be certain. "It says, 'Fondly, Walter Johnson-The Big Train'!"

Chapter 15

About thirty-five members of the Finelli family and Laura, her daughter, and son-in-law from the Santucci family made it to the Pines of Rome restaurant in Bethesda on Thursday night. They were there for two reasons: the first being the chance to see their own All-Star, Alex, and the second being to get confirmation of the rumor that Alex was being traded to Washington. The cousins spent very little time with Alex during the season. Alex would spend the off-season catching up with each member of the family. Financially, he worked out incentives with any cousin from middle school to high school to earn free college tuition from him. Each cousin worked hard to achieve these incentives. They became celebrities with their friends because they were related to an All-Star baseball player.

Alex was worth well over one hundred million dollars. It would be impossible to know by his lifestyle. He owned only two properties, condos, in Kansas City and Cape Canaveral, Florida, overlooking the Atlantic Ocean. He did have three cars, one in DC that his mom used, one in Kansas City, and one in Cape Canaveral. He wore nice clothes but otherwise spent very little on himself. He still lived off of his draft bonus money out of Princeton. The $3.2-million bonus was still in a Goldman Sachs account he started in 1998. His academic adviser at Princeton, Paul Brightman, who had since become a famous economic pundit in the newspapers and on television, helped him initially with some financial decisions. Brightman helped him avoid the tech stock crash that started in 1999 by putting his Goldman account to work in a real estate hedge fund. By 2006 that fund had grown to $9.3 million. Alex then moved the money into a safer Goldman treasury fund, which he continued to live from. When he signed a big contract extension in 2002 and the current contract in 2007, he put a good deal of it into a Berkshire Hathaway hedge fund as well as Microsoft and Google stocks. Alex had given close to $20 million to charitable causes, including support of his extended family.

No one was aware of the engagement news except Laura, and she was great at keeping secrets. All the younger cousins wanted to hear about the All-Star game and about the rumors of the trade to Washington. They thought it was cool that Alex was his own agent and was smart enough to deal with owners and general managers. Alex disappointed most of the cousins when he reported that he doubted that he would be traded to Washington because of his big contract.

He was excited about being on a six-game winning streak with Kansas City. Most of the family was coming to the three-game series in Baltimore. Alex provided tickets and hotel rooms for family members interested in attending his games.

Marco, the owner of the Pines of Rome, continued to meet members of the party at the door and escorted them to the back room reserved for Alex and Sally. Pepe had already put out several carafes of house red wine and dishes of red peppers and anchovies sauteed with garlic and olive oil, broccoli rabe, escarole, white pizza, and Italian bread. Alex sat at one end of the table holding court with his uncles, father, brother, and male cousins. Sally was at the other end of the table with her future mother-in-law, stepmother-in- law, sisters-in-law, and female cousins. In the middle of the table were the twelve and under: children's cousins with the older kids attending to the younger kids. Sally observed that this was an old-world table with the adults talking to each other and controlled silliness from the kids, keeping the men and women apart. Some things never change with Italians!

Most of the men ordered either the succulent roast veal with a side of Pasta, or broiled whole rock fish, a Chesapeake Bay special. The women ordered the melt-in-your-mouth manicotti or the get-your-hands-full-of-sauce lobster diablo. The kids worked on pasta with meatballs or the lasagna with lots of bread.

Seventeen-year-old Guy Finelli sat next to his half-brother Alex. Both were unique athletes for their sports. Guy had sprouted to six-foot five-inches, two-hundred thirty pounds. He noticed that he was now taller than Alex, his arms were enormous, a neck of steel and his behind and thighs dominated the chair. His off-season workouts for football seemed to add a steel casing to his body. Guy had started University of Maryland in the spring semester to play in spring football practice. Those sessions really helped him get ready to play as a freshman, both physically and academically. With spring and summer courses and AP credit from high school, he would enter the fall as a sophomore academically. Summer football practice was only weeks away, and Guy planned to start at safety for the Terps. He would become a game changer in the sport. He was quiet but joyful and loved to talk with Alex about sports.

His half-sister, Grace, was sitting next to Sally at the opposite end of the table. Grace looked radiant in a purple summer dress, with her hair pulled up in the back but still hanging down around her beautiful neck. Alex observed that the two dark-haired beauties were shoulder to shoulder in conversation, acting already like sisters!

• • •

The waiter Pepe, now in his seventies, had first met Grandfather Guy Finelli and Gene Santucci in 1973 at the Pines. He had just emigrated from Nicaragua with his young family after the devastating earthquake in 1972 and knew little English. Guy and Gene soon became his best customers, usually adding a C-note to their regular twenty percent tip to help his family become settled. Soon most of their friends would ask for Pepe and the back room at the Pines. Pepe's oldest son graduated from Harvard Medical School in the late eighties, which Pepe proudly reported. After funerals for Gene in 1991 and Guy in 1993, Pepe personally brought one massive tray each of lasagna and sausage with peppers to the houses, refusing payment as he dished them out with tears in his eyes. Pepe had become part of the family even though they did little socializing together outside of the restaurant. The Santucci and Finelli families were two Italian immigrant families that understood the challenge of the present-day Hispanic immigrant.

The wine and the appetizers were inhaled as everyone continued talking while waiting for their entrees. Alex and Sally rose from the table at the same time, each with a glass in hand, and walked around the table connecting to members of the family. They met behind Laura's seat and asked for everyone's attention. Arm in arm, Alex led a toast to the family, asking for good health for everyone. He then unloaded the news of their engagement, which finished with a kiss to his mom and then with Sally. Quickly, all the adults and some of the kids got up to hug the excited couple.

When the celebration finally subsided, Pepe brought out the entrees, which led to fifteen minutes of quiet at the table as everyone consumed their delicious food. It was a great night with everyone leaving with a full stomach and a doggie bag.

Alex knew he would be back to work tomorrow in Baltimore as he said good-byes to family members. He would see most of them over the coming three days, but his focus would be back to baseball and winning for the Crowns. There were many things on his mind, but he was looking forward to spending one final night at the Westin with Sally.

· · ·

    Back in their hotel room at 9:12, the night was still young. They went for a walk through Georgetown and found a show at Blues Alley to sit and enjoy some live music. They were back at their room before midnight. Sally was fading, already in bed watching *House Hunters International* on HGTV.

    Alex was in the sitting area near the window, which looked north into the city. He picked up the package from the old man that was in front of him on the table. Sally had folded it neatly into the newspaper and back into the plastic. Alex held it in his lap, unsure whether to open it. He wanted to know whether it was really Walter Johnson's handwriting or not. Maybe he could ask Sally to make some calls tomorrow to check it out. He was unwrapping the package, while pondering its authenticity. It was hard to imagine what benefit a fabricated signature would do for somebody and then giving it away, but it would be nice to be sure. He looked into the scorebook and read some old advertisements on the first two pages, then a story about each manager on the next page, followed by the rosters of each team.

    The National League winners were the New York Giants, who had won the pennant the last three years and the World Series in 1921 and 1922. They were managed by the legendary John McGraw and had four Hall of Famers: Frankie Frisch, George Kelly, Bill Terry, and Hack Wilson. They had taken three games to two lead after winning the fifth game of the series at the Polo Grounds in New York, beating Walter Johnson handily 6-2. The "Big Train" had lost the opening game 4-3 and was looking like the World Series goat, giving up twenty-seven hits in two losses to the hard-hitting Giants. Fortunately, Senators left-hander Tom Zachary won the sixth game 2-1, pitching a seven-hitter in getting his second series win and tying the series three to three.

    The Senator roster held four Hall of Famers: player-manager Bucky Harris, Sam Rice, Goose Goslin, and Walter Johnson. He hesitated and carefully opened the next two pages to witness the sanctity of the actual scorebook kept of the game. He felt that it had not been open in eighty-eight years. The white of the pages, the faultless handwriting of the player's names, and the detail of each inning were all perfect. He was aware of the outcome of the game but never remembered the details of the contest. It had been twenty- five years since he heard stories about Walter Johnson and the World Series from his adopted father, Gene, and the one hundredth birthday celebration for Walter Johnson that he attended as a boy.

Bucky Harris started right-hander Curly Ogden for the seventh game, then replaced him after he retired lead-off hitter Freddie Lindstom with George Mogridge, who had won game four in the Polo Grounds 7-4. Mogridge was a veteran left-hander, who had gone 16-11 as a starter that year for the Senators. There was no score until a Bucky Harris homerun in the bottom of the fourth made it 1-0. It was the first hit off of Virgil Barnes of the Giants. The Giants broke out with three runs in the sixth when consecutive errors by sure-fielding infielders Ossie Bluege and Joe Judge allowed the go-ahead runs to score to make it 3-1.

First baseman Joe Judge played for Washington for eighteen years, amassing 2,352 hits with a lifetime .298 batting average. His lifetime .993 fielding average over twenty-one years of playing in the major league was amazing considering 72 of his lifetime 142 errors came in his first six seasons and he had to catch missiles at first base with a glove not much bigger than his hand.

Ossie Bluege was normally a third baseman but had to play shortstop in the seventh game because of an injury to regular shortstop Roger Peckinpaugh. Bluege also played eighteen years for Washington, amassing 1,751 hits and a .272 lifetime batting average.

Alex emerged from his trance of reading the 19 24

scorebook. He was imagining each play and batter from every inning. The score keeping was flawless with perfect penmanship while using a pencil!

It was 1:07 a.m. he rose from the chair and turned off the never-ending *House Hunters International* on HGTV. Sally was in a deep dream stage of sleep imagining real estate abroad. He looked out the window from the tenth floor of his hotel room, northeast toward the intersection of Florida Avenue and Seventh Street, about five blocks north and eighteen blocks east, imagining how the 31,667 attending Griffith Stadium on that sunny, Friday afternoon, October 10, 1924, had handled Washington being down 3-1 in the seventh game of the World Series.

After going scoreless in the sixth and seventh innings, the Senators were running out of outs heading into the bottom of the eighth and down two runs. Alex picked up the scorebook. While standing at the window, he wondered what Walter Johnson had thought at that moment sitting on the bench and watching his dream slip away. The same age as Alex, thirty-six at the time, and in his eighteenth season, The Big Train had a magnificent regular season in 1924 going 23 and 7, pitching 277 innings with six shutouts and a 2.72 ERA.

On the bench he could have been stewing about losing two World Series games in the last six days. Or maybe he was broiling about the throwing error he made in the bottom of the eighth of the fifth game that let in three unearned runs. Or maybe he was fried from the twenty innings he had thrown during that time and how overdone his arm felt from pitching a complete game on Wednesday. At that point, Walter Johnson had won 377 games in his career. The only thing he was thinking about, Alex concluded, was winning this game. He must have noticed that pitcher Fred "Firpo" Marberry was due to bat fourth in the eighth inning and Bucky Harris was sixth.

Alex believed that he went to player-manager Harris before the bottom of the eighth to tell him two thing:, "I'm ready to pitch the rest of the game, and you are going to tie this game up with another hit!"

The twenty-seven-year-old Harris could have looked up to the thirty-six-year-old Johnson and said, "You got it, Big Train!"

Alex stepped away from the glass and sat back down. He had a big day Friday, but he did not feel tired. He hoped to run in the morning and then have a late breakfast with Sally. At two o'clock he was due for an MRI in Baltimore and then an appointment with Dr. Walton. There was a team meeting at four, then batting practice at five thirty and a game at seven. He felt very much alive, feeling the love from Sally, his family, and the KC fans. It was great to be in DC and spend a few more days with the family while playing in Baltimore through Sunday.

Suddenly he had an idea. He turned on his computer and waited for it to fire up. He had to know if the signature was real! How could Walter Johnson write such a note on a scorecard? Was the man who gave it to him named Alex? Did he know he was a "future Star Player" or was that what he wrote to every kid? He could not have been more than nine or ten at the time. Alex pondered all the possibilities as he went to a website where he remembered seeing something that might prove the authenticity. *Baseball-Almanac.com* had a page for every baseball player who ever played. Alex had looked up players in the past, especially Walter Johnson.

He found it was on the first page below the Ty Cobb description of Walter Johnson, which said, "The first time I faced him, I watched him take that easy windup and then something went past me that made me flinch. The thing just hissed with danger. We couldn't touch him...every one of us knew we'd met the most powerful arm ever turned loose in a ballpark." He scrolled down a little farther, and there it was-his signature! It was on a baseball card shown on the site's Walter Johnson page. He remembered seeing it once. He grabbed the scorebook and held it next to the computer. It was exact! "The Big Train" had signed it-there was no doubt in his mind!

Alex sat back in his chair and smiled. It was real: the message and the messenger. He suddenly felt a kinship with Walter Johnson like he had never felt before. For Alex, Walter Johnson was on a mountain of greatness that he always was looking up to. He now realized what it was like to carry the weight of a community and a city on your back. A city desperate to win, daring to hope for greatness. He realized the mission he was on but felt a little confused about the direction. Was it his destiny to lead Kansas City to a championship with such a young team, or to be in DC to bring it back to greatness? He loved what was happening in Kansas City and figured the dilemma of the future would take care of itself. Now he thought to himself, what happened in the game?

Alex zoned back into the scorebook. He imagined the sold-out crowd waiting impatiently for a rally. Did they sense the greatness that was about to happen, or were they ready to accept muted success of the season and hope for another chance in 1925?

Ossie Bluege fouled out to start the eighth inning. Nemo Leibold pinched-hit for Tommy Taylor and doubled to left- center to give hope to the crowd. Slow moving catcher Muddy Ruel was the next batter. He was 0 for 19 so far in the World Series. Was he ready for baseball immortality? He finally got an infield single that put runners on first and third. Bennie Tate, pinch-hitting for the pitcher Firpo Mayberry, walked to load the bases. Then at the top of the order, center fielder Earl McNeely popped up to the shortstop for the second out.

Bucky Harris strode to the plate, already 2 for 4 with a home-run in the game. The twenty-seven-year-old was the youngest manager in baseball and a full-time second baseman while leading Washington to their first World Series. Pressure was apparently something he was equipped to handle because he was about to face a crowd that must have been frantic with anticipation. Plus the iconic John McGraw in the Giants dugout was certain to shout out unprintable slurs to distract his focus. Harris went on to hit .333 in the World Series with two homeruns, while hitting only one during the regular season. This was a moment he must have dreamed of all of his life, Alex realized as he saw the result of his at bat: a single to left field, scoring Leibold and the plodding Muddy Ruel from second to tie the game 3-3. Alex imagined the crowd erupting, feeling relief from the threat of a hopeless loss. Hall of Farner Sam Rice grounded to first base to end the inning.

    Alex visualized Walter Johnson as he walked out to the mound at the top of the ninth; he must have felt a source of energy from a higher power. He would have been pitching on pure adrenaline, having only one day off from pitching a complete game on Wednesday. The crowd may have had mixed feelings about their hero losing two games so far in the series, but most likely they rose to their feet to cheer "The Big Train" to victory. He may have thought back to 1913 when he threw fifty-six consecutive innings without a run or in 1918 when he pitched eighteen innings to win 1-0. There were so many times when he refused to give up a run, because to do so would mean a loss, like the thirty-nine times in his career he won 1-0. It did not matter how his shoulder, elbow, or body felt. Most likely he had no feeling in his body, just determination from the glow of destiny.

Alex turned to the Giants side of the scorebook to read the top of the ninth. Walter Johnson would have to face the top of the lineup, including three Hall of Famers. He got Freddie Lindstrom to pop up to third base, but then Frankie Frisch tripled to deep center field. With a man on third and one out, the chances of a team scoring were high when facing a Hall of Farner. Johnson decided to intentionally walk the left-handed hitting Ross Young, who had three hits against him in the World Series, so he could face, six-foot, four-inch, Hall of Farner George "High Pockets" Kelly. As he stepped to the plate,Johnson was certainly aware of the year he was having.

Kelly had the best year of his career in 1924, batting .324 with 21Hrs and a league-leading 136 RBIs. He had struck out only 52 times in 647 plate appearances. Johnson had to keep him from hitting the ball, other than a double play grounder, which was nothing to depend on as a certainty considering the field conditions back in 1924. He knew he had to strike him out. The matchup must have had the crowd biting their nails on each pitch. Alex could feel every muscle in his body feel the anguish of the pressure. How did Walter Johnson manage to get out the best hitter in the league? He struck him out on three pitches! Then he got Irish Meusel to hit an easy grounder to third base to end the inning.

Alex imagined the dugout as the ninth, tenth, and eleventh innings ended with no runs scored. And "The Big Train" was still going out there pitching his heart out! There must have been a tireless feeling of battle to the last man standing. Johnson gave up a single to Meusel to start the twelfth but struck out Hack Wilson, then got Jackson to ground out and the catcher Hank Gowdy to fly out to left field.

After Ralph Miller grounded out to start the bottom of the twelfth inning, three miracles happened. The first two were in the scorebook; the third one would be remembered in folklore. Muddy Ruel popped-up for what appeared to be an easy out, but the veteran thirty-five-year-old catcher Hank Gowdy stumbled over his mask and dropped it. Given a second chance, Muddy Ruel doubled into the left field corner. Then Walter Johnson grounded to short, which Travis Jackson fumbled for his second error of the game. With men on first and second and one out in the twelfth inning of the seventh game of the World Series, center fielder Earl McNeely strode to the plate.

McNeely was a twenty-six-year-old rookie who came up from the minors to play for Washington on August 8, 1924. He played in forty-three games and hit an impressive .330 for the season. In game seven he was 0 for 5. Many folks and film of the play document the final miracle of the inning, but it was not in the scorebook officially. By the twelfth inning, whoever was keeping score was on the back page writing over advertisements, but written below the inning are the words, "it hit a rock," with an arrow pointing to the hit by McNeely. Earl hit a grounder that third baseman Freddie Lindstrom was in position to field as a double play grounder. However, a pebble that was hidden in the third base chalk line caused the ball to go over his head into the left field corner. A film taken from the upper deck near the left field foul pole shows the ball jumping into left field, Muddy Ruel running home like he has bricks in his pockets with the winning run, and then thousands of fans storming the field in celebration. The feeling for Walter Johnson must have been electric as he went from first to second watching the grounder hop over Lindstrom and head into the corner sealing the World Series. Was he stoic and calm like his demeanor? Or for that moment did he jump into the air and thank God for such a victory?

What a night in DC it must have been on that October 10, 1924, Alex thought. With that imagined celebration in his head, he climbed into bed and dreamed a beautiful scene of baseball happiness that became etched into his memory

Chapter 16

Alex woke up alone in bed at 8:04 a.m., Friday, July 20, unaware that dawn had passed several hours ago. Sally was out, getting some coffee and reading the paper at a cafe on Twenty-Fifth Street. She returned with coffee as Alex got himself into the shower. He missed his opportunity for a long run with the morning rush hour now in full force. As Alex dressed, they discussed the family dinner last evening with great excitement, telling stories from each end of the table.

Alex then shared his experience from last night reading the scorebook. He took her hand and started to feel emotional thinking about the story he imagined. "I feel like something is happening to me-something beyond my life. The experience I had last night was something magical. I mean, it's just a book. But for me it was like the grandfather reading *Princess Bride* to his grandson. I was transformed. I was there in the stadium-on the field. I felt his emotions as he was waiting in the dugout, getting those outs after giving up a triple in the ninth, almost becoming the goat for losing three games in a series! Can you imagine? The pressure was indescribable. I was zoned out feeling him, being zoned in on Walter Johnson!"

Sally brought his hands to her chest, and kissed him deeply and passionately. They fell to the side on the bed, looking at and holding onto each other. Sally was caught up in the emotion of the week, and hearing Alex share such a deep experience was very powerful for her. They continued to be together for the next hour. Then they talked some more about last night while drinking coffee.

Sally, feeling a lot of emotion, told Alex she wanted to call her parents, while they were together, to share the good news of the engagement. He happily agreed to be a part of the call.

Roger and Elena Keegan lived outside of Lawrence, Kansas, about an hour west of Kansas City. Roger was a retired professor of economics, while Elena was a current professor in the School of Social Work, both at Kansas University. The two couples spent twenty minutes on a conference call discussing the excitement of the unexpected but well-received engagement. Roger and Elena were big fans of Alex but had wondered if this day would ever happen. Elena had counseled Sally to be patient with Alex because of his family history of adoption and his current baseball profession. They thought Alex was a kind, selfless, giving, honest, and caring human being.

Roger was an old school conservative, feeling that the world's resources should not be wasted on gaining personal abundance. He believed in the Rockefeller model of making great wealth through capitalism and then giving it back to the community for greater wealth and gain of the society. The Keegan family had become wealthy from a construction business that his grandfather had started at the turn of the twentieth century in the Kansas City area. Roger's father turned most of the wealth into commercial real estate ownership after the Depression. Roger himself was counseled and guided by his parents to pursue academics and then graduate studies instead of being involved in the company. He knew everything about the business from his experience growing up in the family and then studying it while doing his doctorate thesis in graduate school. His trust fund was enormous, but other than using some of it to set up a trust for Sally, most of it went to a scholarship fund at Kansas University's Economics and Social Work Departments. He liked Alex's smart, careful, and conservative approach to his wealth. His liberal wife knew that Alex's strong families ties kept him well grounded but limited in his emotional experiences. When they ended the call, both couples felt satisfied with the result.

Sally and Alex had not talked about a date for the wedding, but they were both excited about making it this off-season, probably in January, which was between semesters for Sally and before spring training for Alex. Her parents were thrilled after hearing that Florida might be a good site for the wedding, considering the weather for January. Details would be discussed at a later time. They had the resources to provide for hotel and airfare for all invited members.

Alex wanted to head up to Baltimore early to get in a workout before the two o'clock MRI appointment. Sally wished to see Cora, a Finelli cousin to Alex, in Owens Mill for a much-needed shopping trip. Cora was thirty- three, a natural blonde, and a size zero, even after giving birth to two children in the past three years. She knew the best stores in Columbia Mall and other shops around the Baltimore Beltway. She loved the adult attention after being with toddlers all day. Sally was thrilled she had volunteered her great shopping skills during dinner last night. Cora was always on top of the fashion scene. Sally was desperate to pick up some outfits and other things (like underwear!), since she decided to stay with Alex for the road trip through the end of the month. She had originally packed clothes for only three days in DC.

Alex had talked to his dad, Phillip, at the Pines dinner about driving to Baltimore early so they could spend some time together and give Sally a chance to take the rental car up to shop with Cora. Alex and Phillip were excited to get some alone time. He wanted to fill in his dad on the medication he was taking, the upcoming MRI, and his emotional reaction to the last week and a half of activity. Phillip had been a psychologist in the 1980s through 1991. He was the best listener Alex had ever known, extremely smart and creative in his thinking and responses. Alex used Phillip as his confidant on personal issues as well as a sounding board during any business contract negotiations. Phillip left the therapy business in 1991 after a period of depression. A series of factors led to the departure from the helping profession, but he mainly needed help on a personal level. Treating kids and their families with their problems for seventeen years had glossed over his years of depression. He had given them everything that he had, but after a while it was not good enough. During six months of paid leave, he finally started to heal and realized it was time to move on to something else. He started writing about his family history, which seemed to help him deal with understanding his problems.

Phillip then found success in business, getting involved in a supply company in the 1990s. He sold his interest to get into real estate, rehabbing homes at the turn of the new century. He was currently semi-retired at the age of fifty-nine, still writing and managing a few properties he owned.

Alex and Sally came into the Everett Street house in Parkwood to see Phillip and Carol. Sally had not seen the finished product since the renovations. Her future step-mother-in-law, Carol, had begged her to stop in on Friday. Carol was a nurse for twelve years before and after the kids had been born. When they reached school age, she finished her master's degree and went back to fulltime work outside the house. She had become very successful in the electronic medical records field working for the government in the Department of Health and Human Services. Now she was in private industry with a major health care company and making big money.

Uncle Anthony and his wife, Aunt Florence, had walked up from Brookfield Drive to say hi to the engaged couple. The three couples were still buzzing from last night's big announcement during dinner at the Pines. Flo was Alex's current financial adviser and tax accountant. She personally managed a twenty-million-dollar part of his portfolio and the cousins' scholarship fund. She ran a small but amazingly successful financial planning and accounting office in Kensington with a staff of less than ten employees. She was tough, extremely sharp, and loved horses. From riding her much-loved horse, Madeira, she kept her youthful-looking face and athletic body, which included very muscular thighs from years of dressage riding. Anthony joked that "her thighs were as muscular as Alex's but not quite as big!"

After thirty minutes of tea and a tour of the house, Alex and Phillip headed out for the forty-minute ride to Camden Yards. Alex expressed an avalanche of emotions that lasted half of the trip before he stopped for a breath. Phillip was stunned but overjoyed with Alex's expressions of feelings. He asked if anything physically had changed over the past couple of weeks. Alex reported changing to the Duloxetine medication based on Dr. Walton's concerns of some kidney and liver tests. He discussed the sonogram test results that revealed some concerns. Phillip held back his feelings of fear and asked if he could stay for the MRI and the follow-up meeting with Dr. Walton. Alex was delighted that Phillip would be there with him.

He then told Philip about the old man and scorebook story, starting in Kansas City after the All-Star game and the many hours of imagining the game last night.

"So you felt like you were on the field last night, following the game's every pitch?"

"Very close to it. I felt like I was one of those cameras over the field that is remote controlled. I would go in and out of the image after reading an inning of play off the score sheet. It was spectacular-like time travel but more like sensing their stress and relief, their pain and joy, their chaos and calmness. I was exhausted at the end. I cried with joy as I witnessed Walter Johnson watching Muddy Ruel galloping around third to score the winning run. You know if the left fielder hadn't given up on the ball when it hopped over third, I think he might have had a play on him at home!"

Phillip was barreled over by Alex's clarity.

Then Alex continued. "You know what 'The Big Train' did after he touched second base while watching Ruel score the winning run?"

Phillip was locked into Alex's storytelling and emotion. He could barely focus on the exit they were headed off from I-95. He quickly pulled into an empty parking lot off of Hollins Avenue, a couple exits south of Camden Yards. He put the car in park and looked at his beautiful son and saw his eyes moistening up. "What did he do, son?"

"He put his chin down to his chest and took a big breath and grabbed his right shoulder with his left hand and stroked it up and down to his elbow. He must have finally started to feel the ache. After a few seconds, he fell to one knee, then looked up to the sky and bowed his head again. Like he was Tebowing!"

Phillip nodded his head, not knowing what to make of the story. But he was sure it was real to Alex.

"Then I saw thousands of people pouring out of the stands toward home plate... like the camera was pulling back in the 'Atlanta on Fire' scene in *Gone with the Wind*. Walter Johnson was still kneeling at second base. It grabbed me like nothing I've witnessed before. It was all about relief for him! Can you imagine what that was like?"

"I understand, Alex. It must have been quite an experience. Did you remember any dreams when you woke up this morning?"

"No, I was out cold, woke up past eight o'clock this morning. I never sleep that late. Even after a late game I get up early to exercise, and maybe I'll nap later. The thing is, I feel great, never better. I feel complete whole, especially emotionally. Dad, do you think it's all real? Is it the medication? It seems kind of crazy, doesn't it?"

Chapter 17

Phillip pulled his Honda Accord into the Baltimore player's parking lot. Hal Baker had called ahead to his friends in security at Camden Yards to let them know about Alex and Phillip arriving. A Baltimore security man named Curt led both men into the stadium to the medical facilities. He asked Alex for an autograph for his son in little league. Alex wrote: "To Curt Jr., To a Great Fan and Future Star, Alex Santucci." He stuck a C-note back with the autograph.

Alex made it through the MRI without his usual Xanax medication. He dreamed about the upcoming series and tonight's Birds pitcher instead. He felt great about his swing and was looking forward to some swings in the underground batting cages.

Dr. Walton looked at the initial MRI and was not pleased. There was definitely some kind of growth on his pancreas and possibly in his adrenal gland. He was waiting for the more advanced MRI spectroscopy (MRS), which is used for a characterization of the tumor and its biochemistry. Physiological aspects such as aggressiveness and metabolism can be demonstrated from this test. It could still be benign or a vascular growth, but now a biopsy was needed. He would perform it himself because it was a tricky procedure. Now it would be question of when. It could not wait to the end of the season. He went to meet Alex and Phillip in the waiting area. He had known Phillip's father, Guy, and was glad to see Phillip. Henry Walton passed along the news of the MRI and the options. He expressed the news with great optimism for being able to solve the issue, internally he was very upset. He asked to examine Alex, who promptly jumped on the examination table and removed his shirt.

Phillip was in awe of his wide shoulders and massive forearms. Like his other children, Alex had been on the swim team during the summers at the YMCA. He enjoyed watching Alex and his half-brother Guy race in a fifty-meter butterfly last January in Florida. Alex had a lead at the turn, but Guy was in swim team shape and beat him at the end by a half-length. It was a great memory for Phillip

Dr. Walton noticed a red area right at his stitches on his stomach. "Is this from the line drive at the All-Star game?" Alex nodded yes. "What are these stitches from?"

Alex related the story about being hit by a bat, catching for a homerun softball game when he was seven. Dr. Walton had never noticed the stitches before because they had been covered by hair and stomach creases, but with the area being reddened by the line drive bruise, they were showing up. Dr. Walton followed up with some questions about the incident history but was now even more puzzled. Maybe there had been some internal bleeding from the bat's blunt force into the area. This may have left a growth that had matured over the past twenty-eight years. He thought, this kind of deep bruising that opened the skin with such a wide cut could also explain the multi-organ connection of the growth.

Both Phillip and Alex agreed to the biopsy procedure on Thursday, his next off day, at a private clinic in New York City. Dr. Walton was very familiar with the personnel and their professionalism at the outpatient surgery unit, which would help keep the procedure out of the media. He would wait to update the Kansas City GM Frank Fellows until after the procedure on Thursday. In the meantime, Alex had a weekend series to get ready to play. He left the meeting totally unconcerned about the news. Alex felt that the growth was something easily explained by his childhood injury. Both Dr. Walton and Phillip tried to mirror those feeling, but privately they were scared to death.

• • •

Laura was getting ready for a special night. Her son was playing in nearby Baltimore, and she was going to the game as the guest of the Kansas City owner, Larry Garson. A car service was picking her up at five o'clock from her Bethesda home. She felt odd receiving so much attention from a man, but Mr. Garson seemed very special and made her feel young again. It had been almost twenty-one years since her husband, Gene, had passed away. During that time, she had never entertained the thought of going out with a man. Being a mother to six children and a grandmother to twelve kept her very busy. She had traveled to Europe several times with special women friends over the years, but having a male companion never seemed to dawn on her. Being Catholic gave her structure in her life without a husband. She believed she had her one marriage in her life until she met Larry. He seemed down to earth but charismatic in his energy and enthusiasm about life. She could enjoy his company without worrying about taking care of him. In their little time together, they had spent a good deal of it talking about losing their spouses. They seemed to share a belief that God had a plan for them, to be strong for their family, and the future would take care of itself. The difference was his family was the Kansas City Crowns, because he had no family since his wife died. They had no children and they were both only children. Laura was surprised how happy she was when he called to invite her to New York City and then called back later in the day to say he was coming to Baltimore Friday night. He wanted to see her all weekend!

Sally met Laura at the stadium player's parking lot to go to the Kansas City Suite and see Mr. Garson. Larry was overjoyed to hear the news of the engagement for his favorite couple. He was convinced that Alex could lead his young team to the playoffs this year and was ready to pick up his option for $16.5 million next year, but his general manager was adamantly against it. He was aware of the trade that was on the table from Washington but refused to even discuss it. He knew in the next ten days, before the trading deadline, if the Crowns faltered badly against the talented American League East opponents, there would be great pressure to trade Alex for future talent and to save millions on this and next year's payroll.

Laura was dressed in a lovely, red silk dress with her

silvery, blonde hair down around her shoulders. Her lipstick, purse, and shoes matched her sleeveless dress. She wore white pearls as a necklace and earrings. Sally was dressed comfortably in a colorful pink and gray blouse with a white skirt and white open-toed shoes with low heels. Her hair flowed over her ears from behind a headband and down below her shoulders. Shopping with Cora had been a very successful venture.

Larry Garson held his hands up to his heart when the two picturesque women walked into his suite. He gave big hugs and kisses to both women as they sat beside him to watch the end of batting practice. He handed each of his guest, a gift box that contained diamond-studded bracelets with a sapphire stone in the shape of the famous blue KC Crown in the middle of the expensive diamonds. It was exquisite looking, and each woman held their breath as they put them on.

Mr. Garson was a happy man as he watched his young trio of sluggers, Homer, Felix, and, Mike, along with veteran Alex, take their swings. All four were putting on a show at Camden Yards depositing balls into the bleachers. Lefties Mike Miller and Homer Watson were trying to hit the brick warehouse building beyond the twenty-foot right field wall about five hundred feet away. Felix Mantilla was hitting souvenirs to left-center and right-center. Alex took his normal fifteen swings in batting practice. Ten of them were bombs down the left field line close to the second deck, and the rest were line drives to right field. He felt ready for the game.

Manager Pete Bowers was still batting Alex Santucci sixth in the batting order even though he had been on a hot streak during the team's six-game winning streak and the All-Star game. He had a hunch in the first inning that Alex would produce from that spot. The first two batters got on base with singles. Homer Watson struck out swinging, and Felix Mantilla bounced a slow roller to third for an out but moved the runners to second and third with two out.

Baltimore manager Barry Neighbors then made the mistake of intentionally walking left-handed batting Mike Miller to load the bases. Veteran right-hander Frank Mathers was a side arming fireballer who was tough on right-handers. Manager Neighbors had not seen tape of Alex lately crushing inside pitches, because Alex crushed the first pitch from Mathers about 475 feet down the left field line into the second deck for a grand slam.

    The crowd was quiet except for the ten relatives in the stands and the two pretty women on either of Larry Garson screaming at the top of their lungs. Larry was speechless, jumping up and down while getting hugs from Sally and Laura. Alex crushed another pitch in the third inning for a three-run homer, followed by two doubles in the fifth and seventh innings. When he came up in the ninth to a polite applause from the Baltimore crowd, Manager Neighbors finally walked him. Alex finished with 8 RBIs, going 4 for 4. KC took their seventh in a row, 12-2.

• • •

    KC owner Larry Garson took out Laura, Sally, and Alex to a private room at the *Don Shula's Steakhouse* on West Fayette Street, a couple blocks from the stadium, for a late dinner. Garson owned a steak supply company used by Shula's, so the owner was excited to accommodate his small party. They celebrated Alex's great night with champagne and prime rib. Alex, at the end of dinner, ordered a dozen bottles of the *Don Shula's Hot Sauce* to be delivered to his half-brother Guy, who had fallen in love with the stuff on vacation in Florida in 2005. Guy and Grace were coming to the weekend games along with twenty other relatives.

    Alex put on a show for the next two weekend games, hitting a homerun Saturday and two on Sunday with seven more RBIs. KC extended their win streak to nine with a rare road series sweep of Baltimore. They were only two games out of first place from Detroit and on their way to New York

City for a three-game series. Larry Garson was invited to stay at Laura's house in Bethesda on Friday and Saturday nights. She cooked breakfast for him as he stayed in one of the guest rooms. He enjoyed more than just the home cooking. They planned to fly to NYC on Sunday night from Baltimore to stay at a suite in the Plaza Hotel for three days starting on Monday night. Laura was having the time of her life and loved to stay in Manhattan. Sally and Alex stayed with the team at the Ritz Carlton, also on Central Park.

At Icon Stadium on Monday night, New York refused to throw the ball near the inside of the plate. Alex walked twice, tripled twice down the right field line in a 4-3 win for their tenth win in a row. On Tuesday night in front of a sold-out crowd of 52,325, left-hander B. B. King threw two cutters that slid toward the inside of the plate against Alex in his first two plate appearances. He hooked both of them down the left field line just inside the foul pole for homeruns along with a clutch ninth-inning single up the middle to drive in two runs to win 6-5, for their eleventh win in a row and a tie for first place.

Laura and Sally were acting like teenagers in NYC, cheering on Alex in the two wins over New York. They spent all day Monday shopping in Manhattan, visiting art galleries and museums on Tuesday, and were going to a Broadway show on Wednesday night. They acted like girlfriends getting their hair, nails, and toes done together, ordering room service at their different hotels, while speaking on the phone and watching *House Hunters International*.

Alex came to the stadium around ten fifteen on Wednesday morning to run on the field three hours before the game. He lapped the famous field for an hour before batting practice, while enjoying the many views of the two-billion-dollar stadium. He imagined the great sluggers, Ruth, Gehrig, DiMaggio, and Mantle, who combined for over two thousand homeruns during their careers wearing a New York uniform. He thought of Walter Johnson having to face Ruth and Gehrig batting third and fourth in the Murderer's

Row lineup twenty-two times a year for the last seven years of his career. Baseballs would have whistled from the mound, swings would be missed, the crack of the bats would have echoed through the crowds as balls were sent to all parts of the field and sometimes over the fence. Alex thought how those matchups in the 1920s may have saved baseball as America's pastime after the 1919 Black Sox scandal. How many in the crowd filling the stands had ancestors who watched those games? When did the excitement of the games become something that had to be watched in person? With the onset of radio in the 1930s and television in the late 1940s, the game exploded in popularity, but still fans had to come and see the real speed of the baseballs, hear the real crack of the wooden bats, smell the real mowed grass, taste the real hot dogs, and feel the instant excitement of that first homerun in person.

    By one o'clock most of Wall Street and their clients were in their box seats and suites while youngsters from day camps all over the tri-state area filled the bleachers in the outfield.

    Alex was playing for first place for the first time during his six years in a Crowns uniform, and he was not about to lose!

    Manager Pete Bowers changed his lineup, putting his three young outfielders up first, second, and third, with Alex batting cleanup, or fourth, in the batting order. ESPN was broadcasting the afternoon game nationwide. For the second week in a row, the Kansas City Crowns were dominating the baseball media scene.

    Mike Miller struck out leading off against the veteran Japanese pitcher Aoki Matsunagwa. He had more moves in his windup than a fast-played chess game. Homer Watson started the rally with a bloop double down the left field line. Felix Mantilla shocked everyone, including his manager, by dragging a bunt down the third base line for a single, moving Homer to third. Alex came to the plate with seven homeruns and an astonishing twenty-two RBIs in the last five games. He was 22 for his last 36, batting .635 during the eleven- game Crown's winning streak. The crowd was so certain they would pitch around Alex, with first base open, that they shared a collective gasp when the first pitch was over the plate and taken for a strike.

Matsunagwa felt that an intentional pass, or pitching around a runner, especially in the first inning, was not worthy of a Samurai-admiring, Japanese pitcher. In fact it was a cowardly act, or in his case, not worthy of a professional pitcher. New York Manager Chuck Grimaldi had given up trying to explain otherwise and was biting his fingernails in the dugout, sweating out this at bat.

Alex stepped out and thought about the next pitch coming, which he knew from experience with Matsunagwa was going to be a high fastball, and how far he was going to hit it. He asked for time from the veteran umpire Hector Morales behind the plate as he made an adjustment in his stance by digging out the back line of the batter's box. He tapped the bottom point of the plate, because he was six inches back in the batter's box, and laid the bat on his shoulder.

The New York, All-Star catcher, Ritchie Urban, laughed as he remarked, "Hey, Alex, man. You're so close to me. I'm going to catch on fire because you're sooooooo hot!" He then made a sizzle sound as he put down one finger for the fastball and tapped his chest, wanting it high above the strike zone.

Aoki nodded, then slowly came to the set for a moment, checked on his runners, and then quickly came to the plate with a high hard one. Unfortunately for the businessman's crowd and the day camp kids, it was not high enough. Alex met the ball with the full intensity of a human swing. It sailed over shortstop Erik Peter's head, then launched high into the atmosphere over center field and ricocheted off the black background, a hundred feet beyond the 407-feet sign. Next it tumbled back into Monument Park and came to rest between Ruth and Gehrig, where nobody sits. It was one of those homeruns!

Alex's three-run homer was the only scoring of the game as they swept the Icons 3-0 for their twelfth victory in a row. The Crowns now sat alone in first place in the American League Central Division. Larry Garson was beside himself with joy as he came into the Crowns locker room for the first time after a game. He was not one for the limelight or hanging out with the players, but he had grown close with Alex and his mom. Rebuilding this team had been a struggle. Seeing the young faces brought feelings that he had trouble putting into words. Manager Pete Bowers asked for quiet as Mr. Garson stepped forward.

The five-foot, six-inch, electrical engineering genius crumbled his Crowns cap as he spoke from his heart. "Boys, this had been the best two weeks of my life. I can't thank you enough for your effort. It has been quite something to witness. I hope you enjoy the day off in Manhattan. Stay out of trouble, of course!"

At that point, winning pitcher Hal Patton walked up to him and handed him the game-winning ball signed by most of the players with words "First Place" written all around it.

Larry was touched by the gesture and told the players, "This is all new to me. But I will cherish this moment the rest of my life. Thank you so much. I'll see you in Boston!"

And with that, a cheer went up and the party began!

• • •

As Alex walked out of the ballpark, he noticed some Crowns caps on fans surrounding the players' parking lot. He went to the fence and signed autographs for the fans, and then quickly hundreds of New York fans were asking for autographs. Alex had become a phenomenon in NYC. *The New York Sentinel* had a feature story about him on the sports page detailing his career in obscurity playing in the Midwest for fourteen years. It went on to discuss the All-Star game performance and his latest hot streak leading KC to first place. Suddenly his number seven Crowns jersey was selling at the stadium, and those fans were looking for autographs. Alex patiently signed for thirty minutes. He paused for a few moments to wave the bus back to the hotel and then continued signing with the fans.

Erik Peters saw Alex as he left the stadium and headed to his car. He shouted out to Alex and announced that he had dinner reservations for him. The fans loved the banter as Erik came over and joined Alex for a few minutes to sign autographs. Soon Erik grabbed Alex's bag and said to the fans," We're starved, guys, and Alex has a big furnace to feed, because he is generating heat!"

The fans obediently agreed and let Alex head off with his friend Erik, who led them off to his red Mercedes SL550 Roadster. They sped north toward the Henry Hudson Parkway to Hudson, New York, and the *Harvest on the Hudson* restaurant about twenty minutes north of the city. The Roadster would make it in about ten minutes, as Erik hit 120 mph on the parkway. Erik had "Mickey Mantle" status in New York: he was hands off by the New York City Police and media. His foundation gave ten million a year to benefit police and media workers in the area. His license plate, ICON 2SS, was a radar buster.

Alex needed this relief from the city and ordered a vodka martini as soon as they sat down at a great table overlooking the picturesque Hudson. It was nearly empty at five o'clock when the waitress came with the drink order. She was in awe, serving two of the most attractive, single, professional athletes in baseball. Erik ordered the mixed olives, bruschetta with red peppers and Anchovies, and the mortadella meatballs for appetizers. Alex appreciated Erik saving him from the fans and escaping to dinner outside NYC. He filled him in on the engagement and other events of the past two weeks. They moved to wine after martinis, as Erik congratulated Alex on the engagement and wondered what the heck was with the MRI results. He was impressed with Alex's calmness about it and listened intently as he talked about his options.

"The biopsy is scheduled for tomorrow in Manhattan, but I'm leaning toward canceling it. The time isn't right with the team on a streak and so forth."
"Yeah, but what if it's something that needs attention?" "I can't imagine that's true. So, I'm going to ruin my season for treatment...now? No way. This is too much fun, and besides, I feel great!"

"You are brave, my friend, and a little crazy, I think. Well, here's to the season, and hopefully we'll meet in the playoffs!" "Wouldn't that be something!"

Wine glasses clanked, and the contents were consumed quickly, along with the appetizers. After that they ordered dinner.

• • •

Larry Garson placed the baseball in front of his plate at *Daniel Restaurant* on East Sixty-Fifth Street on the Upper East Side in Manhattan. Laura and Sally were hopeful Alex might join them, but no plans had been made. They assumed he would be with his teammates celebrating first place this late in the season. Larry was into his second martini, as he had not landed on the ground emotionally after getting the game ball. Having this week with Laura was the greatest time in his life. He missed his wife since her death, but their marriage was anything but exciting. Laura was the woman of his dreams: sophisticated, smart, beautiful, and tough. The dinner and the show tonight would be the icing on the cake. He was scheduled to fly to Chicago for business Thursday but was planning to get to Boston for Friday night's game. He was hoping Laura would join him for the weekend.

Sally finally received a text from Alex explaining where he was and that he would see her at the hotel after the show.

Larry once again picked up the ball and read the names of his players scribbled on the ball. He thought about Alex and the trade that Frank Fellows talked to him about. Larry was usually all business, and logic dictated his decisions- like the flow of electricity-but trading Alex was out of the question. He did not care what was being offered. They were going to the playoffs with Alex leading them and Laura at his side. He was in love for maybe the first time in his life.

The trading deadline was next Tuesday, and he thought, instead of the first-place KC Crowns being sellers, they would be buyers! And, as for trading Alex Santucci. He chuckled to himself, over my dead body!

Chapter 18

Alex awoke at the crack of dawn on Thursday morning at the Ritz Carlton at 50 Central Park South. As he looked north from his hotel room and dressed for a morning run, he watched the first light surface over Central Park before sunrise. He started his run-on Center Street to Park Street, north around the ball fields, the rink, and the Wildlife Center.

He had texted Dr. Walton to cancel the biopsy and offered to pay any costs involved. He called ahead to the clinic as well to help them with their schedule.

The morning turned out to be a humid one with temperatures ready to jump, waiting for instructions from the rising sun. It was not a deterrent to Alex getting in five miles through Central Park. The blood rush to his mind cleared his vision for the future. He believed the excitement of a twelve-game winning streak and first place was the best reason to play the game in the torrid months of July and August. He had been in the playoffs with Minnesota in 2002, 2003, 2004, and 2006, winning only one playoff series in 2002. He was looking forward to staying "Hot in August" and to continue to "Sizzle in September."

While his body received the endorphins from his brain as he ran through the paths of Central Park, he felt serenity about being with Sally for the past two weeks. It was like finding a place at the seat of joy in Heaven. He never knew he could reach such a heightened consciousness.

As he saw an elderly couple walking briskly in front of him, he visioned his mom becoming enchanted with Mr. Garson. On the one hand it made him happy, but on the other hand it was weird-but really a good weird, like seeing an Impressionist painting for the first time. It gets clearer every time you see it. He knew it would continue to grow on him every time he saw them together. To see his mother so happy was worth living the weirdness.

    His energy level for life itself had seemed to go up a notch or two over the past two weeks. As he headed back to the hotel, he thought about his homerun yesterday and hitting in general over the last two weeks. His game plan was almost perfect for every pitcher, and seeing the ball was the clearest in his career. He felt in harmony with his body, and his mind was like the tai chi masters on the lawns in Central Park doing their battles in slow motion. Like honing an attack strategy, his swing felt effortless and right to the ball. The result was the five-hundred-foot homerun that he crushed yesterday that ended up appropriately at the feet of baseball's greatest sluggers in Monument Park. It was number eighteen of the year and put him just four behind the great Senator slugger Frank Howard for his career. Alex was now batting .315 with 70 RBIs, which put him in the top five in both categories in the American League.

• • •

    Laura shared some coffee with Larry in their suite at the Plaza Hotel as he prepared to fly to Chicago on his private jet. A company that he owned was looking to purchase a large herd of Buffalo in Montana and the land where they grazed. It was an amazing opportunity but would take a great deal of capital from Larry. Banks were not excited about financing land in Montana. Larry was looking for a high-protein, low-fat product for his meat supply company. This purchase would widen the type and supply of meat that he sold to restaurants. For public relations purposes, the Montana land would become a nature reserve with part of the herd siphoned off every year for slaughter. He would fly out of LaGuardia and be at Midway by 9:07 a.m. He needed to show up at the meeting with several Chicago banks to help the board of directors secure financing with his backing. Otherwise, he planned to be in Boston for the three-game series.

Larry asked Laura if they could meet this weekend. Laura wanted to be hesitant but could not blurt out yes quick enough. She would fly first class on Saturday afternoon and meet him for an early dinner in Boston. He hugged and kissed her as he left the suite, feeling tears in his eyes from the impending separation for two days.

• • •

Sally was awake in the hotel room as Alex returned from his run. He wanted to rent a car and head into New Jersey to visit Princeton and the town where his grandfather grew up. Erik Peters demanded that he take his Acura SUV for the trip. He could return by Friday and take the train to Boston. It was an offer he could not refuse.

Alex and Sally headed out of NYC, south to the New Jersey Turnpike to the Brunswick Exit, taking Route 18 to US Route 1, pass Trenton and south to Princeton. The traffic was light for the forty-five minute drive. Alex had called Dr. Paul Brightman and was lucky enough to find him available for tea to meet his fiance Dr. Sally Keegan. He was very happy to hear about the engagement and the current winning streak of his team. They talked about public policy, among other topics. Dr. Brightman accepted an invitation from Dr. Sally to come to Park University to make a special seminar presentation during the fall semester. It would be a bonanza for her department to bring in such a celebrity, especially right before the election and the coming federal budget battle.

Alex and Sally then met with Dr. Brightman and Princeton President Shirley Tillman to confirm a one-million-dollar donation that Alex was making in honor of his grandfather, Guy Pinelli. It would fund financial aid scholarships in the Economics Department and any science or engineering departments for athletes in football and baseball. Alex had been working on this for years and was excited to actually have it come together at this time.

After a wonderful lunch in the president's house and a tour of the campus, Alex and Sally headed on US Route 206 for the twenty-minute ride toward Raritan, New Jersey. The Raritan Valley was an area where the Nariticongs Indians, a peace-loving branch of the Lenape and part of the greater Iroquois Nation, lived when the Dutch and English first arrived in 1683.

Hillsborough, which was the town just across the Raritan River, was home to Duke Farms, the 2,740-acre Doris Duke estate. They stopped in to see the newly opened thousand acres of natural habitat that included lush forest, meadows, and her famous century-old orchid house. Doris had pioneered and developed hundreds of hybrid orchid flowers. Alex was aware that his grandfather's life of almost eighty- two years mirrored Doris Duke's life. They were born within a year of each other, in 1911 and 1912, and both died months apart in 1993. As a boy, Guy Pinelli and friends would cross the Raritan River on the Nevius Street Bridge to play along the meandering stone wall that surrounded the Duke property. A story was told that Doris herself played with Guy and his friends until word got back to her father, James Duke, founder of the American Tobacco Company, who put a stop to it. In 1920 Mr. Duke wanted to give forty million dollars to Rutgers University in New Jersey to change their name to Duke University. Eventually he found a suitor in the tiny Trinity College in Durham, North Carolina, to take the forty million, and the rest is history.

After the tour through the estate, they crossed the newly build First Street Bridge into the town of Raritan and turned right on Canal Street to see the grand, three- story, white house where his great-great Grandparents, great grandparents, and grandfather had lived together until 1926. That fall, Guy Finelli entered the nearby Sommerville High School, as his family had moved to a house on Nevius Street about six blocks away. Guy lived there until 1939, when he moved to Washington, DC, to work for the Navy Department. He had met Rose earlier in 1939 at a Finelli cousin wedding in Wilmington. She attended the wedding from her hometown of Philadelphia. They were married in 1942.

Textile Mills, built in 1846 on a canal that paralleled the river, made uniforms for the Civil War and World War I. It attracted Italian immigrants to Raritan from the 1880s until they closed in the 1930s. Sally and Alex walked on Canal Street up to the grand white house restored in the past twenty years to its original grandeur. On the lawn, they turned around toward the Raritan River to imagine the now filled-in canal and mill that occupied the meadow next to the Raritan's riverbanks for ninety years. His grandfather Guy told stories of when he was a boy watching the four hundred workers walking up Canal Road, in front of their house at lunchtime, to go home for a quick hot meal, then back again to the mill within thirty minutes.

They headed up Nevius Street to view the Finelli house and then onto Main Street. They read the history about George Washington spending a winter in nearby Sommerville during the Revolutionary War. They also read how President Harding signed the Treaty of Raritan at the home of Senator Joseph Frelinghuysen in Raritan, which officially ended World War I in 1921. They saw the statue of the great World War II hero and Congressional Medal of Honor winner John Basilone, a Finelli family friend, who for four days and nights almost single-handedly held off three thousand Japanese soldiers, killing hundreds to help win the Battle of Guadalcanal in World War II. After three years of stardom and selling war bonds across the country, he volunteered to go back into combat to train solders going in the Battle of Iwo Jima in 1945. He died while saving hundreds of American soldiers taking a key hill that led to the famous sculpture next to Arlington National Cemetery of soldiers planting the American flag.

They returned to the car for the short ride to

Sommerville High School to see the plaque of Guy Finelli in the sports Hall of Fame. It was very emotional seeing his grandfather as a seventeen-year-old in 1929, in his orange and black wool uniform, the same age as his grandson Guy, who was a foot taller at six foot five and now getting ready to play football for University of Maryland. Alex was a young man entering Princeton the last time he saw the landmarks of Raritan. It had very little effect on him at the time. His grandfather had passed the previous year and was not yet inducted into the Hall of Fame. This felt different, and being with Sally made it feel like the life they were building was a part of a greater legacy-a part of Italian and American history that would he could honor by playing the best he could in the future.

They drove to a local cemetery and found a row of ten Finelli family members under an eight-foot marble statue of the archangel Gabriel. He found his great-great grandparents' headstones, born 1857 and 1864 in Italy, along with his great grandparents' headstones, born 1887 and 1888 in Italy as well. He instinctively knelt down, holding Sally's hand as she joined him. He quietly cried with his head down, praying to God that he be worthy of their heritage. A cloud passed over, hiding the sun as a light breeze swirled from the direction of the angel statue, sending a coolness that chilled his spine in this ninety-degree weather. He sat back on his calves and felt a deep, deep rumbling from his stomach percolating into a spasm of emotion that rocked his body. He doubled over, still on his knees with his hands no won the ground. A wave of sensation forced him to let out a wail of weeping that felt like years of loss and pain.

Sally rubbed his back gently as she witnessed her fiancé let out something deep inside that never had seen the surface of feelings. After several minutes, the sky got darker, and a soft, healing rain began to fall, seemingly cleansing Alex and easing him from his emotional pain. He slowly rose to his feet and kissed each headstone and found shelter under an old, beautiful oak tending to the cemetery. The couple held each other as they gazed at the beauty of the angel watching over his departed family. He missed his adopted dad, Gene, but now he knew he belonged to the Finelli's.

• • •

They went to the Marriott in nearby Bridgewater to find a room. Alex slept all afternoon and woke up feeling refreshed around six o'clock. They got in the car and drove a few miles down US Route 202/206 to see his Great-Aunt Helen and Great-Uncle Ernesto (Ernie). Alex did not call ahead because he was not previously sure of his schedule for the day and did not want to disappoint them if he could not make it. He knew from his dad, Phillip, that Thursday nights Helen and Ernie and their three grown kids, Philomena (Philly), Patrick, and Linda, and grandkids would get together for summer cookouts.

They headed up Allen Road, turned left on Foothill Road and right onto Glenwood Terrace as they headed up toward the Watchung Mountains. Phillip would spend most of August here until eleventh grade. Two of his aunts lived next to each other on acre lots. The pool was a half-mile run through open backyards up the foothills. Ball playing, swimming, fun, and great food were the only agenda all day.

The long driveway was filled with cars. Six of the cousins were playing basketball. As Alex and Sally walked up, Patrick Jr. yelled, "Dad, Grandmom, look who's here. Come on over here!"

Eighty one year old Aunt Helen scurried over to Alex, holding her hands to her face saying, "I can't believe it. I saw you on TV yesterday hit that homerun. What are you doing here? Is this Sally? Your mother called me about you two. Oh! my goodness!" She kissed them both as most of the cousins crowded around for hugs, kisses, and introductions.

Alex remembered that in the car he had a box of a

dozen unsigned baseballs that he kept in his travel bag for this kind of occasion. All the young cousins followed him to the borrowed Acura SUV. When Patrick Jr., a huge New York Icon fan, looked at the license plate, ICON2SS, he yelled out, "Is this Erik Peter's car? Are you kidding me!"

Alex nodded and told the story about sneaking out of the stadium parking lot in the Mercedes Roadster. He started to sign the baseballs to each individual cousin. A baseball star was suddenly in town!

Alex joined Sally who was sitting with eighty-eight-year- old Uncle Ernie and his daughter, fifty-nine-year-old cousin Philly. They were thrilled to see the vibrant and exciting couple. Helen was the youngest sister of Alex's grandfather Guy, and Ernie was the younger brother of his grandmother Rose. Their kids were double first cousins to his birth father, Phillip, and his older brothers. Double first cousins were more like brothers and sisters because they shared the same set of grandparents and DNA pool. Cousin Philly and Alex's dad, Phillip, were nicknamed "Twin Cousins" because they both born on June 7, 1953, within seven minutes of each other. They were named, without consultation, after different great-grandparents. It was confusing but pretty cool, Alex thought, when his dad first explained it to him twenty years ago. The bottom line was that Phillip and Philly were really close.

Cousin Philly, suddenly left New Jersey to do her junior and senior years of high school in France, then college in Italy followed by a sixteen-year failed marriage to an older Greek tycoon-very Jackie Kennedy-like. After twenty-two years in Europe, she returned in August 1991 to live in New York City, divorced and wealthy. But first she came to Bethesda to attend Gene's funeral and lived with Phillip and Carol until Grace was born, taking care of the house while Carol was on bed rest. She helped financially when Phillip left his therapy career to deal with depression and some legal problems. She provided great moral support to both Phillip and Carol, then funded Phillip's supply business for the first year and refused to accept any repayment when it became successful.

Alex sat next to Philly, astonished at how much she looked just like his dad but with perfectly-styled, shoulder-length brunette hair. They had not talked together for many years. Alex did not remember her being so engaging and personable, as he talked about today's journey through Raritan and his feelings at the cemetery. She shared Phillip's empathetic ear and made him feel normal and healthy about his emotional reactions.

"You have gone through quite a lot of success and stress in your life. You just have not had enough time to process the stress. Stay with it; don't run away from it, like I did." She kissed him on his cheek and continued. "Now, when are the two of you going to visit me in Manhattan? I'm jealous about your friendship with Erik Peters-my goodness! After the season you must come and see me. Maybe your dad and Carol will come too. It will be fabulous. Now, how is my goddaughter Grace doing? Aerospace engineering-she is just incredible!"

They continued to catch up on all the family members. Uncle Ernie then motioned for Alex to come sit next to him. "You really put it to my Cons this week! Jeez, what a shot yesterday. I thought only the Mick could do that! You must be pretty excited about the team. Patrick told me you were going to Washington before the All-Star game. Now twelve in a row, jeez, what a streak!" Alex had never seen Uncle Ernie so animated; he had the same beautiful smile as his sister and Alex's grandmother Rose. He had been a great local Philadelphia baseball player but went to fight in War World II during his prime years. He had a tryout with the Phillies during spring training in 1948 but took a lucrative truck driving job to support his family instead of playing in the minors at age twenty-four. He married Helen three years later.

The darkness finally settled on the day around nine o'clock, leading to long good-byes. Alex and Sally retreated to the Marriott and hit the bed quickly and slept soundly.

Chapter 19

The cell phone buzzed several times, bouncing on the night table and acting like a crying baby. Alex cradled it and saw his mom's name on it. The time, 10:43 p.m., was beaming on the bed-side clock as he turned on the light, got up from bed, and sat in a chair. He thought, she is still up, maybe excited about the coming weekend, wanting to check in on my day. "Hey mom, what's up?" He could hear crying on the line. "There's been a crash...His plane went down in the big lake." She paused and was silent.

Alex waited a moment and then asked, "Who mom? Who went down?"

"Larry. Larry's gone. They found him in the plane...and the poor pilot...a good man ...two good men. Say a prayer, Alex. Say a prayer."

"Mom, are you alone?"

"Nina is here. Phillip and Carol are coming over. I'm okay, dear. I just wanted you to know. Be safe, dear. Take care of Sally."

"Mom, I can be there in the morning..."

"No. No, you need to carry on. I am fine. God gave me a gift for two weeks. I'll never forget him, but I have my family. I'm fine, really. I lost your father when you were fifteen. I understand God's plan: it gave you Phillip. You can be there for the team; they will need you. Call me when you get to Boston tomorrow."

"Okay, Mom. Have Phillip call me when he gets there. I love you, Mom."

"Love you, my dear. Please pray tonight."

Alex turned on the television and looked for the news. *CNN* had the wreckage being pulled out of Lake Michigan. The running banner below read: **Larry Garson 78, KC Crowns Owner Dead...Plane Crash...**

Sally was sitting up and cried out while grabbing a pillow for comfort.

"Oh my God! This is insane. Why would this happen? Your poor mom. What did she say? Should we go there? Oh, Alex... What a sweet soul he was. He loved you like a son. I can't believe this is happening!"

Alex switched to *ESPN*. Crowns President and General Manager Frank Fellows was making a statement to the press. The team would play in Boston this weekend and come home to Kansas City Monday for the funeral. Frank was trying to be stoic, but he broke down and left the podium. At the sports desk, Larry Leonard, a University of Maryland graduate, shaved head and all, was on live reporting about the plane crash, being fed information simultaneously into his earpiece. He went on to wing a biography about the self-made billionaire and brilliant electrical engineer.

Another Terps graduate, Bonnie Bramlett, stood outside the Ritz Carlton at Central Park South, trying to catch players coming in from a second full night of celebration before heading to Boston in the morning. She was reporting tidbits of statements received from other owners and players. Suddenly the young trio of Mike Miller, Homer Watson, and Felix Mantilla stepped to the microphone with Bonnie. It was stunning television: truly scared big men, crying, trying to put into words their loss. Felix held Homer and pulled him away to get into the hotel. Mike Miller found some eloquence about keeping up the spirit and carrying on in his honor. Bonnie thanked him and sent it back to Larry Leonard, who was talking slowly and deeply about the young players being in shock.

Alex turned back to *CNN*. The desk reporter was saying something about the lightning hitting the plane soon after takeoff, then losing power and hitting the water just off the Chicago shoreline into the lake!

Alex's phone was buzzing; he was expecting Phillip, but it was Frank Fellows.

"Wanted to make sure you got the news and you were

okay."

"Thanks, Frank. Are you okay?"

"I don't know. Too much to do...too much to think about. The train is leaving about ten a.m. If you can make it, it would help the kids."

"I'll be there at eight a.m., Frank. I'm so sorry just anything I can do."

"I know, Alex. He really loved you, kid. Your mom must be..."

"She's okay. I already talked to her. Her daughter's there and my dad. She's pretty tough."

"He loved her, Alex. I've never seen him so happy. I can't believe it."

"See you tomorrow, Frank. Try to get some sleep."

Alex hung up and the phone buzzed again, a Maryland area code. "Alex, this is Bonnie from *ESPN*. I'm so sorry for your loss. Can I help in any way?"

"Thank you. I know you would like to talk. I'll be at the Ritz Carlton by eight a.m. Call me and we'll sit down."

"Okay, only if you're up for it. I know you were close. I'll say a prayer for your mom."

"She would like that, Bonnie; she would really like that!"

•••

Friday morning at the Ritz Carlton was a mob scene. Hal Baker had flown in at two in the morning to help coordinate security for the Crowns. He called Alex at 6:00 a.m. to give him directions on how to get into the hotel. Erik Peters had a car service waiting for him to go to the hotel after he dropped off the car. Alex and Sally went to the conference room the hotel had set up for the players, wives, fiances, and girlfriends. Immediately Alex sat down with the young trio trying to console Homer Watson, still not accepting the news. The rest of the players stood around Alex's chair. Manager Pete Bowers came over and announced the schedule for the day. After thirty minutes of consoling teammates, Alex got some coffee and called Bonnie Bramlett to set up an interview. Frank Fellows was pleased that Alex would speak for the team after the fiasco last night in front of the hotel with his young trio of budding stars.

• • •

Bonnie had a cameraman and a producer in a hotel suite set up to sit with Alex for an interview. She started with a heartfelt condolence. "Alex, speaking for *ESPN* and most of our watchers, we want to express our sympathies for your great loss of Larry Garson. What would you like to say to your fans, the Kansas City fans, at this time?"

"Thank you, Bonnie. My heart goes out to the Kansas Cit Crowns fans, who were Larry Garson's family. After the death of his wife, Larry's only family was the Kansas City Crowns and their fans. This is a tremendous loss for Kansas City and for baseball. Mr. Garson was about as real as a person can get. He was brilliant in his field and advanced medical services forever in this country. I had the honor of playing for him..."

Alex felt his throat and took a second to recover. "When he first called me in November 2006 on the first day of free agency, he asked if he could send a plane for me to come to Kansas City. I said, please let me take Southwest Airlines out there, but he insisted. We met, and just the two of us toured the stadium and Kansas City. He told me the best place to live, the history of the area. We shook hands on a deal right then. I didn't even look at the numbers-I was so certain that he would be fair. When he sent me the contract, I was shocked at the amount and generous terms. He was a very special man."

Bonnie collected herself, mesmerized by the love Alex was expressing for the fallen Crowns owner. "What happens now, Alex? Your team is in first place on a twelve-game winning streak. How do you go to Boston tonight and play?"

"Bonnie, it would be an honor to play this game and every game this season for Mr. Garson and his memory. We have jobs that he gave us and a great opportunity to do something we love. That part is not tough. We are the lucky ones tonight to honor him by performing our jobs."

Bonnie thanked Alex as she teared up and sent it back to Larry Leonard at the *ESPN* sports desk, still up from last night.

Larry turned to his colleague and said, "There are very few times in this profession when you step out of your role as a broadcaster, but I want to say on a personal level...I know that Alex Santucci lost someone very close to him last night. He is from a great family and is without question one of my favorite athletes in professional sports. He spoke from the heart there-maybe as eloquent as you can speak for your fallen hero. I know his family was very close to Larry as well -especially over the last two weeks. I will be watching the game in Boston along with America tonight..." He trailed off and his partner Chuck Segal went to an advertisement.

Larry Leonard left the set to get some sleep. He got a phone call on the way to his room from Alex Santucci who had been watching from the Interview Suite with Bonnie.

"Thanks, Larry, for your support. I hope we can get in some golf when this is all over."

"Alex...I'm so sorry...going on like that. It was just so special watching you. Good luck tonight. Take advantage of that Green Monster!"

"No doubt about it, Larry!"

• • •

Alex rose from his chair and embraced Bonnie and her beautiful, tall, wide-shouldered, athletic body while she thanked him for the interview. They were similar ages, both college and professional athletes. They dated briefly when she played basketball for the Minnesota Lynx in the WNBA for a year in 2000. She moved on the next year to play for the Los Angeles Sparks for three seasons and then went into broadcasting. They had stayed good friends ever since. She kissed Alex on the check and wished him good luck tonight. As Alex walked out of room, Bonnie reminded him, "Send me an invitation to the wedding!"

Chapter 20

A 5:45 a.m., the cleaning crew from Butler Cleaning in Hoboken, New Jersey, entered the 64th Street Outpatient
Clinic in Manhattan for Sloan-Kettering Institute patients receiving treatments for lymphoma, melanoma, and other types of cancer tumors for the head and neck. The clinic also specialized in endocrinology and pain and palliative care. James Edwards was a recovering heroin addict in his sixth clean month since his release from inpatient recovery who was working on the midnight to eight cleaning crew. His wife was working two jobs to keep up the income while James got himself clean. His boy, James Jr., was a good student and a solid track athlete, thinking about being a walk-on at Rutgers University in the fall instead of Patterson Community College, but funds were vacant. He hoped to earn a scholarship after his freshmen year. Along with other offices on the floor, James handled the trash in the director's office and cleaned the bathroom and vacuumed the huge Oriental rug. He always left this office for the last, like working his way up. Someday his son might have an office like this place. The director had a shredding trash can that was taken in a special purple plastic bag to be destroyed confidentially. His regular trash was usually full of empty Starbuck's coffee cups and food from the day.
On the top of the regular trash can next to the desk was a piece of paper, maybe a memo, laid open on the pile with the words facing up. As James picked up the can, there it was: college tuition for Junior!
The director had come to his desk on Thursday morning and read the phone message canceling Alex's Santucci biopsy. He backhanded it off his desk in anger after reading it, leaving the medical folder hanging on the side of

the desk. James read it and opened the folder. Dr. Walton's notes on the sonogram and MRI, and a general history were on one page. He took off his gloves, picked up the piece of paper by the edge, walked over to the fax/copier/printer, and presto: proof for the tabloids!

• • •

The team arrived at Fenway Park around four o'clock after settling in the hotel and dealing with the crowds of fans and reporters. Fans from Boston had dropped off flowers surrounded by candles in a pile, thirty-feet long and a couple feet high at the bus entrance for the players to see. It was a classy move that the players appreciated. The meeting held by Manager Ron Bowers, batting practice, and interviews before the game were a blur by the time Mike Miller was ready to step to the plate around eight fifteen. After the national anthem, there was a minute of silence for Larry Garson, followed by a flyover of a single Korean War-Era, Grumman FYF-Tigercat that Larry had developed the electrical panels for as a teenage seaman in the US Navy. It slowly circled Fenway and then fired its afterburners, disappearing into the sky. The crowd, already on its feet, roared with emotion and continued applauding for two minutes.

Frank Fellows had told the players via teleconference that Mr. Garson did not want any armbands to be worn by the team in the case of his death. But he did not say they could not wear black socks to honor their fallen owner. The players were proud to wear the black socks.

The crowd gave solid applause for the trio of young hitters in the first inning, but veteran right-hander Dirk Hamlet struck out all three on nine total pitches. When Alex came to the plate in the top of the second, veteran catcher and team captain Mason Williams took off his mask and laid it on the plate as he went out to the mound. The crowd stood and politely clapped and whistled for the veteran and hottest hitter in the league. Mason headed back to the plate as Alex met him in front with his mask. Williams draped the mask on Alex's shoulder and passed along condolences from the Boston players.

Alex tipped his hat to the crowd for a few moments and then settled in at the plate. Working off of a night of no sleep and a day of adrenaline, Alex was looking for an inside fastball to bounce off the Green Monster in left field. Quickly, before Hamlet could start his windup, Alex asked for time. His hands were soaked with sweat as he asked for a towel from the on-deck circle. Under the circumstances nobody would dare protest. He thought again about the pitch sequence and realized Hamlet would start him off with his eighty-three-mile-an-hour changeup. He set up three inches up in the batter's box, tapped the middle of the plate, and laid the bat on his shoulder. Hamlet came to the plate with the right pitch, like a golf ball on a tee. Alex rotated his swing down to the ball, with the meat of the bat six inches off the ground, and golfed the ball high and far over the thirty-seven-foot, two-inch-high Green Monster and into the last row of Monster seats. The Fenway crowd was in awe of Alex and, maybe for the first time ever, rose and cheered for an opposing player to come out of the dugout to tip his hat. Alex obliged, bowed, and held his hat above his head while pointing to his heart. The crowd got louder and louder with more people standing. Alex stepped into the dugout while the crowd continued to cheer. The ball he hit was thrown down to the field and relayed to the catcher, who walked it over to the KC dugout and made Alex come out again to receive it. He put it in his pocket and wished he could give it to Mr. Garson.

The game lasted until 11:43 p.m. with Boston breaking the Crowns' twelve-game winning streak with a convincing 12-1 win. The team had no gas left in the tank after the adrenaline ran out in the second inning.

• • •

At 1211 Avenue of the Americas in Manhattan, four minutes after the game ended, *New York Post* editor Nat Sheridan was staring at an article written by his best writer detailing a potential life-threatening illness to the most popular baseball player in the country. He paid twenty thousand for the information to keep the *National Enquirer* from making a joke out of it. He was trying to figure out the headline to go out on the midnight website update and the morning paper. Nat Sheridan finally decided to go with a real screamer: Baseball Star Alex Santucci Facing Pancreatic Cancer

Chapter 21

Not long after the game ended, Frank Fellows was sitting in his office in Crown Stadium after watching the Crowns lose to Boston, meeting with three lawyers representing the estate of Mr. Garson. The part of the will referring to the baseball team was being read to him. As he was aware, in the event of Larry Garson's death, he would be named CEO of the team with full powers to run the club, but with one big caveat. Other than a generous ten-million-dollar bonus payout to him and several million to other staff members, the club would be financed by its own net assets. The rest of the estate would go into a foundation to be determined by the wishes of Mr. Garson, which were written into the will. Frank would be able to take on partners to raise money to run the team, but essentially he would always control 51 percent of the team as a subchapter of the foundation. His salary would be five million dollars per year, not to exceed ten million dollars in full benefits.

Frank realized that the cash flow for the team would be difficult for several years and that the payroll would need to be well below the current seventy million dollars. He knew he had to take action before 3:00 p.m. CDT on Tuesday, July 31. He picked up the phone to see if Presidents GM Jim Franco was still awake.

"My God, Frank, you must be going crazy. I'm so sorry to hear about Mr. Garson. What can I do for you?"

"I'm ready to make the trade, but I can't finalize it until Tuesday because the funeral is Monday...and I got to work this out the right way."

"No problem, Frank. I understand completely. We really want Alex-that is no mystery. Let's agree on the prospects tonight if we can and see if we can send some paperwork on the medicals without notice."

"Thanks, Jim. This means a lot to me and the future of the Crowns. We can't let this get out, so we have to be careful beyond a doubt."

"I got a security guy that can handle it if you have a go-between you can trust."

"Yes, I do. His name is Hal Baker. What do you think of the guys I sent you in the e-mail?"

Ten minutes later, an agreement to send the hottest hitter and the most-loved baseball player in the country to his hometown was completed.

•••

Early Saturday morning, Alex and Sally took a cab that drove them from the Ritz Carlton at 10 Avery Street in the heart of Boston Common, over the Anderson Bridge, and into Cambridge to roam the town and see the famous Harvard campus. Sally made plans to meet a colleague and her husband for breakfast at their house near campus around nine o'clock. At six-thirty in the morning, they found the air was crisper in New England during the summer than the Midwest. They ran together on the banks of the River Charles as they took in most of the campus. After an hour of running, walking, and sitting on America's oldest campus, established in 1636, they headed for Harvard Square, found a Panera Bread restaurant, and got some much-needed coffee.

As he slowly drank in his first sip, Alex got a call that he realized was Bonnie Bramlett. At the same time, he read the banner running on the *MSNBC* morning show: Santucci Facing Cancer Threat.

"Bonnie, I think I know what you're calling about. I'm reading it on *MSNBC* at Harvard Square."

"I am so sorry to bother you, but the story just broke at midnight. The *New York Post* has some medical notes from a canceled biopsy appointment in Manhattan. They look real, Alex. Are you okay? Please say it's not true!"

"I'm fine, Bonnie-just some anomalies on some tests. I feel great."

"Oh, thank God. Well, you may want to get ahead of this.

It's going to be a wildfire by tonight. Let me know if I can help."

"Okay, Bonnie. I'll think about it and call you."

Alex got off the phone and told Sally about the leaking of his medical notes and tests to the *New York Post*. She was more concerned what all the stress in the past three days was doing his emotions.

"I feel great when I'm with you. That's all that counts. Who cares if they have the tests? What difference does it make? Dr. Walton may get in some hot water for not letting Frank Fellows know, but it's really up to me to get the biopsy or not. I'm still playing. Obviously, it's not hurting my playing."

"You're right about that, my dear. I think we should get Bonnie up here for a sit-down interview with you and me. Like the Bill and Hillary thing before the election... Oh yeah, that was for affairs. I guess this is different, duh!"

"Oh, you're a riot, Alice! I hate to drag you into this, but maybe it will help cool down the story. But you're so hot looking-I think that might make it worse!"

"I can't help that. I'm pure Kansan-Midwest cute and clean!" She did a little shaking of her hair and stuck out her chest, putting her hands on her petite waist.

"Wow, that'll work on television. I can't wait until Bonnie calls you, Dr. Keegan!"

"My students will love it! Let's do it. Come on, let's head over to Claire's house and make out on the way!"

"Like high school students or college coeds? Remember, I'm a baseball player who likes to hit homeruns!"

"Well, nothing wrong with singles and doubles before nine a.m.!"

They got out of Panera with their coffees before the big crowds arrived and found a quiet route to her friend Claire's house. Alex called Bonnie and asked that she come to Boston for an interview with him and Sally. She was in agreement and thanked him for a chance to get into the national spotlight as an interviewer. She could see them by noon at the hotel. It was a relief to set up the interview. The events of the last few days had become so crazy that becoming playful seemed to be the only way to handle the stress this early in the morning for Alex and Sally.

They stopped under several large trees as Alex got in a few bases before 9:00 a.m. Sally loved wrestling with Alex. He was like a large, friendly bear that she could get wrapped up in, put up a playful fight, and still feel safe. She loved to sit on him and hold down his broad shoulders while she teased him with her hair in his face. Eventually he would use his massive forearms and large paws to lift her up like a five- year-old and make her fly like an airplane as she laughed like a kid. His phone was buzzing, and he saw it was Dr. Walton. He reluctantly picked up the phone. They traded emotional thoughts about Mr. Garson, Dr. Walton then apologized for the leak.

"Frank was pretty upset about it. I take full responsibility for delaying the update to him, so then he calmed down and wanted all the medical records sent immediately. But, Alex, I strongly urge you to reconsider about the biopsy. I think it may be from an injury, but it is definitely a growth in there. Not really a good place for something like that. With another impact to the abdomen, you could bleed to death-like an aneurism in the brain."

He thanked the doctor and told him not to worry. They would talk about the issue on Monday in Kansas City.

Alex was glad to be off the phone and snuggled up to Sally, putting his arms around her as they huddled under the tree. He closed his eyes and smelled her scent and wanted to breathe it forever. He pulled her chin toward her and kissed her softly on her lips and down her neck and chest. She felt his warmth but saw his guard down for a tickle attack. She pinned him down and worked on his neck under his ears. Soon he was laughing like a little boy, forgetting about the doctor's phone call or the interview at noon.

They headed to Claire's early and were relieve to hang out with a couple not involved in their stressful last couple of days. Kurt owned a bike store in town. He was an amateur bike racer in his late twenties and still biked five hundred miles a week. Claire was a professor of public policy at Harvard and had been a classmate of Sally's parents. Kurt and Claire had two children, Sandra, seven and Karl, four. They were still in pajamas, calmly playing in the living room.

They had pastry, fruit, yogurt, and nuts on the dining room table with juice, coffee, and tea. Alex toured the turn of the century house with Kurt. He loved the oak molding that edged the ceilings and the walnut handrails on the stairs. It reminded him of his grandfather's work in what was now his dad's house. He started to think about how it would be to buy a house with character and age that he and Sally could work on to make their own. He looked forward to the opportunity to create a home and raise kids. It was only recently that he had thought about these things. His feelings for Sally changed what he looked forward to now.

After a couple of hours, they thanked their hosts for a great diversion. Claire and Kurt insisted on driving them back to the hotel and brought along the kids. They were warned about the potential zoo at the hotel but were to create a home and raise kids. It was only recently that he had thought about these things. His feelings for Sally changed what he looked forward to now.

After a couple of hours, they thanked their hosts for a great diversion. Claire and Kurt insisted on driving them back to the hotel and brought along the kids. They were warned about the potential zoo at the hotel but were oblivious to the situation. Sally and Alex enjoyed the extra half hour with their friends. It was fun to see them act as a family and to witness their love of parenting. As they arrived at the Ritz, none of the press corps noticed them.

"I knew the old Dodge Caravan would be a decoy!" Kurt remarked as he and Claire wished Alex and Sally the best in the next few days. They were certainly going to need it!

Chapter 22

Baseball is unlike any other game on the planet played by professionals in front of large crowds. A team can be at the top of the mountain sporting a winning streak or as a low as the Dead Sea and ready to fire the manager, and a week later those positions can drastically change. Eighteen days in a season can be an eternity for the fortunes of a team or an individual. Alex Santucci rose to the top of the baseball world, where he was loved by his owner, teammates, and fans. Now he was facing questions about his health that could impact whether he could play the game or, even worse, if he was going to be around much longer. Two teams had made decisions about him and his future. Just twelve hours prior, Frank Fellows was looking like Judas selling his savior for pieces of silver. Now Presidents GM Jim Franco was explaining to his owner why he wanted to spend ten million dollars and three top-fifteen minor league prospects for some dying old veteran.

Frank Fellows and Jim Franco still wanted to do the deal for different reasons, but they would both have to finesse the media, fans, and ownership in different cities to get in done. They spoke on the phone several times in the morning and were working up strategies based on the outcome of the noon interview.

"I think if Alex looks fine and doesn't fall apart, it will get down to how he plays tonight. Hopefully he can jack a couple tonight and get us a win," Frank Fellows exclaimed to Jim Franco, hoping they were on the same page.

"I agree, Frank. Our medical guys see no short-term problem with him playing. I hope for the best, please God. But we just need him for three months of baseball."

"All right, Jim, I'll talk to you after the conference probably."

Jim Franco had already briefed Hank Meyers on the

situation. Hank and his father, Frederick, were going to watch the news conference together at noon. Frederick Meyers was not pleased about the potential negative publicity from the medical news when they planned to announce the trade after the funeral. He was planning to be in Kansas City Monday for the funeral. The plan was for a media release of the trade as they were flying back to DC, with a press conference around 6:00 p.m. Frederick Meyers had originally foreseen home sellouts for the rest of the year because of the trade, making the ten million dollars a solid investment. Now he was not so sure about the effect on the attendance.

• • •

    The mob surrounding the hotel had no use for the 1995 Dodge Caravan pulling up to the entrance. Alex and Sally made a quick break into the hotel before anyone noticed. They headed to their suite to await a call from Bonnie informing them of the location for the interview.
    Alex returned a call to Phillip, assuring him the medical news was under control and he would be fine. Phillip was still visiting with Laura, so he put Alex on to talk to his mom, who told him to do what he thought was right and that she was fine. They were traveling to Kansas City on Sunday, and Alex insisted they stay with him.
    Dr. Walton and Frank Fellows had flown into Boston for follow-up interviews with Bonnie and others as a strategy to combat the negative story. No one in the organization but Frank was aware about the pending trade. If a question came up, he would act like Alex was one of many Crown players that he received calls about but had no interest at this time in trading him.
    Alex and Sally were led into a room at the Ritz Carlton with huge windows in the background that showed the Boston skyline. She hugged both of them with great pleasure and then stood holding a hand of each one.

"I hope you don't hate me after the interview. I have to ask all the devil advocate questions involved in this situation. Please don't take it personally. I love you guys."

Sally spoke first, as though they had been best friends for years." Bonnie, this is your job. We are here to make you look good! We can handle ourselves under pressure. Don't worry about a thing."

Alex followed up with a very personable tone. "I think you are the best at what you do. I want everything on the table, otherwise they'll think we like each other too much!"

They all chuckled and sat in their chairs as the technical people signaled two minutes. Bonnie's face became solemn and serious as she went through her notes in the final minutes. She started with some softball questions about how he felt currently and congratulated them on their engagement. Then she threw a fastball question high and tight.

"The medical report shows that you started on the medication Duloxetine some eighteen days ago. Is that for depression, Alex, or because of your medical situation?"

"Actually, Dr. Walton is prescribing it for aches and pains in order to relieve my body from taking ibuprofen and acetaminophen for a while. It seems to be working like a charm."

"Is there depression in your family?"

"As you know, Bonnie, I am adopted. So, I do not have much medical history from my birth mother's side. But my birth father, who is very close to me, did go through some depression. I believe there is some in the extended Finelli family as well. To be honest, Bonnie, I have never felt better in my life, and clearly I am playing well."

Sally jumped in on the conversation. "Bonnie, Alex is doing very well. We are overwhelmed by the support of the fans and hope to continue to be available for questions. Alex has always been available to the press and the fans. I support his decision to put off the biopsy at this time. We believe, after looking at all the medical tests, there is no impending harm in finishing the season."

Bonnie continued with some tough questions about steroids and other drugs that he might have used in the past. She asked detailed questions about the medical MRI showing a growth in his pancreas and adrenal gland. Alex and Sally continued to patiently answer every question without the slightest hint of defensiveness.

Alex finished with this answer: "I believe ultimately we are allowed to control our own decisions about our bodies as adults. If it turns out to be a stupid decision, then I will suffer the consequences. My job is the greatest in the world. I plan to be out there as long as I can run, hit, and throw."

Frank Fellows and Jim Franco high fived over the phone about the success of the interview and agreed to talk further after game. Sally thanked Bonnie after the interview and went to their room to make some phone calls.

Bonnie took Alex to a side room and held his hand. She felt deeply for Alex. Her feelings had passed a romantic phase and moved into a reverence phase with a deep trust in him. She would always want to run away with him but was truly happy that he was in love. She thanked him and said to keep in touch on how he was feeling. She knew he would get swept up in the media dance and go far, far away. Maybe some afternoon she would get a call from that deep voice telling her to come and see her again. Hopefully it would be to talk about better circumstances. They embraced as she kissed him, softly on the lips, while staring into those confident, deep-brown eyes.

After reading every word of the medical report and viewing the unreleased MRI, she was anything but confident about his health. Bonnie was very worried about her friend, but she had to do her job and report the truth.

• • •

Saturday night's game was the Crowns' best of the

year. The team was on fire from the first inning when they scored five runs, including a three-run blast by Alex Santucci, his twentieth, and on through to a seven-run fifth, when Alex hit a two-run homer, his twenty-first of the year. It was a 13-0 spanking with a complete game two-hitter by rookie Parker Paisley. The media were impressed by the healthy looking Santucci, and most of the stories involving the medical crisis were laid to rest. Only the Sunday game and the funeral on Monday lay ahead before the trade could be consummated between Kansas City and Washington. As Frank Fellows and Jim Franco worked on the final's details of the trade, there was a medical clause they were trying to clean up. It involved taking out the usual language regarding physicals and replacing it with, "In the event of unknown or known physical injury that leads to permanent disability of player involved in transaction, the said team will be compensated by like baseball talent and/or monetary funds to be agreed upon by both teams or otherwise an arbitrator appointed by the commissioner."

It might be the first trade in recent history not to be dependent on the involved players passing physicals. After team lawyers reviewed it, the trade would be signed off on Monday around 1:00 p.m. CDT.

Chapter 23

Sunday morning as the sun broke the horizon above the Atlantic Ocean in the town of St. Augustine, Leah sat in her favorite spot on the beach praying to God about her son's health. She had read the story this morning detailing the medical information and the coverage of the interview with her son and that beautiful dark-hair girl in the picture, his fiancé, sitting next to him. After an hour of prayer and meditation, she exercised for the next hour, running and stretching, following her professional routines she honed over the years as an experienced trainer.

She returned to her spot after eight in the morning and held the phone in her hand, pondering her next decision. She had carried Phillip's number on her phone for the past twenty-five years. They had spoken once in the twenty- one years since Phillip had entered Alex's life. After that hour conversation from which she drank up every bit of information Phillip expressed about Alex, she promised God she would never inquire about Alex's life without God's word through prayer or spiritual awareness. She would wait with quiet expectation for the Christmas card from Alex updating her on his family's year. Within that letter, which fell from the card every year when she opened the highly awaited envelope, Phillip would write a paragraph about Alex and his life. She would hang on every word and savor the images they would produce of her beautiful boy.

She finally pushed the send button and slowly put the phone to her ear as her beautiful, long flowing, silvery blonde hair hung down in front of her face. She sat crossed legged on a beach towel, leaning forward, and counted the ring tones because she was petrified at the outcome.

Phillip, finding a spot on his patio for some privacy, answered after the fourth ring. "Leah, is everything okay?"

"Phillip, oh my gosh, it is so good to hear your voice. Is

this an okay time to talk? I am so sorry to bother you this early on a Sunday."

"Leah, it is wonderful to hear from you; it is fine for you to call anytime. I have told you that. Please, what can I help you with?"

"Is Alex sick? Please tell me. I can't bear the thought of him suffering..."

"He is fine. This thing is overblown. He feels great and is playing like an All-Star. I will see him tomorrow in Kansas City."

"Oh God, thank you Phillip, I just needed to know. I don't want to take up more of your time."

"Leah, it is fine. It is wonderful to hear from you. I think of you often. How are your kids and Charles?"

"They are growing up, Phillip. Only Nancy is still around the house. She just graduated Georgia Tech and is starting a job in Atlanta next month. Paul and Claudette are both in Charlotte, working and doing well. Charles is retired, plays golf, and is not around a lot." Her voice fell off from her normal high-energy positivity.

"I'm happy to hear that your kids are so successful. How is your business and your music?" Phillip asked, wondering if Leah was her usual full-of-energy self.

"I'm really busy, traveling more often. I'm singing with a group out of Orlando that I really enjoy. We're doing a lot of my songs. You and Carol should come see us if you're ever at your condo!"

"That would be wonderful. We should really keep in touch more often." Phillip suggested wondering if they could ever be included in each other's world.

Leah's heart dropped while she formed the courage to ask Phillip an important question about Alex. "I would really like that, Philip. You know how much I think of you and Carol. I would never want to impose myself into your lives."

"Leah, you are always welcome. You have decided to stay away...from us..." He hesitated to say the thing he wanted to say: the subject they never talked about.

Leah sensed the opening and said what she had hoped she would be able say. "I know this is crazy, Phillip, but I wanted to ask permission from Laura and you and of course Alex... to...Oh God!" The tears cascaded out as she fell to the blanket and curled up around the phone.

Phillip understood her reaction and waited a moment before he responded. "Leah, you have always been welcomed by us. It would be up to Alex. I would be glad to talk to him later today."

"Oh, Phillip, you are such a loving man. How can you forgive me for what I have done? I'm not worthy of it. It is selfish of me to want to see Alex. I gave him away!" She tried to control herself, but the stomach spasms were taking over her body. She was embarrassed by her reaction but could not control it. She prayed to God for calmness.

Phillip was crying as well, wanting to be there in person to help Leah with her pain.

Suddenly the ocean wind from the north whipped up sand and blew her towel over her, covering her tears. Phillip heard nothing but static for a minute. When it stopped, Leah stood up and wiped her tears and was breathing regularly.

"We had such a special bond, Phillip. I have so much love for you. Please pray and decide if you think it is the right thing and let me know. I trust your judgment."

"I will, Leah. I know it's the right thing to talk to Alex. Keep him in your prayers."

"Always, my love, always." Leah rested the phone on her heart and bowed her head to thank the Lord.

• • •

The Sunday game was at 1:35 p.m. Frank Fellows met with Crowns Manager Hank Bowers before the game about Alex Santucci. "I think it would be a great idea to give Alex the day off today. It's been a grind for him. Maybe he could pinch-hit later, but it would be nice to give Mattos a chance at third and Ramos at first."

Henrique Mattos was a rookie, playing first at times and backing up all infielder positions but was the Crowns future third baseman. Ramos was a young, left-handed hitting, backup catcher, crushing the ball whenever he was in the lineup.

Bowers, oblivious to the manipulation of the situation by Frank, was intrigued by the suggestion. "Well, I kinda hate to take Alex out of the lineup, but I like to see Ramos at first and Mattos at third. Patterson will get a day off tomorrow; he'll get by behind the plate today."

"Thanks, Hank. Talk to Alex for me, but don't mention I thought of it."

Kansas City fell to Boston 8-2 but stayed tied for first after a 7 and 2 road trip. They were glad to take an early flight to arrive back to Kansas City. Alex was surprised at Hank's decision to give him a day off but enjoyed every second of it. He did pinch-hit in the seventh and ripped a double to the left field comer, scoring the Crowns only two runs of the game.

As he sat in the Crowns locker room, Hank announced to everyone, "I'm proud of our effort as a team on this road trip, and we're still tied for first place." Cheers all around.

"Now, Monday will be a hard day, but as a team we will get through it!"

There was rumbling agreement in the locker room.

"We will be home for almost two weeks, which will help. Now I want to make another announcement."

Everyone looked up, wondering what to expect, as Hank headed behind Alex.

"Everyone, let me introduce you to the American League leading hitter at three-thirty-nine!"

A rousing cheer went up, with a chant of "Alex, Alex, Alex" starting.

Hank raised his hands for attention. "Let me say: three- thirty-nine batting average, twenty-one homeruns, seventy-eight RBIs, Gold Glove play at third base...! think we got ourselves the MVP of the league right here!"

The chant of "MVP, MVP, MVP," was even louder.

Hank continued. "Alex, you are worth every penny of that contract. I hope-and I think I speak for everyone here- that you are around here, God willing, as long as I'm here. God Bless you, son." With tears in his eyes, Hank awkwardly hugged a sitting Alex, but he had spoken from his heart for the entire Kansas City Crown community, which "God Willing" would handle the emotional roller coaster coming tomorrow.

• • •

Phillip, Carol, Laura, Anthony, and Florence all made the trip to Kansas City Sunday night for the Larry Garson funeral on Monday. Alex asked all of them to come and wanted them to stay with him through Monday night. He wanted to be around family after the funeral. Phillip asked Alex and Sally to walk down to the sixth-floor garden area to talk about his birth mother, Leah. Phillip had discussed it with Carol, Laura, Anthony, and Florence on the plane ride out to KC.

Phillip spent a few minutes asking Sally how much she knew about Alex's history of adoption. She informed him that Alex had talked about it very little except for some basic details. Phillip then gave a detailed background story of Leah's upbringing, his relationship with Leah, and the circumstances that led to the adoption. He continued talking about how he first became involved with Alex and how he started to keep Leah informed every year in his Christmas card. He then presented Leah's request to meet both Alex and Sally and to ask for forgiveness for giving him up.

Alex's first reaction was to ask about what she needed forgiveness for. He always believed it was a selfless decision to seek the best upbringing for him possible. He always had been loved and never felt given up. Phillip felt relieved at his reaction. Sally was supportive of Alex and was curious to meet Leah.

While Sally was speaking, Alex thought it through and then said, "Dad, it would be great to have Leah in my life, to meet my half-brother and sisters. I understand she is my birth mother, and maybe over time I will develop a relationship with her like I did with you. But Laura is my mom, and that will never change." They all agreed with those words of wisdom. "Do you think she can join us in Kansas City tomorrow?"

Phillip was shocked but delighted at Alex's question. "Are you sure, son?"

"Absolutely, I need my family around me tomorrow."

Phillip called Leah with the great news. She was hesitant at first but then jumped at the chance. For now, it would be a secret from her family.

"Phillip, you are God's gift to me. This is like giving me life. My grandfather lives in Kansas City, and this is a great chance for me to see him. He lives in the downtown area. He is my father's father. I think he's ninety-five or so. You know he grew up in Washing-ton, DC, until he was fifteen or so and then moved to Tennessee and made a lot of money. He ended up buying a lot of property in Kansas City in the sixties after I was born."

Phillip was happy for Leah and was excited that she was coming, but he had never heard about this grandfather before. "Wow, that is great, Leah. Call me when you get in tomorrow, and we can meet up after the funeral. By the way, what is your grandfather's name?"

"Oh my gosh, I never told you, Phillip! I named our son after him-Alex!"

Chapter 24

Crown's Stadium was adorned in black, and the flags were at half-mast. The memorial service was scheduled for 10:00 a.m. By eight o'clock, the parking lots were half full already with thousands of mourning fans drinking coffee, smoking cigarettes, and sharing donuts while talking with each other about the man they were about to honor. As soon as entrances were opened at eight thirty, fans embarked on a procession to get the closest seats available to home plate.

Mr. Garson had grown up in a Quaker home but did not practice the religion as an adult. His wishes for a service involved opening the stadium for the players to express their feelings to the fans and for members of the Crowns organization, including players, to be involved in talking with the fans. Frank Fellows led off the service, explaining what would happen over the next ninety minutes.

In the first half hour, 125 Kansas City Crown personnel, including players, coaches, scouts, trainers, sales representatives, and front office workers, went to sections of the stadium and talked to the fans. They asked and answered questions, listened to tributes, joined in prayers, held hands, gave hugs, and overall tried to soothe the pain people felt about losing Mr. Garson.

The next hour involved tributes from players. Any player wishing to speak was given two minutes to talk. After each speaker, there was at least two minutes of silence to meditate on the words just spoken. Fifteen players spoke, with Alex being the last one.

After a thirty-minute run down to the river in the morning, Alex had stopped on the way back at the City Diner to pen his percolated thoughts as he drank coffee.

The crowd was quiet but slowly rose as Alex came to the microphone. It seemed like he was talking to them, but he was thinking about his friend and mentor.

"It is time to say good-bye to you. When you welcomed me as one of yours, I had no doubt it would be great for me to be here. I was still too young to understand the emotion of being accepted and being treated like a favorite son. But you taught me how to be at home here and how to accept love in a relationship. You made me feel comfortable from the first moment I stepped in this stadium. Now I will remember you whenever I step onto any field in any stadium. This will always feel like home, even when I am away. You will always be with me. Please know that I love you and will miss you forever."

The crowd quietly stirred through the silent meditation, wondering whether the loss of Larry Garson was the only casualty that might happen to their first-place team. Every team was represented by their owner or general manager. Only Jim Franco, Frank Fellows, Frederick and Hank Meyers, and two security go-betweens knew that Alex had said his final good-byes!

• • •

As a gesture to remember Larry Garson across the community, Heartland Depot donated forty-thousand, three-inch-high samplers of flowering dogwood trees to each and every attendee. It was Larry Garson's favorite tree and also the official Missouri state tree. In addition, ten medical trucks with diagnostic equipment were stationed throughout the parking lots for people to get free health check-ups. They were all from one of Mr. Garson's companies, with the personnel donating their time. The medications and use of equipment for tests were all free. Overall, Larry Garson would have been pleased with the simple nature of the service. He would have loved the efficiency of providing the opportunity for medical care and the chance for the environment to be replenished with plant growth.

Phillip, Anthony, Florence, and Sally surrounded Laura as Frank Fellows led them to a grass bank past the outfield fence. He had several maintenance workers there ready to help them plant their trees in memory of Larry. Then the 125 Crown personnel would also plant trees. The grass bank would never have a plaque but would always be known as "Garson Woods."

• • •

Hal Baker was in turmoil sitting in his office after the memorial service. He had been the middle man for Frank Fellows, sending and receiving confidential medical reports and contract information on the players involved in the upcoming deal. Losing Mr. Garson was a personal blow that he was having trouble accepting. Larry had treated his family as his own, at times covering medical expenses for his wife and college tuition for his three children, which Hal would never have been able to afford. No one outside the organization knew how much Mr. Garson had done for his employees. Now Hal was being asked to handle information to help the Crowns get rid of their best player, which would have never happened if Mr. Garson were still alive. He knew it was his job, but he felt like Benedict Arnold. Suddenly there was a knock on the door.

"Hal, I'm glad I caught you here. I wanted you to meet my family. You know Sally of course, but this is my Dad, Phillip, and.."

The Dough Man could barely talk, but he plodded his way through the introductions. Alex noticed that Hal was very emotional.

"Mr. Garson took care of a lot for his employees. I know Hal was very close to him," Alex told his family as he looked straight into his friend's eyes. "We'll just have to stick together, Hal, to get through this. Won't we, Hal?"

Hal nodded with tears coming down his plump cheeks. He held onto Alex's hand after they hugged and asked him to stay a moment. Alex got the message and motioned for everyone to go to the car and wait for him.

"Alex, I have something to tell you. It will probably get me fired...Damn it, I'm just overwhelmed by the stupidity of it!" "What is it, Hal? You can tell me. Are they selling the club?"

Hal settled himself and looked up at the much taller Alex. "That bastard Fellows is announcing it today at one p.m. You're being traded to DC, Alex. This is so outrageous. He will never get away with this insanity!"

Alex was standing but felt his legs go numb. He found a chair to settle into. Air had just left his body, and he was seeing stars in front of him. After about thirty seconds, he could hear Hal ranting on about the team and the city losing their owner and their leader on the field. He started to breathe and see clearly again as he looked at his phone to check the time. It was 12:17 p.m. The phone started to buzz in his hand. It was Frank Fellows. He was too numb to answer the call. He had to get out of the stadium. "I'm sorry, Hal, but I've got to go now. No one will know we talked. Thanks for being such a good friend. I've got to get to my family. Things will be okay. We'll talk later."

They quickly hugged again, and Alex darted out of the office and to the players lot, taking the back way that Hal had taught him. He got to the car and quickly motioned to his family to do the same. Luckily the crowds were mostly sitting in the parking lots with trees in their hands, talking with each other.

Alex was quickly able to take the west end exit and get on Interstate 71 going north. It was smooth sailing as he challenged the handling skill of the Acura TL, speeding to the condo to arrive by 12:35 p.m. Fortunately his family did not notice he was pale and trembling the whole ride. They were talking intently about the service and thought Alex was driving like a maniac to get out of the nonexistent traffic jam at the stadium because he was caught up in his thoughts.

When they arrived at the parking garage, Phillip reminded him that Leah was meeting them for lunch at one o'clock. She had texted Phillip that she arrived from the airport and was taking the car service Alex had arranged to her grandfather's residence at 2004 Grand Avenue, just a couple miles south. Sally had organized a catered lunch in the condo for the family as a way to make Leah to feel at ease meeting Alex's family.

As he walked into the lobby at 909 Walnut, Alex was distracted enough to start imagining meeting his birth mother. Regrettably, Frank Fellows was at the service desk, ready to challenge his imagination!

Chapter 25

Leah had not visited her grandfather since he moved to this place in 2005. Since the early seventies, he had lived on a beautiful ten-acre estate in Johnson County, Kansas. She remembered traveling to visit her grandparents in Kansas with her family before her parents divorced during her sophomore year of high school. Her older sister had been home from college for the summer and joined them on the trip. They took long walks on the grounds and listened to her grandmother tell stories about her dad growing up in Kansas. Leah's dad was a Seventh-Day Adventist Church minister in Maryland at the time of the trip. After the divorce, he went to live in Tennessee and later remarried, leaving Leah alone with her troubled mother.

Leah had made a couple of trips with her family during holidays to visit her grandparents in Kansas before her grandmother died in 1995. Her grandfather held onto the place for ten years before relocating to downtown Kansas City. He was now ninety-five and living with a butler, who doubled as a driver and a fulltime chef. Like his granddaughter, he was strictly vegan.

Leah was feeling settled after having tea with celery sticks and carrots with her grandfather. He was so genuine and kind, that it quickly made her feel at home. She had never told him about his great-grandson living and playing in the same city he resided. She was working up the nerve to inform him and to beg his forgiveness, but she decided to wait after her special meeting at one o'clock. The butler walked into the grand living room to inform them that a car was waiting for her downstairs. She told her grandfather that she had a special meeting with a friend and then stepped on the elevator to head down four floors.

•••

Frank Fellows was not comfortable 1n big social situations. He tried to act surprised when the Santucci and Finelli crowd entered the lobby of 909 Walnut. He shook hands with the men and hugged the women. In less than twenty minutes, he hoped they would all be the happiest people on earth having Alex playing in Washington, DC. Little did he know that Alex was not happy about the trade. He asked the family if he could steal Alex for a few minutes to talk. Sally invited him to come up after the meeting for lunch. He graciously declined he said, "because of team business." No one knew it was a press conference scheduled at three o'clock.

Frank and Alex found privacy on the lobby floor in one of the community rooms with couches and a pool table. The large fifty-inch television luckily was not on *ESPN* or a news channel but showing the noon version of *House Hunters* on HGTV. Frank squirmed in his seat as Alex tried to act civil and pleasant.

Frank got right to the point when he looked at his watch and saw 12:45.

"In Mr. Garson's will and testament, he made several provisions for how the baseball team would be run in the event of his death. Essentially, he put me in charge, which, frankly, I'm not very happy about, but so it is. No longer will the team be run with his deep pockets, unless we sell part of the team, which could not happen anytime soon. You know I think the world of you, but I'm in a position to look after something that affects the whole community. Frankly we can't afford you anymore! Alex... I'm trading you to your hometown, to the Washington Presidents." Frank Fellows hoped the shock would be eased with that fact that Alex would be going home.

But that was not the case, and Alex wasted no time with his angered response.

"Frank, I'm not going anywhere! I know the collective

bargaining agreement backward and forward! I'm a ten-and-five guy, remember!"

A player with ten or more years of service in the professional leagues and five years with his current club could not be traded without his permission.

Frank had not even given this possibility a minute of thought. He had never seen Alex angry or confrontational in their six years together. It was 12:50 p.m., and from reading Alex's face, he could tell his mind was not going to change in ten minutes. Frank excused himself and quickly called his media specialist to put the press release on hold. Next, he dialed Jim Franco and prayed he would pick up the phone.

"Jim, you got to hold the press release. I have a problem with Alex. He wants to invoke the ten and five. I need more time."

"Holy shit, Frank! Let me call you back."

Frank returned to the couch and asked Alex what he wanted in order to agree to the trade.

"I want to win in Kansas City, Frank. Are you crazy? We are in first place, for Christ's sake!" Frank had never heard Alex cuss before, and he was not done." This is nuts. An hour after the service and hours before the trade, you're finally telling me about this. What kind of shit is that?"

"I'm sorry. There was no disrespect intended. I had to keep it quiet, and I didn't want you to feel-"

"Worse? How could it be worse? What, you didn't want me to be confused before the service or get angry at you for betraying me and the fans? You're trying to make Larry's death a good thing by trading me to my hometown? I thought this was the heartland, Frank, not the heartlessland. Christ, you didn't want to make it worse! Are you out of your mind, Frank? I thought you were the smart one!"

Frank took every verbal punch with valor. He treaded the silence for a valuable minute he did not have. He calmly asked again. "Alex, what do you want to agree to the trade?"

"Well, first of all, Frank, how about letting me eat lunch with my family so I can decide the most important decision in my life with a full stomach."

Frank was getting a text on his phone as Alex was staring at him with daggers in his eyes. He took a chance and looked at his phone. The text read: Announcement on hold! Meyers wants to meet with Alex, ASAP!

"You're right, Alex. Can I call you at two or so?"

"How about I call you, Frank!" With that Alex got up and motioned for Frank to leave. He stayed in the room for minute to collect his thoughts.

Frank turned toward Alex and gave it one more try. "Alex, will you at least take a meeting with President's owners, Frederick and Hank Meyers?"

Alex had a spectrum of feelings-anger, hurt, loss, grief, confusion-and there was a sense of curiosity that was trying to leak out, but right now it felt better to be angry. He closed his eyes and looked toward the ceiling as if the heavens had an answer.

"All right, look. Give me until three o'clock. Then we can meet here. I'll leave instructions at the desk where Frederick and Hank should go. Now, please..."

Frank nodded and retreated from further combat to corral the troops for another attack to close this deal. He thought the richest owner in the league, Frederick Meyer, should lead the battle!

Alex felt a buzz from his phone. It was Sally texting, "What's up?"

He kept his head down as he replied, "Sorry for the delay. I'm on my way." He walked toward the elevator as a door opened with a happy couple spilling out, discussing what restaurant to go to this evening. He continued into the elevator and pulled out his pass card to get it to the twenty-fifth floor.

As the doors closed, she was suddenly in front of him, thanking him for waiting. She was wearing a halfway buttoned cranberry-colored cashmere sweater and a matching rounded-neck blouse overlaid with a single row of pearls. Her pleated skirt was deep blue, and her cranberry heels matching the ensemble perfectly. Her body was pushing the limits of outstanding, with the waist of a model and the legs of an athlete. Her hair was mostly blonde with hints of silvery-gray working through the strands. It wasfull of curl and body as it lay down across her large chest. She had light blue eyes painted like the sky and a smile that showed a precious set of teeth. Her cheeks, rosy and flush, surrounded a perfect nose.

Leah checked the floor button that had been pushed and saw twenty-five was lit up. She turned and looked at his eyes, already focused on her, and started to realize who it was. She excitedly reached for his broad shoulders.

"Oh my gosh! Alex? I'm Leah!"

Alex felt no control at this moment. He went with his instinct to hold her tight and lose himself in her beauty. At five-foot seven, she nestled perfectly in his chest and held him the whole ride up. Quietly, she felt the tears rolling down her checks and whispered his name over and over. As the elevator arrived and the door opened, they walked arm in arm the short distance to his condo.

As he entered the door through the kitchen area, he announced, "Look who I found in the elevator! This is Leah, everybody!"

She let go of Alex and was ushered into the living room by Laura and Carol. They made introductions to everyone. Phillip and Sally came from the kitchen and gave big hugs and kisses. She held onto Phillip's hand as she accepted tissues from Laura. She thanked everyone for letting her come and sat down holding Phillip's arm like a life raft.

Alex took Sally's hand and excused themselves for a minute while they went to the bedroom. He sat her down on the bed and told her about the trade. She did not know how to react as she tried to read Alex's face. His eyes looked tortured as he explained the scenario of his options. She felt out of breath thinking about the emotional roller coaster that was finishing the third week of gut-wrenching events. Alex wanted Phillip, Sally, and Florence to be at the meeting with the Meyers and Frank Fellows.

Sally tried to sound upbeat. "Let's do it on the sixth-floor garden in the open air. That will make it like a picnic!" She finished sarcastically.

"This will not be a picnic, my dear, but I do like the location."

They joined the family as they sat around the couch and chairs in the living room. The caterers asked Sally if they were ready to sit down for lunch, but Alex asked for five minutes.

"I need to tell everybody something before we start eating. I have an opportunity..." He took a deep breath as he tried on the dream of a lifetime for size. "To be traded to Washington and play for the Presidents."

There was total silence as they waited to see Alex give away some preference.

He could not go any further in his mind. His voice trembled but he voiced the following. "This is very hard to think about right now. But I have a meeting at three o'clock with the owners from both teams to discuss it." He came up for air and collected himself. "So let's talk about something else for now! Agreed?" As he opened his arms wide and motioned to the table, he announced, "Let's eat!"

The silence was broken with responses of "yes," "for sure," "good idea." For Italians, good food makes life's problems easier to swallow!

• • •

As the eight of them sat at the round glass dinner table, Alex asked that Leah say grace for them. She was humbled and unprepared as she bowed her head and quietly grabbed the hands of Laura and Phillip next to her, which caused everyone to complete the circle around the table.

"Dear Lord, you have given me a miracle to be with this loving family today. I pray to be worthy of their presence.

Please bless this food, and we ask for good health of everyone here. Amen." Her head rose slowly as her eyes opened with tears coming down her cheeks. She could not help but smile as she looked across the table to see her son in the flesh at their first meal together.

Alex found himself looking at her while she was eating, talking, or doing anything, so he could see her beauty. She was truly the most radiant woman he had ever seen.

Occasionally Sally would whisper in his ear things like, "I can't take my eyes off of her!" or "Can you believe that body? Isn't she fifty-six or -seven?" or "My God, she is just delightful!"

Laura and Leah were acting like sisters, laughing together at Flo and Carol telling stories about flying on planes.

As the course of pasta came to the table, Anthony rose from the table and lifted his glass, calling for a toast. He spoke from the heart. "I am so proud of my brother and Carol for bringing Leah into our family. To Laura, Alex and Sally for accepting Leah into their lives. And finally, to the beautiful Leah who, like the song from my favorite singer, Roy Orbison, 'Here I goooo... from the hut to the boat to the seaaaa, for Leeee-ah, Leeee-ah, Leeee-ah! We finally found you, like a perfect pearl from the bottom of the ocean. God bless you being brave enough to be with your son!"

Glasses clinked at the perfect the rendition of the Big "O" lyrics of "Leah" and the wonderful message.

Alex ate voraciously, trying to settle the rising tide of opposing emotions in his stomach. He tried to enjoy every second of the magical lunch with his family and Leah. She eventually sat next to him at the end of the couch for a few moments.

Alex found her to be very calming and just quietly said to her, "I'm really glad you are here, but it seems like a dream to me."

"Alex, I just want to make your life easier, not more complicated. I hope when things settle down for you and Sally, we can. -"

"Leah, I want you here; it makes things easier not

complicated. We can figure out the future tomorrow or the next day. I feel very lucky to have you enter my life, especially after the pain of the last few days. I lost a very close person. You make it easier to handle, like when Phillip came into my life after my father died."

She took his hand and kissed it and quietly whispered a thank you through her tears. For the next half hour Alex asked questions about his half-brother and two half-sisters. It was therapeutic and soothing to listen to Leah's naturally optimistic and cheerful description of her children. He understood how Phillip could have become so enchanted by her. His birth was the uniting of two diverse worlds that tried but then failed to understand each other. It was amazing to him the beautiful outcome that had finally come from this failing. He wondered if his parents' deep love, or maybe respect for each other, made the outcome beautiful instead of a crash-and-burn scenario so often resulting from most real life Romeo and Juliet stories.

• • •

His phone buzzed. The front desk announced Frank Fellows in the lobby with the Meyers on their way. It was two forty-five. He asked Laura, Carol, and Leah to go down together to the lobby and accompany the three gentlemen to the sixth-floor garden. They were all excited to be a part of the plan that would make history. On the way down the elevator, they laughed, discussing ways to unleash their feminine power on the influential men they were ushering to the meeting. Carol led the delegation as they met the men in the lobby. She took the arm of the youngest, Hank Meyers, and started chatting about his crazy day of travel. Laura took Frank Fellows and shared the sadness of their loss of Larry Garson and his tough responsibilities that he was inheriting. Finally, Leah unleashed her southern girl hospitality and beauty on the elder Frederick Meyers, who still saw himself as a dapper dresser and a handsome man.

Alex and Flo had discussed a financial strategy to make the trade happen. If he was going to be traded, he did not want to deal with free agency next year. He wanted to end his career in DC, otherwise he would take his chances with KC this year. If the Meyers were balking at the terms, Phillip and Anthony were instructed to tell stories of the Senators in the fifties and sixties that they remembered. Alex was ready for action. He felt free of anger and sadness after being with his family.

The three couples made it through the doors out to the gardens. Alex made sure it was empty by handing the doorman a couple C-notes to make it so at three o'clock. The five of them were sitting under the shaded trellis on these mid-eighties but humid day. Alex hoped it would be a quick meeting under these circumstances. The usherettes parted ways with their guests as introductions were made by Frank Fellows. They all sat at one table as Frederick Meyers asked if he could address the group. He was an impressive man with charisma and always deadly to the point.

"Alex, we are honored at the chance to have you play in your hometown. As a matter of fact, we want to make it simple. We want you to retire a President. I think you are a fair man; I understand you have never used an agent. Would you mind if I asked you a question?"

He was flawless in his salesmanship. Alex was disarmed as Flo started to say something. Alex held her solid thigh to hold her response. Alex gently nodded to his possible future boss.

"Thank you, Alex. I respect your family so much. They are really lovely. My sympathy is to you and your mother for such a tragic loss. My goodness, what a great man Larry Garson...I'm soooo sorry..." He leaned across the table and looked right at Alex. "Alex, how much longer do you want to play baseball?"

"Well...to be honest, three more years after this year."
"Perfect! What do you think would be a fair contract for three years?"

He turned to Flo, and she handed him the numbers and the terms.

"Sir, fifty-five million dollars for three years."

The group quietly trembled, waiting for master negotiator Frederick Meyers to dismiss the offer.

"Alex, I think if you continue with your fine season with the Crowns, you might get more than that in free agency. I believe that is very fair. Our only problem as an organization is that ensuring that contract might be very difficult."

Professional teams in every sport except football have to guarantee contracts with players because of the competition from other teams. They usually take out disability insurance policies if the athlete gets hurt and cannot play for some or all of their contract. The policies are very expensive, and the costs are company secrets. They usually cover up to 70 percent of the contract and for no more than three years of a contract. In this situation, Frederick Meyers knew that he was looking at several million dollars to cover Alex if he was healthy. But with the uncertainty of his stomach growth, it might be triple that cost or be unattainable.

"Respectfully, Alex, to you and your family, we are open to suggestions."

Florence, who had obtained many disability policies for her richest clients, offered a solution. "Mr. Meyers, if I may offer an idea to this dilemma?"

"Please, please," Came from both Alex Santucci and Frederick Meyers.

"We could write the contracts more like football deals, with some up-front bonus money for Alex and a deal option for each year of the contract."

Alex was intrigued by the idea but knew the Player's Union would be totally against such an idea. He was feeling great turmoil about settling the contract. There were too many thoughts going through his head right now. He knew what he had to do: make a decision.

He suddenly stood up and asked Frederick Meyers a question. "Mr. Meyers, can I have a few minutes with my mom?"

"Alex, Sally, Florence, Phillip, and Anthony, please call me Frederick. We are all equals here and Washingtonians! Please, Alex, take as much time as you need."

"Frederick...sir...I only need a few minutes."

Alex walked over to the corner of the sunny garden area where his adopted mother, birth mother, and stepmother were all chatting away, sitting on the grass, and soaking up the sun. He sat cross-legged between Laura and Carol and pulled Leah to be across from him. He took their hands and asked that each one of them say a prayer, softly but audibly to him, asking God for clarity on his future and his destiny.

They all closed their eyes, and Carol went first.

"God, we are so humbled to serve you. Please help Alex serve you in a way that glorifies your presence in our lives. Amen."

A silence hung for thirty seconds or so until Laura quietly prayed. "Oh God, I beg forgiveness for selfishly wanting Alex to be home with us, but there is work to be done in our community that will honor you. Please help him see his destiny, and help me accept his decision."

Alex squeezed their bonded hands as tears flowed into the corners of his mouth. He felt a lightness in his body as though he was being lifted off the ground. The sounds of the city were muted. He felt the ribs in his chest open as fresh air rushed into his lungs and exhaled the tension in his body. He started to hear a bird singing and then turn into a gentle whisper of Leah's voice, who was praying.

"We rejoice your blessings, this miracle of love that you have bestowed on this family. And you have allowed my presence to soak up this joy. This son and all the children you have blessed us with are here to serve you. Talented Alex can serve you at this time the most and in a way that honors you. Please let him know the path that you clear for him. Amen."

Alex rose without effort to his feet and lifted his mothers to surround him in order to feel their warmth and spirit. They all gently kissed him and wiped his face of tears as they flowed from their eyes. They parted and patted him on his back. He opened his eyes as the sun went into cover behind a cirrus cloud so that he could see the path ahead. He slowly returned to those waiting under the trellis and sat again.

"I am humbled to become a part of the Presidents. I will hit over twenty homeruns and drive in at least fifty runs the rest of the year. We will win for the city of Washington a championship within the next three years. You will pay me the salary that we just proposed and both agree is fair for any month that I play during the six-month baseball season. I will donate a million dollars every month during the season for the length of my contract to your foundation, especially to promote swimming and baseball for DC and the surrounding communities that need support in providing these activities. For any month or year, I don't play because of health or injury, you will not pay me a cent, but you will continue the million a month during the season for the rest of this season and the three extended seasons. We will agree to a small amount of the contract as a bonus payment up front. In my heart this seems right for all of us!" He beamed with energy as if his emotions were recycled into a new power source.

Hank Meyers, who normally deferred to his father in his presence, was caught up in the moment and enthusiastically supported the idea. "Dad, I think this is a beautiful idea, and it could become a great partnership for the foundation and the community!"

Frederick Meyers was calm during Alex's statements and his son's supportive response. Flo and Anthony held hands as they sat and watched Alex intently. Phillip motioned for the three mothers to come over and stand with him behind Alex. Their beauty enhanced the tension for everyone except Alex, who felt protected and calm with his parents surrounding him.

Frederick slowly stood up and put his left hand tenderly on the back of his son's neck and his right hand softly on Frank Fellow's left shoulder. "I'm sorry, Hank. We will do nothing of the kind!"

The trellis seems to shake from a light wind whistling through the vines overhead. Frank and Hank looked frightened. Alex was looking directly into Frederick's eyes. He could see the depth of his soul and a Solomon-like decision in his heart.

"This man is a treasure. We will not treat him like a wounded animal that we discard to the side of the road if he gets hurt. No-none of that! We will guarantee that contract now! Insurance or no insurance-and we will match every bit of that million a month into a joint foundation that our families will run together. Laura, you would honor me to join my wife to chair that foundation."

She nodded with joy as she hugged her son. Frederick extended his hand as Alex rose to accept it with both hands.

"Alex, welcome back to Washington, we have a deal!"

Frank Fellows smiled, very happy to have the ten million dollars of relief for his payroll and the three top prospects from the Presidents highly rated minor league system. Realizing he witnessed the first negotiation where each side tried to outdo each other by giving in, it occurred to Frank that sometimes getting the most out of a deal is not the best deal!

• • •

Frederick, Frank, Alex, Phillip, and Anthony sat around for thirty minutes after agreeing to a contract and talked about Washington baseball history. They traded stories from the 1930s through the 1960s. Hank, Jim, and Florence went over the finer points of the agreement so that the lawyers could make it a legal contract. The main point was that Alex and Hank agreed to an amount (fifty-five million dollars) and the number of years (three) in front of five witnesses.

Everyone but Alex and Sally agreed to fly on Frederick Meyers private plane out of the downtown airport just across the Missouri River back to Washington, DC. There would be a press release at four o'clock announcing the trade and followed by a press conference the next day at noon at Presidents Ballpark.

Alex needed to pack for the rest of the season, and Sally needed to go home and make some arrangements. They would try to catch a late-night flight to DC.

Leah wanted to stay and help Alex pack and then stay overnight with her grandfather before flying back to Florida. She would be facing a tough task telling her husband about seeing Alex and telling her kids about a half-brother that they did not know about. For her there was no doubt it was worth it. If it caused trouble in her family, so be it. She trusted God would lead her through it.

Phillip pulled Alex and Leah aside for one final bit of business. They found a spot on the garden lawn. It felt eerie for Alex to be with his birth parents for the first time alone.

"I think there is one thing that you both should know." Phillip paused, not knowing the best way to put this information. "Alex, you remember the older gentleman that gave you the scorebook after the All-Star game?"

"Of course, Dad, how weird was that by the way? Leah, did you hear about that?"

"Alex and Leah, listen to me! I think it 1s Leah's grandfather!"

"Who is?" Leah asked. "What are you talking about?"

"It hit me the other night when you were telling me about how your grandfather was ninety-five, grew up in DC, now lives in KC, is wealthy, and named Alex!"

"Well, all those things are true-but when did he meet Alex?"

"He gave Alex a scorebook from the 1924 World Series after the All-Star game. He waited for hours in line to give it to him!"

Leah suddenly turned white. She remembered hearing a story about her grandfather seeing the only World Series win in Washington. Her father told it many times during family events, even used it in a sermon once. Could it be that he knew already that Alex was his great-grandson, or was it just a wild coincidence?

"Dad, what are you saying? The old man is my great-grandfather?"

After seeing Leah nodding in agreement, Phillip answered. "Son, I think it is a certainty!"

Chapter 26

Sally was in her house at Niss Lake getting a big suitcase from her walk-in closet in her bedroom. She threw it on the bed and opened it. "What am I doing?" she thought to herself. Finding the only chair in the room, she plopped into it and put her feet up on the night table. She had spent nearly two weeks in a row on the road and was in love with the idea. The notion of teaching in less than four weeks seemed to be in a parallel universe, not at a university! Taking a sabbatical was the only answer. She sat up called her boss, Dr. Daniel Kelly, the head of her department at Park University. He also was a huge baseball fan, born and raised in Saint Louis as a Cardinal fan.

"Sally, I just heard about the trade. Alex must be in heaven. How are you doing?"

"Pretty crazy right now, trying to figure out the next month. I don't think I can teach this semester, Daniel. I have to be with Alex the rest of this season. It's getting complicated!"

"I heard. Congratulations on your engagement! Listen, don't worry about a thing. Come back for the seminar with Brightman in November when the season is over. What are you going to do about the house?"

"I have no clue!"

"Well, I might have a solution. My daughter is in Europe and just called me to say she wants to start graduate courses in the fall and live with her boyfriend somewhere close to school."

"Wow, sounds perfect! This is a great love shack...baby!" Sally started singing the B-52's hit from her elementary school days.

"Please don't remind me."

Boss to employee, friend to friend, they discussed the details of the plan for Sally to take a sabbatical and rent out her house for at least a semester.

She decided to take a smaller suitcase and have the rest of her clothes boxed and sent to Bethesda. Then she had another thought. "Maybe we can find a little house in Georgetown, near a cafe, some shops..." She came back to the task at hand: getting some clothes and the Acura back to the garage and finding a flight to DC.

• • •

Alex and Leah headed back up to the twenty-fifth floor condo after they said good-bye to the five family members heading back to DC in the private jet belonging to the Meyers family. Alex turned on *ESPN* as they sat on the couch trying to catch their breath from the day's activities. Leah had never watched *ESPN* and was amazed at the highlights and the cascading subjects on the left side of the screen showing the stories coming up in order. Most of the subjects were about the Alex Santucci trade at this moment.

"Alex, didn't they just announce the trade a few minutes ago? How do they cover it so quickly? This is pretty cool."

Alex filled her in about the matrix of reporters around the country ready at a moment's notice to jump on a story. The opinions so far were pretty mixed as panels of former players, reporters, and talk show big mouths spouted out their "expert" knowledge of the trade and how it would turn out. Alex turned to PBL Network where they were on-site at Crowns Stadium as fans were coming in the thousands, protesting the loss of the league-leading hitter. Alex felt his phone buzzing.

It was Sally calling from the garage. "Sweetheart, I hope you're upstairs because there are hundreds of people and reporters outside the Walnut entrance. I'll be up in a minute."

Alex realized at that moment there were two ways to get to DC: either rent a jet out of Charles Wheeler Airport where the crowds could be avoided, or drive the 1,063 miles to his mother's house. He wanted to have his car in DC, but it would be hard to do with two drivers.

"Leah, what do you think of driving to DC? You could stay with us at Laura's and fly back tomorrow, Wednesday, or whenever you're ready." Leah loved long car rides. She drove across country before her recent marriage several times. It gave her inspiration for her music and prayer.

"I would love that, Alex. Are you sure Laura doesn't mind me staying there...Or how about Sally?"

"They are both in love with you! How can they not be?" He put his big paws around Leah and hugged her.

"Besides, we may need a third driver!"

Giggling like a schoolgirl, Leah clapped her hands in a Joyous response.

"Oh goody, I love to ride on long trips. Are we leaving soon?"

She remembered that her grandfather was expecting her for dinner. Alex and Leah had not discussed a game plan to meet his great-grandfather, since they were distracted by Phillip leaving for DC and talking about the trade.

"I still need to get my stuff at my grandfather's. Will you come and meet him? You know, just to find out. We don't need to tell him right now. You know, I feel like Lucy Ricardo: 'I got some 'splaining to do' to my family at home first."

"Sounds perfect. We could do an early dinner-bring some takeout. That would be fun. Then we could head out by five or six. I think we can get to Bethesda by seven a.m., Maryland time-before rush hour. My friend Hal Baker installed this anti-radar and cop car thing in the Acura. We can do eighty-five to ninety miles an hour the whole way!"

Sally walked through the door with her luggage. Alex greeted her with a kiss and swept her in the air and excitedly announced their road trip after dinner with the "old man". She was relieved at the news; seeing the crowd outside the building put her on edge. Besides, she thought as Alex finally rested her on the ground, "I'm the luckiest girl in the world:

no work until January, and I'm with the hottest man and hitter in the league."

They headed directly down to the garage with their luggage and escaped the building, unnoticed by media or fans.

Alex drove the few blocks to Constantine's where Sally and Leah headed in to get dinner as Alex found an alley behind the store to hide. After a few minutes of shopping, they made it to the residence at 2004 Grand in three minutes and took the elevator from the garage. The butler escorted them into the living room to sit down. Alex and Sally, hand in hand, looked around the room at the pictures for clues about the "old man". The butler appeared back in the room and announced the takeout from Constantine's was now being served in the dining room.

There, at the end of the table, was the elder Alex, dressed in a suit and tie for the occasion. He was Alex Skarstedt, a first-generation, Swedish-American born in 1917. His father immigrated to the United States in 1899 to work in Gaithersburg, Maryland, as a mechanical engineer in the building and maintenance of The Gaithersburg Latitude Observatory by the US Coast and Geodetic Society. The observatory was one of a system of six international latitude observatories tracking the degree of "wobble" of Earth's north-south Axis and the resultant variation of latitude. The site of Gaithersburg, Maryland, in the heart of Montgomery County, fifteen miles north of Washington, DC, was chosen because, like the other five sites, it sat on the 39.08 northern latitude on earth. His mother came from Sweden seven years later to marry his father and went on to produce seven children, of which he was the youngest. His family bought a farm on land west of Gaithersburg, now known as Seneca Valley, when the observatory was closed in 1915 due to lack of funds. The family farmed the land as his father found work in Washington, DC, in the Navy Department for the war effort. The family sold the farm in 1935 as Alex was entering Johns Hopkins University to study engineering.

After graduation, he worked for IBM developing the first computers used by the government for World War II. He bought as much IBM stock as possible during the 1940s before moving to Kansas in the 1950s to develop machinery for the agriculture business. His value of his IBM stock allowed him to retire and buy a large estate in the 1970s. His personal worth was currently over ten million dollars.

Leah made the introductions of Sally and Alex as friends. The two Alexes' eyes met for the second time. They both remembered the previous encounter. The elder Alex was pleased but very confused. Leah sat close to him and explained that they met through some friends, and when she mentioned she was in town to see her grandfather and remarked about his name and age, it led to Alex's curiosity to meet him.

The dinner was wonderful, full of stories about his work on computers at IBM and developing machinery for farms. But the love of his life growing up was playing and following baseball. The elder Alex's father, before he was married, would ride the train to Union Station in Washington, DC, and take the trolley to Griffith Stadium to see the new American League's Washington Nationals in 1901. Starting in 1907, he became a huge fan of Walter Johnson and continued to follow him his whole career. As early as Alex could walk, he would throw, catch, and hit a baseball with his brothers and father. He remembered riding the train to DC to see baseball as early as three years old when Babe Ruth started with the Yankees. He attended every home game of the three World Series that the Nationals/Senators played in 1924, 1925, and 1933.

Alex was starstruck by the life story and could not get enough of the baseball lore. He looked at the clock on the wall and realized it was clicking toward five thirty. He looked at Leah and Sally to signal the time. Leah started to thank her grandfather for his hospitality but said they had to be in Washington by noon tomorrow.

The elder Alex pushed away from the table and motioned

for Alex and the rest to follow him. Unknowingly, he took his great-grandson's arm. They walked to the elevator and motioned for Leah and Sally to follow. His butler followed quickly as they went upstairs where Alex's bedroom and other private rooms took up the whole top floor. They went down the hall to the last room on the right. The butler opened the door and switched on the light. This private library held shelves of memorabilia and books. They walked over to a table with six chairs and sat down as Alex whispered something into his butler's ear.

"My dear Leah, there is something special about Alex. I knew it when I first saw him on television when he came to Kansas City in 2007. Seeing him in love with Sally and next to you...I can't help thinking there is a special connection there. I can see how you must be dear friends. You even look somewhat alike."

He then turned to Alex and reached out his hand to touch his forearm. "Alex, you feel like family to me." He said, laughing, "We have the same name, similar descent, and the love of base-ball. When I gave you that scorebook, I knew this day would come when you went back to Washington and only you would appreciate it. I want Leah to have all of this when I pass because she will look after it, but I want you to have something special." The butler walked over with an opened box containing many things. "This is my favorite box of memories. Most of it comes from my childhood, but I've collected things over the years. I want you to have it."

Alex stood up and looked in the box. On top was something that could not be real. He reached in, pulled it out, and put it on his left hand. "Whose glove is this, Alex?"

"My hero, Alex. 'The Big Train'-Walter Johnson!"

Chapter 27

Alex had started a new dose of Duloxetine this morning. Dr. Walton had increased him to forty milligrams after seeing him adjust so well over the last three weeks. His recent blood work had shown perfect levels for his liver and kidneys. Dr. Walton explained that the increased dosage should level out some of the intense emotional reactions he was experiencing because the twenty milligram dose was not enough for his size body for the drug to work evenly during a twenty-four hour period.

The Acura TL was flying down Interstate 70 at around 95 mph as they approached the suburbs of Saint Louis at 8:37 p.m. Sally was asleep in the backseat. Leah was wide awake talking a mile a minute about the day's experience. Alex made her play several CDs of the music she had recorded over the past three and a half decades. As each song came on, she would embarrassingly tell a story about the origin. After "Torn between two lovers" played, she told the story of meeting Phillip and their torrid love affair, off and on, over a four-year period. She wanted Alex to know how much she loved him and that she wanted to be with him, but it seemed impossible at the time. She thought having a baby would make their lives come together, but as soon as she found out she was pregnant, she panicked because she was still married. In her family, only her mother, sister, and present husband knew that she had carried a baby and gave it up for adoption.

Alex was enamored with Leah as he enjoyed her exuberance and warmth that emanated from her personality. In addition, her physical beauty was like watching the movie *Avatar* for the first time in 3-D. You wanted to drink in every part of the screen because there was so much going on. He chuckled to himself that this must be what a young boy feels as he goes through the Oedipus stage of development!

Finally, Leah had enough of listening to her own music and stopped the CD and said she had a surprise for Alex. She pulled out a CD from her little collection and popped it in the player. "This was your father's favorite group when I knew him in the seventies. He would play this so loud in his Ford Pinto! At first, I hated it, but I have to admit, it became one of my favorite groups of all time. Every time I hear their music, I think of Phillip." Electric Light Orchestra (ELO) started up the instrumental "Fire on High" off the *Face the Music* album. Alex knew it well because it was one of his favorites. He turned it up and reached out to hold Leah's hand.

There was no talking in the car, just a rocking Spanish guitar riding explosive chords, leading to the swirling violins that provided an interlude before the next round of the rollercoaster masterpiece swarmed their ears. Only crossing the majestic Mississippi River and seeing the Saint Louis Arch in his mirror could match the excitement of the bombarding music as he barreled into Illinois that night.

• • •

Leah finally joined Sally in the world of slumber as it approached midnight. Alex was flying through the Land of Lincoln, going by the small towns of Greenville, Effingham, and Casey in Illinois, coming to the Indiana State line, and soon losing an hour to eastern daylight time. He was listening to his Sirius XM Radio, turned to a late-night game with Oakland hosting Tampa Bay. He was familiar with the players hitting and the pitchers pitching, but he realized that he was going to an unfamiliar National League. He turned to another station to listen to Los Angeles hosting Arizona from the National League. He had been to each city twice to play in his fourteen-year career. Now he would be in Phoenix in August, the hottest place on Earth during the hottest month of the year, and play LA in DC in September. The next two months would challenge his batting skills against strange pitching. He would focus on his advantage, that NL teams had not seen him recently. They could not rely on their advanced scouts since they had not scouted him the last three weeks.

His vision had become keen again, most likely back to the 20/15 of his twenties. Seeing the ball coming out of the pitcher's hand was all he focused on, not the distractions of the windup or his arm angle. Usually after watching a pitcher from the on-deck circle for about fifteen to twenty pitches, he could start locking in on their release point. After that it was a matter of guessing which pitch was coming from their arsenal. Most likely the league would start throwing him inside. He would feast on that strategy.

He was passing Terra Haute, driving on the Till Plains of Indiana's Corn Belt, heading toward Indianapolis at 11:24 p.m. Arizona had taken LA into the twelfth inning in a 4-4 game. Both teams had run out of pinch hitters, which rarely happened in the American League because of the DH, so the pitcher was up late in the game with runners in scoring position. He knew the talented, young Washington starting pitchers could all hit. He was pretty sure that was not the case of their bullpen staff, who rarely batted. The pitcher for LA struck out as the game headed to the thirteenth inning. He was circling Indianapolis on Interstate 74, streaking toward the Ohio border at 12:12 a.m.

The Presidents were opening a series with their Interstate 95 rivals, Philadelphia. Their All-Star lefty, Winston "Smokey" Camels, was scheduled to be on the mound. Alex tripled off of him in the All-Star game, otherwise he had only six at bats in Smokey's seven-year career. With the trade over, Alex was looking to get back into a routine of running and reading the *Daily* in the early morning, fun time with Sally and the family around a good lunch, then film watching and naps in the afternoon. This would be followed with fielding and hitting practice before the game, playing the game, autographs with the fans, late dinner, and hanging with Sally to end the day.

After leaving Indianapolis and returning to Interstate 70, he crossed the Ohio border at 12:25 a.m. and stopped for gas. He loved the Acura's 18.5-gallon gas tank that would let him travel over 550 miles on a tank of gas. They were about halfway home, having been on the interstates for just under six hours. Sally was showing some signs of life in the backseat as Alex smelled the gas fumes mixed with sweet air of the central lowlands of Ohio. She opened the door and hugged Alex, looking sleepy with her messy hair and pretty face. Her lips begged for a kiss as she mentioned bathroom and coffee.

Alex caught several hours of sleep as Sally worked her way through the eastern plateau of Ohio, heading past Zanesville toward the Appalachian Mountains, through a sliver of West Virginia into western Pennsylvania. When she pulled into the "Welcome to Pennsylvania" rest stop at 3:22 p.m. to stretch and use the rest room, Alex awoke and prepared to take over the driving again. Leah showed some life, enough to use the bathroom, and then stayed alert for conversation.

Sally got some more coffee and was still energized by the driving. She started talking about Alex Skarstedt and his amazing life. Leah expressed some emotions, speaking about her grandfather and how much she missed seeing him. She vowed to see him again soon. The darkness was beginning to show a minimal glow. Leah was apprehensive but excited to talk to her husband and children in a few hours. She had much to tell them with lots of uncertainty about her future. Being home was the goal, but she was not ready to leave Alex quite yet.

Alex headed south on Interstate 79, around Morgantown, the home of West Virginia University, to hook up with the 116-mile Interstate 68, known to

Marylanders as the National Highway. It would bring them to Interstate 70 again at Hancock, avoiding the treacherous Pennsylvania Turnpike.

As they passed through Cumberland and the Sideling Hill Cut and into Hancock at 5:35 a.m., brightness was returning to the sky. Alex assured them they would beat the morning traffic on Interstate 270 south of Frederick. He was doing 90 mph on the empty highway. Leah and Sally held hands, barely looking ahead. They were tired and giggling like teenagers. As Alex finally got south of Frederick, it was 6:23 a.m. and Bethesda was less than thirty minutes away. He started talking about his great-grandfather and how sure he was that he knew they were related.

"I could see it in his eyes when he gave me the box and saw me put on the glove. It meant the world to him, like he was passing along his treasure. I felt his trust and his love."

"I know you're right, Alex. I saw it too. He knew you were special to him. I wish we had told him. Maybe when I go back to visit after I talk to my family, I can tell him. I just didn't want him to be confused."

As they headed onto Democracy Boulevard, they passed the baseball diamond at Walter Johnson High School, then a final turn onto Old Georgetown Road for the last mile to Johnson Avenue, Alex thought about the last thing Alex Skarstedt told them. "I still can't believe about the farm they owned. What are the chances of that connection with our two families?"

He looked up and saw Johnson Avenue and the Johnson house on the corner. The Acura made a final right turn down Johnson Avenue to his mom's house and pulled into her driveway. As relief came over his body from his emphatic push of the gear shift into park, he leaned back in his seat and expressed a silent hallelujah to the heavens. Sally leaned over his shoulders from the backseat and laid her head next to his ear and her arms on his chest. She pulled back after a kiss.

Leah quickly leaned in and buried a kiss on his check and

whispered in his ear.

"I'm so glad you're finally home with your mother!"

He felt the full weight of her slender frame and the fragrance of her body.

"Leah, I'm so glad you're with us now." Alex kissed her on the cheek and pulled away as he opened the door and leaned on the roof.

As Leah and Sally got out of the passenger side doors, Alex remarked out of the blue, "I can't get over it! They really sold their family farm to Walter Johnson?"

Leah smiled, thinking of her grandfather. "I think it's great that his father wouldn't seal the deal unless 'The Big Train' gave Alex one of his mitts!"

"My guess is that he was happy to do it," said Sally. "Didn't he write 'To a Great Fan and future Star Player' on the scorebook? I think he knew it would get into the right hands." Sally smiled as she slammed the door and hugged Leah next to her.

"I still can't believe it!" Alex muttered.

Leah spoke with verve. "And now, dear Alex, all of DC is expecting you at that noon press conference. I believe God has let this quirk in history be a chance for you to bring a World Series to DC like Walter Johnson did. You have a destiny-a spirit of winning for DC that has been passed down to you. Now you'd better get inside and get some sleep! It's almost seven o'clock in the morning for God's sake!"

Chapter 28

Laura and Phillip joined Alex and Sally for the trip to Presidents Park and the noon press conference. Leah wanted to stay at the house and make calls to her family in Florida. Laura was thrilled to have such great activity at her house. She had everyone's room ready for them. Alex had built for her a guest suite on the top floor of the house's addition. All of her children were married, had children, and needed privacy. When they visited, the four-room suite was perfect. Leah stayed in the regular part of the house with Laura.

Alex had arrived around eleven o'clock north of the ballpark to take a tour of the facility. They entered from the center field gates, where all the crowds taking Metro (the DC area subway system) would walk down Half Street, southeast into the park. Alex had never played at Presidents Park since it opened in 2008.

He remembered playing at RFK Stadium in 2007 and loved every second of it. Built in 1961, it was the first of the modern ballparks built specifically for football and baseball. It was the last standing of the enclosed circular-shaped stadiums, now used for professional soccer and the occasional college football game.

Alex had gone hitless during a three-game series in the cavernous RFK Stadium. Admittedly, he tried to put every pitch into section 500 of the upper deck so he could be like his homerun-hitting hero, Frank "Hondo" Howard. Hondo had three seats painted white from his days as a Senator. Section 500 was the second section of seats in the upper deck Alex tried to reach section 532, which was the first one in fair territory. He figured that pulling an inside fastball would be his only chance.

Hondo's titanic shots hit sections 536, 538, and, the Holy Grail of bombs in straightaway center field, section 542. Before the series had begun, Phillip took him up to the white seat in section 542. Behind him he could see the

Anacostia River and over it the Greenway Apartments in Anacostia, where his grandparents lived, before moving to Parkwood in 1951. The center field fence was 410 feet, and he felt over a hundred feet in the air. He figured the homerun might have gone 600 feet if the stadium had not been in the way.

As they walked through the gates of Presidents Park, Phillip led them to the most important spot in the stadium, the seemingly moving statues of the three greats of Washington baseball: on the left, Walter Johnson, in the middle, Frank Howard, and on the right, Negro League great, Josh Gibson. Alex quietly looked at each statue starting with Josh Gibson and closed his eyes as he touched each one. He envisioned a relentless force emanating from the statue that was powerful but graceful at the same time. When he was in Kansas City, he visited the Negro Leagues Baseball Museum several times for inspiration, especially during the past two years when the museum installed ten statues on a studio-size baseball field. Each player was a life-size bronze replica standing in baseball-ready positions. When he stood next to Josh Gibson, it was something special. At six foot one, 210 pounds, he would physically match up with power hitters of today. His muscles came from surviving the grind of becoming an athlete, when black professional athletes were rare. He hit over 800 Hrs during his seventeen years of professional baseball, while batting .359-numbers that are unimaginable in this day and age, especially from the catcher's position. His death at age thirty-five was an enormous tragedy.

Alex stopped at the Frank Howard statue, looking up at the monster of a man. He was a big man from his feet to his head. Even today he would make the six foot six, 290-pound Adam Dunn look average.

When he made it to Walter Johnson's statue, Sally walked up to Alex and held his hand. They looked quietly at Alex's idol, seeing his athletic presence in the statue.

Sally noticed something that most people miss. "Alex,

there it is. He's wearing it!"

Alex looked at the statue. "What is he wearing, Sally? Is it his uniform?"

"It's on his left hand! It's your mitt!"

• • •

As they left the statues and approached the outfield seats, Alex looked across the span of the magnificent stadium structure that was built in seven stages over a sixteen- month construction schedule. To save time, each section was completed while drawings were being finished on the next section. Kansas City-based stadium architects, HOK, led the project. Alex realized the stone-and-glass architecture was meant to mirror many of the famous landmarks throughout the capital city.

They climbed up to the upper deck to see several of the viewing areas in between sections. One on the third base side gave beautiful views of the US Capitol Building's rotunda, and another behind home plate overlooked the Washington Monument. The first base side looked south over the intersection of the Anacostia and Potomac Rivers with the historical city of Alexandria in the background.

At eleven forty-five, Alex headed down to the dugout to meet with Manager Charley Jackson and his coaching staff.

The Presidents had battled injuries all year while their young pitching staff continued to keep them in the Eastern Division race with a 51-49 record and trailing seven games behind the leaders, Miami. When Charley asked Alex how he felt about being in the lineup tonight, he assured him he was ready to go. Injured Team Captain Bruce Hammersly, sensational nineteen-year-old rookie Blake Hopson, and veteran infielder Jerry Gonzalez were there to give him support.

Alex entered the packed press room with Phillip, Laura,

and Sally at his side. Presidents GM Jim Franco stood at the microphone at 12:02 p.m., with Frederick and Hank Meyer to his left. Alex and Charley sat to his right, as Phillip, Sally, and Laura sat on seats out of camera range.

A few minutes earlier, at 11:55 a.m., the Alex Santucci Era officially started for the Washington Presidents as he signed his contract extension in Jim Franco's office next to the press room. Jim Franco did not announce the signing to the press in his opening remarks because Frederick Meyers, at 11:58 a.m., told him to wait. Jim introduced Hank Meyers, who looked puzzled by the absence of an announcement. Hank then spoke enthusiastically about bringing a veteran All-Star talent to the team. Alex stood with Hank as he put on the throwback "W" uniform being worn for tonight's game.

As the cameras clicked a thousand digital pictures, Alex winked at Sally, wondering what he got himself into. He looked down at the W on the left shoulder sleeve, and it started to dawn on him what kind of pressure he was about to face. He thought about the words he had spoken at Larry Garson's service and how they had really been a farewell to the Kansas City fans. Tears started to come to his eyes as he realized how that bond had been so quickly broken after almost six years. Less than a week ago, he was in New York City celebrating first place and a twelve-game winning streak. The next day, his world changed when that plane crashed into the lake.

In a rare scene, Frederick Meyers asked his son if he could say a few words. Frederick had stayed behind the scenes since the first press conference in 2006, when Professional League Baseball announced the Meyers group had won the bidding for the Presidents. It took PLB eighteen months to select an ownership after they moved the team to Washington for the 2005 season. PLB had owned the team for three years after the Quebec franchise had gone into default. The team and the minor league systems were depleted of talent, but PLB got $4 70 million for the team anyway.

Frederick Meyers stepped in front of the microphone to face the press for the first time in six years. "I want to announce that Alex has signed a three-year, fifty-five-million-dollar extension with the Presidents. He will retire as a part of this organization. This was my decision! I believe destiny brings Alex here and that destiny will bring a championship to Washington!"

A silent press room suddenly became busy texting and tweeting the shocking news. Frederick Meyers did not spend money easily, but when he saw a good deal, he was all in.

"Alex has graciously agreed to donate six million dollars a year to the Presidents Foundation that will focus on baseball and swimming programs for youth in the Washington area. His lovely mother, Laura, and my wife, Hanna, will co-chair the program. The Presidents will be honored to match this donation. I am proud to introduce the newest member of the Washington Presidents, Alex Santucci!"

Being introduced at a press conference after a trade is pretty routine stuff. The general manager usually pats himself on the back and spouts out cliches like, "It's a great opportunity to make our team better" or "We got the guy that we wanted all along." The manager smiles and ogles over the great talent they just traded for. He says how productive it will make the lineup, or that the starting staff just became the best in the division, or the bull-pen just found the missing piece. The press always asks the same questions like "How does it feel to be here?" or "Are you looking forward to hitting in front of so-and-so?"

When Alex Santucci stepped to the microphone, every reporter in the room knew this press conference would be different. Reporters Ron Roswell and Bonnie Bramlett sat in the front row, looking up at a tense athlete who had changed the baseball world over the past three weeks.

"I am grateful to Frederick Meyers for bringing me here to my hometown. When I first heard about the trade yesterday after the service for Larry Garson, I was angry. I felt it was disrespectful to me and the fans of Kansas City. I initially refused the deal because as a fourteen-year veteran that has played in a city for six years, it was my right according the Collective Bargaining Agreement. I then had a meal with my family and thought about how an organization is as good as its leader. When Larry Garson died, Frank Fellows became their leader. He thought he was doing the right thing for the ball club. I disagreed and then thought about the owner of the Presidents. Did they really want me, or did they want to rent me for the rest of the season? So I decided to make them an offer that would prove to me they wanted me for now and for the rest of my career. Frederick Meyers proved to me that he is the type of leader I want to play for the rest of my career. I promised Mr. Meyers I would bring a championship to this city during that time period." Alex felt proud to say those words. At the same time, he realized that he just started a media frenzy from his statement and especially his prediction. "Now, if you promise to be gentle, I will try to answer your questions as long as I can. I did just drive all night to get here!"

The inquisition came quickly. Kelley Browner from *Big Atlantic Sports Channel* (BASC) wanted to know: "Do you think you're worth all that money?"

Julia Newmar of *Washington Reporter Newspaper* asked, "Have you been lucky during your hitting streak? And why should it continue in a different league?"

Pedro Carew lectured, "You've been treated like royalty by your friends in the media. They seem to ignore the medication issue, which clearly is making you play better!"

Clark Battle finished the barrage with, "Will you give all the money you make to charity if you bomb in August and go into a major slump?"

Alex felt very little energy to take on these questions, but he was very competitive and so it became a game to be friendly. His answers ranged from "Hell, yes, I'm worth it!" to "The medication is a miracle, and it's supposed to help me" to

"I'm not going into a major slump because I know what I'm doing."

Bonnie Bramlett raised her hand asked, "Alex, I'm a friend of yours, and yes, we used to go out, but really, are you over me?" The room exploded with laughter, which was a perfect tonic for Alex to share his true feelings about being in Washington. "Seriously Alex, what do you want to say to fans of the Presidents?"

Alex felt an inner strength from seeing Bonnie in the front row and Sally, his father, and mother on the side of the room. "It is truly hard to put into words, because I guess it has not hit me yet. I know everything about Washington baseball: Clark Griffith, Walter Johnson, Josh Gibson, Cecil Travis, Mickey Vernon, Roy Sievers, Harmon Killebrew, Bob Allison, Frank Howard, and now great owners in Frederick Meyers and his son Hank, and a great player in Bruce Hammersly."

"I know many dedicated fans. Like ninety-five-year old Alex Skarstedt, whose father immigrated from Sweden in 1899 and found comfort in America riding a train on weekends from Gaithersburg to Union Station and then hopped on the trolley to see baseball at the original Nationals Park starting in 1901. Then Alex himself grew to love baseball and went to every Nats World Series home game played in Griffith Stadium starting when he was seven.

"Marvin Hampton, a janitor at my high school, Walter John-son, told me stories about growing up watching baseball in the thirties and wondering why the Homestead Grays players, who won eleven Negro League Championships, including nine in a row, could not play in the American League. Players like James 'Cool Papa' Bell, Buck Leonard, and Josh Gibson would have led the Nats to baseball domination. He also watched Nats great Cecil Travis play in anonymity from 1933 to 1941, batting three-twenty-seven in nine seasons, including a fabulous 1941 season when he batted three-fifty-nine, second to Ted Williams's four-oh-six but ahead of Joe DiMaggio's three-fifty-seven, even with a fifty-six-game hitting streak. Cecil Travis then spent almost four seasons fighting in World War II curtailing an almost certain hall-of-fame career at age twenty-eight.

"My Uncle Anthony, who grew up watching the great two-time batting champion Mickey Vernon, then fell in love with slugger Roy Sievers who won the 1957 homerun and RBI crowns, beating out greats like Mickey Mantle and Ted Williams. Then he watched Rookie of the Year Bob Allison and Hall of Farner Harmon Killebrew before they were ripped from the city and sent to Minnesota for greener money pastures in 1961. And finally..."

Alex was feeling pure emotion-a stage achieved when your whole body understands something so deeply it becomes open to the full pain of the experience. He knew he had stepped over the edge, but he had to go on talking or his body would explode. He paused and looked at Sally, who blew him a kiss, and then Phillip, who motioned a baseball swing showing he should keep hitting it out of the park. The embarrassment he felt for that moment streamed out of his body. Intense adrenaline shot throughout his being as he continued the tale of history from his memory.

My father, who grew up adoring the expansion Senators, went to his first game at age seven in 1961 to witness a Gene Green grand slam at Griffith Stadium to beat the mighty New York Yankees. His Hero, Frank Howard, played the game like Paul Bunyan, crushing homeruns like he was creating legends. In 1971, my father was a ball boy for one game during the Senators' last year. He got to wear a Senators uniform and walk past Ted Williams in the dugout. After the game, he huddled in the locker room with the other bat and ball boys around a big tub of ice loaded with soda and beer. 'Hondo' dominated a stool as he dipped his feet in the tub, handed out sodas, gulped beer, and told great baseball stories. My father then witnessed his beloved Senators and Frank Howard sent to Texas for blood money."

Alex looked at each reporter who had tried to challenge him, and he continued to tell the truth as tears flowed down his eyes. "Finally, a great man, Frederick Meyers, said, enough is enough! He decided to make Washington a baseball town again to ease the pain and torture of the past farewells and create the fantasies of baseball joy for the future. I'm here on a mission." Alex started to feel disoriented but continued. "I'm here on a mission. It's time to stop the era of pain and the sorrow of loss and time to free the feelings of hope to love baseball in this city again." He felt numbness in his legs and held on tight to the podium, hoping to regain his orientation. "By September first, you can judge me if I'm right or wrong." He felt some strength return to his legs, but a pain in his stomach started to swirl.

Ron Roswell stood up in the midst of the tension in the room and broke the silence of the muted reporters. "Alex, I called for you to be traded here three weeks ago. Now it's happened. Do you think a month is long enough to prove yourself?"

Alex nodded yes as he took a few steps from the podium toward his family. Sally stood up and watched Alex crash to the floor!

Chapter 29

Dr. Henry Walton had traveled to Washington, DC, on Tuesday morning after laying his resignation letter on Frank Fellows's desk late Monday night. He needed some time off after blowing up at the Crowns GM in a meeting after the trade announcement. He called ahead to Presidents Park medical staff to ask for access to the press conference and to consult with them on Alex's medical condition. He told his clinic in Kansas City he needed two weeks to figure out his future. Privately, Dr. Walton knew it was time to sell his interest in the clinic and move back to DC. Losing his friend Larry Garson and his favorite patient, Alex Santucci, created a void in his life. He was concerned about Alex and wanted to offer his help. It was the least he could do for Laura and the late Gene Santucci.

Dr. Walton had entered the back of the press room and witnessed Alex's long historical perspective of baseball in DC. He observed a man in emotional pain and physical discomfort. He had worked his way toward the side of the room where Sally, Phillip, and Laura were standing. He broke through the crowd during Ron Roswell's final question as he saw Alex clutching at the podium. Laura looked at him with a big smile, totally unaware that her son was in distress. Dr. Walton turned back to see Alex seemingly nod yes to Roswell's question and take a step and a half as he quickly lost all balance and fell headlong toward the back of his empty chair next to the podium. Alex struck his forehead directly as his body turned enough from the impact to have his right shoulder bang on the carpet as the rest of his body bounced behind it and finally came to a rest on the floor. Dr. Walton sprang in front of a standing Sally and saw blood sprouting all over Alex's unconscious face. He grabbed a cloth napkin from the table, pressed it over the wound, and felt for a pulse and signs of breathing.

"Get me a stretcher and an ice pack!" he screamed, as

the crowded room filled with shrieks and moans.

Three of the Presidents players sitting on the other side of the podium appeared in a flash. They quickly picked up their fallen teammate and listened to instructions from Dr. Walton as he led the way out of the room toward the locker and medical rooms. A gurney appeared as they fled down the hallway. Dr. Walton kept pressing the wound as they transferred Alex to the moving table. He quickly found a pulse and heard breathing sounds.

Alex started to spit out his blood that dripped into his mouth and opened his eyes to see Dr. Walton. Henry slowed down the gurney as they stepped into the training room. He asked Alex how he felt.

"Doc, you're killing my head. Other than that, I need some water."

"Alex, you need stitches. Try to relax."

Alex grabbed Bruce Hammerly's good wrist and pulled himself to a sitting position against protests from Dr. Walton. Jerry Gonzalez gave him a cup of water and a wet towel to clean his bloodied face.

Blake Hopson howled with exuberance as Alex made himself look presentable.

"Bro, that was awesome. What a comeback! Are you all right?"

Alex gulped the water and motioned for more. He chugged another full cup as Dr. Walton motioned for him to lie back down. The best stitch man on the training staff appeared as Henry pulled back the icepack and bloody cloth napkins.

"That's going to need about thirty-five stitches, Alex." Mark Lansing said after Dr. Walton introduced himself to him. "I know you, Dr. Walton. I'm honored to have you here. You saved Alex a trip to the hospital and about a pint of blood!" Dr. Walton breathed some relief and let Mark take over.

Mark laid out his tools. "Alex, this should take about thirty minutes. Let me clean this up so I can shoot some Novocain around there."

"Don't worry about it, Mark. It already hurts. Just get to work. I got a game tonight."

"Alex, you probably have a concussion. You're not playing anytime soon."

Alex sat up and towered over Dr. Walton and Mark Lansing. They were intimidated by his presence. "I'm going to be in uniform tonight. Whether I play or not is up to Charley Jackson, not you two. I've got a hard head, and I feel fine since I drank some water. I was dehydrated from being in that room and drinking too much coffee and driving all night. Give me some more water, Blake." He layed back down and took his punishment for the next half hour.

• • •

Dr. Walton walked outside and found Sally, Laura, and Phillip waiting in the hallway wanting an update on Alex. He hugged Laura and Sally, who were beyond relieved and very happy to see him. He told them about quitting the Crowns organization and coming to DC for a few weeks to follow up on Alex and to get some time for himself to figure out his future. Laura insisted he stay at the house in Bethesda where he could keep an eye on Alex while he became settled. Dr. Walton felt it was an offer he could not refuse.

Jim Franco caught Dr. Walton outside the training room and took him to the side. After getting an update on Alex, he asked Dr. Walton if he would come to the press room and soothe the still-shocked press corp standing in silence. He told Jim he resigned from the Crowns.

"Well, that's perfect because I can hire you as a consultant right now! Please fill them in on what's happened. This thing has gone viral on the Internet."

Henry felt energized to help. He knew he was in the right place at the right time. At 12:32 p.m., he walked into a blood-stained press room and went right to work for the Washington Presidents. He answered twenty-five questions about Alex's health in perfect detail until everyone in the room was exhausted by the subject.

The news headlines running as a banner on *CNN* stated:

Santucci Predicts Championship, then Crashes to the Floor

MSNBC was running video tape highlights of the press conference. The banner read: **Santucci Says: Judge Me by September 1st**

This was followed by a warning about the footage to be shown of Alex's injury and the banner of: **Alex Santucci Collapse Leads to Bloody Head Injury**

ESPN's banner had the latest from Dr. Walton on Alex's condition: **Santucci Alert After Fall, Receives 35 Stitches, Plans to Play!**

Bonnie Bramlett cornered Dr. Walton after he finished settling the circus. She asked if she could see Sally or wait outside the trainer's room. Henry walked her down to meet with Sally, who had just come from being with Alex, Phillip and Laura. It was one fifteen as Phillip and Laura decided to catch a cab to Laura's house. Sally hugged Bonnie as they found a place to sit. Bonnie asked if there was anything she could do. Sally just wanted company. They sat with each other outside the training room as Alex slept for two hours. Dr. Walton checked on him every few minutes and reapplied an ice pack to the wound.

Finally, by three thirty, Alex emerged from the training room to see Sally and Bonnie sitting together. They both hugged Alex at the same time, examining his wound intently. Sally flipped his hair down over the stitches, reporting that his dirty blond locks would completely cover all thirty-five of them. Alex was starving. They went to the main kitchen and got some food. Bonnie told the suddenly famous first couple of baseball that tonight's game would be watched by millions. She also thought he should be aware that pitcher Winston Camels was known to be intentionally wild. Alex might be a perfect target for receiving a special "welcome" to the National League.

Alex shrugged it off saying," You cannot play baseball and ever worry about it; besides, it doesn't really hurt, it just makes you more intense and focused. It gives you a purpose to conquer the guy that hit you. That jolt of pain seers that into your brain forever!"

Bonnie and Sally looked at each other, wondering if they just heard the phrases, "it doesn't really hurt" and "the pain seers" within the same answer. They chalked it up to guy talk!

Bonnie tried to say good-bye, but Alex begged her to get Sally to go home and get some rest. He suggested Bonnie stay at his mom's and meet Leah. She was thrilled and accepted right away. She was hoping to have a longer piece on the Santucci story for the weekend. Otherwise, she was free to watch the beginning of something special in Washington, DC.

• • •

Alex entered the empty locker room at 3:47 p.m. A throwback uniform and the batting practice jersey for tonight's game were hanging up. His number seven was on the back of each. Alex was eager to get dressed and then found manager Charley Jackson in his office. Charley was relieved to see Alex in one piece. He believed it would be better for the team if Alex did not start the game but to be available for a double switch or a pinch-hitting role when the starting pitcher was replaced. Alex was happy with the clarity of his role for the game and headed for the batting cage under the stands. He was relieved to have a bat in his hands and swinging at a baseball. Suddenly the headache was eased by the perfection of his swings. He hands felt alive, and the bat seemed like a toothpick. The pressure of the day seemed to leave his body. In a hour, he would be on the infield dirt taking grounders and getting in his fifteen swings in the batting cage.

He headed back to the locker room, which was filling up with players. It was like a rock star had entered the house. A crowd surrounded Alex as each player took turns with their versions of passing out and falling on their faces. Alex was immediately at home with his teammates and anticipated the real welcome coming in a few hours from hometown DC fans. Finally, it dawned on him that passing out was his way of being reborn...as a member of the Washington Presidents!

Chapter 30

Alex read the lineup posted in the dugout and was not surprised to see Ryan Hudson playing third base on this last day of July. Rookie Bryan Hackett had been playing there since the injury to Hammersly three weeks ago. When Washington added Alex to the twenty-five-man roster earlier in the day, Hackett was reassigned to AAA Richmond Rabbits with an almost certain September 1 call-up back to the majors. He asked Manager Charley Jackson if he could leave Wednesday morning so he could be in the dugout to watch Alex debut as a President. Since Alex's head injury earlier in the day, that debut was in doubt. Nevertheless, it did not stop the pregame activities from becoming a circus with *ESPN, PLB, Fox, CNN, Comcast,* and *BASN* all having television crews covering batting and fielding practice. Alex did an interview with every channel, going over the reasons, patiently, for his passing out earlier in the day and assuring everyone he was healthy enough to play. He enjoyed taking fielding practice on the Presidents infield, getting a flavor for the heat in the clay dirt and the sweetness from the grass. His fifteen swings in batting practice were mainly for show, since he had already worked for an hour in the under-the-stands batting cage. He hit every ball to right field, working to bring the end of the bat, where his hands were, directly to the ball. During the underneath-the-stands session, he was doing exactly the opposite, working on pulling every inside pitch for power. He felt his power stroke was the best it had ever been in his career. Maybe there was chance he would get to show it off tonight.

After batting practice, he spent forty-five minutes signing autographs during Philadelphia's time in the cages. He loved to see swings from ballplayers. It was like a fingerprint you could catalog. After watching a batter for about fifteen swings, his memory marked the player for his swing as well as his name. Some swings were so enchanting and irresistible; it was like remembering an attractive woman. Those types of swings you could take on a date, dream about them later, and never forget how they looked.

The series with Philadelphia had sold out because Independence fans would come to Washington by the thousands. They could get tickets cheaper and enjoyed leaving Philadelphia for a few days. As he finished his swings, Indie fans razzed him about his passing out, telling him they would join him at the end of twelve beers. Never one to miss a chance to win over fans, Alex stopped at the railing and took off his cap and showed them his wound. He turned razzing into high-fives as he signed autographs for about fifty soon-to-be-drunk fans.

Fans from both teams booed when the starting lineup did not include Alex Santucci. As the Presidents took the field, "We want Alex" chants took over the humidity on this hot end-of-July night. For a rare minute, Washington and Philadelphia fans were brought together. Left-hander Phillip Fields was throwing for POTUS. He was the fifth starter in the rotation, regaining his spot in late June when veteran Ming Sun Chang was traded for infielder Bryan Hackett and a minor league prospect.

Fans from both teams booed when the starting lineup did not include Alex Santucci. As the Presidents took the field, "We want Alex" chants took over the humidity on this hot end-of-July night. For a rare minute, Washington and Philadelphia fans were brought together. Left-hander Phillip Fields was throwing for POTUS. He was the fifth starter in the rotation, regaining his spot in late June when veteran Ming Sun Chang was traded for infielder Bryan Hackett and a minor league prospect.

Alex settled into the dugout, sitting next to veteran backup catcher Henson Scott, who played at Harvard when Alex was at Princeton. He was the first player in the locker room to meet Alex before four o'clock and introduced him to the rest of the players as they arrived. He survived fourteen years as a catcher by being a left-handed hitter who could hit homeruns and was a wizard defensively. He was sitting out tonight against the All-Star left-hander Camels, but was starting half the games, providing some part-time power with twelve homeruns on the season.

On his other side was the injured franchise player Bruce Hammersly, who was quiet but sticking to Alex like glue. He was a smart, twenty-eight-year-old star, still soaking up any knowledge he could from Alex. He was so impressed by Alex's speech, which included a nod to him, that he was feeling chills down his back and legs before Alex passed out. His adrenaline had kicked in when he saw Alex go down. His wrist injury had really depressed him until the Santucci trade was announced yesterday. After hearing the fire from Alex during the press conference, he was high as a kite. The soft cast would come off in a week, and he was hoping to be back in a month.

The Presidents were down in the game 3-1, coming to the bottom of the sixth. Fields was due to bat sixth. Charley Jackson had Mario Ramos ready in the bullpen to pitch the seventh inning if there was a rally; he told Alex to be ready to bat for Fields. First Baseman Abel LeMont grounded out to first to start the inning. Right fielder Marty Morris doubled to left-center, followed by an RBI single to right by left fielder Carlos Mendoza to make it 3-2.

Alex had his bat and helmet ready as he waited in the hole for his turn. The crowd continued to cheer as Alex high-fived Morris coming into the dugout with the second run. Camels was clearly struggling with location and got a gift when catcher Vito Valencia swung at two pitches in the dirt for the second out. Hammersly and Scott yelled "Here we go Alex" as he headed to the on-deck circle for the first time as a part of the Washington Presidents. Alex felt the rumbling from the stands as the crowd stood to cheer both second baseman Chris

Patek, who was coming to the plate, and Alex, who was standing twenty-five feet away taking practice swings. Patek responded by doubling down the left field line as Mendoza had to hold at third because of a strong relay back to the infield.

Alex was introduced to the 43,656 fans, part of a sold-out crowd with standing room only tickets available. The chorus of boos by Philadelphia fans were covered by a mountain of emotional DC fans cheering a prodigal son.

Alex felt amazingly comfortable in the batter's box because the continuous roar from the crowd was drowning out the pain in his head for the first time since his tumble this afternoon. He was prepared for Camels to come inside, but the pitcher missed the target badly and luckily caught the outside corner for a strike. Camels made sure the next one was inside, throwing right for Alex's head. Only a cat-like back somersault kept Alex from the training room for the second time today. Learning gymnastics as a kid and yoga as an adult kept him from getting beaned. Umpire Marshall Randall came toward the mound and warned Camels and both benches that any more pitches like that would mean an ejection. The POTUS dugout was ready to jump onto the field, but Manager Charley Jackson came out in front of the dugout to calm matters. He screamed at Randall for warning his bench, even though he knew Randall was following PLB protocol.

Alex dusted himself off, checked the bandage on his wound, and secured his helmet on his head. He stepped closer to the plate, forcing Camels to pitch outside, which he did. Alex laced a liner down the right field line that finally sliced foul by two inches. As he sprinted around first, Alex felt his legs stretch out as he got into his sprinter's gear. The standing crowd recovered from the heartbreak foul ball and started stomping, clapping, and screaming "Let's go DC!" Alex returned to the plate as the runners got their leads from second and third. On a 1-2 count, Camels threw a changeup toward the lower part of the plate. Alex forced a defensive swing and topped the ball about twenty-five feet down the third base side of the infield. He got a great jump out of the batting box and started flying down first, determined to beat the throw. Camels came off the mound, spun around toward third as he picked up the ball, and fired to first as his left foot slipped away from him. Alex was a step and a half away from first as his left foot landed and then his right hit on the bag, beating the throw by a clear margin. As he sprinted through the bag and beyond first base, he looked left to see the first base umpire's safe sign. Suddenly he felt the car wreck of Philadelphia's second baseman Rico Rodriquez plow into his side like a special teams player on punt return duty. Rico was backing up the throw to first and ended up watching the play at first instead of running past the base line. This time Alex did a nice side roll and popped up to his feet. Rodriquez took the brunt of the collision and knocked himself out for a moment. Alex picked him up and grabbed Rico's mitt as he sent him back to his position at second with a pat on his behind.

Veteran first baseman and prolific homerun hitter Tim Thume put his glove arm over Alex's shoulder as he stood on first dusting himself off. They had spent two years together in Minnesota, which had been a nice right and left-handed power duo, batting back-to-back in the lineup. Tim wished him the best in the new league.

Camels got the last out in the inning and pitched perfect eighth and ninth innings as Philadelphia got a ninth-inning homerun by Tim Thume, his 608th of his career, to win 4-3. The crowd left disappointed by the loss but excited by the athletic presence of their new addition.

Tomorrow was the beginning of August; the real pennant race was just beginning and would be decided by the end of the month. Tonight, was a dress rehearsal for the real show that was premiering tomorrow night. There was a new player in the starring role, and his name was Alex Santucci!

PART III: THE SEVEN STREAKS

Chapter 31

The morning of the press conference, Leah had spent thirty minutes on the phone with Charles telling him about seeing Alex and her grandfather in Kansas City and driving to DC. Charles was not happy about her decision and called it a midlife crisis that she needed to figure out on her own. He had a tee time at 8:15 a.m. and could not be late. Then at 1:15 p.m., she had received a text from Charles wanting an update on Alex's condition. Suddenly he was a big fan. She was relieved by his uninterest/interest in Alex. It would help give her time to figure out her life.

She used *Skype* to talk with each of her children. All three were shocked but overjoyed at the news of a half-brother who was older and famous. "Can we tell all our friends?" and "When do we meet him?" were the first two questions. Then they acted like the wonderful young adults that had become by asking "How do you feel?" and "What made you wait so long?" and giving her permission to "take as much time as you need, Mom!" She spent most of the afternoon and evening walking in the neighborhood with Laura, seeing Alex's playgrounds and elementary school. She did some swimming and exercising at the YMCA with Sally, and afterward she rested and prayed in her room.

Now Leah was on the couch in the living room drinking tea, watching *House Hunters International* with Laura and Sally. It was closing in on midnight and the beginning of August, a month that would change history in DC and in Leah's life.

Alex walked into the Johnson Avenue house exhausted from the day's events. Laura greeted him with a big hug and a look at his bandage. Sally slid her arm around his waist and lifted up his shirt to search for any bruises from his collision beyond first base. Laura led him to the kitchen for some food as Leah stayed on the couch waiting for her turn and sipped more tea.

Alex engaged Leah from behind the couch and swept her up in his paws and told her he missed her. This caused a prolific smile as she balanced her tea in her hand, trying to survive the mugging. After a few more gulps from her tea, she joined them in the kitchen and gave him a bear hug from behind and kissed his bandage. Laura warmed up some pasta and served it with a salad and fresh tomatoes from the garden. Close to 1:00 a.m. on August 1, they finally all went to bed, feeling happy and close like a family should.

Alex took a cold shower for all of his ailments. He hoped to feel fresh tomorrow. His wound was surprisingly clean and beautifully stitched. It had been iced off and on for five hours, which really kept down the swelling and gave it an appearance of normalcy. His side was a little sore but nothing painful. Sally was fast asleep when he got into bed and did some reading. He finally hit the pillow at one thirty and fell into a deep sleep.

The dream must have started sometime before dawn, but time is uncertain when one travels to another world. He found himself wearing a 1969 Washington Senator uniform, standing in the locker room with the other ball boys. His friend, Jack Frasier, had invited him to come to the stadium after the regular ball boy went on a last-minute vacation. But that was his dad's friend from WJ!

It felt dark and dusty as he tried to find his way around the room. Suddenly he heard a booming voice: "Hey, kid, come join us! Grab a soda from the tub."

Around the corner, he saw a giant of a man, lying back on a bench, wearing long-john underwear and no shirt, with his right arm and shoulder in the ice tub.

"Hey, what's your name? Is it Alex? What can I getcha? An orange or cream soda?" Hondo handed him a cream soda. It felt cold to his face.

Then a man wearing a Senators jacket appeared and grabbed a beer. Hondo shook his hand as the man sat down. "Is this the kid you were telling me about, Hondo?"

"That's him, Ted! Hey, what should we tell him about hitting a baseball that he doesn't know already?"

Ted Williams, The Splendid Splinter, stood up in his batter's stance to show his point. "Get your pitch, son, and drive it hard. Get your money's worth on each swing. I like your swing: it gets right to the ball. You're going have a big month in August, I betcha. Call me when you're in Florida, and we'll go fishing and talk about hittin'. You're gonna do great here and have the month of your life. Tell him, Frank!"

"You're the hitter, Ted. I just try to kill the ball, every time, nothing like the feeling of a longball. I think you're a bomber, Alex. You don't always have to pull it to get it over the fence. I think you got big power. Ted, tell him the truth."

"I can't do that, Frank. Only he can do that!" Ted pointed into the darkness.

"You mean him!"

Suddenly out of the shadows, he appeared in his uniform with a *Won* his left shoulder sleeve.

Frank pulled his arm out of the tub. "Hey, it's The Big Train. That shoulder must be sore. Wanna put it in the tub for a while?"

"Feels fine, Hondo. I'm glad I didn't have to face you guys! Foxx, Ruth, Gehrig, Wagner, Hornsby, Jackson, Speaker, Sisler, and that bastard Cobb were enough for me! They sure kept me up at night. Ted, thanks for letting me see Alex. He's the one for sure! But I have to go now...You know I'm buried in Rockville. Alex, will you come and see me? Maybe tomorrow, or soon I think. We have to talk so you are ready for what's coming-you know it's coming soon!"

Alex looked in his eyes. It scared him enough to wake him out of the dream. He sat right up in bed breathing hard. It was just becoming light outside. His head was sore as he felt his wound. In their suite was a little kitchen that was stocked with coffee and ice packs. He started coffee and pulled out an ice pack. It immediately soothed his head as he closed his eyes again trying to feel some peace in his thoughts. He started to remember the dream: Hondo, The Splendid Splinter, and The Big Train all talking to him. He smelled the coffee and grabbed a cup. Wow, he thought, that was some headache from yesterday. Then he wondered, is he really buried in Rockville?

• • •

Alex headed out to the deck with his coffee. Sitting in the outdoor glider seat was Leah wrapped up in a blanket, listening to music through some earplugs, singing in a whisper while reading lyrics from a small notebook on her lap. She was startled when she smelled the aroma of coffee as Alex neared. She pulled out her ear-plugs and put them with the notebook to her side as she opened the blanket and stood up to meet Alex. He slid in next to her and nestled in on her shoulder. She stole his coffee and sneaked in a couple of sips. Alex closed his eyes as she played with his hair and gasped at the stitches in his scalp. She leaned over, with her full breasts hanging free under her nightgown, and kissed his forehead while saying a prayer to heal his wound. Alex, feeling warm and comfortable, drifted off into a meditation while Leah sweetly sang a Beatles lyric: "All you need is love, love..." After twenty minutes, he gently came back to life, feeling strong and loved.

Leah told Alex about talking with her family. He was happy about the kids' reactions and told her to get them here as soon as she wanted. She also shared that she might to stay for a while, maybe as long as a month, and then go to Kansas City to visit her grandfather. Alex was pleased and offered his condo as the perfect place for her to stay, especially if the kids came as well.

Alex then shared something with Leah. He had not thought of until this moment. "I think I want the wedding on Labor Day. We play St. Louis on Sunday the second and then play Chicago early on Labor Day Monday. We could do it in the evening, September third."

Leah had her mouth wide open and wondered about Sally's reaction. "Have you told Sally?"

"No, but she would love it! You three could all work on it in August!"

Leah started to smile, wondering what had shaken his head so hard yesterday!

"I think that might be a great thing, my dear!" She smiled looking sheepish with her Swedish blue eyes as she continued. "You'd better wake up that little bride-to-be of yours and let her know that she getting married in thirty-four days!"

Alex popped up, kissed Leah on the lips, and ran in to give Sally the news! She was still asleep when Alex attacked her from behind. She rolled over bleary eyed, wondering what woke her up.

"Sally, let's get married on Labor Day! It would be perfect! Leah wants to stay for a month. I think Mom would love it. We'll fly your parents into DC for the weekend. It would be perfect!"

"I think you must have a concussion or too much coffee already, my dear!" She sat on her folded knees, holding onto a pillow for comfort. "Did you take your medication yet? And get me some coffee-please!" Alex did as order and pleased his fiancée for the next hour.

Alex did a short run through the neighborhood and the Ayrlawn field. The day and probably the month both were going to be hot. It was always like this at the beginning of August. He remembered the recreation centers would close after the first week in August, leaving empty dust in the fields. Families went on vacations, and those left behind felt the loneliness of the playgrounds without kids playing on them. Alex would swim and hang out at the YMCA and play at night in organized baseball leagues. But he still woke up early to run down to the park and see if there was going to be a game only to find the absence of activity. The wait for the next summer break was incomprehensible; a sadness would prevail in August without homerun softball.

After a shower, he got on his computer to read some e-mails, and then his fingers went to *Google* and looked up "Walter Johnson Buried." It obeyed and exposed the listing: "Walter Johnson, Died December 10, 1946. Buried at Rockville Union Cemetery." It must have been in his subconscious from all the times he read about him, even though he did not remember. Why should I visit? He wondered. It was just a dream. Big Train said there was something he needed to tell him. How silly!

He returned to the main living room and found Sally, Leah, and Laura giggling like schoolgirls. His mom greeted him with a hug and tears in her eyes, overjoyed at the news of a wedding on Labor Day. "So much to do," she said, but it seemed to be the perfect tonic for her eventful last few weeks.

Dr. Walton was sitting in the kitchen when Alex walked in. Alex was glad to see him, almost forgetting he had come to the house an hour before him last night. Henry got out his blood-pressure thing, his heart-listening thing, and the look-through-the-light thing to do a quick examination of his patient. Everything seemed fine, but he still wanted to talk to Alex about his overall body diagnosis. He hoped to find the right moment in the next few days.

Laura was in her glory with almost a full house and a wedding with an unlimited budget to plan. She knew the priorities: they would have to find a location, which would be impossible, but maybe a conference room at the stadium, or a church if necessary, and a guest list. Thank goodness for e-mail, she thought, because this would not follow regular protocol.

• • •

Alex asked Sally if she wanted to go out for breakfast and then take a ride for an adventure. She was excited for any time alone with Alex after this morning's decision. They quickly jumped in the Acura TL and exited west down Johnson Avenue past North Bethesda Middle School. After many turns and several miles on back roads to avoid the traffic, he turned right on Falls Road, which crossed over I-270 and into the old part of Rockville, the third largest incorporated city in Maryland with 61,000 people. Several houses on Great Falls Road dated back to the 1800s, with some landmarks predating the Revolutionary War. They headed towards Rockville Pike now a ten-mile avenue of shopping and commercial buildings, and the main artery for Civil War troops as they headed north to deadly battles such as Gettysburg and Antietam. The downtown Rockville area was a beautiful few blocks of stores, restaurants, apartments, and town houses. Alex, excited to be scooting around in his Acura TL, pulled into a spot right across from the First Watch Cafe.

After the waitress brought two coffees, Alex quickly ordered the eggs Benedict with a side of corn beef hash; Sally went with the French toast with bacon. She was starving after being woken so early with life-changing news. They wolfed down the great breakfast as Alex shared with Sally the dream, he had last night.

She responded, "Wow, you are really carrying this pressure around with you. I hope you are okay, Alex." Alex continued with the part about the cemetery. "So, wait," she said. "This adventure is an Easter egg hunt through a cemetery. Do you even know where his headstone is?"
"It will be fun to find it, sweetheart. I said it was an

adventure!"

With her professor eyes, Sally looked at him like he was a student turning in a paper a week late. She then took a final bite of her French toast, brushed back the hair hanging in her face, and wiped her mouth with a napkin that left a beautiful smile. She uttered in her best Scarlett O'Hara imitation, "Now, I didn't come to talk silliness, Rhett Butler." She paused and allowed her southern accent sink in with Alex. "Now, my dear partner, let's hit the cemetery!" She jumped up from the table, grabbed the bill, and paid for something for the first time in a while. It gave her a passion to help her man find the message he was looking for-as crazy as it sounded!

The Rockville Union Cemetery was established in 1738 and was located at 1350 Baltimore Avenue, next to the Civic Center Park, a couple miles from downtown Rockville. It became famous for being the original resting place for F. Scott Fitzgerald in 1940, until his remains were moved in 1975 to nearby St. Mary's Cemetery to be next to his wife, Zelda Fitzgerald.

Sally gathered the two cups of coffee she had bought for the road as they pulled into the twenty-four acres of cemetery. A caretaker gave them directions to the Walter Johnson grave site, and they happily took their time to get to the right spot. The plain three-foot high headstone appeared first, with a simple "Johnson" carved into the stone. Two stone markers were placed six feet in front. The one on the right read: Hazel Lee Johnson 1894-1930. The one on the left read: Walter Perry Johnson 1887-1946. The top of the headstone was adorned with a couple baseball hats, left by fans, and a few items had been left at the base. Alex grabbed Sally's hand and bowed his head, looking down at the man he literally dreamed about. He had felt his spirit at times as a kid, playing in his backyard, but he had never been this close to the remains of his body. He noticed that his wife, Hazel, died at age thirty-six in 1930, leaving him with five young children. Walter Johnson's mother came from California to care for the children after Hazel's death while he was still living on Old Georgetown Road and managing Washington until 1933 and then Cleveland through 1935. He then finally retired from baseball after twenty-nine years of playing and managing and bought the farm in Germantown to be with his children full time.

Alex wondered how his life became so intertwined with this great man: as a kid pitching against a wall in Big Train's Backyard, as a teenager going to a high school named after him, and as an adult getting a chance to win a championship for a team in Washington. He accepted the possibility of a destiny to lead this team to a championship like Walter Johnson did in 1924, but he was a pitcher and Alex was a third baseman. If they could talk, what would "The Big Train" say to him about hitting or fielding? Would he just give him insight into leadership, or was there something else for him to learn from "The Big Train"?

Sally walked around the Johnson headstone, picking up each cap left on the top. The last cap was blue with an old W on the front, similar to the Senators in the 1920s. Something fell out of it and landed behind the headstone. She picked up the piece of paper and laughed as she read it to herself. She put the small note back in the hat and placed it back on the headstone.

Alex was in a zone, still at the stone markers, with his eyes closed, thinking about the dream. Sally tugged on his arm and asked if he was all right. He opened his eyes and looked puzzled.

"I can't quite figure the dream out. I guess it was kind of silly to come out here, even though it is a beautiful area. I guess I thought there would be something out here for me... like a message from him as if we were talking. You know what I mean."

Sally tried to make sense of his frustration but could only laugh when she thought of the note in the hat. "Well, I guess there was something in that old ratty blue What that could be considered a message." She laughed, trying to make a joke.

Alex was still shaking his head, feeling puzzled, until he heard the word "message." "Sally, what message are you talking about?"

"Oh, it was a silly little note somebody left in a hat. Look, I'll read it for you." She took three steps and picked up the hat again and pulled out the note. "See, here it is. You, see? It's silly, Alex. Read it!"

Alex took a quick look and saw the message. "DC Needs You. Keep on Pitching -Big Train."

Chapter 32

The trade deadline had ended on July 31 with the Presidents making the biggest making the biggest splash by acquiring Alex Santucci. National League East division leaders, the Miami Sugarcanes, received the best pitcher available, left-hander Joe McDowell from Arizona. The Presidents would be hosting the 'Canes for an important four-game series starting on Friday, August 3, with a doubleheader. McDowell would start his first game as a 'Cane in the first game Friday night.

Tonight against Philadelphia, number one starter Travis Tyler would take the mound with an extra day of rest after pitching his first complete game in a 6-3 win against the Milwaukee Millers on Thursday, July 26. He gave up a three-run homer in the third but shut out the Millers for the last six innings. Tyler was a mountain of a pitcher at six foot five, 235 pounds, and just turning twenty-four. He and Blake Hopson were both first picks in the entire PBL draft- Tyler in 2009 and Blake in 2010-with incredible hype and expectations. Both were meeting expectations and beyond. Tyler was the National League starter in the All-Star game and was a leading candidate for the NL Cy Young Award with a 14 and 2 record and a 2.24 ERA in his first full season.

Alex came to the ballpark around three o'clock to get some treatment for his bruised left side, his sore right shoulder, a tender stomach area, and a forehead that was black and blue. He saw the chiropractor, the physical therapist, the trainer that stitched him up, and Dr. Walton, who took blood for some follow-up tests on the inner workings of his organs. He spent forty-five minutes going from the hot whirlpool to the ice-cold tub to get his body ready to play tonight. Most days Alex did not need these intense healing sessions to play. His running, yoga, swimming, and limited weight work kept him in premium shape. The last three weeks gave him some bumps and bruises from on and off the field that challenged his normally great body health.

Manager Charley Jackson came to visit Alex when he was going from hot to cold treatments. Alex grabbed a robe and sat with Charley for a few minutes. Jackson wanted him to feel welcomed but to know there would be no orientation time to become the leader of this team.

"I wanted you to get settled yesterday, but apparently you fell on your head. So, I held you out last night. But starting tonight I'm batting you third. When Hammer comes back, we'll figure out who bats third or fourth. Alex since you're a veteran, I can be straight with you without worrying about putting pressure on you. It's simple really. You need to carry us through August. I hate to put that on one player...but it's the truth. You know it and I know it!" Charley, at age sixty-nine, was a truth guru. He knew reality, talent, and how to win championships in baseball. He won two World Series as a player and one as a manager, and played in four All-Star games. He once hit forty-three homeruns in a season. This occurred after never hitting more than eighteen because he batted in between two great players who hit over forty homeruns that season as well.

"Alex, what I need out of you is power! I don't care what else you do, but go for the fences. I know your swing. It's a classic homerun swing. You swing like a combination of Hank Greenberg and Harmon Killebrew, but more athletic like Bob Allison or Roy Sievers. Those guys were great right-handed power guys! Now Robby, Hondo, Schmitty, and Dick were something special. They could chop down a tree with a flick of their wrists, but the greatest I've seen was Hammering Hank. He could hit a pitch almost behind him for a homerun. He would wear pitchers out with an at-bat. They would get so flustered by pitching to him that when I came up, they would throw me a BP fastball right down the middle. That's how I got forty-three in 1973."

Charley had Alex's attention. He knew every swing that

he mentioned, even nicknames like Frank "Robby" Robinson, Frank "Hondo" Howard, Mike "Schmitty" Schmidt, and Ritchie "call me Dick" Allen. He even knew Charley tied the record for homeruns in a season for a second baseman, which had been held by Rogers Hornsby since 1922. He was also aware that Hornsby was arguably the greatest overall hitter in baseball history with a lifetime .358 batting average. Over a five-year period, from 1921 to 1925, he hit an astonishing .397, .401, .384, .424, and .403 while averaging 29 homeruns and 120 RBIs. "Not bad for second baseman," Alex thought.

"When I saw you get going right before the All-Star break and then kept it going on the nine-game road swing, I said to Franco, 'Let's get this guy!' He said they wouldn't let you go, and then somehow, he pulled it off after the owner died. I got to tell you, it was an up and down couple days! You know what I mean?"

Alex silently nodded his head in agreement, totally mesmerized by their synergy.

"Well, I'll let you get back to getting some treatment. You got Grantham tonight and Reed tomorrow. I'll go over both with you later. I think you can go deep on both of them." Charley, with a nod from Alex, quickly rose and headed back to his office.

Alex went back to the hot whirlpool one more time, pondering the directive from Manager Jackson. He was in full agreement with him and felt ready to play long ball!

• • •

Travis Tyler, taking his warmup tosses, looked like a turbocharged pitching machine. Henson Scott threw the last warm-up pitch down to second baseman Chris Patek, who flipped it to shortstop Jerry Gonzalez, who fired it to Alex on the infield grass.

Alex walked the ball to pitcher Travis Tyler. As he laid it in his glove, Alex said, "This one's a winner, kid. Enjoy the ride."

Tyler smiled and headed to the mound to capture the crown of winning over the Independence.

• • •

Alex doubled off the wall in left-center in the first inning but did not score. In the fourth inning with no score, he came to bat with Hopson on first after a single. Grantham was nervous on the mound with Hopson on first base. After several throw-overs to first base, he finally fired high to Alex for ball one. Alex stepped out and checked his bat, looking for the sweet spot, and lined it up perfectly in his hands. He saw his family standing along with the other 44,243 fans.

Sally, Leah, Laura, Phillip, and Dr. Walton sat in the Diamond section behind home plate as guests of Hank Meyers. Leah held Phillip's arm, feeling the electricity of the ballpark and the moment. She blew a kiss in his direction while Phillip cheered, "Let's go DC!"

Alex stepped back into the plate and took the slider on the outside corner for a strike. Charley had told him that Grantham would fall in love with his slider if he got it over early in the count. It was coming again. Alex turned on it quickly and put it over the bullpen in left field for a 2-0 lead. He lapped the bases quickly with his head down. He pointed right to his family after crossing home plate and received double high-fives from the rookie Hopson. No one except Alex noticed that he had just tied Frank Howard for career homeruns with number 382.

Washington added two in the seventh for a 4-0 win and a complete game shutout for Tyler, the first of his career. The crowd had been in a frenzy in the ninth as he struck out his tenth, eleventh, and twelfth batters to nail down the victory over Philadelphia. Alex was the first to the mound to congratulate Tyler as Henson Scott stuffed the winning game ball in his glove. Alex went to the stands to quickly talk to his family then headed inside for some much-needed fluids. After fifteen minutes he came out to sign autographs for an hour with fans.

Sally stayed patiently in her seat, sending everybody else home. Several wives came to her seat after the game and introduced themselves. She had met Charlotte Scott and Patty Peterson previously, during spring training in Arizona. Marcia Hammersly, Maria Gonzalez, and the young Alexis Tyler were new to her. They made her feel very welcome while interrogating her about the wedding news. All of the women except Alexis Tyler were blondes of some sort and dressed beautifully in summer dresses. Alexis was something special. She was a natural redhead with freckles all over her body that made her look seventeen. She was Sally's height, with a very petite body that was filled in the right places like Sally's. She was quiet with green eyes that smiled right through you, almost like she was a prototype for the perfect natural country girl gone Hollywood. Both Alexis and Travis were from San Diego and both had that sunshine look from a lifetime of playing, swimming, surfing, and running on the beach. Alexis was the youngest Presidents wife at age twenty-two, but she was a quiet leader and sat down next to Sally after giving her a warm welcome hug. Alexis held Sally's hand and wrist with both hands as the other women peppered Sally with questions. Sally did her best to have a late-night conversation while her fiancé was signing hundreds of autographs. Every few minutes, Sally noticed the warmth of Alexis's hand, smelled her intoxicating presence, and heard her whispery voice laughing or commenting on a question or answer.

Sally was an only child and longed for a sister or close friend to enjoy. Her parents taught her independence from an early age, and the teaching profession had become her closest friend. Sally enjoyed Alex so much because he had become her best friend over a long relationship. They spent six months together before becoming intimate, mainly because they met as the season started and never spent more than six hours with each other. There never seemed to be a rush, even though she was so attracted to him. She knew that Alex was distracted by the season and that only ten-day road trips kept them from being together until the season was over. They spent a week at his condo in Florida after the season was over in 2007. It was the greatest time in her life and well worth the wait.

    As she sat in the stands, she wondered how her dream of being engaged to Alex had finally happened so quickly over the last three weeks. She knew it would be quite an adjustment in her life. Where would they live? Would she go back to teaching in January? Would they have kids sooner or later? The scariest thought was about Alex and his health. Did all of his feeling for her become more intense because of the medication or his possible stomach ailment? Or was that just a natural progression of their relationship? Surrounded by these women and holding hands with Alexis made her feel settled with the situation. All she knew was that she was the happiest and luckiest woman in the world right now.

Chapter 33

Alex woke up six o'clock, Thursday, August 2, ten minutes before sunrise. It felt like almost a normal night of getting six hours of sleep after a home game. No crazy dreams, no extra pains, just the smell of coffee in the morning. He took a quick swig of his cup as he put on his running shoes and shorts for a long run. The dew point, which is the temperature below which water will condense into liquid, had dropped below seventy, making the morning comfortable before the sun became a factor. He ran across Old Georgetown Road and headed down hill on Cedar Lane for almost two miles until he crossed Rock Creek. He turned left on Beach Drive and ran for another two miles until he crossed through Puller Park and onto Parkwood Drive. Quickly, he picked the pace on the last quarter mile up the hill until he came to Everett Street. He went up to the door to see his father, Phillip, who was sitting on the patio, next to his garden, reading the paper and drinking coffee. After covering about four miles and thirty minutes of running, Alex enjoyed the chance for a break. Phillip greeted him with a big hug and offered him his coffee cup. Alex took a much-needed sip, even though it was decaf. They sat and talked about the game last night. Phillip was very animated talking about the experience of the night, pulsating about the introduction, relishing the two-run homer and double, and beaming about the ninth inning strikeouts. He became very emotional talking about seeing his son play in Washington, DC. It seemed Phillip was having trouble grasping that his son was really playing for the Presidents. Phillip paused for a minute, trying to regain his speaking ability.

"I was sitting there soaking it all in-the crowd, the athletes-and then you were at the center of everybody's attention. It was like a dream, seeing the whole thing. Then you hit the ball off the wall and then the homerun! I thought right then if I didn't take another breath, I would be happy to go..." Phillip felt memories from years of concern for Alex and disappointment in himself. He tried to breathe through his emotions and stabilize his shaking body. Alex sat next to him, rubbing his shoulders. He took another sip from his coffee and muttered to Alex, "So did you get any sleep last night?"

"Actually, I had a routine night for the first time in a while. It was a pleasure to wake up without a crazy dream or something else going on."

Phillip wiped his eyes and nose with a napkin as he noticed the words "crazy" and "dream." He cleared his throat now that he was out of his emotional state and his body was not shaking. "What kind of dreams?"

"The night after my fall, I had a crazy dream about being a ball boy." Alex continued to report the details of the dream and the subsequent trip to the cemetery.

"Did it help to go out there?"

"Well, kinda! But it got a little mysterious after Sally found this note on the headstone." Alex explained the note and the hat she found it in.

Phillip sat up straight and pondered the complexity of this" Walter Johnson" thing. He had some concern that it was bordering on an obsession. "What did Sally think of it?"

"She thought it was funny, actually. We did not talk about much on the way back." Alex stood up and walked around the garden, clearly uncomfortable with the next question coming up.

"Well, son...What did you think?"

"It's a crazy note-just some fan leaving it there. It has nothing to do with me." Alex looked straight at Phillip, who knew better.

"That may be true, but what is important here is what you think, because it may not be reality, but at least you have to talk about it."

"I can't tell you what I think. You'll think I'm crazy!"

"Crazy is a country I used to work in. And believe me; you're not within a continent of crazy."

Alex smiled and for the first time felt some relief. He took some time thinking through the options in his head. As soon as he heard the words from Sally, "DC needs you. Keep on Pitching. -The Big Train," he knew what he was supposed to do. Now the question was, should he keep it to himself or talk about it to another human being. He finally decided his father, Phillip, ex-therapist and confidant, was a good place to start.

"I think he wants me to pitch!" "Who wants you to pitch?"

"The Big Train!"

Chapter 34

Thursday night was a slugfest with left-hander Leo Lawrence giving up seven runs in six innings of work. Luckily the Presidents bats were effective against Joe "Skate" Freeze, the Canadian-born left-hander who usually shuts down DC, with seven runs as well. Alex had an RBI single and a walk in three Abs. In the bottom of the eighth, he came up with two on and two out, facing right-handed reliever Woody Franklin.

The Presidents media relation department was quickly disseminating information that Alex Santucci was tied with Frank Howard for career homeruns with 382. Somehow this fact had eluded the staff member in charge of keeping the head of the department, Patty O'Neil, informed. Patty was becoming red-faced, to go along with her red hair, trying to make sure the announcers had the information. The embarrassment went to panic when a cameraman somehow found Frank Howard sitting with a couple of scouts from the Presidents organization. The scouts, Chuck Cottier and Hank Allen, were teammates of Hondo in the 1960s. They had called Frank and invited him to the game after the tying homerun in yesterday's game. Frank was excited to be at the game and was hoping to meet the newest President after the game. The Presidents game announcers, Wayne Woodworker and Nick DePillis, received the media note about the homerun information, just as they were hearing their director tell them a shot of Frank Howard in the stands was coming up on screen. Luckily, the on-the-field field reporter, Sarah Miles, asked manager Charley Jackson to go out to talk to the home umpire to stall for a minute. Charley had a death stare going on with GM Jim Franco, who was sitting in the front row behind home plate with Hank Meyers. Jim held his hands up, claiming innocence in the calamity.

Finally, the field announcer, with Alex still in the on-deck circle being held up by the umpire, introduced the great Frank Howard to the crowd. He stood like a normal aging giant, seeming human-like, only six days away from his seventy-sixth birthday-forty years to the day before Alex Santucci was born!

The crowd starting politely clapping but then started to get louder when Alex went to the stands and asked to shake Frank's hand. He graciously came down from the tenth row seat to meet Alex. The announcer then proclaimed that Alex was tied with him in career homeruns. Hondo bent over and took Alex's right hand with both of his giant paws. Alex felt a brutal strength from Frank's hands, something he never felt from another human.

"It's an honor, Mr. Howard, to meet you. You were a hero to both of my fathers!"

"Alex, I remember your birth father, Phillip. We met one time at a conference in San Francisco in 1989. He told me about a son that he gave up for adoption that might become a ballplayer. We chuckled about him playing in DC if they ever got a team. We talked about him being a ball boy for a game. It was a great night-had quite a few beers!" Frank rubbed his stomach and laughed. "He was an impressive man, like yourself, Alex. I never forgot him-especially once you became a ballplayer. Been following you ever since. People like your father keep me going, son. Now let's get this thing over with. Hit one out for me!" Hondo winked at him as he turned to wave at the crowd. They were chanting "Hondo" and "Alex" at the same time. Alex headed slowly to the batter's box on a mission from Hondo.

Pitcher Woody Franklin was being visited by pitching coach, Herm Willard, with a message from the manager about pitching to Alex. "Keep it down and away, nowhere near the plate. He is way too hot to pitch to right now. I don't care if you load the bases. With two out and a lefty corning up, I got Knowles ready to face LeMont if we have too."

Woody was not listening to Herm. He was staring

straight at the plate, ready to throw ninety-eight miles an hour. "Knowles is not doing my job," he thought to himself.

Alex stepped in, feeling a little unsettled. Franklin fired strike one right down the middle. Alex stepped out, collected himself, and thought about Hondo in his dream saying, "I think you're a bomber, kid. You don't always have to pull it to get it over the fence. I think you've got big power." Alex dug in for the next fast-ball and fouled it straight back. His swing felt nice and easy, like a toothpick in his hand. He stepped out again and thought about the statutes as you walk in to Presidents Park. It became clear to him: "This one's for Frank."

Woody could have thrown any pitch but a fastball and had a strikeout, but he figured, "This guy can't catch up with my heater." He shook off his catcher twice and finally got the heater sign. He came to the stretch, the runners took their leads, and the crowd hushed as he fired to the plate. Alex dove at it with a Hondo swing that parted the air around it. The sound of the bat on the ball was supersonic, like four F-22s doing a flyover of the stadium. The fans in the left field stands heard the explosion of the bat a fraction of a second later as the ball flew over their heads toward the plaza entrance. The baseball acted like a missile, quickly hitting its apex and promptly heading straight down to the ground some 550 feet from home plate. Fifteen feet from a hard landing, the ball hit squarely on the swinging bat of Frank Howard's Bronze Statue, sending it hopping toward the entrance gate and out of the stadium! Several security men watched in awe as the ball seemed to be on a mission to leave the stadium. It rolled through a turnstile and then finally nestled on N Street before it was retrieved.

Alex circled the bases and paused to wink at the gentle giant in the tenth row. The crowd would not let him sit down on the bench. He tipped his hat several times, trying to digest the feat they had witnessed. Closer Clay "Bean" Counter finished up the ninth to seal the 10-7 victory, their second in arow.

• • •

    The first place Miami Sugarcanes were in town for an important four-game series starting on Friday, August 3, at 7:05. Washington was now three games over .500 at 53 and 50, and six games behind Miami. Alex had little time in the morning to enjoy his game winning blast last night.

    Frank Howard had joined him after the game, happily signing autographs for an hour. Reporters were circled around the power hitting couple, asking questions about the ball Alex hit to move ahead of Hondo in career homeruns. The story was running continuously on *SportsCenter,* showing replays from fan's- camera-phones of the ball hitting the Hondo statue and bouncing out of the stadium. The *Washington Daily* had a front page picture of the game-winning homerun, calling it "The Natural Blast" and reporting it as the farthest ball hit in DC since Mickey Mantle's 565 foot blast left Griffith Stadium in 1953. Ron Roswell wrote a column titled "Is Alex the Savior?" Feeling vindicated about calling for a trade for Alex earlier in the month, he intimated that the "blast" was a signal that "Santucci was ready to take this team to the promise-land like Moses himself."

    Alex finished reading the paper and drinking his coffee before heading out for a run. This time he grabbed a baseball on the way out, alternating between bouncing it off the pavement or tossing it behind his back and up into the air, either catching it in front of him with his left hand or between his legs with his right hand. He performed this self-- pleasing show for about a mile down Johnson Avenue to North Bethesda Middle School.

    He found a back wall of the school, unnoticeable to other runners in the morning. He put his back to the wall and stepped off twenty perfect paces of a yard, then dug a mark in the grass. It was a perfect sixty-feet and six inches, the distance of a pitcher's mound from home plate. He surveyed the brick in the wall and imagined a strike zone and started to throw. Each toss produced a bounding ball that he fielded with his bare hands. After about ten throws, he started to feel a windup and a snap in his wrists. The ball started to come off the wall quicker. The faster pitches were leaving marks on the bricks of his imaginary strike zone. These marks were all over the place, mainly high in the strike zone. After thirty pitches, his arm felt loose, and his shoulder was leading his follow through. The marks started to get closer and lower in the strike zone. After his fiftieth pitch, he grabbed the grounder with one hand and put it in his pocket. He walked up to the wall and observed the marks in detail as he closed his eyes and imagined being a young boy and checking "The Big Train" house for any dents he might have left on the back of the house. Luckily he had used a tennis ball to warm up back then.

Alex finished his run and came in to see his mom, Laura, who was sipping morning coffee while reading the headlines in the *Daily*. It was hard for her to contain her excitement after reading about Alex's winning blast. She watched very little television, so unless she saw his games in person, she never saw the actual games in real time. Laura had been busy working on the wedding and was making great progress lining up a Presidents stadium conference room and a caterer for the reception. Leah was working on the invitations and was ready to send them out to a list of guests as soon as Sally approved. Laura wanted Alex and Sally to consider marrying in a church, even though both had not been in one since high school. Both families were Catholic and would like a Catholic venue, but she would settle for any church at this point.

"Alex, I know you have a lot on your mind, but can you find a church near the stadium for the ceremony? It will be hard to explain to your kids twenty years from now that you got married in a stadium!"

"Well, does home plate sound better, Mom?" Alex stole

a gulp of coffee from his mom's cup and laughed at the look on her face. "I get it... I'll see what I can do. Today will be tough with a doubleheader starting at four. Roswell has me parting the Red Sea today, I think!"

"Maybe Sally can help, Alex. Just talk to her about it... please!"

"I promise by the weekend we'll get you a church for the wedding, Mom."

"That's my boy! Now win those games today and hit some more homeruns."

"Let's see, Mom... a church, a couple of wins, some homeruns. Should I pick up some milk on the way home tonight?"

"That will be fine, my dear. Oh, I could use a check for fifty thousand. I have lots of things to pay for this week!"

"Wow, whose idea was this wedding anyway?" Alex joked. "Check with Sally for money-she's loaded!"

• • •

Alex headed to the stadium around ten o'clock. He took his usual route, which included going west on the beltway to the Cabin John Parkway exit south to Canal Road, hopping on the Whitehurst Freeway, passing the Monuments to the Southeast-Southwest Freeway, or better known as 1-395. As he headed pass the Fourteenth Street Bridge exit, he merged onto the freeway and was immediately slowed to a crawl by the normal stop-and-go conditions. He crossed under the Twelfth Street overpass and the beginning of the three blocks of the L'Enfant Plaza on the left. Famous architect, I.M. Pei, designed the late-1960s plaza currently occupied by government agencies.

Alex moved over to the right-hand lane to exit from the traffic mess and zoomed off the Ninth Street exit, making several illegal turns to get onto G Street going east across Seventh Street. Suddenly he felt torque in the steering, tugging him left. He pulled into a townhouse parking area to look at his tires. He coasted to an area shaded with large oak trees in the back of the lot that bordered the 1-395 expressway just about thirty feet below. It was a pleasant spot except that he had a flat front tire on his car. His friend, Hal Baker, had hooked him up with a premium car repair service that included a hyperactive tow-truck/start-your- car/change-a-tire service that would be at your car within fifteen minutes anywhere near a metropolitan area. A five- hundred-dollar bounty would go out on a text to certain tow drivers in an area to fix a VIP car in a hurry.

Alex finished the phone call to the service and walked to the four-foot high retaining wall bordering the highway. He looked down at the poor souls below in some sort of purgatory, moving like snails late to a picnic. The temperature was being reasonable today, hovering around the upper eighties. He thought about the dichotomy of how smooth things had really gone for him and Sally, driving halfway across the country, enduring the craziness of the last month. The flat tire was the first "bump" in the road. He wondered if divine intervention had led him to this place of a feeling of destiny with this team. His birth mother and adopted mother were very religious and spiritual people, but Alex himself found little time for religion since early high school. Spirituality was a part of his emotional renaissance during the past month, but it was still in the early stages of development and all very confusing.

He slowly looked up from the patiently moving cars in the chasm below and saw the buildings above on the other side that made up L'Enfant Plaza, the headquarters of HUD(Housing and Urban Development) and a NASA administration building. Parting these towers of federal bureaucracy like the Red Sea was a heavenly structure as old as baseball in the National League. It was a beautiful church of some sort, with dark red stone highlighting its' twenty-seven stained-glass windows.

Alex struggled to focus on the outside beauty of the building. There was something inside, an inner beauty that was summoning him to visit. He wondered if this was what some meant when they talked about a "calling from God." Abruptly a loud roar seemed to descend upon him. He looked up, wondering if the heavens might be opening up a storm or if maybe a sign would appear from above. Instead, the noise behind him became louder. He finally turned around and saw his savior!

Premium Service Towing, a thunderous and massive diesel truck with a long bed for several cars on the back, had come to the rescue. Reginald Chaney, a six-foot eight-inch, 255-pound, former power forward for the Georgetown Hoyas, jumped out wearing a nearly clean set of white overalls hiding a shirt, a bow tie, and a white hat and matching gloves. He was used to dealing with high-priced clientele, but getting a ballplayer was a treat. Being a homegrown DC product himself, he was all over the Alex Santucci story. Cocaine use in the 1990s ended his promising career. Now clean for fifteen years, he was a deeply religious family man running his own business. He was ready to literally lift up the Acura, Lord willing, and repair the soul of that fallen tire!

"My brother, how can the Lord help you today?"

Alex looked at the smiling, large African-American and recognized the talented rebounder and defender who helped the Hoyas compete in the Big East for two years before going to the NBA for a multimillion-dollar contract. Most of it went up his nose, but there was enough left over, after a medical rehabilitation, to start the tow truck business and buy a three-bedroom townhouse in the southwest neighborhood where he now stood.

Alex felt an immediate kinship with Reggie and laughed to himself about his latest daydream with the church. But he hoped that Reggie could answer a question about it for him. "You have come to save me...I hope." Alex extended his hand and received a bear hug back from Reggie.

"I saw that homerun last night at the ballpark. Seen nothin' like that in all my young years on God's Earth. I saw it hit big Hondo's bat and bounce out of the stadium from the bleachers I was in! I think the Lord wants you to make a statement."

"Well, Reggie, the Lord is making a statement to me today about making illegal turns over curbs and such, no good for the tires apparently!"

They shared a laugh as Reggie took Alex by the shoulder, sharing his love for the Lord.

Alex looked up to Reggie and asked, "By the way, do you know what that red stone building is across the highway?"

"I sure do, my friend. That is the cathedral of my Lord Savior, Jesus Christ: Saint Dominic's!"
"What kind of church is it, Reggie?"

"Straight from "The Rock" of Saint Peter and Jesus Christ, my brethren-Catholic!"

Chapter 35

It was still early in the day, before noon, and thanks to Reginald Chaney, the Acura TL was ready to drive. Reggie invited Alex to church on Sunday morning with his family. It was an offer Alex could not refuse but begged for it to be the early service at eight o'clock.

With time on his hands and a working vehicle, Alex decided to drive across Seventh Street to bear witness to the inside of St. Dominic's. Somehow the structure had survived all the highway and building booms of the 1960s and was sitting on a sliver of land at 630 E Street, in Southwest DC. Alex walked up the front steps and opened one of the fifteen-foot high mahogany front doors and entered the nave adorned with stained-glass windows and a side chapel. He immediately felt comfortable, with his emotions in control, as he walked through the next set of doors into the sacristy of the church with a roof that rose some seventy to eighty feet in the air. Each side wall had eight, twenty-foot-high stained-glass windows projecting a spectrum of colors on the golden oak pews. The twelve Stations of the Cross lined the wall in between four side chapels inside the main church. Alex noticed the electronically lit candles paying homage to St. Agnes Ortepal Ciano, St. Rose of Lima, St. Francis of Assisi, and of course St. Dominic, or Santo Domingo, the founder of the Dominican Brothers, who spread the use of the rosary, starting almost a thousand years ago. He was also known as the patron saint of astronomy.

Alex returned to the main aisle and walked toward the Sanctuary tabernacle. Hanging down from the ceiling in front of the altar was a fifteen-foot wood sculpture of Jesus on the cross with his Mother Mary and Mary Magdalene kneeling at his feet. Alex sat in pew a few rows back and took in the grandeur of the eight-hundred-plus seat church. Behind the altar, and lining the domed ceiling, were nine stunning stained-glass windows, five with figures, including Jesus, Mary and Joseph, St. Thomas Aquinas, and St. Dominic. Alex started to understand the icon history of the Catholic Church. As a kid, he never related to the adornment of the church and all the old history. The Catholic Church was about tradition and ceremony, which created a vision or atmosphere for people to meditate and pray-a quietness from all the day's activities. The rosary was an example of this with its ten Hail Mary's between other prayers. It was becoming clear to him why people sought out these oases in the cities to bring order to the chaos in their lives and peace to the turbulence in their souls.

As he sat in the pew, Alex wondered whether, like the Catholic Church's attachment to "The Rock" of St. Peter, he had been trying all his life to become connected to "The Rock" of baseball in Washington, DC, Walter Johnson. Baseball stadiums had become his sanctuary tabernacle to reach his athletic spirit; home plate had become his altar to offer his talents to the world; and third base was his confessional to a higher power. Was his chance discovery of St. Dominic's a new place for him to expand his spirituality? Could Leah entering his life be a signal that this religious thing could work for him? Did his sudden need to get married become a statement of becoming right with the Lord? It was all so confusing. As he continued looking around the church, he saw to his left a plaque at eye level on one of the many pillars holding up the ceiling. He slid over and read it:

To The Memory Of PRESIDENT LYNDON B. JOHNSON

who during his term of office frequently came

to St. Dominic's Church and chapel to pray and to seek divine guidance in the fulfillment of his responsibilities as President of the United States.

He sat back in the pew wondering about the man who changed history in the 1960s. He knew LBJ was a Texan who, before he was president, had already been the most powerful man in America as leader of the Senate. He brought rural electricity to Texas and many states in the Midwest and South in the 1940s and 1950s. As president he passed civil rights and Medicare legislation that changed the country after the Kennedy assassination. He was the most popular president since Roosevelt until his second term, when he led the country into the Vietnam War and sent thousands of troops to their deaths. Alex wondered if he found divine guidance in this church as Senate leader and early in his presidency, especially after JFK's death, but then after a while maybe he just stopped coming, feeling paranoid about having too much power from the presidency.

    Alex escaped the beauty of the church, leaving through the giant mahogany front doors. He knew Sally and Laura would be happy about his discovery. He was not so sure about St. Dominic's Church being his place for spiritual awakening, but it did provide him great comfort. A place near the ballpark that could provide him quiet and solitude -it c o u l d become a sanctuary for him at a time when he was discovering his feelings about himself and his old and new families, including Sally.

• • •

    The doubleheader with first place Miami was like a double feature at an old drive-in theater. The first game was like a B-movie horror film for Miami in front of a sparse crowd of less than ten thousand fans. Briles Martin, the 'Canes first-round pick in the 2010 draft, was making his first major league start. They decided to rest their regular rotation for the doubleheader because they had been overworked the past two weeks. Manager Manuel Santos had ridden his starting pitching as hard as a horse jockey because the division was up for grabs with the Presidents falling behind them. He believed that the trade for Joe McDowell, along with the rookie call up, would provide much-needed support for his pitching staff.

He was wrong in the first game. Martin looked like the baby-sitter in the movie *Scream* wondering where the killer was going to strike next. Alex was first among the killers in the POTUS lineup, hitting two homeruns by the second inning. After giving up eight runs and twelve hits, Santos took his rookie out of the horror show with one out in the third inning. Blake Hopson and Marty Morris added homeruns in a 12-3 rout.

As a capacity crowd arrived for the second show of the double feature, they were ready for a sophisticated thriller like Hitchcock's *Vertigo,* patiently waiting for the killer to be revealed. Presidents' starter Tony Johnson out-dueled Joe McDowell, pitching a five hitter, going the distance in a 2-1 win. After tying the game 1-1 in the top of the ninth, the 'Canes were murdered by Alex's walk-off homerun in the bottom of the ninth. For the fans it was a delightful ending to a day of entertainment, watching the Presidents take their fourth victory in a row. Their newfound hero, Alex Santucci, had starred in both games and rescued his team in the last frame of the feature, keeping his fellow cast members from an uncertain ending.

Like his childhood world, Alex got to play baseball all day Friday, August 3, starting with his morning run down to the field to practice his pitching, to playing homerun baseball in the afternoon and evening. He stayed on the field signing autographs and taking pictures until midnight when the security staffs, finally got him into the locker room and out of the ballpark. To his surprise, Laura and Dr. Walton had come down for the second game after touring St. Dominic's with Leah and Sally earlier. They had been dropped off by Sally and Leah, who then went dress shopping for the wedding.

Before he left the ballpark, Dr. Walton took some blood from Alex after checking blood pressure, performing an abdominal exam, and inspecting his forehead injury. Henry was uneasy about Alex's abdomen situation. He felt like it could be a ticking time bomb. He hoped it was an old injury flaring up and not a cancerous tumor. He was going to do some more serious blood tests to get some answers. Conflicting his decision-making was the fact that he was staying with all of these women at Laura's house. He was having the time of his life and becoming quite fond of Laura. He was too much of a gentleman to reveal these thoughts to her, but Sally and Leah were making him talk about himself much more than he was used to. Hopefully, he thought, he would not reveal something inappropriate.

Finally getting home at 1:07 a.m., August 4, the kitchen was the place to be in the Santucci home. Sally, Leah, Laura, and Henry joined Alex in celebrating the doubleheader win and the discovery of St. Dominic's Church. Even Leah felt comfortable with the church because of its history and beauty. When Laura revealed to everyone that St. Dominic was the patron saint of astronomy, Leah spoke out. "It seems that St. Dominic has helped us line up our lucky stars starting tonight so the Lord can watch over us!"

Alex raised his glass of wine to Leah as if he wanted to make a toast.

"There is no doubt something or somebody has been watching over us during the past month. As far as I know, Reginald might have been Jesus himself or an angel sent by him. He was so spiritual, in a real way like my mom and Leah. He invited my family to join him on Sunday morning for the eight o'clock Mass. I hope we can all go; it might be something we can do together."

Laura suggested that Alex and Sally go alone this Sunday. A long silence commenced for a minute or so. Finally, Henry Walton stepped forward. "I'm really not a religious man, but I would follow Alex anywhere. I agree with Laura that Sally and Alex should check out the Mass alone. I feel like I'm the doubting Thomas sometimes, but this is special to be welcomed into this house." Laura and Leah took an arm each and said words of encouragement to Henry. His head was clearly in the stars with St. Dominic.

Chapter 36

The game on Saturday, August 4 was a quick turnaround at one thirty. Alex was looking forward to finishing early for an evening alone with Sally. Pitcher Phillip Fields led the Presidents to their fifth win in a row with a 7-4 victory over Miami with seven solid innings, giving up two runs. The homeruns kept flying, as Alex roped two liners barely over the left field fence, driving in four runs. The low-flight missiles were both two-run homers. The first one came in the opening inning to put them ahead; the second one in the seventh lengthened the lead for an easy victory.

Before the game, Miami Manager Manuel Santos was convinced, based on watching film, that throwing inside to Alex would silence his bat.

After the game, POTUS Manager Charley Jackson commented that the film must not have been old enough to show Alex feasting on inside pitching while playing for Kansas City. "Right now, Alex is hitting at a level that happens once or twice during a decade. The way he's seeing the ball now, I'm not sure how you would pitch to him."

Instead of signing autographs, Alex went into the media room after the game to answer some questions for the first time since his initial press conference. After about ten minutes, most of the reporters were filled with enough information to make them giddy. They hung around Alex for the next twenty minutes as he went off the record talking about his upcoming wedding and living at his mother's house. He asked advice on how to thank the Kansas City fans that he left last Monday. They all agreed on him taking out two full-page advertisements in the *Kansas City Post,* one in the front section and the second in the sports section. Ron Roswell with the *Daily* said he would make a quick call to the editor at the KC *Post* to see if they could get it in the

243

Sunday edition. Julia Newmar from the *Reporter* offered to write copy for him. Kelly Browner with *BASC* Sports Channel suggested he do an interview over a Cisco feed with the KC Crowns Sport Network on Sunday.

After five days in DC, Alex had the fans and media totally behind him. They were joining in for the ride of excitement that was hitting the city. At this time, there was no energy to be contrarian. Most of the reporters were getting chances for national appearances, being asked for their insight to this new phenomenon taking over the capital of the free world.

At 5:15 p.m., the *Kansas City Post* received this statement from Alex Santucci to be placed on a single page for two sections in their Sunday edition for a total of twenty thousand dollars:

To the Great Fans of Kansas City,

I want to express my deep appreciation for the honor of playing in front of you as a major league ballplayer with the Kansas City Crowns. Losing my friend and mentor, owner Larry Garson, forced the Crowns organization to trade me because of my age and salary for future talent.

I hope these young players become stars for the Crowns and join the already talented trio of outfielders and young talent in the organization. I am very excited to be playing in my hometown city but will miss forever the love of the Crowns fans. I plan to keep my apartment in Kansas City and will visit from time to time.

Sally picked up Alex at the stadium, as she had taken the car to go shopping and visit reception venues. The last few days had been all about preparing for the wedding. With the help of Laura and Leah, it had been fun and exciting. She felt a wonderful kin-ship with both women and especially Leah. The more time Sally spent with her, the more she could see Alex in her personality and actions. Besides being beautiful and one of the most radiant women she had ever seen, Leah added positivity to every conversation about everything. Sally noticed that it added a bounce to her step and an upgrade in her confidence. The two of them would get long looks from men and women wherever they walked because of their opposite looks of beauty and style. For the first time in her life, Sally enjoyed giving and receiving physical affection from another woman. In seemed natural for them to go arm in arm down the street, give each other hugs when greeting or leaving, and holding hands occasionally during a conversation. There was a mentor-protege aspect to their relationship, with the roles changing at times depending on the subject. The age difference of twenty-five years did not seem to define their relationship. Sally and Leah felt respect and warmness for each other, almost like sisters.

Alex was amazed how hard the three women were working on the wedding plans. He was relieved how well Leah had connected with Sally. Listening to Sally describe how much Leah reminded her of him, he was stunned to hear the comparison, considering they just met a short time ago. He wondered if positivity and spirituality could be inherited in one's genes. Either way, he was glad to have Leah in his life

Sally and Alex headed for the Adams Morgan section of Washington to walk the streets and find a place to eat. It did not take long for people to recognize him. Fortunately, it was mainly greetings and appreciative acknowledgements from Washingtonians. In the previous two cities that he played in, he found there was no panic from fans when he was recognized outside the ballpark. He believed this was because he was so accessible before and after games with autographs and interactions. They knew that this guy put sin his time at the ballpark-go see him and he will be available. It seemed to be an unwritten covenant between Alex and local baseball fans.

They *found Meskerem,* an Ethiopian restaurant named for the first and most favored month in the Ethiopian calendar, which corresponds with the Roman calendar of September and ends the three months of the rainy season. They had sambusa, an appetizer, and Meskerem tibbs, a lamb dish, and gored-gored, a beef dish for their main meal. They had fun sitting at the lower tables and using the sponge-like bread to slop up the food.

After finishing the spicy meal, they headed north on Sixteenth Street for a few miles, just crossing into Maryland and downtown Silver Spring to go to the *American Film Institute's Silver Theater,* refurbished ten years ago as a part of the redevelopment of the downtown area of Silver Spring. They watched Hitchcock's *Vertigo* with Jimmy Stewart and Kim Novak. It was a wonderful experience in a beautiful theater. They left the theater and strolled north on Colesville Road. There they noticed the neon signs across the street of the year-old *Fillmore* music hall, which had been built using an art deco]CPenney fac;ade from the 1930s. They turned on Fenton toward the parking garage and soon found hundreds of people walking up and down Ellsworth Avenue, home to movie theaters, restaurants, shops, and places to hang out.

As they turned up Ellsworth, Alex spotted *Galaxy Billiards* and pulled Sally in for a game and a beer. The fifteen-thousand-square-foot facility had twenty-seven pool tables, a sixty-foot bar, and thirty-five big televisions. They grabbed two beers at the bar and a pool table for a real match. Sally was a pool hustler from Kansas. During her rebellious teenage years, she learned pool from some locals and secretly got quite good. In college, she made hundreds from dopes who would not take her seriously in the pool halls when she was fooling around on a table with a date or some friends.

Alex played during summers of high school and college when he was around with his cousin Joseph, Anthony's son who was seven years older. At six foot three and a half, and a muscular three hundred pounds, he commanded a pool hall. He quickly noticed Alex's hand-eye coordination and bought him his first pool stick. Joe played in pool leagues twice a week and loved to have Alex join him whenever possible. Alex missed spending time with him and thought of him tonight when lining up the cue ball for the first break of the night.

They started with several games of eight-ball, which Sally won easily. Sally was mechanically perfect with her petite five-foot-four frame moving like a cat over the felt of the table. Alex was slow to warm up, trying to get the right feel of the angles of the shots. Finally, after a second beer each, they switched to nine-ball, and a few folks noticed the popular couple seriously competing on the table. Sally won the first three games in workmanlike fashion, getting high fives from the twenty to thirty people watching her dismantle baseball's hottest hitter. Alex finally found his stroke in the fourth and fifth games, making the best of seven game series competitive. Sally returned to form in the sixth game, running balls four through nine straight for the victory. She jumped into Alex's arm, who landed her on the table as she held both hands in the air in celebration. The patrons cheered with congratulations, and Alex signed several autographs and posed for a few pictures.

Sally finished a third beer and Alex drank an ice tea as they found a quiet table to discuss Sally's victory. Her face was flushed red from the activity and the alcohol, and her blue eyes beamed with excitement. Alex found her youthful exuberance very attractive and was looking forward to going home to Johnson Avenue. This would be their last night in Bethesda together before the Presidents started a grueling ten-day road trip to Houston, Phoenix, and San Francisco. Sally was planning to meet Alex in Phoenix next Friday. It would be the longest stretch of being apart in a month. She had a lot of wedding stuff to do and wanted to see her parents in Kansas for a day and night on the way to Phoenix.

The famous DC couple spent another hour talking about Sally's beat down of Alex in pool. They enjoyed the time alone off in a quiet spot of the vast pool hall. It was a perfect place to get lost in and still interact with people at times. They finally headed to the garage and retrieved the

Acura TL at 12:24 a.m. on Sunday, August 5, for the ten-minute ride home to Johnson Avenue. The house was dark and quiet as they made it to their suite in the house. They were ready to be together and had a beautiful ending to what had been a special night. They finally found slumber at 2:14 a.m.

•••

The final game of the home stand with the Sugarcanes was set to start at one thirty. Alex wanted to be there by ten o'clock. So even with their late night, Alex and Sally woke up at six thirty so that they could make it to St. Dominic's for the eight o'clock Mass with Reginald's family. They hit a *Dunkin' Donuts* on the way for two coffees and Alex's favorite: vanilla cream-filled doughnuts. Sally admonished him about stuffing his face with worthless carbohydrates and sugar as they rode through DC. She giggled about the white powder he was accumulating all over his face and clothes as he ate the monster doughnuts. Alex pointed out that his favorite doughnuts had only 380 calories-less than the normal 450 calories for a regular glazed doughnut that most people eat. Sally rolled her still tired eyes at the rationalization as she struggled to sip her morning coffee. They talked about their great night out and wondered if they would still be able to do that for much longer with all the public attention coming upon them.

Even though they were tired, they were quietly excited about the morning church experience. Sally was impressed with Alex's discovery and looked forward to a special place for their wedding and a spiritual community in the future. They arrived at a parking space several blocks away at 7:48 a.m. and walked arm in arm to the entrance, following several families up the steps and through the opened grand mahogany doors. The church took on an added magnificence of humanity with hundreds of people in the pews, music from the massive organ in the loft behind them, and flowers surrounding the altar. Beautiful garments adorned the priests and the servers as they entered the sacristy. The choir and the church members belted out several hymns that filled the arches of the church. After some initial prayers to start the Mass, Reggie walked from the front row and went to the lectern to read the liturgy for the morning. He was adorned in a beautiful double-breasted suit with a Pan- African-colored sash around his neck. His wife and children sat proudly surrounding Alex and Sally in the front row.

Pastor Father Higgins rose to read the Gospel and give a sermon after Reggie had finished. The seventy-six-year-old Bronx native had studied at Fordham, a Jesuit university in the Bronx that counted the great Vince Lombardi as a proud alumnus. Father Higgins grew up a Yankee fan in the 1940s and 1950s before entering the seminary after graduating Fordham in 1958. He was sent to Washington in 1961 to be a young parish priest at the growing Holy Redeemer parish in Kensington. With many duties to keep him busy, including training the altar boys, he still was able to sneak down to Griffith Stadium to see his beloved Yankees that season and through their last pennant win in 1964. When Frank Howard was traded to the Senators in 1965, he became an immediate fan, as he remembered Hondo mauling the Yankees in the fourth and last game of the 1963 World Series, hitting a double and a homerun off Whitey Ford, the only Dodger hits of the game, to win 2-1.

Father Higgins followed the Presidents "religiously" since they returned to DC in 2005. Standing at the lectern, he thought he was seeing a vision from God when he noticed the new Presidents hot hitting star, Alex Santucci, sitting in the front row next to Reginald Chaney, his most enthusiastic parishioner. He tried to stay steady through reading the Gospel but then left the lectern before the sermon to walk down to the front pew to personally welcome Alex and Sally, among others, to St. Dominic's.

When he returned to the lectern, he ignored his notes and spoke from his heart about the importance of community and commitment to the city with all of the great gifts God had brought to them. He talked about being a kid and following local heroes of baseball in New York that gave him enjoyment. He believed kids needed mentors and real heroes in every community, not corporate-produced idols from Hollywood or Manhattan. Deep inside he realized he wanted his values to be included in God's plan because he loved community, which included cheering for your home baseball team-not exactly in Christ's teachings.

The rest of the Mass was celebrated in record time as Father Higgins led the procession out of the church to the nave to greet the parishioners. He was almost lightheaded as a teenager meeting the Beatles when Reginald, as he called him, brought Alex and Sally to meet him formally. Father Higgins asked if they would wait a few minutes for a tour with him and then share some tea. Alex and Sally agreed and enjoyed seeing the inner areas of the church. They shared tea in his upstairs residence. Father Higgins related a story about his first trip to Griffith Stadium. He mentioned Kensington, Holy Redeemer, altar boys, Roger Maris, Gene Green, and a grand slam.

Alex could not speak as he listened to a story he had heard before from his father, Phillip.

When the pastor was done, Sally turned to a white-faced Alex. "Didn't your family go to a church in Kensington? And your dad was an altar boy, wasn't he?"

Alex was sorting through the facts and nervously looking at the Mass pamphlet in his hands.

In the silence, Pastor Higgins spoke up. "Were they Catholic, Sally?"

"Yes, Father, they had four boys: Anthony, Mark, Greg, and Phillip. They were the Finellis."

Father Higgins looked puzzled as he put the names

together. "You mean Guy and Rose Finelli. The oldest son was Anthony... the homerun hitter at Puller Park. My goodness, what a coincidence!" Pastor turned to Alex and continued.

"Alex Santucci, how are the Finellis related to you?"

"Phillip is my birth father. I was adopted by Gene and Laura Santucci of Bethesda. You may have known Dr. Gene Santucci; he was an internist and blood specialist at NIH."

Father Higgins stood up and held his chest. He took a deep breath and tried to ask a worthy question. "Alex, are you saying that Phillip Finelli, the football player with great hands who tore his knee up making the greatest catch in county football history for Walter Johnson to win the championship and ran the hundred-yard dash in nine-point-seven seconds, a county record at that time, is your father? And Anthony Finelli, who had the greatest power swing I have ever seen since Mickey Mantle, before Frank Howard, is your uncle?"

"That's all true, Father. Did you know them at Holy Redeemer?"

"Yes, of course. They were altar boys and played CYO ball. I played softball with your uncle at Puller Park. Phillip was too young to play, but it was a special time when I was still a young adult myself." He smiled and then remembered the last part about the adoption. "You were born in 1976 and then were adopted?"

"Yes, Phillip was twenty-three. He fell in love with my birth mother, Leah, who was twenty-one, and she became pregnant. She was Seventh-Day Adventist and married. It's a long story! Anyway, they decided they couldn't be together, but Leah wanted to have me, so the two families made an agreement to find a local family to raise me so at least the Finellis could be around when I became older. Gene and Laura were family friends with five children, all over ten, who were excited to have me. My adoptive father, Gene, died in 1991 when I was fifteen. Soon after, Phillip entered my life, and we have been close ever since. Just last week I became reunited with my birth mother, Leah. It has been quite an overwhelming experience, but I'm learning that it may be a gift from God..."

Alex stopped for a moment and noticed Father Higgins in prayer, holding his cross hanging from his neck.

"I'm sorry, Father, to upset you."

"On no, Alex. I just can't believe that God has granted me this chance..."

Alex was puzzled by his response but had one unanswered question to ask again.

"I'm sorry, Father Higgins, but I not sure if I heard you or not. But, did you say whether you knew my adoptive father, Dr. Santucci?"

Father Higgins, looking right at Sally and Alex, grabbed both of their hands and answered with a fervor. "I knew Dr. Santucci very well...He saved my life!"

Chapter 37

The Sunday showdown with Miami was a sellout. Washington had cut the lead to three games with a five-game winning streak. The national media had descended on Washington and were crowding the field during batting practice. They were all following the big story: Alex Santucci tearing up the National League. He had hit 7 home runs in five consecutive games, batting .571 in six games for DC with 16 RBIs and an amazing 1,333 slugging percentage.

Riley Preston, a veteran reporter now with *ESPN* and a Walter Johnson graduate, was brilliant in coming up with new statistics in historic terms concerning present-day baseball. He was reporting that Alex Santucci could become the first player in baseball history to lead the major leagues in batting, homeruns, and RBIs (The Triple Crown), and not qualify for awards in either league because of the lack of plate appearances. In the American League, Alex had 420 plate appearances for Kansas City before being traded. If he played the rest of the season for Washington in the National League, he would get, at most, 250 to 280 plate appearances. To qualify for a batting, homerun, or RBI title in any league, you needed 501 plate appearances based on 3.1 appearances per game over a 162-game season. Currently Alex was hitting a combined .351 with 28 Hrs and 94 RBIs, on pace for the first Triple Crown since 1967. But it would not be recognized by either league because of the rules of statistics. Riley Preston was now proclaiming Alex Santucci could win a Professional Baseball League Triple Crown. This was a greater feat than winning one in either league because a player from either league could win just one category and shut down a Triple Crown.

Travis Tyler was on the mound for Washington, coming off his first complete game shutout of Philadelphia. His wife, Alexis, had called Sally to make sure she was coming to the game so they could sit together. Before the game they were interviewed by *Hollywood Access* and *Entertainment Tonight,* each doing close-ups on the young and the veteran stars of the Presidents. They also had plans to cover Alex and Sally's wedding because they were becoming the couple to watch in DC. It was only a matter of time before *House Hunters* booked them for an off-season appearance to find their dream home in Bethesda!

Alexis was very nervous about all the attention. Between interviews, she asked Sally about how she did, if she looked at the right camera, and if her make-up was okay in the heat. She was not trying to gain notoriety, just show some competence to Travis. Sally was becoming a pro at this by now and calmed Alexis and her nerves down with positive feedback. Besides, she thought, Alexis had movie star looks and youth on her side-what could go wrong?

After the interviews, Alexis wanted to know all about the wedding. After filling her in on all the details of the week, Sally stunned Alexis by asking her to be in the wedding party. She was truly overwhelmed but accepted immediately. Her make-up was taking a beating because her eyes kept tearing up until the game started. It seemed to Sally the smart thing to do, including a Presidents wife as a bridesmaid. Besides, she really liked Alexis and loved her red hair and green eyes, which would go great with the pale green dresses she had in mind. She also decided to ask her friend and colleague from Boston, Claire, to be her maid of honor. Claire would never refuse her, even with two young children. But just in case, Sally was planning to hire full-time nannies, a couple of hotel rooms, and plane tickets to seal the deal. She already asked Grace and Cora to join Alexis to be the three bridesmaids. A true brunette, a natural blonde, and a real redhead would add variety to the wedding party!

The outcome of the game was simple in terms of winning. Only the Santucci Streak was in doubt for the overflow capacity crowd of 43,353. Travis Tyler threw another complete game shutout, and Alex Santucci drove in all three Presidents runs in a 3-0 win over Miami. Their sixth victory in a row cut the Miami lead to two games. Alex had RBI singles in the first and third innings. He was walked in the sixth and came up with two outs and nobody on in the eighth. 'Canes reliever Hector Lopez was brought in to keep it a 2-0 game in the eighth so the 'Canes could rally in the ninth. He struck out Hopson and Gonzalez on six pitches to start the eighth. Alex was watching his tailing fastball falling away to right-handers as he came off the mound violently to his left. He knew that the two strikeouts gave Hector confidence to stay with the tailing fastball. Besides, they must figure it would be hard to hit the pitch for a homerun.

    The crowd was in a frenzy knowing that this would be Alex's last at bat in the game. They stood clapping and hollering as he came to the plate. The outfield was shifted to left-center, leaving a gap in right-center a mile wide. Alex wanted to drive one into the gap for a double or triple to get into scoring position. He was not thinking about elevating it for a homerun unless Lopez left the ball up in the strike zone. The first two pitches were in the dirt as Lopez got ahead of himself in his delivery, trying to produce some extra juice on his fastball. The crowd cascaded loud boos after each ball, trying to will a hittable pitch to the plate for their hero to smash. During the fifth inning walk to Alex, fans became delirious about him not getting a pitch to hit. Hector lightened up on his delivery and threw a fastball that had little tail and stayed up over the outside corner of the plate. Alex stayed down on the pitch with his swing, made solid contact, and watched as it sailed on a line to center field, too low to go over the fence. Alex knew it had a chance for extra bases. Center fielder Marcus Weathers, the fastest outfielder in baseball, had a long run to get to the ball and seemed to have a bead on it, but Weathers dived a tenth of a second too early as the ball climbed slightly over his glove, finally landing on the warning track. It then took a short bounce, hit off the fence, then like a golf shot to a green with backspin, came to a dead stop. Alex raced around second base with no intention of stopping until the dugout.

The left fielder finally reached the ball as Weathers slowly got to his feet. Alex hit third as the ball was thrown in to the cutoff man, who never bothered with a relay as he watched Alex score standing up for an inside-the-park home-run, his eighth homer in six consecutive games. Once again Travis Tyler struck out the side in the ninth to seal the victory, and the crowd reached a rock-concert encore level of noise.

After the game, with nowhere to go until the flight out to Houston, all the ballplayers followed Alex to the stands to sign autographs as kids ran the bases. A good deal of the capacity crowd stayed to soak up the groovy feelings of the beautiful scene at the ballpark.

For the first time, Alex was the first one into the trainer's room to meet with Dr. Walton. He was dying to tell him the story about Father Higgins and his adoptive father, Gene. Apparently in the 1980s, Father Higgins was being treated at NIH for a congenital blood disorder that affected his pancreas and adrenal gland. After months of testing, Dr. Santucci was brought in to check out the diagnosis. Father Higgins had blood tests showing continued high enzyme levels in his liver and kidney for months. X-rays had shown a growth on his pancreas but no other symptoms had shown up to believe it was cancer. Dr. Santucci figured out he had extra blood vessels between the pancreas and Adrenal glands that had most likely formed during the pregnancy or from an injury. He also concluded they were very weak and ready for an aneurism. Back then it was major surgery, and Father Higgins was saved. Like LBJ, who gallantly revealed his gall bladder scar to the media in the 1960s, Father Higgins showed Alex his scar to prove it. Henry Walton was both relieved to hear the news and scared to death.

"Alex, your symptoms fit that scenario. Obviously, I have to check out the details, but if it is true, you have a ticking time bomb in your abdomen. We cannot wait much longer!"

"Are you kidding, Henry? First of all, aren't you amazed

that this fell into our laps? Do you think the universe is going to line up all of these actions in the past month and let my abdomen explode? I don't think that is how this works. I mean, God... or whomever...the forces of nature are prevailing here! I don't think another month will be too late. And yes, I'm willing to take that chance! We'll do the wedding on Labor Day, and I promise to go to surgery the next morning if that's what it takes, okay?!"

"Alex, you're right. I'm sure we have some time, but it will be risky, and my job is to make that clear to you. We can probably do it laparoscopically, which will minimize the recovery time."

"I'm sorry, Henry. It just seems like a relief. There must be a way not to derail this train. We've got a lot of work to do to win this thing in the next month. Hammersly said he would be back by Labor Day. He can take my place for a while!"

"No problem, Alex. I understand everything you're feeling. Until then: silence about this thing. Maybe some extra prayers to St. Dominic! Maybe we have to find the patron saint of abdomens! Really though, I want to see Father Higgins and dig up those records if we can. Stay safe and play with caution, my friend!"

• • •

Saying good-bye to Sally was not easy. They got a few minutes in the trainer's office after Alex got his stitches removed from his forehead. Phillip and Carol, Grace and Guy, Leah and Laura, and Anthony and Florence all came down to the ballpark for the send-off. They brought enough food to have an impromptu picnic in one of the two-hundred-level suites. Laura had made an antipasto, Flo her special salad, Carol her cheese tortellini with squash, and Leah, a tofu lasagna. Alex was starving and ate half the food, along with Guy, Phillip, and Anthony. The women survived on salad and tortellini as wine flowed quickly through the room.

Alex was happy to spend a few minutes with Grace and Guy. Grace was heading off for her senior year in a week to NC State in Raleigh, and Guy had finished a week of football practice for the Terps at UMD. Both were in their first serious relationships, which started in the spring. Alex caught up on the details and activities since the Pines of Rome dinner. They were excited about the wedding plans. Luckily for Guy it was on a Monday evening, because his game was scheduled for the previous Saturday night and practice was Monday afternoon. Guy wanted to fly out to Phoenix next Friday to see the weekend games because they had that weekend off from practice. Alex was ecstatic about the news and would make plans for him to be at the hotel with him.

Having that hour with the family was a perfect tonic and send-off for Alex. He was leaving DC again, but this time it was home and he was just going away for ten days. A big crowd at the stadium player's lot, including Reginald Chaney and Father Higgins, watched as the players entered the buses to head to the airport. The team was on a mission to bring back first place with a comfortable lead ahead of second place. The Santucci's and the Finelli's were getting ready for a reception and a wedding in a month, while DC was getting ready for a party in the next two months to celebrate a post-season for the first time in almost eighty years. The players knew this road trip would make or break the season, and they were all in.

Chapter 38

The presidents plane arrived at Houston Hobby Airport at 7:58 p.m., ten minutes ahead of schedule. Alex was in his room at the Four Seasons Hotel, about a half mile from Minute Maid Park, by 8:30 p.m. He pulled out a book and started reading for the first time in weeks. Since they were in Texas, he thought it would be appropriate to start the most recent Stephen King novel, *11/22/63*. At 849 pages, it would keep him busy for the road trip. He was actually looking forward to these four days by himself in Houston. It was also the first time for him playing in the new ballpark, which was a dream for right-handed pull hitters.

After reading the opening thirty pages of the King novel, he decided to head down to the lobby and find some teammates for dinner. It was exciting that he could sleep, eat, or go out whenever he wanted. But when he went down to the lobby to check out the bar and restaurant, he was not prepared for the media hanging out in the hotel or the Presidents fans that were all around the hotel. It was a minor inconvenience.

He found Henson Scott, Travis Tyler, and Blake Hopson in the bar and convinced them to walk over to the *Quattro Restaurant* in the hotel for a decent Italian meal. Alex told Blake to call them for a reservation in 30 minutes in one of their private dining rooms for up to twenty-five people. Blake followed orders and then asked, "Why are we waiting if it is right next door?"

"Because it will take Travis fifteen minutes to call or text the rest of the players on the team to get their asses there, and fifteen minutes in the lobby to sign autographs on the way out!"

Both Travis and Blake followed orders. Their phones were buzzing in seconds with responses from teammates. Twenty-one of the players were going to be there in thirty minutes. Only "Bean" Counter, who was sleeping, Jerry Gonzalez, who had his wife and kids in town, Tory Taylor and Ross Williams, who were both at a local strip club already, could not make it.

Henson mentioned that "bullpen guys are not really ballplayers anyway" and "only Gonzalez has a real excuse not to be there." Blake and Travis doubled over in laughter at the comment.

The crowds gathered around the unlikely quartet and got their money's worth of signatures and pictures. Except for Gonzalez, who was from San Antonio, all the players' wives or girlfriends would join them in Phoenix. Blake and Travis drew the most attention from the women, while the male fans hung out with Alex and Henson. Most of the women were not Presidents fans, but for four days they would hound these two young, budding superstars. The quartet finally acted like they were leaving the hotel and grabbed a cab to escape. Alex paid the driver a C-note to drive them around the block to the other entrance to the restaurant. Alex got his number and said to be ready to get them when he called in an hour or two. The cab driver, Rodrigo Perez, was shaking his head in joy: Alex already made his fare for the night!

The private dining room was being readied when they walked in at 9:47 p.m. A few players were already there and excited about a team dinner. Pitchers Leo Lawrence and Danube Rivers and infielders Chris Patek and Abel Lamont wanted to know the big story from Alex about the dinner. He told them eating the right Italian food would make them better ballplayers! As they finally sat down around a long oval table, most of the players were calling Alex "the Swedish godfather" for sitting in the middle. Veteran bench players Madison Bennett and Renaldo Rivera sat next to Alex as Ryan Hudson and injured Bruce Hammersly sat across from them next to Henson Scott.

Alex spoke with the head waiter for a few minutes and ordered the appetizers and wine. He announced to the players they were getting either a veal dish or fish with plenty of pasta on the side. There was no mutiny, so Alex told the waiter to bring out plenty of food and not to bother them otherwise.

Alex had never been an overt leader on Minnesota or Kansas City. He never felt the emotion to organize the team and tell them how to play. There were times he felt he lacked leadership skills, but wanted to lead these teammates. Recently it was starting to come naturally to him and his recent power hitting added credibility. He remembered his father, Phillip, and his Uncle Anthony running local teams in football and softball. They were naturally passionate in their leadership. Even when they were not coaching, teammates would look to them for answers to the team's problems.

After drinking a couple glasses of wine and eating just enough antipasto to not spoil his upcoming roast veal, Alex stood and quieted the crowd. He welcomed everyone and thanked his teammates for showing up on such short notice. Alex then spoke from the heart. "This next month through Labor Day will change our lives! I know I've only been here a week-"

Marty Morris reminded him, saying, "Actually only six days, Alex!"

The room erupted in laughter.

Alex knew this might be a tough crowd. Alex thought to count out the seven days, but it was losing argument. "Anyway, it's great to see that somebody can almost count in this room. Let's see: Tuesday, Wednesday, Thursday..."
The crowd went nuts!

Alex turned serious. "I may need to get a procedure done the Tuesday after my Labor Day wedding, which I want all of you to attend with your wives or girlfriends, or in Williams's and Taylor's case, a couple of strippers!"

The players laughed nervously, and they leaned forward to listen to Alex.

"My friend Dr. Walton thinks something needs to be fixed in my abdomen ASAP. I think it can wait a month until Hammersly gets back. I can't leave now." Alex made a fist with his left hand. "We just got this thing started this month. I know this is going to be something special to remember for the ages. I can really feel it." The room became silent. "We need to win this thing by Labor Day so Bruce doesn't have to rescue you shitheads when he comes back!" Silence still prevailed. "Bruce told me he'll return by Labor Day to play. We need to give him three weeks without the pressure of a close pennant race to get ready to lead us in the playoffs!"

Alex pointed to Hammersly, who stood and threw off his soft cast and proclaimed with authority, "I'll be god damn ready, Alex, to fill in when you're gone! But let's get real guys...procedure, my ass. He's going on a honeymoon-in the middle of a pennant race, for Christ's sake!" Bruce raised his glass to Alex as the laughter calmed down. "Alex, my friend, we are behind you one hundred percent. Get that stomach thing fixed, because we're going to the playoffs, and we need you to win it for us!" Players leaped out of their seats, clanging glasses, guzzling wine, hugging teammates. Then to seal the commitment, like out of a scene from a gangster movie, Bruce Hammersly walked around the table and embraced Alex and whispered in his ear. "You be careful, my friend. I don't want you dying on us!"

Alex responded, "I don't think St. Dominic would let that happen!"

Young catcher Vito Valencia rose next and asked everyone to bow their heads. "Please God, watch over our friend Alex and his family as they work hard to lead us to our destiny to serve you. You have brought Alex to us to teach us the way. Please give us the time he needs. Amen."

Carlos Mendoza, a quiet outfielder who had signed a big contract in 2011 and was just starting to show some of his talent because the attention was away from him, stood up after many glasses of wine and spoke eloquently. "I want to say two things. First, I think we forget how hard it is to perform in a new setting under the bright lights of the media, which this man has done so well. Second, if anyone talks about this dinner to anyone besides your teammates, you are making a big mistake. Please respect the team. What is said here, stays here!"

The team, in unison, agreed and sealed it with drinks, handshakes, and hugs all around. Henson Scott and Frank Peterson, who had been guarding the door to keep the waiters out during the discussion, proceeded to quietly open the doors and allow the dinner entrees in to feed the hungry crowd. Alex shouted out, "The food's here! *Mangiamo!*"

Chapter 39

The Houston heavens were celebrating their fiftieth anniversary in the PLB in 2012. They started as the Houston Colt .45s, one of the great nicknames in sports history. This expansion franchise played outdoors in the hottest and most humid weather in the country in 1962. They played in Colt Stadium for three years with their only highlight being in 1964, when Ken Johnson became the first pitcher to lose a complete game, no-hitter, 1-0, because of an error by the pitcher. Luckily civil engineers invented the indoor stadium and built the Astrodome in time for the 1965 season.

The Colt gun company suddenly decided they did not like Houston using their famous gun's name as a nickname. So the newly named Astros moved into the Astrodome instead of the Coltdome! Initially the roof of the massive new stadium had clear panels that allowed the grass to grow indoors. But the glare from the roof was so bad that players had trouble catching a pop-up or a fly ball, so they painted the roof. Soon the grass was dying because they painted the roof, and as a result Astroturf was invented. Once installed, the new industry of sports medicine was discovered. Orthopedic surgeons treated new ailments like turf toe and surgeries for knees, ankles, and hips became a gold mine.

The Astrodome became the Eighth Wonder of the World, drawing crowds from everywhere to visit, especially when the Astros were not playing. They did not make the playoffs until 1980 when Nolan Ryan showed up. It took the Astros seven playoff appearances and another nineteen years to finally win a playoff series in 1999. They went to the World Series in 2005, only to be swept by the Chicago White Sox.

In 2000 they moved out of the Astrodome and stopped playing on joint-killing Astroturf and into a retractable roof stadium with natural grass. Then last year the sale of the Astros was approved to a local businessman who, like many Texans, was a born-again Christian. In deference to God and to change the luck of the team, he changed their nickname to the Heavens. The new ownership was given an eighty-million-dollar discount to move the Heavens to the American League in 2013-a godly feat to even the number of teams in each league to fifteen.

Currently the Heavens had the worst record in the National League, but glory is given to those who wait until next year. Leo Lawrence was leading the Presidents to their seventh victory in a row, nursing a seven-hitter going into the eighth inning with a 3-2 lead. Houston pitchers were under strict orders to pitch away from Alex Santucci. He had walked twice and grounded to second in three at bats. He came up with one on and one out, facing righthanded reliever Drew Monday, who threw a wicked changeup and a low nineties fastball. Drew did not like to walk anybody, but he fell behind with two fast balls outside.

Alex figured a changeup on the outside corner but got crossed up with a high and inside fastball for a strike. This next pitch has to be a changeup, Alex thought, but then he called for time from the umpire. Alex stepped out and looked at the nineteen-foot wall in left field, only 315 feet down the left field line. Behind the wall there was a train that ran on top of a Roman-looking arched railway to honor the site of the old Union Station that the stadium was built on. He was disappointed not to see the railroad loco-mote so far without a Houston homerun. He thought," too bad it won't choo-choo for my next shot."

Alex stepped back in the box convinced that Monday was throwing a fastball right over the plate because he thought it was his day. As Alex remembered the *Mamas and the Papas* singing "Monday, Monday can't trust that day," Alex parked his thirtieth of the year over the railroad for another titanic, two-run home-run that sealed a 5-2 victory-his ninth homerun in seven games. The crowd, realizing they were watching history in the making, clapped rather loudly. The applause caught Alex's attention, and he tipped his helmet as he entered the dugout.

Alex stayed on the field signing autographs for an hour and a half. Ten Houston players came out with bats or balls for him to autograph. Alex was a machine, signing his name so that the *Al* had a line trailing it; the *Sa* was followed by a line that looped into two *Ts* and came back up and over to cross them. He could do it in his sleep but generally enjoyed looking at every fan. He had no messages and made no calls when he arrived at his hotel room. He watched *David Letterman* for a while, then read *11/22/63* until 11:22 p.m., and fell into a deep sleep until dawn.

• • •

Alex went for a long run in the business district of Houston with the streets vacant of cars. He went to the workout room in the hotel to do his weight work. *ESPN* was doing highlights of the Houston game last night.

Suddenly an alarmingly beautiful redheaded woman, soon to be twenty-nine, stood in front of the television and watched the highlights showing the homerun and Alex tipping his hat to the Houston fans. She turned around to check out Alex, an alarmingly handsome, blond-headed man, and held her breath when she realized her discovery. They were alone in the room, so it was difficult for Charlotte to hide her embarrassment. She walked over to Alex to introduce herself and tried to be cute by asking if she could get him anything.

Alex responded quickly. "I would love a coffee and your lovely company for a few minutes, Miss." Alex was used to aggressive women and liked to be direct about his intentions. Charlotte turned red with embarrassment but jumped to her assignment and came back in five minutes with two coffees and some fruit.

She was in Houston for a week working as a consultant for Rice University, revamping their computer systems for the administration offices. They hit it off right away, sharing stories about running early in the morning and being on the road. They were both in serious relationships, both got hit on a lot, and both loved baseballs. She grew up in Saint Louis watching the Cardinals but now lived in Austin, Texas. She knew all about Alex and was a big fan. They agreed having sex would be great but a bad idea. Instead, she talked about how staying exclusive with her boyfriend was sometimes hard.

For Alex, it was never an issue until today, because before the medication, he never thought about it much. Since then, his emotions were on full alert, but Sally was always with him. They talked about how it was unusual for each to have an opposite-sex friend, so they agreed to run together for the next three mornings and work-out afterward.

Both of them were amazed at each other's bodies. Alex thought Charlotte had him beat, but she disagreed because of his shapely butt. He countered, pointing out her lovely chest and beautiful hair were something special. She disagreed, saying her chest got in the way of her running and her hair was too long and too curly to handle. He understood her point, but he liked the way both features looked just the same.

Alex got her game passes for the three remaining games. She would go alone to Tuesday's game and bring amazed colleagues to the Wednesday game.

• • •

Tuesday morning Charlotte and Alex caught up on a lifetime of events and quickly found out they were both adopted. Like a lock mechanism on a safe opening up, they realized their connection and embraced while Charlotte cried for minutes on Alex's shoulder. She desperately wanted to meet her birth mother but was always scared to pursue it. Alex shared his recent reunion with Leah, which inspired Charlotte with the courage to find her birth mother. At that same moment, Alex's phone buzzed for the first time on the trip. It was a text from Leah saying she was coming to Houston with her daughter Nancy to meet him Wednesday. He laughed and shared it with Charlotte. She wiped her eyes, got herself together, and thanked Alex with a big kiss.

By the end of the day, she had obtained her birth mother's number and called her. It brought to mind *The Moody Blues* as they sang about "Tuesday Afternoon". I'm beginning to see, I'm on my way.

• • •

Tuesday afternoon, Alex walked to the ballpark, attracting fans on the way. He signed autographs but kept walking. He went to the training room for a Jacuzzi, then a rubdown, yoga, ice treatments, then another Jacuzzi before batting practice. Danube Rivers was on the mound tonight for Washington facing a rookie callup, James Hunter. Houston's starting pitching was in transition from inning-eating veterans to young, high-heat arms. Hunter was the future for the Heavens, but not tonight. Hopson doubled to start the game and Gonzalez homered, which was followed by a Santucci walk and a LeMont homer. It was 4-0 in the blink of an eye. Hunter settled down and followed with five shutout innings. Rivers got tagged for a two-run homer in the six and left the game with a 4-2 lead.

The national media was in full force watching Alex's current streak of homeruns. With a homerun tonight, he would tie the record of eight straight games held by Don Mattingly (ten in eight games) and Dale Long (eight in eight games). Both men were left-handed hitting first basemen.

Mattingly did it in 1987, and Long in 1956. Ironically, Long played for the 1961 expansion Washington Senators, hitting 17 Hrs and 49 RBIs, making him second in Hrs to Gene Green, the grand slam-hitting hero of Phillip's first baseball game at Griffith Stadium.

Alex was 1 for 2 with a walk as he faced Drew Monday for the second day in row. He had watched film on his changeup before the game with Charley Jackson. The manager had picked up a hitch in his motion, which gave away his changeup. He would only look at his glove when he came to his set on his changeup.

Jackson lamented, "I don't know if it will help you see the ball better, but you'll know it's coming. It still drops a foot or two. Get your two-iron shot ready!"

Alex stepped in and moved up in the batter's box. The rare sellout crowd was tense. Thousands of Washington fans were chanting "Alex, Alex, Alex." Monday came to the set, looked at his glove, and threw the changeup high and tight. Alex leaned back but stayed settled in the box. Monday came to set, did not look at his glove, and fired a strike on the outside corner. Alex was focused on center field, all 435 feet of it as it rose over Tal's Hill, a 30 percent incline named after former team president Tal Smith. Charley Jackson was right about needing a two iron. Drew Monday came to the stretch again, looked at his glove, and threw the changeup right down the middle. Alex saw it and stayed low, hitting it in front of the plate like the sinker in New York City that landed in the monuments-except this one was in a hurry about 475 feet to dead center. He nailed the two irons, dropped it to the side for the caddy to handle, and roamed the bases for his thirty-first homerun. It sealed another 5-2 win, making it their eighth in a row and tying them for first place with Miami at 59 and 50.

• • •

Alex celebrated with the fans after the game. Thousands of people crowded the railing trying to get close to Alex. All twenty-five members of the Presidents stayed for an hour signing autographs to disperse the crowds. Finally, security had to force Alex into the dugout and back to the hotel. He was hungry and called Charlotte to come by for dinner. She was not hungry but was glad to be company for the most famous guy in baseball. Alex asked Blake Hopson to escort her up the locked elevator.

He laughed when Alex called her a friend and explained, "Hey, bro, you know I'm cool with whatever you do. She's a looker for sure, but I think you're playing it the right way, man. Sally has sharpshooter looks and a body to match, so there you go, bro!"
"Thanks for the advice, Blake. You're pretty special!" "Anything I can do to help, bro!"

"Well, then come back in a hour to walk her back to her room." Blake looked at his phone and announced, "I'll be back at midnight, Red-Dog Leader!"

Alex rolled his eyes as his Private Hopson ran down the hallway.

• • •

Charlotte sat in the chair nearest the window, wearing a light green blouse with a V-neck and tight designer jeans. Her hair was curled around her pretty freckled face, highlighting her light brown eyes. She could have been dessert.

Alex was famished, ready to start on his rib-eye steak, a sweet potato, broccoli, and a large Caesar salad. He turned off the television and focused on Charlotte for entertainment, as she could not stop talking about finding her birth mother.

Her animation and joy made her even more attractive

as she leaned over the whole time, expressing her emotions like she was an Italian with cleavage. After their long phone conversation, she could not wait to meet her mother in person.

"Where does she live?"

"In Kentucky, just south of Cincinnati, she has three grown kids in college and out of the house. Her husband does well. She writes off and on, some poetry, short stories, and articles for the local paper."

"Tell her to get on a plane tomorrow and come to Houston. Leah will be here-you'll love her, and it will take any awkwardness out of the scene. The game will be a big party. I'll pay for her ticket and hotel room."

"Alex, why would you do that? That is too generous."

"Charlotte, life is too short, and I have way too much money!"

She was suddenly hungry and grabbed vegetables off his plate. Soon they were side by side, laughing and eating every morsel on the plate.

She said, "This emotional stuff makes me so hungry. I think I'm going to sleep well tonight." Charlotte leaned over and put her head on Alex's chest and felt his heart beat. She thought it must be very large to be the type of person he is. She wiped her eyes and kissed him on the lips. "I think your chest is definitely bigger than mine...for sure. I'll see you at the crack of dawn, my friend. Sleep well. "She left his warm body and walked toward the door.

Just then Private Hopson knocked on the door reporting for duty-right on time!

Chapter 40

Alex met Charlotte Roberts for a predawn run at six o'clock on Wednesday, August 8, followed by a workout at the hotel's gym. For the third day in a row, they were alone in the workout room from six thirty to seven. Still sweaty from their hour of running and lifting, Alex grabbed some coffee, juice, fruit, and bagels from the executive lounge and headed for the streets of Houston for the two-block walk to Kinder Lake for a picnic breakfast.

Charlotte was still bouncing off the wall with emotions from her interactions with her birth mother. Alex tried to get her to focus on a plan to see her in person and learn more about her. Alex shared, that he approached meeting Leah with total positivity because he knew she or any other birth mother already felt so much guilt about giving up their child. He thought it was important to view it as the biblical "Prodigal Son" story; where Christ taught that any act of returning to the family, after deserting or leaving, should be viewed with acceptance and love, even if it seems unfair to those who have been loyal the whole time. Alex believed it was a very powerful story that highlighted the essential tenet of forgiveness in the life of a Christian. Alex had always been impressed by the concept of forgiveness in the Christian religion. It was one of the few things that would reach him emotionally, especially watching it in movies or reading a story about it in a book. It was practiced rarely by people in real life, he thought, even those that call themselves Christian. Alex told Charlotte he did not practice a religion, even though he was brought up Catholic. But being a Christian always seemed to fit his values or, he thought, "was it the other way around?"

Charlotte was overwhelmed by Alex's wise counsel and friendship. She thought it was improbable that he would have time for a friendship connection in the future, but she was willing to go along for the ride to keep learning.

Alex was meeting Leah and her daughter, his half-sister, Nancy at ten o'clock. Charlotte would be free for lunch at noon and meet up with them at Rice University. Alex and Charlotte headed back to the hotel after an enjoyable picnic. Charlotte hated to leave him as well as the conversation but had a full slate of meetings in the morning at Rice.

Alex took a shower back at the hotel and called Sally, who was in Kansas visiting her parents. She was excited to get the call and wished him happy birthday, adding that his present would have to wait until she arrived Friday morning in Phoenix. Alex gave her a report about the player's dinner and meeting Charlotte, the beautiful redhead. Sally reminded him that only good boys get birthday presents! She had no time to worry about Alex being with other women. It never seemed to be his nature, so worrying about it was not going to prevent it from happening. They were together because he did not want other women. On the other hand, Sally noted to herself, Alex, like herself, had a soft spot for redheads!

• • •

The media was all over the lobby by ten o'clock, with fans crowding the outside of the hotel. Alex asked for a suite on the penthouse level to move into with Leah and Nancy. It would give them privacy until Thursday. They were escorted by the concierge to the suite after they arrived in the lobby. Leah was wearing a red sateen blouse with tight designer jeans and her hair in a ponytail. Nancy seemed to hide behind Leah, wearing a beautiful blue summer dress cut above the knee that lay nicely on her thin frame. Her blonde hair was pressed to lay straight just above her shoulders, making her look like a model straight out of a J.Crew catalog. She weakly shook hands with Alex after he warmly hugged Leah. Alex showed her the suite and her bedroom. She brightened up after looking out the windows on to the Houston skyline and the stadium in the distance.

"Could we come to the game tonight?" she asked politely.

"Of course, Nancy, do you want to meet some of the players during batting practice?"

She responded like a teenager and answered with, "Are you kidding me, Mom, can you believe it?" She asked questions about his half-sister Grace, the closest in age to her, and where Guy was going to school.

Alex filled her in and hoped she, Claudette, and Paul would come to the wedding on Labor Day.

"I'm sure we would all love to come to Washington. Mom, could we stay in Georgetown?"

Alex answered. "Of course, there's a Four Seasons in George-town. I could get you rooms."

Leah wanted to stop the candy being distributed. "Honey, I'm sure we can find a Hampton Inn or Homewood Suites that would be just fine."

Alex could see that Nancy had Leah's lovely blue eyes but seemed to have a very different personality than her mom. She was a girl who had graduated college, lived and knew about the real world.

• • •

They headed to Rice University around eleven forty-five after only a four-mile cab ride south from the hotel to the University near the Houston Museum District. A prestigious, private research University, Rice started under shaky circumstances only fitting a Texas institution. William Marsh Rice, a prominent Massachusetts businessman in real estate, railroad development, and cotton trading in Texas had wanted to leave his fortune to start a free-tuition educational institute in Houston after he died. Unfortunately, he was murdered in 1900 by his

New York lawyer and valet driver, who together forged the will, trying to steal his fortune. By 1901 they were charged and convicted of murder, and the money finally went to establish Rice University in 1907.

Alex filled in Leah and Nancy about Charlotte on the way. They were happy to give her support but were curious about the connection. Charlotte was very nervous about the meeting, but Leah's infectious personality loosened her up very quickly. Leah talked about the years of guilt she lived through and how she finally broke free to let herself meet Alex. Nancy sat amazed hearing her mom talk about another world she had just learned about. As they walked toward the administration building, Charlotte and Nancy finally connected by talking about the computer systems upgrades Charlotte was working on at Rice. Nancy had an undergraduate degree in computer science, so she was full of questions. Charlotte was excited to share the job with her and told her about her graduate studies involving information systems.

Looking at a map, Rice University is shaped like an upside down triangle with the right corner partially clipped off. The beauty of the campus gave Alex and Leah a chance to walk together in another world away from the business of a city and surrounded by youth. She talked about how sad she was that Phillip would not be here for the game, but Alex sensed it was his company she really missed. Sadness was generally a leap off the cliff of emotions for Leah because of her natural positivity, but this time it seemed like just a few steps down. Being with Alex and Nancy was helping her make the adjustment.

The four of them met in front of Lovett Hall, majestically built with a nee-Byzantine style similar to other Rice buildings. They walked through the middle of campus without recognition from the partially abandoned summer campus. As they arrived back at the hotel together, fans crowded the driveway excited to get a glimpse of Alex. Everyone was ready for the game. They hoped it would be a record-breaking night!

Leah and Nancy headed to their room in the suite while Alex got ready to head to the ballpark. Nancy was excited to have spent time with Charlotte and shared with Leah a couple of details. "Her birth mother is flying in for the game tonight at five, and guess what? It's her birthday! She's meeting her mother on her birthday. How cool is that? Mom, let's find a *Lululemon* store and get her some running clothes as a gift, maybe a card and flowers. She has no family around and is by herself!"

Leah had a confused look on her face as she finally realized what day it was. "How could I forget?" She thought to herself. No wonder this was the first time she was not depressed on August 8-Alex Santucci's birthday!

"Oh Nancy, that is a great idea!" She then whispered quietly, "I just remembered: it's Alex's birthday as well!"

"Well, you've had a lot of your mind, Mom. This is going to be a really great party-especially after he hits that homerun!"

"What homerun, Nancy?"

"He's hit ten homeruns 1n eight straight games, and tonight he's going to break the record!"

"How do you know this stuff? That seems almost impossible to do under this kind of pressure! How can you be so sure he's going to break the record tonight?"

"It's easy, Mom-he's, my brother!"

Leah felt a great rush of warmth in her chest and soul and then burst into tears as she hugged her all-knowing daughter. "Okay sweetie. Let's do some shopping!"

• • •

Alex arrived at 3:45 at the ballpark for the 7:05 p.m. game. He found a lap pool at the stadium used mainly for rehab therapy. It was refreshing spending a half an hour slowly doing laps. His mind seemed to clear out from the day's activities, and he could focus on tonight1s starter:

veteran lefty Harper Martinez, better known as "Harpo" for his wild, springy hair.

After swimming, Manager Charley Jackson pulled him into his office to watch some film on Harpo. Once again he had figured out a game plan based on the pitcher's delivery.

"This guy rarely throws a fastball from his normal three- quarter delivery, almost always slightly sidearm, maybe just sixty-percent, instead of seventy-five. See, here it is-just a slight tilt. The more he drops, the more it comes inside. In your first two at bats, you got to pull this guy." Charley stood up and walked around the cramped office and sat on the desk next to Alex. "This is unanimous coming from the team. Hammer just came to see me with Gonzalez and Beans. They'll win the game for us. All they want you to do is hit one out. Don't worry about the situation or nothin'. They want you to jack it out and break the record! You understand? This means a lot to them!"

Alex nodded and smiled at this one-of-kind manager.

"Oh yeah," Charley added. "Happy birthday, number thirty-six for an old man, be ready for some whipped cream in the face after you go deep! And one more thing, Alex, no one is going to be talking to you or the other team tonight. I think they're pretty serious about this thing...You may not want to disappoint them." He did not crack a smile as he shook hands with Alex. With an equally serious face, Alex answered. "Thanks for the heads up about the whipped cream-I hate that shit!"

• • •

Alex took batting practice underneath the stands, and then found the bullpen coach to play some catch and do some pitching. There was a mound next to the BP cage. It felt great to let go of the ball with an incline.

Bullpen Coach Wes Coats commented on the velocity.

"That's got to be mid-nineties. Where have you been

hiding that?"

"I use to pitch in high school, feels great. A friend of mine told me to start pitching again. You know, DC needs me!"

"You got that right, Alex!" As Alex fired his last pitch, Coats made a mental note to have a speed gun around next time.

• • •

The sold-out crowd was hurrying into their seats for the first inning so they would not miss Alex's first at bat. Hopson lined the first pitch down the right field line for a double, and Gonzalez walked on four pitches. The crowd stood, mixing cheers with silence, wondering if they would see history. Alex took two sliders outside for balls. Harpo checked the runners and came sidearm with a fastball inside. Alex was waiting and fouled it off his foot, failing to get his hands in front of the ball. He stepped out, ignoring his foot, and stood noticing the crowd for the first time. Leah, Nancy, and Charlotte were sitting about thirty rows behind the Presidents dugout. He saw Charlotte's red hair; she was clapping, screaming, and bouncing along with Leah, while Nancy stood, biting her fingernails nervously. Charlotte was hugging another redhead next to her-Alex realized she found her mother! He glanced to her mother's right and saw Phillip and Laura had come in for the game on his birthday. Phillip was pulling his hands through the ball, demonstrating to Laura on his right. Alex finally noticed the pain in his foot and knelt down to stretch it out and collect him thoughts mentally.

Manager Charley Jackson came out as Alex concealed his wet eyes. "Got yourself pretty good. You all right, Alex?"

"I thought nobody was talking to me!" Alex said with a smile as he headed back to the batter's box.

Umpire Earl Derwood, a twenty-eight-year veteran, asked him as he cleaned the plate, "All right, son?"

"Never better!" Alex dug in.

Martinez came to the set and fired another sidearm fastball. Alex swung hard and hit a two-bouncer to third. He hurdled out of the box as Heavens third baseman Wayne Piersall looked to second for a moment and recocked his arm to throw to first. But his throw was late by a step as Alex blew by the bag for an infield hit. The bases were then loaded for lefty first baseman Abel LeMont, who took the first sidearm fastball to left field for a short porch Grand Slam to give the Presidents a 4-0 lead. Three more hits in the inning increased the lead to 5-0. The men in the lineup continued to take care of business.

Tony Johnson pitched a scoreless bottom of the first, bringing the top of the order up again for Washington at the top of the second inning. Hopson struck out, but Gonzalez singled to center. Alex came to the plate, thinking Harper was coming inside on the third or fourth pitch. He might waste a couple outside with a slider or two. But he wondered if he might get lazy and throw a fastball outside instead, which might needlessly tail over the plate. Harpo was known to be impatient with his approach to pitching sometimes, especially when he fell behind. Alex prepared for a three-quarter delivery fastball tailing over the plate. The first pitch was a slider way outside. Martinez scuffed the rubber on the mound, talking to himself. Alex stepped out to let him finish the conversation.

He allowed himself a quick look into the stands. Phillip was pointing at something in left field and swinging toward it. Alex realized what he was pointing at and laughed as he stepped into the box.

Veteran Houston catcher Mike Runnels noticed and asked him, "What's so funny, Santucci?"

As Alex tapped the bat on the plate and brought it to his shoulders, he answered. "The Citgo sign!"

Harpo went to the set, and as he started to deliver, Alex blurted out as he pulled back his hands. "Just thinking about hitting..."

On cue, Martinez delivered the tailing over-the-plate fastball. Alex got his hands through and sent the baseball to it's destination for history.

As he finished his swing, he finished his answer to Runnels: "... the Citgo sign."

The ball hit between the G and the O part of the sign, and then plummeted down about eighty-feet from the sign back onto the field. The ball was thrown into the Presidents dugout for the Hall of Fame. Runnels was standing in front of the plate, looking out to the Citgo sign, shaking his head in disbelief as Alex rounded the bases.

As Alex crossed home plate, Gonzalez was first to congratulate him, followed by the rest of the team. Alex lifted his helmet to the cheering crowds. Henson Scott threw him the ball from the dugout. He caught it, pointed to Phillip, Laura, Leah, Nancy, and Charlotte, and blew kisses. He held the ball out high as he came out of the dugout for a curtain call. He avoided the whipped cream for now!

Mike Runnels was stewing mad and talked out loud to no one in particular as he finally returned to behind home plate. "You got to be freaking kidding me, Santucci. You're something else. I ain't telling anybody what you said-nobody!"

Umpire Derwood waited for Runnels to get in his crouch for the next hitter before setting him straight. "Don't be such an ass-hole, Runnels. You want *me* to be one to tell the world or *you*? I heard it too you know, as clear as day-no doubt about it!"

Runnels quietly put his fingers down for the next pitch to LeMont but then had to blurt out one final comment. "That is one lucky son of a bitch...that Santucci!" Umpire Derwood called strike one. "Lucky, my ass, Runnels. He's something special, and you were a witness to it!"

Chapter 41

The Presidents drained the Heavens pitching of their dignity with a 16-5 win for their ninth victory in a row. Alex went 4 for 4 before Jackson took him out after the seventh inning. He was allowed to skip the media and leave for the hotel before it was impossible to do so. The Presidents bused a media contingent to a hotel conference room with heavy security. The hotel lobby was checking for hotel keys at the door. Alex answered questions for fifteen minutes and begged off because it was his birthday, his family was in town, and he was starved. He offered to meet with anyone on Thursday morning at eight o'clock; they reluctantly agreed.

Alex returned to his suite and was the victim of a surprise party! Leah ordered a cake in the shape of a baseball with thirty-six candles and a second cake for Charlotte in the shape of an iPad with twenty-nine candles. Leah and Nancy had also done a great job shopping for birthday gifts, getting workout clothes from *Lululemon* for Charlotte and an iPad and an iPod for Alex. They were both thrilled with the gifts and made quick work of the cakes.

Charlotte and her birth mother, Margaret Williams, had been introduced by Leah to Phillip and Laura at the stadium. By the time they got to the suite five hours later, they were comfortable friends.

Phillip and Laura excused themselves quickly after cake and retired to their rooms because they were heading out on an early flight in the morning, leaving the hotel before Alex rose at 6:00 a.m.

• • •

For the fourth day in a row, Alex joined Charlotte

for a run and a workout. It would be their last morning together, and already Alex was missing her. There was something very special about her, especially her love of running and workouts that was making her a close buddy. For an hour between seven and eight o'clock, after their workout, they talked in detail about Wednesday. For Alex it was explaining his feelings about breaking the consecutive homerun record, while Charlotte talked about meeting her birth mother.

"I'm still pinching myself to see if this is real. Just three days ago, I was a different person. Alex, you changed my life!" Sitting side by side on a park bench, Charlotte leaned on Alex, overwhelmed with happiness.

Alex lifted up her head to look at her pretty face and luscious hair. "What was the coolest thing you learned from Margaret?"

"Well, I found out who my birth father was, and guess what? We're both half-Italian!"

"I knew there was something special about you. Is he alive, and where did they meet?"

"No, he died over twenty years ago, and they met at a conference on the East Coast in November 1982. Maybe it was New York or Boston-no, it was at NIH, I think."

"Well, NIH is in Bethesda; that's where I'm from. Did she tell you his name or profession?"

"No, no. We didn't get that far. Margaret is a nurse at the University of Cincinnati Cancer Center. She's hoping to retire in a couple of years. She's Phillip's age."

Alex was putting the pieces together in his head. "Where is your mom, now?"

"She's leaving this morning to catch a flight back home. She has a shift later tonight."

Alex rose up quickly, carrying Charlotte up with him.

"Let's try to catch her at the hotel."

"She's not going to leave before eight o'clock."

"I'm not so sure!"

Alex led the way to the hotel, crossing the three blocks

in less than two minutes. They caught Margaret as she was walking out the hotel's revolving door. Alex stepped in front of the doorman and took Margaret gently, placing his arm around her shoulder and ushering her inside to a side sitting area.

"Alex, what are you doing to Margaret?" Charlotte turned to her mother, gasping for breath. "And where are you going? You're leaving without saying good-bye!"

Margaret could not make eye contact with either of them. She was a lovely looking woman who had kept herself in good shape but was worn out from thirty-five years of giving direct patient care. She did not follow sports, including baseball, and did not know about Alex Santucci until she came to the stadium last night. After she heard Alex's named announced and all the excitement, she knew she was in a tight spot. She knew her daughter would want to know about her father, so she gave her some information-just too much information as soon as she mentioned "NIH"!

"Margaret, I apologize for being so direct, but I think you have something to tell Charlotte." Alex said while directly looking into her eyes.

Charlotte replied, "What is it? Please, someone tell me, Alex how do you know?"

Margaret said, "Charlotte, it is about your father. He was a doctor. It was a one-week affair in Bethesda, Maryland."

Charlotte was still confused and looked at Alex as her mother looked for the courage to say it out loud.

Charlotte said, "Alex, wasn't your adoptive father a doctor in..." She fell back and waited for the final verdict from Margaret.

Alex held her tight with both arms, hoping to keep her calm.

"Yes, dear," said Margaret. "His name was Dr. Gene Santucci... Alex's adopted father."

• • •

Alex was due to meet with some press in the restaurant. He let Margaret and Charlotte have time to accept the consequences of the information just exchanged. Before he left, he told each of them that no one else could know this secret until he said otherwise. They happily agreed. Margaret was relieved to be able to share it with Charlotte even under the stressful circumstances.

Alex did an interview with Riley Preston of *ESPN*. They were starting to trust each other and agreed to spend time together in San Francisco talking about background information that could help him report better about Alex in the future. Julia Newmar and Kelly Browner did Washington area interviews. Ron Roswell, with the *Washington Daily,* was doing a long article for Friday's edition, and he wanted some quotes from Alex. Jim Jeffries from *Fox Sports* tried to coax him to do a radio call-in show with him, and Alex declined for now but did do a live interview with him. Many more reporters were spurned by the POTUS media department since Alex did not have an agent or publicist handling the press.

He found Charlotte and Margaret in the lobby along with several fans wanting autographs. He signed quickly as he dashed to the elevator with the two women. They met with Leah and Nancy in the hotel suite, as both were just getting up, and explained the newest revelation from the galaxy to land in his lap. Alex called it an ever-expanding family universe!

"Something is bringing us all together," said Alex. "Let's call it 'God,' for the lack of a better explanation. We all have to see this as positive energy for each of us to learn and grow from. We are here to support each other."

Margaret's face had dropped ten years of age, and Charlotte was mesmerized by her new step-brother. She was not sure of their official status, but it had her buzzing with love.

Leah was praising the Lord with affectionate prayers, writing down poetry for new lyrics.

Nancy was standing up straight while keeping her fingernails out of her mouth. Alex once again pleaded for secrecy until he could talk to Laura. It was gaining momentum inside of him to tell her about Gene's imperfection with another woman and the daughter they had together. It made him gain a different perspective of Phillip, who now seemed heroic to him compared to Gene's narrative. Needless to say, there was a lot to sort out. He wished Phillip and Sally were here to talk to about his feelings. He needed to call Phillip and get him to fly out with Guy on Saturday. He decided to take Leah into another room.

"Leah, I trust you to talk to Laura. I think she needs to know right away before somebody from the press or social media finds this story. She respects you and will accept it from you. It's really not about me, so it doesn't matter who tells her. I just happened to have met Charlotte."

Leah hugged Alex, feeling his energy that was abounding it great quantities. She closed her eyes for a minute and soon understood the reason she was sent to Alex. She looked up and said to Alex, "I understand. I'm here to help with the healing-first it was me, then Phillip, Nancy, Charlotte and Margaret-and now Laura. We all have been blessed with power to fix our pain and help others. You are here to heal the big stuff, like baseball fans in DC. I get to help the family all connected to you somehow." They parted holding on by a hand. "God loves you, Alex Santucci!"

Alex twirled her back to him like Fred Astaire would do to Ginger Rogers.

"I'm glad you understand him better than I do. This is all new to me. I do love you, Leah. You gave me life-and had to give me up-but you never gave up on me." Alex let go of his bear hug while Leah held on to the feeling as long as she could.

She turned around before opening the door and shined him a beautiful smile while pulling her hair out of a ponytail and shaking it out onto her shoulders. "My dear Alex, I think you just gave me some lyrics for a hit record!" She sang as though she were channeling Whitney Houston in a church. "The Lord gave you life, but I had to give you up, though I never gave up on you!"

• • •

After Leah took Margaret and Nancy to the airport and got on a plane herself to Washington, Alex told Charlotte he wanted her to stay with him until at least the Labor Day wedding. He would hire her to be his assistant. She was overwhelmed to be needed and gladly cleared her Friday schedule after finishing up her work at Rice University. She luckily had three weeks of vacation time starting on Monday, which would take her through Labor Day. Her boyfriend had taken an assignment in China working for Cisco Systems. She was considering plans to visit him but never made a final decision because it was such a large time and relationship commitment. She realized now that she was meant to do something else, to support Alex and learn more about her birth father and her new family in Bethesda. It was all so exciting, and she could barely wait for Alex, who picked her up at Rice at four o'clock in a cab and brought her to the ballpark.

During the day, he spent time on the phone with Phillip and Sally explaining the bizarre connection between Charlotte and Gene. Phillip agreed to come out Saturday, while Sally looked forward to being with Alex and meeting this new redhead in Phoenix.

Alex spent the first hour at the stadium workout pool talking with Charlotte about his fifteen years with Gene. It made him really miss him and mad at him at the same time to share stories about him. They joined in laughing about the good times and his last days with him. "I think he died pretty happy after seeing me hit a homerun in a summer league game. He was gone so quickly. I've never really thought about it much because I didn't know any better. I was too busy being a ballplayer and a kid."

Charlotte was in awe of Alex's openness. She swam a lap and came up out of the water right in front of him and put her head on his chest and put her wet arms around his waist. "It seems so weird that he was your adopted dad and you lived with him for fifteen years, and he was my birth dad and I never met him!"

He kissed her on the top of her head as he gathered her hair and wrestled the water out of it, laying it back on her neck as he thought about what she said. He was past noticing Charlotte as a knockout in a bathing suit, even though it was an unflattering one-piece, made for serious swimming. He saw a great athlete, a workout partner, and some kind of sister.

• • •

Alex barely dressed in time for batting practice, and for the second night in a row he stayed off the field. He told Manager Jackson that he probably was not ready to play but might have his head together later in the game.

Charley Jackson understood and surprised him with a wise guy answer. "I already had you out of the lineup, Santucci. You're just not hitting the ball!" He passed him in the dugout and slapped Alex in the back. "Be ready if I need you after the fifth inning!"

Alex smiled and saluted his general.

Ryan Hudson started for Alex at third. The capacity crowd booed the announcer when Hudson batted in the second inning, because they came to see Alex Santucci go for his tenth game in a row with a homerun. Presidents' pitcher Phillip Fields was not locating any of his pitches and had to be removed in the third inning when the score reached 7-0.

Ross Williams came in and shut down the Heavens through the sixth inning, giving the Presidents a chance to close the gap to 7-2. Morris led off the seventh with a walk, and Mendoza followed with a double off the wall in left-center. Henson Scott singled in two runs to cut the lead to 7-4. Madison Bennett pinched hit for Williams to a chorus of loud boos, because they wanted Alex and struck out. With one out, Hopson singled up the middle, and Gonzalez walked to load the bases. Manager Clint Parker went to the bullpen for left-hander Harlan Catchings to face Abel Lamont.

Alex had been taking some swings under the stands in the bottom of the sixth to stay loose. Manager Jackson told him to grab a bat, knowing that Alex had seen Catchings many times in the American League when he pitched with Detroit. Parker did not figure Jackson would take out his only first baseman in the lineup and bat Santucci-certainly not as early as the seventh inning. Jackson asked his equipment manager to find a right-handed first base glove for Alex to use in the field.

Jackson said, "Alex, don't worry about playing first base. It's a piece of cake!"

In the on-deck circle, Alex laughed at his manager who was trying to distract him from the situation. "That's what they said about the iceberg on the *Titanic!*"

The crowd was getting louder, delirious about their new hero getting ready to pinch hit.

Jackson waved him back for one thing. "He always throws a first pitch cutter in on righties. I think you can pull one down the line. Try to keep it fair, though!"

Alex got to the batter's box and turned his front foot out a couple of inches. Catchings came to the set and quickly fired a fastball right down the middle. Alex watched it for strike one and immediately stepped out and looked at Manager Jackson, who shrugged his shoulders that he got one wrong. The second pitch did the same thing, and this time Alex stayed in the box. He decided to take his chances on the next pitch. He thought, *Pitchers, in their* hearts, are show-offs, and Catchings is dying to throw that cutter inside to move me off the plate.

Catchings once again wasted no time coming to the plate, this time with the cut fastball, but the pitch refused to move inside.

Catcher Mike Runnels muttered, "Oh, shit" as Alex pounded it off the railroad arches.

It was a grand slam, or as the Finelli's called it: a grand salami! His twelfth homerun in ten consecutive games and thirty-third of the year.

Charlotte was out of her mind, cheering in the stands. The entire dugout was at home plate to greet Alex. Houston fans looked to the Heavens for answers, but the players had none, going nine up and nine down in the seventh, eighth, and ninth innings. The bullpen of Ramos, Peterson, and Counter saved the comeback victory 8-7. Their tenth win in a row now put the Presidents safely in first place with a two-game lead over Miami. It was now time to streak on to the Valley of Sun, where it would be easy to stay "Hot in Phoenix"!

Chapter 42

The late-night charter flight arrived in Phoenix at 1:35 a.m. on Friday, August 10. The mood on the flight was festive to say the least, with being in 'first place' the dominate theme of celebration. Charlotte was given a seat on the plane with the training staff because she was now Alex Santucci's official workout partner and assistant. His teammates had no care or concerns about his relationship with her. They had not been filled in about the sister status yet.

She wore tight blue jeans and an eye-popping, lime-green blouse with the top three buttons undone, revealing an eyeful for interested ballplayers standing over her in the aisle. Her shoulder-length red hair was cutely curled and parted on the side, revealing her slender neck. Of course, it was her witty personality that kept her in constant conversation with a handful of players, especially nineteen-year-old Blake Hopson and thirty-nine-year-old Ross Williams. She enjoyed the attention from the athletic men ten years younger and ten years older. She was used to wearing boring pantsuits, with her hair up and little or no makeup, spending most days around nerdy engineering and computer types. Alex came up a couple of times during the flight to check to see if she needed rescuing, but both times she seemed to be enjoying holding court with the players.

• • •

Alex and Charlotte agreed to meet at eight o'clock for a short run, a swim, and a longer weight workout. They finished by nine and went for oatmeal, eggs, and coffee in the hotel cafe. They both showered and dressed for a cab ride to the airport to pick up Sally and to rent a car for Charlotte for the next three days. She would have most of the days to herself for exploration of the Phoenix area. Alex wanted her to come to the games but left that up to her each day. After meeting Sally at the airport and seeing the affectionate greeting between Sally and Alex, she finally knew she was in the right place. Sally made her immediately feel comfortable with a big hug and an offer to go shopping in the afternoon and going to the game together.

"Charlotte," said Sally, "now that we are going to be sisters-in-laws, we need to know everything about each other and be the best friends possible."

Charlotte's heart lit up with love from the idea of such inclusion with Sally. She focused on Sally's neckline-cut, red cashmere sweater with a modest-sized set of white pearls adorning her chest. Her perfectly cut black hair was held back with a matching red hair band, revealing a young, royal-looking face with outstanding black eyebrows. Charlotte thought to herself, Sally could really teach me how to look like a real woman, not just a cute redheaded computer engineer. A budding friendship was about to begin.

Charlotte dropped Sally and Alex back at the hotel while she was off to explore the "Valley of the Sun." They could not wait to get back to their room; being apart since Sunday seemed like an eternity. There was not enough time to talk before Sally could give Alex his birthday present.

• • •

The three-game series with the Phoenix Firebirds started with Travis Tyler pitching his third straight complete game shutout for a 2-0 victory. The Phoenix starter refused to pitch to Alex, initially walking him in the first and the fourth innings. In the seventh inning with two on and no outs in a scoreless game, they had to pitch to him, trying to keep the ball outside. Alex hit a hard line drive base hit to right field that loaded the bases. Alex LeMont and Marty Morris each drove in a run to seal the victory, the eleventh in a row for the Presidents.

• • •

Charlotte had done some exploring on Friday and on Saturday morning took Alex to Squaw Peak in the north-central part of the city to run. The sights and terrain were majestic as they realized they were now in the West with open blue skies and mountains in the distance. They ran five rough miles but then sat for a while to view the sunrise over the Superstition Mountains. It was their first sunrise together as siblings. Holding hands and feeling the warmth of the sun, they sealed their bond as family. They returned to the hotel for a long swim but no weight work and then retreated to their rooms for showers.

Sally was sleeping in, enjoying the extra morning hours from the time change. When Alex arrived, she groggily reminded him that Phillip and Guy were arriving on a 9:30a.m. flight. After another hour of sleep for Sally and an hour of relaxing reading time for Alex, they joined Charlotte for a drive to the airport to corral Phillip and Guy.

Alex wanted to take them all for a late breakfast to the *Elements* restaurant in the Paradise Valley's Sanctuary at the Camel-back Mountain Resort. He had arranged for Phillip's close friend Stanley Freeman to meet them there for a ten o'clock reservation. Stanley had grown up in the Washington area but moved to Phoenix over thirty years ago. He had mentored Phillip in his first full-time job at the YMCA. Stanley was a counselor at a junior high where Phillip worked with pre-delinquent youth. Even with their ten-year difference in age, they became lifelong friends. He came east in 1991 for two weeks to meet Alex, stand in as a Jewish godfather for Grace at her Christian baptism, and help Phillip with his depression. Stanley had built a solid private practice as a psychotherapist in Downtown Phoenix, including many professional athletes and politicians. Little did anyone know that his god daughter was joining them for breakfast.

Grace was the first one to come out of the baggage area to see Alex. He jumped into the air in delight as she ran to him and then to Sally for big hugs. Phillip and Guy followed close behind. Charlotte was manning the car in the pick-up zone. Luckily they had rented the largest SUV that *Hertz* had available, a Chevy Suburban. As the entourage made it to the car, an airport cop was trying to escort Charlotte away. She was doing her best to keep him distracted until Alex walked up and asked if he wanted to go to the game tonight. Once he recognized him, he was soon helping with the luggage as Alex introduced Charlotte to Guy and Grace. Alex gave the policeman a number to call for tickets saved under his name at the will-call window. A dozen airport cops would show up at the Saturday night game and became Santucci fans forever.

Grace sat up front with Charlotte while Sally sat illegally on Alex's lap with her legs stretched across Guy and Phillip. It was a cozy ride up to Paradise Valley. Stanley was waiting at the table when the Alex party was seated. He was overwhelmed, seeing Grace and meeting Charlotte. The breakfast lasted until noon, and was followed by mimosas on the beautiful terrace until two o'clock. It was a joyous atmosphere with various fans, including all the servers, coming by for autographs and short chats with Alex. The owner came out and gave Alex and Sally a fifteen-minute tour of the restaurant and the resort. He invited them to brunch at his private residence on Sunday. Alex thanked him and said they would get back to him.

Stanley did not want to leave the party and planned to meet them at the ballpark at five o'clock. Grace and Charlotte really connected, talking about their brutal engineering classes in college. Guy looked enormous after months of working out and two weeks of intense football practice. He was looking forward to batting practice tonight and a workout in the morning. At the same time, he was having trouble keeping his eyes off of Charlotte. She was a dozen years older than him, as well as his half-brother's step-sister, but other than that, she seemed his type: an athletic, redheaded beauty.

• • •

The second game of the series was another pitching duel with Presidents left-hander Leo Lawrence going the distance in a 3-0 victory for their twelfth win in a row. Manager Charley Jackson was ecstatic that his bullpen was getting rested for the second game straight game. Once again Phoenix decided not to pitch to Alex until the seventh inning. This time when he came up, the bases were loaded and there were two outs in a scoreless game. On a 2-2 count, he lined a triple down the right field line, similar to the one in the All-Star game off of "Smokey" Camels. The hit cleared the bases for three RBIs, which gave Alex a total of 30 RBIs in his thirteen games with Washington. For the season, Alex was batting .366 with 33 Hrs and 108 RBIs. He was not leading either league in any statistics, just the majors in everything!

• • •

On Sunday morning Grace took an early flight home to get ready to head to Raleigh for her senior year at NC State. Charlotte and Guy decided to work out together, and Alex took the morning off to spend some time with Phillip. They walked from the Ritz Carlton at 24th and East Camelback Road toward the Bilt-more Hotel and Golf Course facility just a couple of blocks away. It was named "the Jewel of the Desert" when it was built in 1930, designed by Albert MacArthur, a Frank Lloyd Wright protege. William Wrigley, gum magnet and owner of the Chicago

Cubs, became sole owner in 1930 until 1974, when it was expanded and refurbished several times over to become one of Arizona's largest meeting and event venues. They found a private spot in the hotel's cafe for some breakfast.

Alex said, "I'm having mixed feelings about Gene after learning about Charlotte. It's painful to explore. I'm missing him and angry at the same time. Before it was just a story, now it feels like it just happened. I remember him being away on my seventh birthday. It's one of my first memories, along with being hit in the stomach that summer, and now I know why. He was in Cincinnati when Charlotte was born. I guess that was a good thing. He was taking care of his mistake, making sure of the adoption and Margaret's health. It just seems so bizarre!"

"I guess it hurts to know that he was human, just like me. I wouldn't call it a mistake, Alex. I mean, Charlotte doesn't seem like a mistake to me, and you certainly weren't a mistake."

"Well, you were twenty-two and not married. He had six children and was in his fifties."

"I think you're splitting hairs. Every man loves attention. He was just gaining success in his profession and met a pretty nurse, and they hit it off. I mean, making love is not such a bad thing. Obviously there are consequences, but he took care of them. No one would have ever known if not for an amazing coincidence that now seems like an act of God, along with the season you're having."

Alex sat back and tried to take in what Phillip was selling. It was all about forgiveness, like with Leah-no more or no less. He needed to get out of the judgment business and just accept what happened and enjoy the gift of Charlotte in his life.

"What did you think when you heard about Charlotte and Gene?" Alex was looking for Phillip's honest reaction.

"I was floored! How did you put it together so quickly?"

"Somehow, when she mentioned NIH, I saw her face like

it was a mirror to me. I knew it was Gene-it all made sense in a micro-second. I think we made it back to the hotel it under two minutes. It was like racing through the block from Big Train's backyard to the recreation center. It was timeless...That's what it was-it was timeless." Alex paused and closed his eyes to seal the thought.

Phillip reached out and touched his hand. "What is it, son? What is timeless?"

Alex opened his eyes as though he were in a trance.

"I get it now...the whole thing, the dreams, the messages, the coincidences... It's all going to happen again."

Phillip stayed still, waiting for eye movement from Alex.

Finally he blinked and looked at Phillip. "It's going to be amazing, trust me."

Chapter 43

Danube Rivers pitched six shutout innings and was followed by a rested bullpen of Ramos, Peterson, and Counter to combine for an 8-0, three-game series shutout of Phoenix. Alex had a first-inning sacrifice fly and a third-inning infield hit. Morris and Mendoza each had a two-run homerun to lead a fourteen-hit attack for their thirteenth win in a row and a four-game lead in the NL East.

Before the game, Alex sat out batting practice to watch Guy take his swings with his regular group of Hopson, Gonzalez, and Mendoza. Blake was giving him some tips on his swing, which led to some moon shots to left and center field stands. Guy exchanged a signed Terps jersey for a signed Hopson POTUS jersey after batting practice and stood for some pictures. Both thought they got the better deal.

Blake Hopson said to Alex, "That bro is going to be a force in college football. He's a monster, and he's faster than me. He's going to be a first rounder in a few years. You wait and see bro!"

• • •

Charlotte and Guy spent a few hours together after the game on Squaw Peak. They seemed worn out from a long run, or some-thing, when they met Phillip, Sally, and Alex for dinner. They both seemed pretty happy and nobody asked any questions. They all had a great time at dinner. Then Phillip and Guy headed east on a plane, and Alex, Sally, and Charlotte headed northwest.

The plane ride Sunday night to San Francisco was a mirror image of the ride from Houston to Phoenix, except a little looser. The coaching staff was clearly relieved at the level of play from the club, especially the pitching.

Manager Charley Jackson did not know if they could play any better. He told a reporter, "This is how I thought they could play this season with some clutch hitting. The starters are relaxed, not worried about run support. I guess at some point we'll lose a game and deal with the fallout from it. Santucci has to cool down at some point. Phoenix didn't pitch to him, and he still got three hits!"

Sally and Alex were sitting together in the plane. She was looking forward to San Francisco, her favorite city in the USA. They would be staying at the St. Regis, less than a mile from AT&T Park. It was a glorious area at 125 Third Street, next to the Yerba Buena Center for the Arts and a few blocks from the French Quarter, Chinatown, The Mission District, Knob Hill, and Union Square. It would be three days of shopping, attending art shows, and people watching. Oh yeah, she thought, and some baseball games with the hottest team and player in baseball.

• • •

The players, wives, girlfriend, fiancées, and other team personnel all continued to hang out at the hotel bar after the flight. They found a *Four Seasons* Restaurant two blocks away for a very late dinner. They continued to celebrate to midnight, when most of the players headed back to the hotel. Sally, Charlotte, Alexis Tyler, and Patty Peterson decided to hit a few bars to find a dance spot after midnight on a Monday morning. They ended up in the Mission District, rocking and rolling until 2:30 am. Two redheads, a blonde, and a jet-black brunette showed the locals how to live it up.

On the ride home, Alexis was curled up and sleeping on Charlotte's lap with Sally and Patty hanging on either side of her in the backseat. Charlotte thought, "I guess the working out is paying off!"

• • •

At 5:30 a.m., Alex was knocking on Charlotte's door. She stumbled to the door in a long T-shirt with her red hair, full of curls, in her face. Alex entered as Charlotte held on to him and backed up to the front of the bed and sat down.

Alex put his arm around her, trying to see a face under those red curls. "Rough night with the girls, I'm guessing?"

"Can you get me to the shower and find my workout clothes? They're all together in a pocket of my suitcase." Alex walked her slowly to the bathroom and turned on the shower. "Can you bring me coffee...Please!"

Alex backed out as the shirt came off, searched for the clothes, and made some coffee. He listened for the shower to finish and said through the cracked door, "Are you decent, Charlotte? I've got your coffee and clothes."

She muttered yes as she sat on the edge of the bathtub wearing a towel and hand drying her hair. She took a sip of coffee, hoping for a miracle. "I'm so sorry, Alex. It won't happen again. I never do that-I don't know what got into me."

"Don't worry about it. It was a special night of bonding! Did you have fun?"

She brightened up, her light brown eyes coming to life.

"Oh my God, it was a blast. We had so many guys hitting on us. And that little Alexis...Wow, can she shake a tailfeather. I think she got pretty drunk!"

Alex squeezed her solid shoulders and kissed her wet hair. "Take your time getting dressed, and meet me in lobby."

Charlotte grabbed Alex. "Oh, no, don't leave me. I'll be ready in a minute."

As Alex left the bathroom, she was already dressing and came out in sixty seconds carrying her socks, shoes, and a scrunchie for her hair.

When they came out of the elevator, Charlotte was dressed and raring to go. They ran down Third Street toward the ballpark and turned north on the Embarcadaro, a wide boulevard that borders the waterfront all the way to Fisherman's Wharf. They made it there just as the sun was ready to rise over Oakland across the bay. Charlotte was happy to not miss this moment with Alex. They found a bench, where she curled up like a little sister in his arms. She wondered how, during an otherwise mundane life, she had won the lottery of a brother without even buying a ticket.

After witnessing a wonderful sunrise without the normal fog that can flow into the bay, they walked through Ghirardelli Square and found some coffee at six fifteen. Charlotte talked about the past week and her recent discoveries about her origins. It had seemed to awaken many dormant feelings within her. Like Alex, she went through life having very few natural reactions to emotions. She was learning from Alex that as an adopted child, you learn to shelter your emotions and move through life not developing, nurturing, farming, or growing those feelings. Entering the engineering field guaranteed she would not develop those feelings, as opposed to entering, for instance, the psychotherapy field like Phillip did. Alex and Charlotte were learning to grow those feelings together: Alex taught her about Gene, who he lived with for fifteen years. Alex witnessed how Charlotte displayed half of Gene's DNA even though she had grown up outside the Santucci family.

They decided to make a torturous run by heading up Powell Street through North Beach and Chinatown. Finally taking a left on Geary Street for a few blocks, they ran to Third Street back to the hotel. They raced the last few blocks and arrived at the St. Regis Hotel, bent over and begging for oxygen. It was just seven o'clock as they entered the hotel full of life after a day's worth of exercise for them, or a month's worth for normal people. They made it to the infinity edge pool for a cool down of slow laps followed by weight work at the gym. Alex discovered that after a week of challenging workouts with Charlotte, his weight work routine had become easy. He slowly increased the weights on each exercise, which would increase his strength.

They headed to the restaurant for some fruit and oatmeal, but when this did not fill them, they ordered omelets, bacon, and juice. When Charlotte finished her meal, her lack of sleep quickly hit her. She was escorted back to her room by Alex for some slumber.

Alex then answered some phone messages and went downstairs to talk with some media people. The first one was Ron Roswell, who was doing a Sunday piece on the "Presidents Miracle Run," as he put it. He asked for some background information on Alex, especially his Bethesda connection growing up on Johnson Avenue and his idol Walter Johnson. Alex was concerned about the public perception of this information and asked Ron to use it carefully. Roswell was a well-known student and historian of the game, and most likely he would only use it in a way to make the history of Washington baseball more available to new Presidents fans.

The San Francisco Goliaths, better known as the Go's or Go-Go's, had won their first World Series in 2010, since moving to the West Coast in 1958. They did it with tremendous starting pitching, a great bullpen, and clutch, timely hitting. They were headed back to the playoffs this year using the same formula, now in first place over Los Angeles by 2.5 games in the NL West. Playing at AT&T Park, the Go's had a distinct home-team advantage. From the temperature changes to the winds, to the angles of the outfield fences and the capacity crowds, it was a tough place for a road team.

The Presidents Tony Johnson was on the mound for the Monday night matchup against the Go's two-time Cy Young Award winner, Jim Timmons. He overpowered the POTUS lineup through the sixth inning, giving up only an infield single to Alex in the fourth inning. Johnson had given up seven hits, but spectacular plays by the infield of Santucci, Gonzalez, Patek, and LeMont kept any runs from scoring. The two teams continued a scoreless game into the eighth inning. Timmons was still on the mound and had barely reached ninety pitches. He quickly put down the Presidents in the eighth and ninth innings. Paul Angelucci took over for Johnson after seven and struck out six in a row in the eighth and ninth inning.

    Gonzalez led off the tenth with a triple, the second hit off Timmons and the first POTUS base runner since the fourth inning. Alex shocked everyone with a suicide squeeze bunt to third that did not draw a throw and scored Gonzalez with the first run. LeMont hit a slow grounder to first base, moving up Alex to second. Morris drove a fly to center that was deep enough for Alex to tag and make it to third with a slide under the tag.

    Manager Charley Jackson put on the steal sign for Alex as Go's Manager Boyd Beach came to mound to talk to Timmons. Jackson had watched film of Timmons and noticed that he used a windup with a runner on third. Jackson had timed the windup and the pitch to the catcher's mitt at 3.2 seconds. With a running lead, he figured Alex could cover the last twenty-five yards to home plate in three seconds. He also had a left-hander batting in LeMont, and Alberto Rivera, the Go's third baseman, was nowhere near third base. He instructed LeMont to swing and miss to distract the catcher just a fraction of a second. Otherwise, he thought stealing home was a piece of cake!

    Alex had a fifteen-foot lead when Timmons stepped off the mound. He was worried that he gave it away too soon. He went back to the base as Timmons went to the rubber to get his sign from the catcher. Alex's heart was racing as he took a lead off the base again. Timmons gave him a quick look, and turned away as Alex took off like a dart. Timmons was still stuck in his windup as Alex was halfway down the line. When Timmons finally released the ball, Alex was ten feet away from home plate. As the ball got to the plate, LeMont swung wildly through the strike zone as the catcher, Vernon Morrison, tried to jump forward and catch the high pitch. Alex was into his slide toward the plate as Morrison dove toward his feet. Alex touched the plate as LeMont dove out of the way, and Morrison's mitt hit a fit a foot.

The umpire spread his arms like an eagle and screamed, "Safe, safe, safe!"

Alex hopped up and ran to the dugout. The players were screaming and mobbed him like he had just hit a grand slam.

LeMont then struck out. Clay "Bean" Counter came in to close for the tenth inning. He quickly gave up a single and a double to the Go's for their eighth and ninth hits. Counter struck out right fielder Cody Williams for the first out. Morrison then hit a rising line drive toward the hole between short-stop and third. Somehow Alex dove straight across toward second and nabbed it at the top of his glove. He crashed to the infield and felt his left shoulder pop. He got to his feet and held his shoulder to his side as it slowly found its place in the socket. He threw the ball to Counter and finally took a knee on the infield as he tried to catch his breath. The team almost ran out on to the field, but only Jackson, a trainer, and the entire infield made it to Alex.

He laughed as they gave him time to recover. "How many outs boys: two and one to go?"

Jackson retorted, "Beans, try not to let them hit this one!" Lefthander Alberto Rivera was up for the Goliaths. He was the NL All-Star third baseman and owned "Bean" Counter, hitting 12 for 21 against him. Jackson thought about bringing in a lefty but wanted to trust his closer to finish the game. He could have walked him with first base open but got him leaning on a changeup and popped him up behind shortstop. Unfortunately, Gonzalez was playing on the other side of second in a shift, and the left fielder Mendoza was nowhere near shallow left field.

Alex had just caught his breath before the pitch but was dying for some ice for the pain. He was in great position to see the ball over his left shoulder as he put his head down and ran to a spot in the outfield. After a short sprint, he looked up and saw the ball coming down to his mitt. Suddenly the wind caught it and kept it going toward the outfield. He had to leap but could not stretch his left shoulder, which was screaming at him to stop the torture. He turned on his back in midair, like going from freestyle to backstroke. He grabbed the ball with his right hand while falling directly on his back as he tucked his wounded left shoulder into his chest. He ended with a backward somersault and popped up holding the ball high over his head and then ranback to the dugout. Rivera already rounding second base, tipped his hat, as did many of the Go's on the top of the dugout steps. The Presidents had won their fourteenth game and fourth shutout in a row, 2-0.

• • •

The weather was spectacular for a Tuesday and Wednesday in the middle of August. Soon enough they would be facing the humidity and ninety-degree weather of DC. But for now Alex, Sally, and Charlotte would enjoy the respite of perfect San Francisco weather. After morning workouts, the days were spent seeing some of the San Francisco area: riding the cable cars, catching buses to Golden Gate Park and Lake Merced, or taking a cab over the Golden Gate Bridge to have lunch in Sausalito.

Tuesday's game was a workmanlike affair with an early lead by Washington that held up for a 3-0 victory. Phillip Fields made up for his last start with six scoreless innings. Tory Taylor and Ross Williams pitched scoreless innings for "Bean" Counter to close out the ninth. Alex had a run-scoring single in the first inning, followed by a Morris two-run homer to finish the scoring. It was the fifteenth win and the fifth shutout in a row, with a team record of fifty-two innings fifth shutout in a row, with a team record of fifty-two innings.

Ace Travis Tyler would be on the mound for the Wednesday afternoon matinee at AT&T Park. Travis was on his own personal streak of thirty-three shutout innings in a row, including three straight complete game shutouts. In a word, he was unhittable with a high-nineties fastball, a high-eighties slider, and a high-seventies curveball. The game was on national television and was attracting attention from all the news media, including *CNN, FOX, and MSNBC.* Starting at noon, *ESPN* and *PLB* were doing live shows from the stadium. The game would start at twelve forty-five. Players decided to take their plane home on Thursday at 9:00 a.m. They wanted to celebrate their winning road trip for one more night in the "Golden City by the Bay."

Charlotte and Sally had bought special summer dresses for the game. A meticulously planned shopping trip had harvested several new outfits and shoes for Charlotte and a dress for Sally. They sat with their new dancing buddies, Patty Peterson and the nervous Alexis Tyler. She was concerned that Travis was so hyped up about the game that he would not find the plate or, worse yet, hurt someone with a fastball.

All-Star right-hander Howard "Dusty" Streets, whose nickname implied he left the field with filthy stuff behind him, would face Tyler. At this time in the NL, they were the two best righthanded pitchers.

Alex had received treatment and an X-ray on his left shoulder. The good news was that his shoulder was fine and in place; the bad news was the cracked rib high in his chest toward the shoulder, which only hurt every time he took a breath. Before the game, he skipped batting and infield practice, but received ice treatments and shot up with Novocain. He hoped to make it through today and then have forty-eight hours before Friday's game to recover. Right before the game started, he took a few practice swings under the stands and warmed up his arm without any problems.

Manager Charley Jackson's strategy against Streets was to hit him early in the count and look for the fastball every other inning. For the even-numbered innings, he wanted them to take the first two pitches and look for off-speed pitches. Before each inning, he reminded the batters which strategy they were installing that inning.

In the first inning, Blake Hopson hit the first pitch down the right field line for a homerun. Jerry Gonzalez doubled on the next pitch, and Alex Santucci singled him home on his third pitch of the game. Travis Tyler started out strong, striking out the side in the first; Alexis let out a huge sigh of relief. The second and the fourth innings did not produce any runs, but the patient hitters threw Streets for a loop, who was having trouble locating his breaking pitches. In the third, Hopson again hit the first pitch for a triple to right-center, Gonzalez again doubled on the next pitch, and again Santucci singled him home on the third pitch of the inning. Tyler had cruised through the first four innings only giving up one hit. Streets was finally sent to the showers in the fifth after Hopson doubled, Gonzalez singled, and Santucci doubled on three consecutive pitches to make it 6-0. Hopson singled in the seventh to hit for the cycle-the youngest player in history to do so. Jackson removed Tyler after the sixth inning breaking the record for team consecutive shutout innings at fifty-eight. He finally agreed after much protest, which saved him some innings on his young arm after four spectacular starts. The Presidents bullpen ran the streak to sixty innings with two more scoreless innings, but San Francisco finally scored two runs in the ninth to avoid a series shutout. The 6-2 victory was the Presidents' sixteenth win in a row and a sweep of their ten-game road trip. They sat atop the NL East with a 67-50 record, and by the early evening they would be five games ahead of Miami.

In the locker room, Hank Meyers congratulated the team and asked for all team members, family, and friends to join him and his father on a special dinner tour of the San Francisco Bay on *The Spirit of Two Thousand Ten,* a 120-foot chartered yacht. Only one hundred grand for the night, the all-night evening cruise included a five-star dinner for up to eighty people. He assured everyone they would be safe in their hotel rooms by ten o'clock if they wanted, otherwise they had the yacht until just after sunrise. The room exploded in excitement as buses waited for them outside the stadium.

One person was not in the locker room. Alex Santucci was still on the field with his side wrapped in ice, next to the dugout railing and signing autographs. Sally, Charlotte, Alexis, and Patty acted as group hostesses, providing water for everyone in line and keeping everyone happy by greeting people and having fun with the kids. Both *ESPN* and *PLB* stations showed segments of the signing marathon of mainly San Francisco fans, although there were plenty of President's jerseys waiting in line as well.

Eventually word of the special team dinner reached Alex. E-mail addresses were collected and a special autographed note would be sent to those left in line. People appreciated the idea, especially when a pretty hostess took their e-mail address personally. Charlotte came up with the idea in her new role as Alex's assistant. She also realized he needed a website and a Twitter account. It would give her a day job along with her morning job as workout partner, at least until Labor Day and probably beyond, judging by the growing excitement surrounding Alex's playing and the Presidents w1nrung. She planned to fly back to Austin Thursday morning and collect clothes from her apartment, sort her mail, and pay some bills. She would join Alex and Sally Friday evening at the Presidents ballpark.

Alex would rest his cracked rib until then, and it would give him time to measure Laura's reaction to the news about Charlotte. Phillip had offered their guest suite in a newly empty-nested house if necessary.

• • •

The evening started with drinks and appetizers as the yacht headed for a slow circuit around Alcatraz Island and then crawled under the Golden Gate Bridge. Before the seven o'clock dinner, President's owner Frederick Meyers and his son, Hank, with their wives Hanna and Audrey, spoke with team members individually. Most team members and personnel had never met Frederick Meyers. He was not one to mingle with his team. He left that chore to Hank and his GM, Jim Franco. This was a special once-in-a-lifetime occasion to personally thank his players for getting his team into first place. Now he wanted them to finish the task and get Washington in the playoffs for the first time in almost eighty years. He put out the word to gather just the players and the coaching staff in the dining area downstairs. Champagne was passed out to all thirty-five people crowded into the room. Frederick Meyers rose from his seat and stood in between Jim Franco and Hank. The room became quiet as the presence of the richest owner in baseball overwhelmed the room.

"Please, I want everyone to relax and enjoy the evening. I just wanted to say a few words before we enjoy a toast together." He paused a few seconds to gather his thoughts. "We're not just playing a game of baseball. We're here to successfully lift the emotions of everyone who associates themselves with Washington. I am convinced that we live in the greatest city on the planet that lacks a group identity. This community is almost like a lost child who needs to be adopted." He paused and met eyes with Alex, and they enjoyed a smile together. "For those of you, who don't understand that, spend some time with Alex Santucci and you'll get it. He gets it and is putting his career and his life on the line to get us to the playoffs. We have him for another sixteen games before he gets married and then gets his body healed. Hammersly will be ready by then to take over until we get him back." A silent room got even quieter as reality started to set in with the players.

"I went to the last World Series in 1933 in Washington. It was a childhood experience I can't explain with words. Read up on the 1924 team that won the Series and the 1925 team that lost a heartbreaking seventh game of the Series. You guys will become heroes like them. Not just the Hall of Famers, like the great Walter Johnson, or Sam Rice, Bucky Harris, and Goose Goslin, but guys like Muddy Ruehl, Joe Judge, Ossie Bluege, Firpo Marberry, and Tom Zachary."

Players had their mouths open, impressed by the knowledge and memory of Frederick Meyers. They realized this guy was not just a rich owner but a real baseball fan.

"When you guys get home, you will be shocked by the fan reaction; they have adopted you as heroes! What you have done has lifted the city in the dead of August, when everyone is on vacation. But baseball doesn't take a vacation, and after tonight neither do we. I'm here to congratulate you for your winning streak and to remind you to keep the winning focus at home. I want to finish with a toast to the city of Washington. Let's get this city out of foster care and find them a permanent home with the Presidents!"

Chapter 44

The night on the bay was a big hit. The players could celebrate and relax at the same time in a safe atmosphere. Sally and Alex were part of the fifteen that stayed on the yacht after the ten o'clock drop-off. Others included players Henson Scott, Frank Peterson, Travis Tyler, Bruce Hammersly, Jerry Gonzalez and their wives, as well as Charlotte and her groupies, Blake Hopson and Ross Williams. The six couples were given access to the six private rooms when they needed to retire. Charlotte, Blake, and Ross would have to use the rest of the yacht to hang out, or pass out if necessary. Most of the night, the party of fifteen hung out together on the front deck of the yacht. The crew provided drinks, food, and blankets as needed.

At midnight, Alex led the party to the nine-hundred-gallon hot tub. The crew provided bathing suits for everyone. The intimate setting literally warmed up the party The eight guys were in first, having no trouble finding and getting into swim trunks. The women came in the tub one by one, announced by Alex and Bruce, who were playing masters of ceremony. Charlotte Scott, Marcia Hammersly, and Maria Gonzalez entered wearing modest one-piece suits. Sally, Patty, and Alexis dazzled the crowd with bikinis, receiving whistles and catcalls as they presented their best parts. Charlotte Roberts was the last one introduced, wearing a revealing black bikini that increased the water temperature in the already hot tub. She was cheered on to show her exceptional cleavage hidden behind her folded arms. She finally leaned forward as she slowly got used to the temperature.

Champagne was flowing as Alex started to talk about Charlotte. He had a high tolerance for alcohol, but it helped him become very emotional when he revealed that she was his step-sister. He told them about their chance meeting in Houston and how he figured out about his adopted father's affair. The players stayed silent listening to the stunning scenario and were impressed by Alex's investigative instinct. They felt honored to hear the secret and promised together it would never leave the hot tub.

Feeling pretty loose, Travis Tyler stood up with Alexis and pledged, "You are now my brother, Alex."

Alexis added, "Charlotte and Sally, you are now my sisters."

Travis continued, "We have nothing but love for you guys, and so does the Lord!" He raised his glass for a toast to seal the deal.

By 2:00 a.m., most of the party was retired to rooms. Ross Williams was passed out in the dining room. Sally and Alex were resting under a blanket on the deck. Charlotte and Blake looked at the stars in the sky. Only Alex and Charlotte made it to sunrise awake, telling stories all night about childhood mischief. Alex added experiences with Gene that he could remember, and Charlotte hung on every word. By sunrise Charlotte was sitting in front of Alex, leaning back on his chest like she was a baby bear enveloped by a big bear. Several blankets surrounded both of them, keeping them warm as they sat on a deck bench watching the eastern horizon perform its daily miracle.

• • •

Leah had settled in at Laura's home, quickly becoming her best friend. After performing her duty as an emissary from Alex over a week ago, she flew home for a couple of days to see Charles and to settle some business concerns. She came back Monday morning to help Laura cope with her new life, now knowing about Gene's daughter. Dr. Walton spent the weekend making sure Laura was okay while Leah was gone. When she returned, they took long walks all week and exercised at the YMCA. They prayed and sang together like girlfriends. Leah played the guitar and shared her music with Laura. Finally by Thursday, Laura was getting excited to see Alex and meet Charlotte. She had only feelings of love for Charlotte, who was the only innocent one in the affair. Perhaps Charlotte would have more privacy at Phillip's house, Laura thought. Otherwise she was welcome at her big house. She purposely had not talked to Alex about how she was adjusting to the news. She wanted to do that in person, if necessary. She felt Alex should not be bothered by her concerns, because he was in the middle of a pennant race.

    Alex and Sally arrived at 6:45 p.m. from the airport. When she saw them, Laura was overwhelmed with emotions, not realizing how much she missed them. She was disappointed not to meet Charlotte but understood about her coming in tomorrow after a much-needed stop in Austin. A warm home-cooked meal awaited them. They sat at the table-Laura, Henry, Leah, Sally, and Alex-to say a prayer. Leah asked the Lord to help the five of them act as a family to help Laura with her thoughts and feelings and to help Charlotte to feel their love as a family. They all agreed with simultaneous, "Amen."

• • •

    The New York Firemen were not expected to be a very good ball club due to last season's change of general manager and manager who were committed to rebuilding. But surprisingly, several things fell into place to help them compete for the playoffs this year. The pitching was vastly improved with the return of a former Cy Young winner Sebastion Montez and the development of knuckleballer P.B. Johnson, better known as PB&J, who was leading the league at the All-Star break with fifteen wins. The hitting was helped with the return of several injured players, most notably former All-Star third baseman Craig Affirm, who was batting over .350, and young first baseman slugger Dale Harmon with twenty-two homeruns. But the most important thing that helped the Firemen this year was moving in the fences at Citifield in Queens. For three years, the pitcher's park had reduced Affirm from a thirty-homer guy to a twelve-to-fifteen homer guy and ruined the swing of highly paid, free agent, left fielder Joel Black, from which he had never recovered. The monster sixteen-foot fences in left- center were shortened to eight feet and brought in fifteen feet, and the 415-foot right-center field fence was brought in twenty-five feet to make it 390 feet.

New York had scouted the pitching approaches of Phoenix and San Francisco to Alex Santucci. They were trying to unpuzzle how they stopped the homerun streak, yet had not ended his hitting streak, which was now at seventeen games, or his RBI streak of five games, and RBI's in sixteen of his last seventeen games. New York would continue to pitch him outside and low whenever possible.

• • •

Alex arrived at Presidents Park at 4:37 p.m., Friday, August 17, stiff and in pain from the rib injury. The night of celebration and a long plane ride home did not help his rehabilitation. He met with Dr. Walton for an examination, an **MRI,** and some blood work.

"I know this will fall on deaf ears, but you may want to sit out a few games. Another direct shot to that side might start a chain reaction of bleeding we can't control."

"I promise: no more celebrations or alcohol or hot tubs or diving at balls until at least Sunday!" Alex joked, trying to get the serious look off of Henry's face.

"You know, Alex, I'm starting to feel like Michael Jackson's doctor-except I'm not getting a multimillion-dollar retainer!"

Alex felt in his pocket and pulled out a cash roll and started to peel off hundreds. "Let's see...will five hundred keep you quiet?"

Henry finally smiled. "Oh, sorry, let me guess...You're Henry Hill in *Good Fellas.* Right! Either way, I'm going down!" Alex pulled in Dr. Walton for a bear hug and looked him in the eye. "Henry, I told you, I'm not going down. Remember, I agreed to surgery right after Labor Day. Hell, Mr. Meyers told the whole team about it-so I have to do it now!"

Henry waited for Alex to pull away and turn toward the door." Well, that's the best news I've heard since the winning streak. Now listen: stop playing baseball like a contact sport!" Henry smiled, feeling good about getting in the last word.

He returned to his office to find a FedEx package on his desk. It was from the National Library of Medicine at NIH in Bethesda. It contained all the research and surgery notes from thirty years ago when Dr. Santucci diagnosed a rare abdominal blood disorder in Father Higgins. He had been nervously waiting to research the Higgins case and to see what Alex was facing with his surgery. Dr. Walton had been quietly recruiting several surgeons from Georgetown and Johns Hopkins Hospital teams to game plan a laparoscopic surgery to remove, contain, or fix the growth in the area between Alex's pancreas and adrenal gland. Now that he had the notes of the Higgins case, Alex's MRI and blood work, he would have a video conference with the surgeons to plan all contingencies. If things went well, Alex could return in two weeks or less. If the surgery did not go well for Alex, then the season would be lost and maybe his career as well.

• • •

Certain players in baseball do not perform well

on the road. Sometimes ballparks have different hitting backgrounds or the infield grass is longer or the hotel's beds are not comfortable. In the case of Carlos Mendoza and Vito Valencia, they just missed their families. Each had three young children and wives who did not ever travel. Mendoza especially was under great pressure with a big contract that had the hometown fans complaining about his subpar 2011 season. Recently, since Alex Santucci arrived almost three weeks ago, the press had ignored him completely, and slowly he was feeling comfortable with his stroke. During his batting practice sessions with Alex, they talked about pitchers and their power strokes. He was just as strong and athletic as Alex but had ignored his instincts to pull the ball since his slump began last year. He had learned two things from Alex: run thirty minutes every morning to clear out your mind and to increase your body's blood supply during games, and get your hands through on every inside pitch. After a night of home cooking, he was ready to rock New York's pitching.

Manager Charley Jackson had a hunch about Carlos Mendoza and moved him up to fourth in the lineup behind Alex for the New York series. Abel LeMont was more than happy to move down to seventh, where pitchers would not game plan for him. Jackson had met with him to explain his decision.

The veteran LeMont told his manager, "I'm just a ballplayer who's glad to be in the lineup. You've got no explaining to do for me."

The six-game home stand was sold out except for standing room only tickets and some diamond seating behind home plate selling for close to two hundred dollars. Leo Lawrence was starting for the Presidents, coming off two impressive wins on the road, including a shutout in his last outing in Phoenix. The crowd was delirious in the first inning when Mendoza hit a three-run homer for an early 3-0 lead. Mendoza's power hitting continued with a grand slam homerun in the third inning to boost the lead to 7-0. Lawrence was cruising with a two-hit shutout into the sixth inning, when he lost his location on his fastball. Before he could get the second out, the Firemen had exploded with six runs. Angelucci came in to contain the backdraft and a 7-6 lead. Alex got his third hit of the game in the seventh inning with a two-run double. He then stole third, cautiously sliding on his right side, and scored on a sacrifice fly by Medoza, his eighth RBI of the game. When nobody was paying attention, LeMont added a two-run homer in the eighth to finish the scoring for a 12-7 Presidents win. It was their seventeenth victory in a row and gave them a six-game lead over Miami.

Cool air had arrived as the game ended, which made it pleasant for several players to stay on the field, especially Carlos Mendoza. Carlos was staying close behind Alex Santucci, signing autographs and slugging the ball like him. He thought to himself, "It sure is nice to be home."

Alex hardly noticed the cracked rib in his left side as he signed for thirty minutes after the game. The trainers had to drag him inside for ice treatments to treat the inflammation. He closed his eyes for a while as he got comfortable on a training table, with a couple of pillows under his knees and one under his head. His ribs were wrapped in ice, and the trainer was rubbing his calf muscles, which knotted up after games sometimes. He had been forcing fluids for the whole game but probably needed an IV bag.

Slowly the sounds of the room became quiet, and he found himself on a pitching mound, staring down at the plate for a sign from the catcher. He thought, "What are all these signs? I only throw one pitch!"

He looked over at third base and saw no one was playing third.

He saw his high school coach yelling, "Hurry up and pitch the ball so you can cover third!"

"That's weird," Alex thought. He fired a fastball at the plate and then tried to get over to cover third, but as he ran toward the base, it kept getting farther away. Gene Santucci was coaching third, "You're doing a great job, son. I thought Charlotte could help you out-that's all I was thinking-since I was gone. She's here now!"

Alex first felt her touch, then smelled her scent and heard her soft voice.

"Boy, he's out cold, huh?" she said to the trainer as she took Alex's hand.

Alex fought to wake up, feeling her warmth on his right hand. He tried to focus, seeing her red hair hanging down in front of her face as she leaned toward him to check out his face. She was wearing a red Presidents home jersey with Santucci and a number seven on the back, fashionably unbuttoned to show a pretty necklace. But in her current leaning position, there was plentiful cleavage to wake up the average man. "Wow! Now that's a pretty sight to wake up to!" Alex muttered. Charlotte was clueless to her exposure as she hugged him.

Alex sat up to get her upright and help him unwrap his ice treatment. He was glad to warm up after the chaos of his dream, wondering what Gene was trying to tell him.

"Did you get everything done in Austin that you wanted?"

"Yeah, it was good. Felt kind of lonely. I'm glad to be back.

Hey, quite a game, huh? What got into Mendoza? I guess he liked moving up in the order!

Alex jumped down from the table and pulled a shirt on.

"I think he likes being home... I guess everybody does."

Chapter 45

The weekend was blessed with a preview of fall football weather in August and enough scoring in the two games to preview the coming pigskin season as well. Danube Rivers was on the mound on a lovely Saturday evening. He pitched as though he wanted to be out enjoying it instead of throwing a baseball by giving up seven runs in the first three innings. Luckily the Presidents bats were not cooled off by the weather. Sebastion Mendez could not get loose and was rocked by Carlos Mendoza, who once again struck early and often, with two more homeruns in the first three innings, keeping the score close at 7-5. Ross Williams pitched perfect fourth, fifth and sixth innings, dominating the Firemen with six strikeouts. Vito Valencia showed that his homecoming was going well with a go-ahead three-run homerun in the seventh inning. Alex singled in two insurance runs in the eighth inning to seal the 10-7 victory. Their eighteenth victory in a row, gave them a seven-game lead over Miami.

Phillip and Carol came to the game with their new house guest, Charlotte, and picked up Guy at UMD in College Park. The four of them met Sally and Alex after the game for a late-night dinner at the *Old Ebbitt Grill* at 675 Fifteenth Street in DC, within shouting distance of the White House. They enjoyed the raw oysters, steamed clams, jumbo shrimp, crab soup, and crab cakes.

Guy held court, talking about playing college football how the game was different from high school and the challenge of covering speedy receivers. He missed playing quarterback but knew he could get on the field quicker playing safety. Alex asked him if he hit anybody yet in practice. Guy smiled and said he didn't care about running into people; he just tried to intercept the ball or break up the pass on defense. He liked tackling runners because it was so hard to do. He had to predict moves, like guessing on pass routes.

Alex said it sounded like guessing pitches. They agreed it was a part of the game plan, to know what your opponent would do ahead of time. Charlotte said it was like being an engineer, where you had to learn all the systems before planning out a particular new one. Phillip said it was like listening to a client and surmising their behavior based on their story. Carol said it was like mining the medical data to figure out what a community needed for health care and what the costs would be. Sally said it was like teaching a class and researching what the students could learn from the course based on their results on their first quiz. They all realized they were playing their game in their profession. It involved homework, research, planning, prediction, and being physically as well as mentally ready to make the right move.

Phillip had been listening most of the night. He felt proud of his wife and children and felt glad being a part of the family. His emotions were building inside, becoming harder to communicate during the evening. He raised his glass and asked to speak. "I feel so lucky having Alex in DC, Guy at UMD, and now Charlotte to bring life to the house when Carol is on the road. I need a coach to become fit again." He looked at Charlotte, gesturing with his glass. "Maybe you can help me, Charlotte, in the next few weeks to become physically in shape again. I still want to be able to throw the football with Guy and hit a baseball with Alex. I want to feel alive again!"

Phillip had lived with heart disease and neck pain for the last ten years, which kept him to sports like golf and pinch- hitting in softball instead of running and biking. He never talked about a knee injury forty years ago that destroyed his football career or having to abandon his counseling career over twenty years ago. Taking care of his kids and his family was his life.

The tears rolled down his face as he lifted his glass to finish the toast. The table exploded with emotions. Charlotte expressed excitement about being needed. Carol nestled affectionately with her man, missing the young athlete that she first fell in love with as a teenager. Both Alex and Guy were overwhelmed with their dad's show of emotions. They both hugged their father and agreed that he was their guiding light and it was time for him to take care of himself physically.

As the time approached midnight, Alex asked for volunteers to attend Mass at St. Dominic's at eight o'clock. Reluctantly everyone agreed, and with that they quickly headed for the exits to get some sleep!

• • •

Father Higgins was proud to have his superstar back in town and in the front row. The Alex Santucci entourage was now up to eight. He was happy to see Laura, Henry, and Phillip, but had to guess that Carol and Guy were Phillip's wife and son. But he was dazed by Charlotte and her resemblance to Dr. Santucci. He quickly finished the Gospel reading and presented another off-the-cuff sermon about how the purity of the sport of baseball was like the purity of Christ. Most parishioners were too sleepy to notice the odd purity metaphor. They did know that the Presidents were in first place and that Father Higgins was a big fan. What they did not know yet was how it would bring them closer to God!

• • •

The final game of the New York series was an afternoon affair on Sunday, August 19, at 1:35 p.m. The Presidents, with Tony Johnson on the mound, were facing the knuckleballer P. B. Johnson. Alex, unlike most major league hitters, loved to face a knuckleball pitch. He thought it was like playing slow-pitch softball where you looked under the ball to drive it out of the ballpark. Before the game, Alex was preaching to pick a spot in front of the plate where they wanted the ball, and swing through that spot if the ball came out of *PB&J's* hand above it. He said to get low enough in the box to see it coming down instead of watching it drop. The troops followed orders and scored eight runs in the 1st inning. Mendoza hit his fifth homerun of the series, driving in three runs, which was followed by Valencia's second three-run homerun in consecutive at bats. Tony Johnson could not hold the lead and gave up a touchdown of runs in the fourth inning and a field goal in the fifth inning. The 10-8 lead by the Firemen was extinguished by a three-run homer by Alex Santucci in the sixth inning to retake the lead, 11-10. It was his first homerun in nine games since his historic streak and his thirty-fourth homerun of the season. Clay "Bean" Counter blew a save in the ninth, giving up a go-ahead two-run homerun to Craig Affirm. Then Dale Harmon added the extra point with a solo homerun to extend the lead to 13-11.

    The bottom of the ninth inning had every seat in Presidents Park empty because all the fans were on their feet to either witness an end to the winning streak or to experience an amazing comeback to get one game closer to breaking the all-time streak of twenty-one victories in a row held by the 1935 Chicago Cubs. Chris Patek led off the inning with a strikeout. Pinch hitter Madison Bennett popped up to the second basemen for the second out. The crowd was cheering through their anxiety as Blake Hopson came to the plate. Firemen reliever Pete Anderson threw two sinkers in the dirt that Blake chased after. Blake stepped out and heard Jerry Gonzalez yell out, "Calm the hell down, and stop chasing women in the dirt," referring to the baseball. Blake fouled off a couple of high fastballs. Finally, Anderson left him "a women to date-over the plate," another Gonzalez phrase, and Blake smoked it to deep center. Travis Sanchez got a glove on it but smashed into the wall, causing the ball to fall to the ground. Hopson made it to third easily. Gonzalez was next up and worked the count to 3-2, then fouled off three pitches before taking ball four.

The crowd reached jet-engine-level noise on the decibel meter when Alex came to plate. He was three for three so far, needing a triple to hit for the cycle, but he was thinking a field goal would win it. Anderson thought about walking him, but Mendoza lurked in the on-deck circle with a hot bat that the Firemen had not put out yet. The first sinker to Alex did not make it to the plate. The second one was a bit inside but a little higher for ball two. The third sinker was the charm, hanging in the strike zone to become a Santucci screamer, a low liner that hung for a moment near the warning track in center field. Sanchez raced back and jumped for it at the fence and again smashed into the wall for a second head-ringing. Alex rounded the bases with glee, ready for the celebration at home plate. The field goal was good, over the center field fence, cementing an unforgettable 14-13 win. The Presidents nineteenth victory in a row gave them an eight-game lead on Miami and Atlanta, who was coming in town for a three-game series.

• • •

Alex was looking forward to a morning routine until the Labor Day wedding and the following day's surgery. The ribs were sore but definitely healing. The Presidents would have an easy two-hour ride to Philadelphia on Friday for a weekend series, then home on Monday for a day off, followed by a short two-game series in Miami. They would close out the month with two at home against St. Louis and then two more with St. Louis to start September. A four-game series with Chicago would start on Labor Day.

Alex planned to run this morning starting at five forty-five to meet Charlotte on the newly reinforced Cedar Lane Bridge over Rock Creek near Beach Drive by six. They would run for another thirty minutes along the park, ending up at Phillip's house a little after six thirty. They would then corral Phillip and drive up to the Bethesda YMCA for some swimming and weight work. Phillip spent most of his time on the stationary bike and doing leg weights. Charlotte was up for the challenge to keep up with Alex and supervise Phillip at the same time.

After a successful ninety minutes of exertion, Alex enjoyed the short walk home to check in on Sally and grab some fruit, protein, and coffee with Laura and Leah. Of course, Laura had invited Phillip and Leah to join them. They were already sitting at the kitchen counter and sipping hot coffee, having beaten the clueless Alex who had walked.

• • •

Dr. Walton was at the Cisco Network room at the NIH National Library of Medicine, ready to discuss Alex's surgery. He had spent all weekend examining Dr. Santucci's research on the blood work involving Father Griffin's diagnosis. He was stunned at the similarities of the network of blood vessels and tissues, which had grown from the adrenal gland to the pancreas. He had several potential aneurisms that had developed within the blood vessel network, apparently from a short boxing career at Fordham University. Like the finding from Alex's MRI, there seemed to be a combination of a natural growth from injured tissue and blood vessels that could lead to the deadly possibility of an aneuristic bleed.

The Georgetown team of surgeons, feeling a home team advantage, went first, reporting confidence that the laparoscopic procedure was doable without incurring major surgery possibilities. The Hopkins group countered that it was highly likely that there was a foreign object in the tangled web of tissue and blood vessels of Alex's stomach. They believed it was the only explanation for the size of the mass and that it might not be able to come out laparoscopically.

There were three things that both surgical teams agreed upon. First, Alex would have to stop taking the Duloxetine immediately and all NSAID medications. Second, Alex was risking death on the baseball field if he continued to play for the next two weeks. Third, Dr. Walton was going to tell him.

Henry asked Dr. Ross Chang from Johns Hopkins to lead the surgery, with Dr. Natalie Woodson from Georgetown University to assist. The rest of the doctors agreed on one thing: they all wanted to be there!

• • •

Dr. Walton made it back to the Johnson Avenue house in time to join the breakfast crowd. He pulled Alex aside and told him to stop the Duloxetine and any NSAIDs, as recommended by the surgeons. Alex had not taken the medication since Saturday because his prescription was out, and he had forgotten to pick it up. Henry made it clear that any mood changes be reported to him immediately. Alex was not concerned, because he was getting used to the ice treatments and the ice tub for pain relief. It would be more of a challenge than he thought!

• • •

The Atlanta Chops were coming to town playing their best baseball of the season. Their name derived from the beef and veal industry and was an unnamed homage to the Tomahawk Chop, made famous with the last politically incorrect nickname.

All of their injured players had returned to their starting lineup, and the signing of a veteran former All-Star pitcher had rounded out their rotation. Right-hander Hudson Lake would be asked to be the first Chop to slice up the hungry Presidents lineup. Atlanta had brought with them a humid Gulf of Mexico air mass of ninety-five-degree weather with them to replace the beautiful weekend off all-type weather in Washington, DC.

Throngs of sports media were camped out at the ballpark doing pregame broadcasts covering stories of the Presidents winning streak. The celebrity media was updating the upcoming Alex and Sally wedding on Labor Day and the new redhead working out with Alex.

ESPN Reporter Riley Preston did a long piece on *Baseball Tonight* covering "The Seven Streaks of August" for the Presidents. He led off with, "Not only did Alex Santucci hit twelve homeruns in ten consecutive games, and the POTUS pitching staff went sixty innings without a run-both new Professional League Records-but the Presidents are on a nineteen-game winning streak, within two victories of tying the major league record of twenty-one games held by the 1935 Chicago Cubs."

Ever the stickler, Riley pointed out that the 1916 New York Giants won twenty-six in a row with a tie game in the middle of the streak, which would make it the longest streak without a loss. The big surprise to viewers was his uncovering of four other streaks that were currently under the radar. Three were by Alex Santucci. The first was for the most homeruns in a month: currently he had fourteen homeruns in August; the record was twenty homeruns, held by Sammy Sosa since 1998. The second was the most consecutive games in a row with an RBI: currently he was at eight games; the record was seventeen games, held by Ray Grimes since 1922. The third, and the most obscure of the streaks, only to be uncovered by Riley Preston, was for the most games in a row with three or more hits: currently he had four games; the record was six games, held by George Brett since 1976 and Jimmy Johnston since 1923.

The last streak was the most prestigious because it involved pitching. Presidents' ace pitcher Travis Tyler was on the road to beat the streak of consecutive innings without a run: currently he was at thirty-nine innings; the record was fifty-nine innings, held by Orel Hershiser since 1988.

Riley pointed out that the "Great" Walter Johnson still held the American League record of fifty-six scoreless innings, unlikely to ever be broken in the designated hitter league. Riley Preston ended his report with a humorous yet errant insight to the grandness of the baseball being played by Alex Santucci and the Presidents. "By the way, Alex Santucci has a hit in all twenty National League games he has played so far. But hey-who's really keeping track of that!"

Chapter 46

Nat Sheridan, editor of the *New York Post* tabloid newspaper, was following the Alex Santucci story, trying to get a picture. Ever since he broke the story of Alex's health problems, he had been trying to get his hands on the MRI of his abdomen. The price was up to fifty thousand with verification on authenticity. The last thing he needed was to spend money for nothing. He already did plenty of that. His next breaking story on this could not be so easily ignored by the mainline press or denied by Santucci with such ease. He wanted to show that thing growing in his pancreas. Sheridan was convinced it was cancer, but his last lead at Sloan-Kettering had grown cold.

Now he had something else that might hold him over until the evidence arrived proving a cancerous growth. It was a great picture of a redhead with cleavage wearing a Presidents Jersey with a number seven and "Santucci" on the back. He noticed she was very cute with a great body; too bad he had the truth about her. Reporting an affair, even before the big wedding, about baseball's new hero would have been something special-millions of hits' worth on the paper's website. But even Nat Sheridan could not report a blatant lie, especially when he was the first to discover the real story. A step-sister from Alex's adoptive father's affair: interesting but not currently sexy, murderous, or close to death-his three best sellers for a leading headline. Well, this one had to do for now:

Santucci's Redheaded Gal Is Long-Lost Step-Sister

• • •

Atlanta was not ready for the carnival atmosphere

at Presidents Park. Hudson Lake's sinker was not working in the humid air, and the hot POTUS lineup went through Lake without getting wet or cooling off. Three runs in the first inning and three runs in the second gave Phillip Fields enough confidence to go six innings while giving up only one run. The bullpen of Ramos, Peterson, and Counter recovered from their weekend of giving up touch-downs and field goals to sizzle the Chops. Alex had three straight singles and a first-inning RBI to help the Presidents get a 6-1 win, their twentieth in a row.

Alex was bushed after the game and had a quick ice bath instead of his usual autograph hour with the fans. He went home and was in bed by 11:10 p.m. on August 20. He barely noticed his radio alarm at 5:45 a.m. on August 21, when it played his current favorite CD, ELO's *Face the Music* and the first track, "Fire on High." He had played it every morning since hearing it from Leah on his trip east on July 31.

Sally was out cold. Still young enough to sleep through anything, he thought. He set out for his run, starting slow until he woke up halfway to Wisconsin Avenue. Charlotte was leaning back on the Rock Creek Bridge railing, looking up at the new sky when Alex finally made it to their meeting place. Without a sound, she put her head down and led Alex toward Beach Drive. She had a lot of energy this morning and forced Alex to get in gear. Always the competitor, he quickly bought into the challenge, and they made it to Phillip's house in record time.

Phillip was looking at his lap-top on the patio when they both arrived out of breath, landing their backsides into chairs like nine-year-olds. Phillip was on the *MSNBC* website, which was reporting the *New York Post* story about Charlotte and Alex. They both laughed at it, especially when Charlotte realized her cleavage-revealing POTUS uniform.

"Why didn't you say something to me about the girls hanging out like that!" She playfully requested from Alex.

"Are you kidding me? And ruin the view? I couldn't do that to my fellow man or teammates!" He argued chauvinistically.

She smacked him several times on the arm before dragging him off to the YMCA. "Just for that I'm kicking your ass in swimming today!"

Phillip grabbed his stuff and followed quickly behind the nine-year-old kids!

• • •

Alex went back to sleep after breakfast and slept until 2:12 p.m. It was his first extended nap since July. He felt great when he woke up and made it to the stadium by 4:00 p.m., where all eyes tonight were on Travis Tyler and his scoreless innings streak. Tying the winning streak did not seem as important as winning for Travis, even though it would produce the same result. Every interview was answered with how they were supporting Tyler instead of answering about the winning streak. Certainly it put tying the three-hit streak for Alex was on the back page. Alex enjoyed the chance to be a supportive teammate.

Alexis Tyler was a nervous wreck, surviving on very little sleep, making sure everything at home was perfect for Travis. She was sleeping on the couch before his starts to make sure he got a good night's sleep.

Charlotte, Patty, and Sally were being helpful friends listening with all ears before, during, and after the game.

Travis was all over the place in the first inning, walking the bases full before striking out the side to end the mess he created. He walked two more in the second inning and one in the third inning, but two double plays helped keep down his pitch count. He found a groove starting in the fourth inning, getting nine in a row through the sixth inning. He was hovering around ninety pitches, but Manager Jackson threw that statistic out the window as long as the scoreboard showed no runs and no hits. Travis finally noticed his teammates had left him alone after batting in the sixth inning. It first dawned on him starting the seventh inning that he had a no-hitter going. He mowed down the Chops in the seventh and the eighth innings.

Alex started the seventh with his first hit of the game but was stranded at second base. Finally, Travis gave up an infield single to start the ninth inning, which was wiped out by a great double play started by Gonzalez up the middle. He then finished the ninth with a strikeout, hoping for a run in the bottom of the ninth.

With two outs in the bottom of the ninth and Gonzalez on second base, Alex lined a single to left field. The crowd went wild as Gonzo headed home, but a perfect throw struck him down to keep the game scoreless. Travis refused to give up the ball even though he was at 115 pitches. He pitched a scoreless tenth and eleventh, and then finally hit the trainer's table for an IV bag.

Alex came up in the bottom of the eleventh with the bases loaded and two outs. Charley Jackson said later, "It was like a pregnant woman two weeks after her delivery date: something had to give!" With the winning streak on the line, the sell-out crowd was trying to make the Chops pitcher crazy, banging on their seats, bouncing off the ground, and chanting, "DC wins," trying to will the Presidents to victory. Alex felt no emotion being in the batter's box. He felt rested and clear minded. He was in singles mode, choking up an inch on the bat and aiming for the middle of the diamond. He smashed the first pitch off the pitcher's mound and up in the air almost twenty feet. He flew down to first and beat the throw. The run scored and the Presidents won 1-0, tying history for their twenty-first victory in a row!

• • •

    Ron Roswell led off his column the next day with his feelings about Alex.

    "And by the way, Alex Santucci got his third hit of the game tying George Brett for the record and his tenth game in a row with an RBI, but who cares? The Presidents got their 21st win in a row and lead the NL East by an incredible 10 games!" He filled in the rest of the column with the story of Travis Tyler's performance and his gut-check performance. He ended by quoting himself. "But the real story 'BY THE WAY' is Alex Santucci, whose 22-game performance with the Presidents is becoming legend. At this point, I only have this left in me to write, God Bless You, Alex. God Bless You!"

Chapter 47

Leah, Laura, Sally, and Charlotte were told to watch the Wednesday night game at home. Alex was more comfortable knowing that they were safe because of the impending celebration at Presidents Park. Alex was confident they would win the game and break the winning streak record. He wanted to experience the situation without worrying about their safety before, during, or after the game.

Dr. Walton was at the game as a part of the training staff, and Phillip was watching the game from the owner's box. Alex had installed a sixty-inch Samsung LED television in their suite's living room, which gave Sally a chance to host the women in their private part of Laura's home. Guy and the entire Terp football team were ready to watch the game from the lounge area of the practice facility. Grace was hosting a Presidents Party and had a dozen friends over at her townhouse in Raleigh. Nancy in Florida had all of her friends over to the house to watch the game while her siblings in Charlotte, Claudette and Paul, were together with friends watching the game. Even their father, Charles, had his friends at the country club check it out in the lounge. The president of Princeton, her fund-raising committee, and Paul Brightman were having tea on the front portico of her residence with the game on just inside. Margaret and her fellow nurses were ready to check in on the action in the staff lounge between patient care. Cousin Philly in Manhattan had a cocktail party with a television put in the living room for the occasion. The fall-like Kansan weather allowed Roger and Elena Keegan and fellow Jayhawks to enjoy the game on television out on the back porch.

Most Kansas City Crowns fans were not watching the Crowns, including Alex Skarstedt, Hal Baker, everyone from Anthony's Restaurant, and many residents of 909 Walnut. Instead they watched their distant hero, Alex, on *ESPN*.

Every media member from every newspaper, sports

channel, cable and national news outlet that could get media credentials were at the game, including Bonnie Bramlett, Ron Roswell, and Riley Preston. There were rumors that the president of the US himself was trying to get a ticket, but the owner of the baseball Presidents had to say "not today." Some were calling it the toughest ticket in town since the Congressional Watergate Hearings.

・・・

Alex changed his routine in the morning, instead choosing to meet Charlotte and Phillip at the YMCA at six to swim and then go down to the Ayrlawn field to work on his pitching and do some sprinting. Phillip was excited to play catcher on the baseball field in the far corner of the park. It was rarely used for baseball anymore because most of the infield was grown-in for the soccer field. But there was still a pitcher's mound with a rubber and a home plate, sixty feet, six inches apart.

Charlotte was asked to hold a stick and stand in the batter's box. Her five-foot six-inch height did not exactly present a major league target, but Alex was not really focused on his red-haired sister with a ponytail hanging out of the special pink Presidents hat. Alex first tossed ten pitches directly into Phillip's mitt without much effort. Charlotte became braver as each pitch hit its target precisely.

"Is that all you got this morning, Alex? I wish I had a real bat... I'd be crushing those lollipops!"

Phillip tried to temper the trash-talking. "Alex, keep them coming just like that-nice and smooth!" Phillip shouted.

Alex used the next ten pitches to get used to the rubber, pitch from the stretch, and use a little bit more sidearm. A few zipped in around Charlotte's waistline into the mitt.

"You think that's supposed to scare me? Come on, Santucci. Those are all frozen ropes back up the middle!"

Alex thought, "This woman has been hanging around Blake Hopson too much!" He pitched from his windup in the next ten pitches and started to feel loose with his regular, two-seam fast-ball on the outside corner.

Charlotte could see the increase in velocity and finally had a solid comment. "There we go, brother. I think you got something to build on there!"

Phillip stood and threw back the ball for first time. "I'll give you some targets, okay?"

Alex nodded and hit each spot with his next ten pitches, switching between his two-seam and four-seam fastball. He grabbed the last throw back from Phillip and walked behind the mound, thinking of the thousands of hours he spent on this field. He wondered whether his adoptive father, Gene, if he could see him today, would remember all those catches with him starting at the age of five until he left him at the age of fifteen. He felt emptiness in the pit of his stomach, realizing how much he missed his adoptive father. His eyes teared up as he turned back. Trying to ignore his tears, he turned back toward the plate.

"Okay, Miss Charlotte, only ten more pitches to pose for!" Alex closed his eyes and thought about being in a game and focusing on the catcher's mitt. He opened his eyes as he started his windup and let loose a 95-mph fastball, then another, then another. He switched his grip to a four-seam fastball and fired three more 95-mph fast-balls tailing away from Charlotte over the outside corner.

Charlotte was silent, with sweat beading up on her neck, feeling like she had an apple on her head with arrows coming, missing her by inches. She stood very still, counting only four more left.

Alex went back to his two-seamer for the last four pitches, moving his arm slot below his normal three-quarter delivery. The first one started at 98 mph, then came a 99-mph pitch, then 100 mph, and finally 101 mph. Alex was guessing of course, but he knew it was very close to reality.

Charlotte fell to her knees and let out a big sigh of relief as

Phillip ran the last ball out to Alex.

"Great job, son. I see you've been working on your pitching since we talked about the dream." Seeing the tears in his eyes, Phillip put his right arm around Alex and patted their mitts together. "Brings up some stuff?"

"Yeah, just good stuff, feels great to be out here. I miss it a little bit!"

"That is good stuff. You're living it out every day. Nice pitching too!"

They returned to home plate and helped Charlotte collect herself off the ground. "I'm bringing a bat next time to defend myself. How did you learn to throw like that? Does Jackson know you throw like that?"

"Are you kidding? I wouldn't give him a chance to throw me out to the wolves. Those guys can hit fastballs all day. I would get killed. Maybe if we were down by fifteen runs and we needed to save some pitchers...It might be fun."

Phillip and Charlotte looked at each other and laughed, knowing they had seen something special!

• • •

Thousands of people were lined up and down Half Street, partying and waiting for a glimpse of any player coming into the team parking lot. Alex drove in his Acura TL, got out, and came to the fence with a Sharpie to sign some baseballs and connect with some of the fans. Security cut off the session after a few minutes as hundreds crowded the area.

Alex was looking forward to batting practice under the stands and out on the field. He was feeling surprisingly chipper considering it was his fourth day without any medication. He had been sleeping very soundly and without any dreams he could remember. There was very little soreness in his body. He was hoping it was from his increased workouts since Charlotte had been around. The humidity had broken and the night would be perfect for baseball.

• • •

Leo Lawrence was on the mound for the Presidents hoping to make up for giving up six runs in his last outing. The rest of the team was loose after winning the thriller last night. They felt that the pressure was off since tying the streak already put them in the record books. And besides, they were ten games ahead in the NL East race.

Carlos Mendoza and Alex Santucci put on a show in batting practice, each hitting ten balls in the stands. The crowds in the bleachers, scattering for the souvenirs, were like ants coming together for a fallen crumb off the dinner table. Alex's hands felt smooth and quick to the ball. They both knew they were ready for the game.

Carlos caught Leo heading to the bullpen for warm-ups.

"Don't worry about runs tonight, my friend. You relax and pitch your game, and we will provide enough for you." Leo let loose his contagious smile and gave Carlos a thumbs up.

The crowd cheered for every strike in the first inning as Leo struck out the first two batters. He showed some frustration after walking the third batter after not getting a call on a 3-2 count. Then he misplayed a grounder up the middle and loaded the bases with another walk.

Manager Charley Jackson took an unusual trip to the mound to send a message to Leo. "Look, I don't care if they clear the bases; the troops are ready to run tonight. Start locating your fastball now and you'll get through sixth innings at least. That's what I want."

Leo nodded without a smile.

Atlanta twenty-year-veteran Junior Smith was the batter, a switch-hitter batting right-handed. He loved fastballs and took Leo's second one to right-center for a bases-clearing double. Leo struck out the next hitter on three straight fastballs.

In the first five innings, Mendoza and Santucci combined for four hits, three homeruns, and six RBIs, doubling Atlanta 6-3. Leo Lawrence was following orders, using his fastball 80 percent of the time, accumulating ten strikeouts in five innings. In the sixth, Lawrence gave up two solo homeruns between three strikeouts that brought Atlanta within a run at 6-5. Leo was done for the night with thirteen strikeouts through six innings.

Manager Jackson gave him kudos as he came into the dugout for staying with his stuff. "Leo, don't worry about those runs. You went with your best stuff...like I told you. Now, we got some more runs coming. Don't worry this will be your win!"

His teammates in the dugout followed suit as they tried to get the disappointment out of his system. The crowd was on a perpetual high, ready for the Presidents to take their swings in the sixth. Henson Scott singled, moved to second on a Patek sacrifice, and scored on a Ren Rivera pinch-hit single. The top of the order stranded Rivera with two fly-outs. Mario Ramos pitched a scoreless seventh inning. Alex led off the bottom of the seventh with the crowd howling like the wind, trying to squeeze out a third hit from Alex to break the consecutive three-hit record.

The players in the dugout were very aware that this might be Alex's last chance to extend the three-hit streak and break the record, which was first set the year Alex was born. Ahead 7-5, the players were very confident of getting the win streak, but most cared more about Alex's current streak. His leadership and remarkable play had moved the Presidents on to a higher scale of team play. Most losing teams focus on individual goals, whereas winning teams focus only on team goals. This team had broken new ground of team play. They cared so much about the team that they were willing to guarantee a win to further a teammate's individual record, or records in Alex's case. In other words, this player's pursuit meant so much to the team's overall makeup that it took the possibility of losing out of the formula. In Alex's case, breaking the record meant nothing to him. He would forfeit a hit if it meant a walk, a sacrifice fly, or bunt would win the game. Fortunately, leading off an inning meant he could do what he usually tried to do-get a hit!

While Alex was in the on-deck-circle taking swings, Manager Jackson yelled at him "to be a hitter," which meant, "do not take a walk." He was facing Arnold Nichols, a side arming right-hander with a rising fastball that was almost impossible to hit. Alex's only success with him was to pull the ball with a downward swing to catch the rising fastball or to hope to hack at an outside pitch to right field. Nichols came right down the middle for a strike. Alex thought it was high but he had no swing for it anyway. Then came a pitch in the dirt for ball one, followed by a foul back to the stands for strike two. Alex was hoping for the inside pitch, and he got it. He swung down on it and hit a high chopper toward third base and past the diving third baseman's glove in foul territory. The ball headed toward the corner where the ball girl sits near the stands as Alex rounded first and the crowd went delirious.

Before Alex could start digging for an easy double, he saw the third base umpire heading to meet the home plate umpire. As their eyes met halfway between third and home, they both in unison pointed toward foul territory. Alex stood motionless. Manager Charley Jackson was out of the dugout like a jackrabbit, pointing to the third base bag. The crowd was in disarray, starting to realize it was a foul ball. The replays on three different network cameras showed it clearly bouncing once in fair territory about halfway up the third base line, then crossing third base in the air, and finally landing foul-the definition of a fair ball!

Alex headed quickly back to the plate and took some swings, waiting for his manager to get thrown out of the game. Charley would get his money's worth for his first ejection of the year. To their credit, the crowd, unaware of the replay, tried to help Alex get focused for the next pitch with a collection of cheering, stomping, and clapping. He was ready to get a piece of the next pitch, which rose at an angle and crossed the outside corner. Alex tried to follow it across his vision and slapped at the pitch, sending it in the air toward shallow right field. Three Chops headed toward the line behind first base; all three dove and missed the ball. The first base umpire, running down the line, had his vision blocked out by the first and second basemen in front of him. After the ball bounced near the line, he saw it bounce foul and went with his best guess: call it foul! The Presidents bench coach and first base coach converged on the umpire before he could turn around. The replay again showed it hit fair. Both coaches were thrown out, and Alex returned to the plate. This time he swung through a letter-high fastball for strike three. The crowd gasped, realizing their hero had done his best to continue the streak.

    Pitching coach Pete McNeil, third base coach Mo Howard, and hitting coach Rex Epstein were the only coaches left in the dugout. Mendoza lined the first pitch back up the middle for his third of the day, Morris walked, and Le Mont had an infield single to load the bases. Left-handed hitter Henson Bennett hit a sacrifice fly to drive in a run. Pinch hitter Ryan Hudson struck out to end the inning.

    The Presidents quietly took the field to defend their 8-5 lead, relieved that their teammate would bat third in the bottom of the eighth. Frank Peterson gave up a solo homerun to make it 8-6 but got his three outs in the eighth inning.

    Blake Hopson started the eighth and zoomed a homerun to thankfully send Arnold Nichols to the showers. Gonzalez patiently fouled off eight pitches in a thirteen-pitch at bat against fireballer reliever Bryson Mason. Gonzo did his job exposing all of Mason's pitches for Alex to see from the on- deck circle.

    Alex was done wasting time. The crowd was

screaming at the top of their lungs, trying to intimidate Mason, who worked from a windup and fired a first pitch fastball to Alex high and inside. Alex had his hands high and pulled them in tight as he got the barrel of the bat on the ball. He slashed it toward the left field corner and ran with his head down toward first, hoping it was fair. The crowd roared as the left fielder picked up the ball in the corner and flipped it underhand to the shortstop. He slowly walked to the baseball to pick it up as Alex headed toward second base, finally seeing Chop second baseman Hank Paleski high-five him and hearing him scream, "It hit the foul pole," just audible above the high-decibel crowd. Alex continued around the bases after his thirty-seventh homerun of the year, sixteenth of the month, and second of the game.

The dugout stayed quiet not recognizing the record-breaking feat as the crowd stayed delirious. Carlos Mendoza refused to step into the box as he pointed to Alex, who finally came out of the dugout to tip his cap. Suddenly the dugout erupted in unison and blocked Alex from returning. They stood clapping, as did the rest of the crowd, for the next three minutes. Alex could see Phillip from the owner's box wiping his eyes and clapping. Three minutes felt like hours as he had no feeling in his body. He was floating from the energy of the fans in his isolation on the field.

He finally stepped down into the dugout and into the tunnel toward the locker room, trying to find some isolation. He made it the trainer's room and found a quiet spot. He slumped up against a wall and slid down to the floor and pulled his knees into his chess. He finally felt his breath and then a surge of emotion. His stomach went into spasms as he let out a silent cry to catch another breath. After ten of these, he went into quiet sobbing for a few minutes. In those moments of ultimate isolation, Alex finally felt the loss of his adoptive father, Gene. Only through feeling anger about the affair did it unlock his anger at losing him at age fifteen. Once recognizing that feeling, it allowed him to feel the real love that he missed from him. It had been hidden away while learning to be a professional athlete and replaced with love from his birth father, Phillip. Finally, after finding real relationship love with Sally did, he understand what he had received from Gene for fifteen years-unconditional love!

• • •

Vito Valencia was the only player left on the bench. He replaced Henson Scott at catcher, who went to the outfield as Marty Morris came to the infield to play third. No mention was made about Alex's whereabouts as Clay "Bean" Counter closed out the game with a one-two-three ninth inning for a 9-6 victory, a record-setting twenty-second win in a row, and a 73-50 record.

• • •

Alex finally got himself up, found some towels to clean his face, and headed back to the dugout just as "Beans" was pointing toward the sky after the last out. Manager Jackson and the other ejected coaches were in front of Alex in the tunnel, heading out to the field. Alex made it to the dugout, clapping his hands as the team celebrated in front of an adoring crowd. Carlos Mendoza, Blake Hopson, and Jerry Gonzalez came to the dugout and pulled a reluctant Alex Santucci to the field. He was surrounded by his teammates with back slaps and head rubs. Somehow it energized Alex to wave to the crowd and enjoy the moment. He quietly headed to the dugout after a few minutes with the rest of his teammates, thanking a higher power that he had a day off tomorrow before heading to Philadelphia for a three-game series. By his count, there were thirteen days left in his life before his surgery!

Chapter 48

Nat Sheridan watched the end of the record-breaking game from his office. What a great morning it will be, he thought, to break the news to the nation that their new hero was going under the knife soon. It would be a poor tonic for the hangover that DC was going to get from tonight's partying. Nat remembered those nights in Georgetown drinking until the break of dawn and then trying to go to class at George Washington University in the morning during his days in the nation's capital. He recalled fondly when the Redskins first started winning in the early seventies, how the town came together during the Nixon protest years and the ending of the Vietnam War. The summer after he graduated in 1974, he was interning at the *Washington Post* when Nixon resigned. Boy, that was a party, he remembered fondly! Then he remembered how the real baseball fans started to realize that baseball was not coming back after the tease of the San Diego Padres moving to DC. The deal was quashed by *McDonald's* magnate Ray Kroc when he came in at the last minute to save the team for San Diego. No such thing happened for DC.

The NHL's Capitals and the NBA's Bullets started playing in Landover, Maryland, in 1974, and college hoops at Maryland and Georgetown became hugely popular. He remembered baseball turned its back on Washington for good when Redskins owner Edward Bennett Williams bought the Baltimore Orioles and sold the Redskins to Jack Kent Cooke in the late seventies. The great irony being that Jack Kent Cooke bought the Los Angeles Lakers in 1965 from businessman Bob Short, who used the profit as leverage to buy the Senators in 1968. Cooke went on to build the Fabulous Forum for the Lakers and made a ton of money that helped him buy the Redskins from Williams, who used that money to buy the Orioles, which gave him leverage to keep baseball out of nearby DC. Both the Orioles and the Redskins became winners in the 1980s, which helped them get new stadiums in the nineties. Even when baseball expanded in 1977, 1993, and 1997, they ignored Washington. It was embarrassing for DC, Nat thought, the way the great city was treated.

When Nat Sheridan finally made his journalistic pinnacle in 1995, becoming managing editor of *Time* magazine, he knew that his conservative leanings would rile the liberal staff who would eventually conspire against his power and drive him down and out. He always thought it interesting that two powerful men in the Democratic Party, Bob Short and Edward Bennett Williams, were the primary forces in destroying baseball in DC and keeping it out for over three decades. Bob Short died of cancer in 1982, but the team that he sold in 1974, the Texas Rangers, were bought in 1988 by a group headed by George W. Bush. His tenure as president of the Rangers made him fifty million dollars and got him elected governor of Texas. As Nat Sheridan recalled, the rest is history.

The *Fox News Network* was gaining an audience when Nat was fired from *Time* in 1998, and he smoothly moved into the new empire of "Fair and Balanced News." He then became editor at the *New York Post* at the start of the second Bush term, and still loved every second of it. Now he was having some mixed feelings about crushing the balloon of the DC baseball world. Yes, he would "feel their pain," but business was business, and someone was going to break the story that was sitting on his desk-so why not him!

The minutes of the Dr. Walton/surgeons teleconference and the notes of the NIH file on the Higgins case were costly. He negotiated the forty-thousand-dollar price tag with great trepidation, but this was too big to pass up. Nat was now back into "hard news," not just celebrity gossip news. The whole country would take a look at this story:

Presidents Slugger Santucci to be Sidelined by Surgery Baseball

Hero's Health in Danger by Waiting after Labor Day Wedding

• • •

The water was getting colder as he swam toward the edge. His backstroke kept running him into the rope, and he could not remember the next stroke. Was it breast stroke or butterfly? He could not hear the yelling from the crowd because his head was under the water as he tried to turn over. He was tangled in the rope, but he did not struggle, uncertain of his next move. Then he heard the full orchestra being led by long violin strokes and the booming timpani. He finally awoke to the sound of the Spanish guitar from Jeff Lynne of ELO from *Face the Music.* Alex's first thought after remembering the nightmare was: I need to switch CDs in my alarm.

He was close to shivering and quickly got into the warm shower, something he had could not recall doing during the summer months. His thoughts were cloudy as he struggled to remember the day of the week or his purpose in life. The pulsating water finally jarred his memory in time to remember his workout date in the morning. He slowly dressed and walked out his deck to check the temperature, and noticed media trucks parked down the street. He quickly went back inside and whispered to Sally,

"Hey, sweetie, call me in hour. Do not go outside, okay?"

She nodded and went back to sleep. He went from his suite to his mom's bedroom and found her sitting in bed reading a book.

"Mom, don't go outside to get the paper; don't answer the door. Make sure Sally gets up in an hour, okay?"

She nodded and removed her glasses. "Alex, where are you going?"

"Sally and I are headed out of Bethesda if I can make it without... Oh, don't worry about it. It's just the media is outside. They just want to talk to me. They'll go away when they think I'm gone." With that explanation, he leaned down to kiss his mom and headed out the back door.

He hopped the back fence and then rushed through a couple of neighbors' yards toward the "Big Train" house, then across Old Georgetown Road and down Cedar Lane.

He arrived at the Rock Creek Bridge in fifteen minutes to see Charlotte stretching her hamstrings. When Charlotte saw Alex, her leg quickly released off the ledge and helped her jump into his arms to hug and praise him for last night's performance. She looked in his eyes and unexpectedly saw sadness. "Are you okay, Alex? Why did you come out of the game last night?"

"Just tired from the pennant race, I guess. Last night was pretty powerful."

She took his hand and headed toward Beach Drive in a slow trot. They talked the whole way about his breakdown in the trainer's room. It felt good to be moving and talking about it, but there was something in his head he could not shake.

• • •

Phillip was standing at the door when they arrived. He motioned for them to come in as he pointed to the television. Reporters were in front of Laura's house, and the newscast was leading with the *New York Post* story about his upcoming surgery.

Alex turned it off and told them he left instructions for everyone to stay inside. "Sally is going to call me in a little while. What do you say we do a little morning trip?" It was the most animated Alex had been this morning. He asked Phillip if he could drive his car. Phillip happily agreed, and Charlotte cheerfully followed.

Alex drove through the entrance of Gates of Heaven cemetery, which was about five miles North of Kensington at the intersection of Connecticut and Georgia Avenues. Phillip drove to an area just west of the mausoleum building and pulled over the car to park in the shade. Guy and Rose Finelli's grave markers were under several massive oak trees bordering the road. Alex paused to kneel and say a prayer to his grandparents. Phillip and Charlotte stood behind him, giving him distance and time. Alex felt numbness come over his body as he looked at the grave markers. He wanted to visualize his grandparents but could not focus on them. He remembered to say an 'Our Father' before he stood up.

Charlotte wanted to ask about her father's grave but could not find the words. Alex had been quiet the whole ride, so it had been a surprise to her when they entered the cemetery. She had never thought to visit her father's grave until just now, but she stayed quiet as Alex took her hand. They walked north about twenty yards and then west another hundred yards. She walked peacefully but with anticipation as she noticed that Phillip stayed at his parent's graves visiting for the time being.

Alex then stopped and turned toward Charlotte. He held her by the shoulders and said with a slumberous gaze, "I hope you're okay with this. I really needed to see him."

Her eyes filled with tears as she found a safe spot in his chest. "This is wonderful...just wonderful, Alex. I'm really glad to be here!"

Alex stepped forward a few rows and found Gene Santucci's grave marker under another large oak tree. Gene and Guy had traveled to Gates of Heaven in 1973 after an Italian club meeting to pick out sites. They were assured the newly planted oak trees would be fully grown in twenty years. Almost forty years later, they were fifty feet high. Charlotte wanted to feel the marker, so she got on all fours to get as close as she could to her father's grave. She crawled on the grass and laid her body down wanting to soak up the soil. It was a warm place for her to feel connected and to be next to the origin of her family.

At the same time, Alex sat cross-legged staring at the

grave marker. He tried to be in touch with his yoga breathing, wanting to inhale hope. He remembered as a fifteen-year-old hearing the news early in the morning, then wondering what would happen to him. Would he be sent somewhere? Could he still play baseball? The loss to his family-Laura, and the older kids, all over twenty-five at the time-hadn't occurred to him at the time. He did remember grabbing his mitt and a ball and running out the back door to his favorite spot to throw the baseball all morning. He had just wanted to pitch like the "Big Train" that morning because everything could go back to normal again!
Oh my God! He thought. I need to talk to Phillip.

• • •

Sally took her time in the morning gathering clothes for herself and Alex for the trip to Philadelphia. She enjoyed the extended time with Leah and Laura over coffee. By ten o'clock, the media had thinned out to a couple of local stations getting ready for a noontime report. By twelve thirty, they were gone and Sally pulled out the Acura TL for the forty-minute ride to Glenwood, Maryland.

• • •

Alex spent the morning walking the cemetery grounds with Phillip and Charlotte, talking through his just realized dilemma. There were moments of clarity for him but mostly sadness and a feeling of desolation. When there were long pauses, finally Charlotte would try to add hope, sharing her feelings of gratefulness to Alex at his immediate acceptance of her in the family. She tried to breathe life back into him by using her touch and whispering praises in his ear.

Phillip was a master at family therapy, especially in

the surroundings of the cemetery, which added somberness to the subject. He helped Charlotte and Alex share their different perspectives of loss about Gene: Alex's real, Charlotte's perceived.

After two hours on the grounds of the cemetery, they found a breakfast spot fifteen miles north out Georgia Avenue in the little town of Sunshine, Maryland, where they continued talking until almost noon. Alex made arrangements to meet with Sally at his Cousin Helen's mansion on a hill in Glenwood, Maryland. Anthony's daughter made arrangements for them to have the house to themselves after getting a phone call from Alex. They were at the beach for a week and were thrilled they could help out. Sally, Alex, Charlotte, and Phillip would stay there through the night.

• • •

Phillip was concerned that Alex had slipped into a mild depression caused by the cessation of the medication and the pressure of the winning streak. The appearance of Charlotte and the news about his dad's infidelities stirred his forgotten memories of fear and loss over Gene's death. The dreams and messages from "The Big Train" were comforting and familiar places for his subconscious to seek value and motivation. The whole situation was complicated by the paradox of his health condition and his amazing performance on the field. Phillip wondered how he could best help his son.

He decided at that moment that he would not leave Alex until the date of the surgery. He called Dr. Walton about his conclusions and agreed to meet him at the house in the morning. Henry wanted to do a physical assessment and discuss medications Alex could take that would not threaten his surgery. Phillip felt energized to have a meaningful role in his son's life and was determined not to have any harm come to Alex. He needed to reconstruct and understand the events that started July 10 in Kansas City and came to a head last night in Washington, DC. As he realized insights from these events, he would be able to weave a story to soothe Alex's subconscious about the loss in his life. At the same time, he could rebuild Alex's confidence and purpose in the world as a national figure. It would be a delicate operation, because one thing was clear to him: too much had happened in the past forty-five days for it to be coincidence. He was convinced that his son Alex was on a path of destiny!

Chapter 49

Sunday morning at five fifteen, Alex was staring at the Delaware River from his hotel window at the Omni Hotel, at 401 Chestnut Street in downtown Philadelphia. For the first morning since Wednesday, he felt hopeful and was determined to get Charlotte awake for a workout. He had spent hours with Phillip on Thursday, Friday, and Saturday talking and going in and out of therapeutic trances.

On Friday and Saturday nights, he had played sparingly in two Presidents losses. Amazingly, he had a hit and a RBI in each game in four at bats. Manager Charley Jackson did not start him either game but put him in by the fifth inning. He had been shuttled by security to and from the hotel, protected from media and fans. Being in the dugout and being on the field pumped energy into Alex. It was comfortable to be one of the guys. None of his teammates ignored him, but no one crowded him either. Other than greetings, they waited for him to initiate a conversation. Phillip had spoken to the team and coaches with Alex in attendance before Friday's game about his condition, trying to establish a new normal for the team.

Alex phoned Charlotte, who answered immediately. She was dressed at 5:05 a.m., and had been watching the same river and praying that Alex would want to work out. They had the streets to themselves as they did forty-five minutes of running, followed by thirty minutes of swimming and twenty minutes of weight work. Sally was awake when they returned and had coffee, juice, fruit, and oatmeal ready for them. Phillip joined them and asked Sally and Alex if they were ready to talk to the media. The decision was a unanimous yes, starting with a taped appearance on *Meet The Press.* Host David Marks was a huge Presidents fan and had been in touch with the team since

Wednesday night trying to talk to Alex and Sally. They would follow with a short interview with Bonnie Bramlett on *ESPN,* a print interview with Ron Roswell, and a press conference at the ballpark after batting practice that would focus entirely on baseball questions.

Phillip talked with Alex after each interview to assess his status. He was pleased with his progress. With David Marks, Sally Keegan initially stole the show explaining the background of the surgery and the surgical teams assembled. She also talked about the upcoming wedding and the reception at Presidents Park. Alex talked about the importance of the team winning in August and being in first place but deflected any question about his recent record- setting performances.

When David Marks asked him about the possibility of "dying on the field" before the surgery, he answered, "We have troops still dying every day in Afghanistan; they are the real heroes facing death every day. I'm lucky enough to be playing a kid's game for a living. People in construction, the coal mines, on oil rigs-they face death every day. Millions of Americans have jobs that pose a greater risk of death than I do-and without the luxury of doctors to take care of them. I'm getting a chance to create hope for people; to me that is a privilege, not a risk."

David Marks sat motionless for a few seconds and then realized there was nothing else to say! He shook both of their hands and looked at the camera. "That's why Alex Santucci has become my new baseball hero...and much more to the residents of the nation's capital and to fans of baseball, and all of America! We'll be back in a moment."

• • •

Once the interviews were done, sitting in the dugout had a quiet excitement for Alex and being on the infield felt normal again. Phillip Fields was coming off two excellent starts and was full of confidence to get the Presidents back on their winning ways. The team was excited to have Santucci's name in the lineup, especially after his batting practice, which looked like fireworks landing in the bleachers.

Left-hander Winston "Smokey" Camels was again the ornery opponent on the mound, fresh off a $130 million contract extension. He signed after efforts to trade him were extinguished by owner Franz Chopin, a music publishing billionaire, who could not bear to part with his World Series hero from 2008. Camels was the only one of the three all-star pitchers in the rotation having a great year for the bottom-of-the-division Independence. He had been the last pitcher to beat the Presidents before their record-setting win streak started on August 1. This afternoon he would try to finish a sweep of the first-place Presidents.

• • •

Alex's grandmother Rose Finelli grew up 1n South Philadelphia; back then she was known as Rosina Angelucci. Born in 1914, she left Overbrook High School, alma mater to the great Wilt Chamberlain, at sixteen to work as a seamstress to help keep the family afloat after the Depression hit the country.

Alex made a point, every time in Philadelphia, of taking a cab or his car through the neighborhood where his grandmother grew up, just off Broad Street north of the stadium complex. The ten-foot wide row-houses seemed barely possible to house the seven people in her family. In the 1920s, they moved to West Philadelphia near City Line Avenue to a decent-sized row-house on 67th Street. Sally always was amazed at the size of the living spaces and the streets in the East after having grown up on the plains of Kansas. Alex envisioned hard work every day without complaint while retreating to the love of the family at night and on Sundays.

During a hot August weekend like today, Rose and her sisters would take the train from the Thirtieth Street Station to Atlantic City, along with thousands of other Philadelphians, for a day of fun in the ocean. Now forty- five thousand current-day Philadelphians were packed into Citizen's Bank Ballpark to see a Philadelphia grandson perform on the field.

There has always been something special about the sound of a wooden bat crushing a baseball. The perfect swing synchronized with a blazing pitch makes a supersonic sound unlike anything in sports. Add to that formula a special player who is a slugger on a streak, and you have a crowd on pins and needles every pitch of his at-bat.

On a perfect baseball summer Sunday afternoon, Alex Santucci was ready to give the Philly crowd four supersonic moments. He roped a first inning changeup off the left field line that one-hopped into the seats for a ground-rule double. This was followed in the third inning by another rope to dead center off the fence for another double. He saved the last two at bats for his best performance. By the sixth inning, the Philly crowd, behind 4-1, stood with anticipation as Alex stepped to the plate with two on and no outs. They tried to muster some support for "Smokey" Camels, but really, they were ready to see another bomb off the Santucci bat. He did not disappoint, getting a down-the-middle-of-the-plate fastball and hitting it into the club level seats in left field, about 475 feet, for a sweet-sounding three-run homer, his thirty-eighth homerun of the year and seventeenth in the month of August.

In the eighth inning, down by 7-1, the Philly fans were again standing, this time openly cheering Santucci for another special moment. They understood they were witnessing a special moment in baseball history, like Phillip seeing Roger Maris hit his forty-third homerun at Griffith

Stadium in 1961, on his way to sixty-one homeruns, which they could talk about fifty years later to their children and grandchildren. Now they would be able to talk about the Sunday when they saw Santucci hit one into the visitor's bullpen in right-center that broke the sound barrier, landing close to five-hundred feet from home plate and caught by reliever Paul Angelucci, an unknown distant Cousin to Santucci.

    After the game, the two players and mates went to *Bistro Romano* Italian Restaurant on Lombard Street in Philadelphia's Society Hill, a special invitation by Alex to congratulate Paul for catching the baseball and to get to know the fellow Italian on the team. He was a quiet twenty-eight-year-old in his third season on the Presidents. Not originally favored to make the team in spring training, Angelucci puzzled the opposition with his sinker and mid-nineties fast-ball. He had been solid all year as a set-up man in the bullpen and strong enough to pitch several innings on back-to-back days. After several bottles of wine, they realized their Angelucci families were from the same town in Italy, Castel Frentano, near the Adriatic Sea in the Abruzzo region. Paul had spent time there during a semester in college. He told great stories about the region and the little town of four thousand people with wonderful churches and palaces. By the end of the night, they were referring to each other as Cousin. He promised to bring in the history of his Angelucci family and share all that he had gathered in the homeland.

    Weeks later they discovered Alex's great, great, great-grandfather Filippo Angelucci, born in 1825, had a brother Stefano Angelucci, born in 1821, who was Paul Angelucci's great, great, great, great-grandfather. This made them fourth Cousins once removed, meaning that they shared between 3.125 and 6.25 percent of their DNA! They laughed as they agreed that it was somewhere between a good ERA for a pitcher and a great slugging percentage for a batter. Either way they would take it, because it made them family!

●●●

Alex hoped the interviews on Sunday morning and his performance in the afternoon would calm down the media hype around his health. The team was playing well, and he would have a procedure in seven days that would sideline him for a couple of weeks. He was relieved when this was how the media reported it on Monday.

Tuesday morning was a chance for Alex to get back some anonymity and his regular routine. He woke up at 5:30 a.m. feeling pretty normal for the third day in a row. Dr. Walton had given him a B-12 shot and put him on a low dose of serotonin on Thursday to help his depression symptoms; it seemed to be working. Alex did not have time to read the paper in the morning in order to meet Charlotte for their morning workout. It was nice to have a great run, and then pick up Phillip followed by an easy swim, and light weight work without having to discuss baseball or his current state of mind. He made a point of asking Phillip how his body was feeling after beginning the workouts and what he was currently writing about.

It was fun to enjoy Charlotte's excitement about deciding whether to accept Alex's offer to pay her to move to Bethesda and become his full-time assistant, workout partner, agent, or whatever you call it. They had been talking about it over the weekend, and he was certain she wanted to do it.

He felt freedom that morning from the heat of the personal and team streaks. He believed that he had accomplished what he set out to do in Washington. With the surgery a week away, the team solidly in first place, and President's franchise player Bruce Hammersly just a few days away from joining the team, he was feeling some peace.

•••

    Alex, Charlotte, and Phillip took a private flight provided by Frederick Meyers to Miami. Phillip and the team agreed it would be best for all parties involved for the Santucci entourage to come separately from the team. Sally, Leah, and Laura were in the last week of preparations for the wedding and would stay in Bethesda for the two-game series in Miami. Leah was working with Father Higgins on the music for the wedding. Laura was finalizing details with the caterer and the guest list. Sally had to finish getting her dress and the bridesmaid dresses ready and make sure her family and friends coming in from out of town were taken care of by the Marriott in North Bethesda. Otherwise, she had thousands of little things to do to get ready for the biggest day in her life!

    The new stadium for the Sugarcanes was The Taj Mahal compared to the Sun Life Stadium they shared with the NFL's Dolphins for fifteen years. They were fifteen miles closer to Miami International Airport in the Little Havana section of Miami but still a couple miles away from downtown Miami. The attendance was up over 50 percent because of the new, intimate, art deco style, retractable-roof stadium but still on a pace to be the lowest attendance at a new stadium since the new generation of stadiums started with Baltimore's Camden Yards in 1992.

    The Presidents were staying at the Ritz-Carlton Key Biscayne on the Atlantic Ocean, about ten miles from the stadium. It was worth the ride for the privacy and the view of the ocean. For Charlotte it was the first time coming to the Atlantic Ocean. She was curious to understand why Alex and Phillip were both in love with it, both having condos about 200 miles to the north overlooking it. Checking in early at 1:30 p.m., Alex was able to get into his room and called Charlotte to meet him for a quick swim in the ocean. The fairly calm ocean was warm as bath water, which was perfect for thirty minutes of fun and relaxation. After some time, sunning on an uncrowded beach, they headed in at three o'clock.

Riding in the elevator across from Charlotte, he noticed the unforgiving Florida sun brought out the freckles and lots of red to Charlotte's skin. It made her look youthful in her modest orange and green bikini, which matched the hometown, Dolphins. Alex had a spiritual moment standing in the elevator with Charlotte. He truly still could not comprehend that she was in his life becoming almost an alter ego he could witness in person. He wondered if Gene had witnessed her life like Phillip had done with him for fifteen years. Could he have flown to Cincinnati or Saint Louis many times before he died in 1991 to see her grow up from afar? Maybe appearing as a family friend and having dinner with her and her adopted parents or seeing her at a school activity. Alex had a sense, after he reached seven, that he found solace in baseball because Gene was so busy with his medical practice and career. Or was it also emotional distance because his mind was on Charlotte or Margaret in Cincinnati? Did all these factors lead to his early death? He started to understand the dilemma that Gene went through and was glad that they had that last year of baseball together before he died.

As the elevator stopped at their floor, Charlotte took a moment to latch onto her big brother. "How come I'm all red and you're just getting darker?" Charlotte noticed. Alex jokingly explained he had the right combination of Swedish blond locks and the Italian skin, which generally got darker with sun exposure. He held onto her as the elevator closed slowly. She extended her hand to open the doors and looked up at him. "It's nice to see that handsome smile of yours again. I hope you're ready for tonight!"

They headed off into the hallway together as Alex

thought to himself how lucky he was to find love and soon marriage with Sally and to receive in the last month two important parts of his family in Leah and now Charlotte. He wondered if this meant life was becoming complete. Or would it just become more complicated, like Gene's life after he adopted Alex and had an affair with Margaret to bring Charlotte into his life? The sudden rumbling in his stomach was a clue that "complicated" was just around the corner!

Chapter 50

Travis Tyler was going over the Miami lineup with Manager Charlie Jackson. They had watched film on their hitting tendencies, but Charlie had an easy message. "Tyler, trust your mechanics. They have been so good that they've made your stuff almost unhittable. It reminds me of Bob Gibson in sixty-eight. Everything he threw was at the knees - same thing with McLain and Lolich that year. Your arm angle is perfect right now. I would not change a thing." Jackson did not mention his fifty scoreless innings streak because he knew the kid was stressed about it. He had a chance to tie the record tonight of fifty-nine innings.

Tyler's wife, Alexis, was driving him crazy because most of the wives had stayed home for the two-game trip and was antsy. When he saw Alex enter the locker room at 3:35 p.m., he jumped at the chance to talk to the center of attention and ask a favor. "Alex, is Sally here? Alexis is a wreck; she needs some lady attention."

"Well, Charlotte is at the hotel. I'll tell her to call Alexis. You know those redheads need to stick together!" He texted Charlotte an assignment!

Charlotte was excited to hear from Alex and have a reason to get to the ballpark early. She had seen the banner running on *ESPN* first thing in the morning and was amazed that Alex was so calm about it. She quickly got in touch with Alexis and met at the hotel bar. They ordered drinks and talked for a while about her anxiety about Travis pitching tonight. They caught a cab to the ballpark, both feeling pretty loose for the game.

Travis sat with Alex before batting practice, asking him about the pressure he went through with the homerun streak. Alex thought for a moment and responded. "It seemed like it was out of my hands because the team seem to make it happen. I think tonight you won't have pressure because we will win the game for you. And you just get to do what you love: play, pitch, and catch with Valencia. Nobody cares if you give up a run. What you have done is already amazing. That's the only thing I remember... Breaking the streak was fun!"

Travis seemed relieved to have a mission and was impressed that Alex was so calm and happy tonight. "Well, damn, I know I can do that. Hell, we'll just have fun tonight!"

• • •

Alex had been unaware that GM Jim Franco had shielded the media from him since Sunday. Franco told the media today Alex would be available after the game for questions if he felt all right. Otherwise they could talk to him around the batting cage off the record. Riley Preston, Ron Roswell, and two dozen other reporters stood quietly as Alex took his first five swings, while Franco eyed them across the cage.

As he finished, Alex walked over to Ron and Riley, who were good friends with each other, and said, "You guys are awfully quiet today, nice ballpark, huh?"

Ron and Riley looked at each other as Alex towered over them with a big smile.

"Yeah, great place, Alex. How are you feeling about tonight?" Riley inquired.

"Great...great, I think me and Carlos will hit a couple out tonight for Travis. I think he's throwing great and has a shot at the record! What do you guys think?"

Ron found his voice, "Yeah, big kid with a great arm. Do you feel any pressure about your..."

Alex headed back into the cage and hooked a couple around the pole in left field and then came back. This time the two dozen reporters had filled in behind Ron and Riley.

"Sorry, Ron. What were you asking about?"

"Well, we were just wondering about...what you thought... about hitting four hundred?"

Alex stood with his jumbo hands on his thirty-six-ounce bat and slowly swung.

"Yeah, I guess I have been hitting for average the last few games since the homerun streak. You know not as many juicy ones over the plate..." He headed back to the cage for five more swings.

All the reporters looked at each other. Finally Pedro Carew from a local DC station spoke. "Ron, ask him if he knows what he's hitting for the year-not just for the month."

Kelly Browner added to the conversation.

"Do you think he knows what he's hitting for the year?"

Riley answered, "We'll find out soon, Kelly."

Alex returned after feeling great about his stroke.

Riley tried again. "Alex, have you read the paper since Sunday?"

"That's weird. Now that you mention it...It's usually the first thing I do in the morning, but I've just been laying low since Sunday with all the interviews."

Riley paused. "Well, in case you didn't know...You're hitting four hundred for the year!"

• • •

The temperature was a controlled seventy-two degrees with the roof closed. Travis Tyler had never been so comfortable on the mound, pitching the bottom of the first inning with a 3-0 lead on back-to-back blasts from Mendoza and Morris. He looked calm but determined, plowing through the first five innings and giving up only an infield single and a walk.

Alex stepped into the box in the top of the sixth inning, still batting .400 with a 1 for 2 nights. Since joining the Presidents on July 31 and playing in twenty-six games, he was 60 for 92, a .652 average with 18 Hrs and 63 RBIs. Indescribable numbers for almost a month of baseball. He was still leading the PBL in all aspects of hitting with Triple Crown numbers and now attaining the magical .400 batting average this late in the summer. And to quote Riley Preston, "By the way," he had a twenty-six game hitting streak.

He had faced 'Canes pitcher Briles Martin in DC earlier in the month, who had treated him rudely. Alex thought Martin had lasted in this game too long. He was leaving his slider over the plate all night, but the Presidents lineup was impatiently popping the ball up consistently, except for the first-inning: fireworks. Martin peppered the outside corner with three pitches to get the count to 2-1. Alex knew he was not going to walk him with only one out in the inning and with Mendoza and Morris coming up. He threw a fastball high over the plate for another ball.

Alex stepped out and noticed The Clevelander Restaurant next to the bullpen in left field. He dazed for a minute daydreaming about sitting in the pool and having a drink with all the pretty girls swimming around him. He thought about his four-hundredth career homerun he was about to hit and wondered if the ball would float, so he could give the ball to Phillip. He refocused as he stepped into the box and waited for the slider on the inside of the plate. It came as ordered, almost too flat, and his swing was almost too level. He stung the ball on a line straight toward the bullpen, hitting the back wall before any pitcher could get a glove on it. As Alex rounded the bases for the fortieth time this year, he was glad to see the ball being thrown into the dugout and thought maybe he would get another chance at the pool!

Alexis and Charlotte were on their fifth drink of the night as Alex rounded the bases. Charlotte was thrilled about the accomplishment that was announced to the cheering crowd who waited patiently for Alex to come out to tip his cap. It was enough of a distraction to keep Alexis happy as she watched Tyler finish the sixth and seventh innings without much competition. The lead stayed 4-0 going into the bottom of the eighth.

Charley Jackson was pleased with Tyler's pitch count

and the way he was going after hitters. The first two pitches in the eighth were hit for singles. Mendoza, Hopson, and Morris in the outfield came in ten steps to cut off liners or to get to singles quickly. The infield was playing at double play depth. Tyler kept firing his upper-nineties fastball to get ahead of the batters, and they kept swinging. Another line drive headed to center field; Blake Hopson took off like a bullet and snagged it with a diving catch. The next pitch was rifled to left field for a base hit; Mendoza charged it and fired the ball to Valencia, but the runner was held at third.

For the next hitter, Alex played even with the bag, looking for a bunt while the rest of the infield was at double play depth. Alex saw the top hand of the hitter move up the bat as Travis fired another fastball. As the bat made contact, Alex bolted from third to spear the ball going down the third base line. Alex knew it would stay fair, so he had one chance to keep the run from scoring. He dove for the ball to his right and with his glove hand swung at the ball backhanded to send it to the catcher for the force at home. Vito stretched to snag it barehanded to complete the force, and then spun to fire the ball to first for an inning-ending double play. The Miami fans were in disbelief that the score was still 4-0 when the Presidents came off the field. They had to watch the replay on the scoreboard before they could figure out what just happened.

Alex led off the ninth and received a standing ovation from the Miami crowd. They continued standing and cheering as he found The Clevelander with the first pitch fastball for his forty-first homerun of the year. The baseball did get wet when it landed over the fence, just short of the pool but right into an oversized cup of beer. The fan was not pleased about losing his ten dollars' worth of beer, so he threw the ball and his drink back over the fence and onto the field, not realizing the significance of the homerun. No announcement was made about it being the record-tying twentieth homerun of the month. To the crowd it was just another long homerun to make the score 5-0 in between a four-hundredth career homerun and a possible record- setting pitching performance that could happen next inning. Blake Hopson ran into the outfield to retrieve it from the Miami left fielder. The 'Canes media department was having trouble keeping up with all the streaks, even though POTUS announcer Wayne Woodworker was screaming at them from several broadcast booths away.

Travis Tyler was completely in the zone as he struck out the side in the ninth inning on nine pitches to tie the consecutive scoreless innings record at fifty-nine innings and win the game *5-0* for his twentieth win of the year.

• • •

As they celebrated in the locker room, several players suggested bringing the party back to the pool bar at the hotel.

Only nineteen-year-old Blake Hopson took time away from his teammates surrounding Travis. He found Alex in the ice bath to give him the ball and congratulate him for his record-tying home-run. He remembered when he was five years old that Sammy Sosa hit twenty homeruns in June 1998 to set the major league record. Alex was happy for the recognition but even happier that all the attention was on Travis tonight.

• • •

Charlotte had done a nice job medicating Alexis for most of the night. She had switched to seltzer water after her fifth drink, but Alexis needed a few more to settle her anxiety around the fifth inning. She fell asleep on Charlotte during the sixth inning, and then awoke from the nap when Charlotte jumped out of her chair in the bottom of the eighth during Alex's great defensive play to preserve Travis Tyler's shutout. After ingesting some nachos in the top of the ninth,

Alexis was able to enjoy her husband's strike-out-the-side performance to tie the record in the bottom of the ninth 1nn1ng.

• • •

The hotel beach setting on the Atlantic Ocean was remarkable, with a perfectly clear sky and the moon at 93 percent full. The second full moon of August, better known as a blue moon, was only three days away.

A handful of players along with Charlotte, Alexis, and Phillip graduated to getting in the pool to play volleyball. Travis pulled together the pitchers around Alexis on his side, while Blake corralled the position players around Charlotte on the other side of the net. Travis's team finally gave up after being swept in four games. Phillip, Alex, Blake, and Charlotte were strategically placed in rotating corners, making up for the rest of the crew who played with one hand while drinking a beer with the other.

After a quick swim in the ocean, Travis made the mistake of bringing out the football for a game on the beach. The moonlight and light from the hotel provided some ability to see the ball. It was decided that Alexis and Charlotte would quarterback each side. The game quickly turned into a rout as Charlotte flashed her big arm and great speed to produce four quick touchdowns using Blake and Alex as her main targets. The game finally ended when Charlotte was tackled and piled on by the pitchers and Alexis was hoisted on the shoulders of the position players and dumped in the ocean. Fortunately, all clothing was kept intact. Final drinks were ordered at the poolside bar as they enjoyed telling stories about the great night in Miami.

• • •

The final game of the series on Wednesday night

was a predictable letdown with a 6-2 loss, as most players were mentally already back in DC. Alex made his last attempt to get a ball in The Clevelander pool but fell short with a double off the wall to drive in both runs in the fifth inning.

The Presidents quickly recovered their winning ways on Thursday night with a commanding 12-2 win over the St. Louis Scarlets. Danube Rivers struggled through five innings, but the POTUS bullpen fresh from their hangovers Tuesday night, shut down the St. Louis hitting machine for four innings. The thirteenth consecutive sell-out crowd loosened up the POTUS bats for twenty hits. Alex contributed an infield single in the first inning and a sacrifice fly in the eighth inning, which tied the all-time consecutive games with an RBI at 17 games held since 1922 by Ray Grimes of the Chicago Cubs. No mention of the record-tying event was made before the end of the game.

The Presidents media head, Patty O'Neil, missed the event, going home early because she was suffering from undiagnosed pneumonia. The rest of her staff was organizing a post-game press conference centering on the return of Presidents superstar Bruce Hammersly for Friday night's game. Fortunately, *Daily* reporter Ron Roswell called the *BASN* play-by-play announcer Wayne Woodworker to alert him of the news so that he could at least announce it on the post-game show.

The players in the clubhouse were focused on the news about Hammersly and having their bats show up at home. The post-game news conference was held by Manager Charley Jackson, who said Bruce would be in the dugout Friday night but would not be activated until Saturday night's game on September 1, when all the major league rosters were increased from twenty-five to up to forty players. Before he introduced Hammersly, he noted that veteran Jerry Gonzalez had played an almost flawless shortstop for seven weeks and would not start for three days; instead, he'd be a defensive replacement late in games. Otherwise, Gonzalez would take some extra infield practice to get to ready to play third base on the Tuesday after the upcoming Labor Day weekend. Nobody asked, "Why on Tuesday?" They knew that hot-hitting MVP candidate Alex Santucci was metaphorically "going under the knife." The procedure was known medically as a laparoscopic procedure, which ironically was being done to avoid going under the knife!

• • •

August 31 had arrived on a Friday night in the nation's capital. This usually meant half the population would be at the Maryland and Delaware beaches for the Labor Day weekend. The other half would be settling in after starting school or college in the area. Many of those would play or attend the opening night of area high school football. Others were forming foursomes at the local golf courses, betting to beat their handicaps. Gardening plots would be getting extra attention as ripe tomatoes, peppers, squash, cucumbers, zucchini, and eggplants would be ready to pick. Biking trips were being planned for the weekend from DC to Mount Vernon, or from Bethesda to Lake Needwood, or from the north-west branch of the Anacostia to Bladensburg, or from Reston to McLean in Virginia. Community pools would be open for their last weekend of the year, providing a site for cookouts, parties, and of course, swimming. Boating and sailing on the Potomac and the Chesapeake Bay would provide for great recreation and entertainment for thousands. Eating crabs at least once over the weekend would be a main event for many of the eight million residents of the Washington-Baltimore Metroplex. For the first time since Washington, DC had its own mayor and self-government, would anybody care about a baseball game before, during, or after Labor Day weekend.

•••

From her hospital bed at Sibley Hospital in DC, Patty O'Neil, on IV antibiotics for pneumonia, was on her Blackberry at 12:07 a.m. She was texting to the *Washington Daily* sports editor that Friday's night game would be a chance for Alex Santucci to break two records and set new ones: the first for Hrs in a month at twenty-one, and the second for consecutive games with an RBI at eighteen. She knew her job was on the line after she received a call from Ron Roswell that Hank Meyers was throwing things in the Presidents Media room after they did not announce that Alex Santucci had tied the record for consecutive games with an RBI at seventeen in the bottom of the eighth inning. Since the call from Roswell, she had been harassing the managing editor at the *Daily* for a front-page headline and a story about the records, even while she was feeling the effects of her pain medication. She found that her condition helped her not accept no for an answer!

Unknown to her, both Ron Roswell and Presidents owner Frederick Meyers were lobbying the editor themselves for a front-page headline and story. At 4:00 a.m., the *Washington Daily* was ready for delivery with a front-page headline:

Superstar Santucci's Streaks Soar! HR, RBI Records on the Line Tonight

On the left side of the front page was a column that explained the significance of the record-breaking month of August to all Washingtonians, in case anybody had not been watching television, listening to the radio, cruising the Internet, or reading the paper in the past month. The short article by Roswell would be the centerpiece of months of reporting that would cement a Pulitzer Prize for sports reporting.

"Hot in August" ends an "Era of Pain" By Ron Roswell
Every century a character comes to a town and transforms the region in an instant. At a Press Conference on July 31, Alex Santucci said, "I'm here on a mission. It's time to stop the era of pain and the sorrow of loss and time to free the feelings of hope to love baseball in this city again." He then finished with, "By September 1st, you can judge me if I'm right or wrong." Well, the returns are in. It's Santucci by a landslide! never has a player taken on an "Era of Pain" in a city and cleanse it within a month. Thousands of Washingtonians over fifty now can come out of the closet and scream with pride: I'm a Baseball Fan!

Only words by Lincoln at Gettysburg or M. L. King at the Lincoln Memorial have been spoken more eloquently about pain. Those were great prepared speeches to the nation after a barbaric battle in the Civil War in the 19th century and an often-violent battle for Civil Rights in the 20th century. In the 21st century, sports have replaced Civil Wars for the Right for a region to be the most Civil in the Land! Most will criticize this comparison, but let us look at the facts. The federal government takes care of the war business by spending over $700 billion a year on the Defense Department and another $50 billion on Homeland Security to ensure that any war we fight will be on foreign soil and never another "Civil War". The only civil rights arguments left over are about abortion and gay marriage. Those issues will be decided by the courts and legislators.

Cities and states have spent hundreds of millions on separate stadiums for football, baseball, basketball, hockey, and even soccer! DC spent $611 million on Presidents Park stadium alone. You may not like it, but sports for a large percentage of the population have become the armor we wear for pride metaphorically and physically. They do not call it *Under Armor* for nothing!

Tonight Alex Santucci has a chance to break two unthinkable records in baseball history. He has already erased the "Era of Pain" in Washington; tonight, we can watch him reach baseball immortality with one swing of the bat. It is time for Washingtonians to "step up to the plate" and wear their baseball pride and watch a miracle season of our own American Idol!

• • •

Patty awoke at 12:10 p.m. on August 31 after a solid twelve hours of sleep for the first time since college. It was first sleep of more than an hour without coughing in two weeks. The nurse walked in, checked her vital signs and IV hookup, and announced she had some visitors waiting to see her. She felt pretty fuzzy but refreshed and wondered who even knew she was in the hospital besides her two assistants and an intern. Her family was in Ohio, and she had little time to make friends in the past year. The nurse raised her bed, propped her pillow, and said, "Best you stay in bed until this evening. Are you ready for your visitors?"

Patty ran her hands through her shoulder-length red hair, attempting to give it some extra body. "Sure...I guess so. Who is it?"

The nurse smiled and winked as she headed out the room. "I'm sure you'll recognize them!"

Seconds later there was a commotion in the hallway as a crowd of people seemed to be talking outside her room. Patty cleaned her ears, wondering what all the noise was about as she took a sip from a glass of water. Suddenly the first couple of Washington walked into her room.

"Patty, do you mind if we come in for a minute? We

were so worried about you!" Sally Keegan carried a beautiful bouquet of red roses as she approached the bed first.

Alex followed holding a final edition of the *Washington Daily* in his hand. He unfolded it and presented it Patty. "I think your job is pretty secure Patty, and I told them they'd better give you a raise and some more staff!" Alex and Sally laughed, while Patty was speechless from the kindness of these strangers. Sally offered a hug after Patty starting crying when she took a moment to smell the roses.

Alex held her hand and gave her one of his baseball bats signed by the entire team.

"I wanted you to have this in case they don't listen to you in here. Get some rest. You're a big part of this team, and we need you back as soon as you feel better. I hope you can come to the wedding Monday if you're up for it. My assistant Charlotte can pick you up from here or home. She'll call you, all right? Remember, all the players love you!" What Alex forgot to mention was that he was flying her parents in from Columbus, Ohio, and that the card stuck in with the flowers had a check in it for ten thousand dollars, which included contributions from every player.

Alex and Sally talked to Patty for the next ten minutes about where she went to college, how much she likes DC, her frustrations with the job, and when they should get together after the season was over. She was gaining strength by the minute from the personal attention from the famous couple. Alex predicted they would win tonight for her and the record breaking would take care of itself. Sally could see that Patty was getting tired, so she pulled Alex away and they said their good-byes. Alex checked the TV on the way out to make sure that the right channel was on for her to watch the game tonight.

They walked out of the room to over a hundred hospital staff members who had congregated on the nursing floor trying to catch a glimpse of the good-looking couple. Most were eating the leftovers from the catered lunch Alex and Sally had arranged for the nursing staff during the hour they spent seeing Patty. They waved and shook hands as security helped them to the elevators. Everyone told the happy couple to enjoy their wedding on Labor Day and wished Alex good luck tonight and Godspeed on Tuesday.

Chapter 51

The Presidents had started the month of August with a 51-50 record after a free-fall for the last three weeks of July. They were 25-3 in August with one game to go and three Professional League records to break. They had already broken two all-time records for a team, twenty-two wins in a row and sixty shutout team innings in a row, and two individual all-time records, ten consecutive games with a homerun and seven three-hit games in a row. All eyes tonight would be on Alex and his attempt to hit his twenty-first homerun in August, which would give him his eighteenth game in a row with an RBI. He was also batting .400, sporting a twenty-nine-game hitting streak, and on track for an unofficial Triple Crown.

Before the game, infielder Ryan Hudson was put on the fifteen-day disabled list dating back to August 26 when he sprained his ankle running in the outfield. He had traveled with the team to Miami but did not play. Manager Charley Jackson was anxious to get Bruce Hammersly back in the lineup. Alex volunteered to bat second to give Bruce back his normal third spot in the order. Both Bruce and Charley would not agree to move Alex from his successful third spot in the order.

Tony Johnson was facing his team from the last two years. He won a World Series game and a championship ring with the Scarlets last year in a memorable seven-game classic. He was juiced up early, hitting 98 mph on his fastball in the first three innings. Switch-hitter Barry Ortega hit a homerun to start the fourth inning, breaking a scoreless tie. Hammersly got his first hit in the fifth with an RBI single to tie the match at 1-1. The crowd was getting restless as the game went into both teams' bullpens to begin the seventh inning. The Scarlets or the Presidents could not muster a rally in the ninth and the game went into extra innings.

Both teams had only three hits and five base runners during regulation.

Alex had gone hitless in four at bats, hitting a couple of long fly balls that excited the crowd for a few seconds. The ballpark's overcapacity crowd-of a record-setting 44,567 fans-was very nervous, sitting on their hands most of the night. They seemed scared to stir up the Presidents who were concentrating so hard in the game, like students pulling an all-nighter to cram for an exam. The game continued scoreless through the tenth, eleventh, and twelfth; only left- hander Ross Williams was left in the bullpen for Manager Charley Johnson.

Tory Taylor started his third inning of relief in the fourteenth by walking the first two batters. Travis Tyler grabbed his mitt and headed out to the bullpen without warning as the POTUS pitching coach went out to the mound for a visit.

Manager Charley Jackson asked everybody left on the bench, "What the hell is he doing? He can't get ready in time!" Taylor was clearly struggling as Jackson called for several throw overs to first base. Then he sent Valencia to the mound to talk over signs. Finally, the home plate umpire had enough of the stalling and warned Jackson to make a decision. As the count got to 2-1, he called the bullpen for an update.

"He says he's ready, Charley. I think he's throwing a hundred miles per hour!" said the bullpen coach.

When ball four crossed the plate, Charley took the slow walk to the mound to remove Taylor, who had walked the bases full. Travis Tyler came running in from the bullpen with fire in his eyes.

• • •

Patty O'Neil was sitting in her hospital bed with her knees pulled in tight to her chest. She had finished her third meal of the night and was still hungry. Several nurses were watching the game in her room, handing her sandwiches left over from the catered lunch. As Patty saw a pitcher come in from the bullpen, she realized it was Travis Tyler. She grabbed for her purse and her Blackberry. "Listen, if he gets three outs, he breaks the record-even if some runs score! Don't screw this up! Look up the record to get the names and numbers straight!" She listened to the reply on the other end and then said, "All right, let me know how it goes." When she clicked off the phone, she said to no one in particular, "Oh God, they can't make a big of a deal about it because Alex still has a chance to hit. Oh shit!"

The three nurses in the room looked at each other and nodded. One whispered, "Type A personality. She'll be dying to be outta here tomorrow!"

• • •

Travis Tyler finished his warm-up pitches after getting an earful from Manager Jackson when he arrived at the mound. "Travis, I know you're trying to help. Talk to me next time you get an itching to be a hero. Now just get me three outs. Don't worry about the guys on base-we'll get some runs to win it!"

Travis grabbed the ball and fired a first pitch fastball to Barry Ortega, who crushed it to center field sending Mendoza to the fence. A gust of wind held the ball while he jumped as high as possible. The ball nestled into his glove, and he came down and fired the ball to the infield. It was too late to stop the runner on third from scoring the go-ahead run.

Tyler recovered to get a strikeout for the second out. The runners had moved up to second and third base on the fly- out, so Travis worked carefully to the right-handed batting Steven Stream, the World Series hero. The crowd was almost relieved at the run scoring and started to show some life, clapping to encourage the third out. Tyler had thrown all fastballs, working the count to 2-2, then snapped off a curve that fell off the plate as Stream's bat swam threw it without contact. Valencia looked in his mitt, found no ball, and spun around to locate it ten feet behind him. Stream took off for first base as Vito grabbed the ball and Travis headed to cover the plate. The catcher hesitated a moment and decided to throw it to first base but it was too late-the run scored. Travis Tyler headed back to the mound with his head down.

Santucci and Hammersly were waiting for him while playing with the rosin bag at the mound. They spoke to each other, ignoring Tyler. "I guess it's time we get some runs, Alex. Don't you have some business to take care off?"

"I think you're right. You'd better tell Mendoza too, because I'm not coming out here again tonight. I need my sleep!"

Travis turned to home plate and finished off the inning with a strikeout, breaking the consecutive shutout innings record at sixty.

Vito collected the ball and patted Travis on the butt with a "Nice job-my fault."

The stadium announcer had all the right information and informed the crowd of the fifth record-breaking streak of the month.

The crowd stood with applause, trying to pace themselves for the possible end of a magical month. It was like the last night of summer before the neighborhood kids would be returning to school. They wanted to catch every firefly before their parents called them in. Tonight, they hoped they could catch one last firefly to provide that spark to come back from a 3-1 deficit in the bottom of the fourteenth inning.

Travis Tyler had to lead off the inning because there were no pinch hitters left. Luckily he was batting .314 and could handle the bat, but this time he flied to center field for the first out. Blake Hopson was hitless in six at bats, striking out four times. He worked the count full, fouled off four pitches, but finally grounded out to second base for the second out.

Bruce Hammersly was two for five with a walk in his return. He saw enough pitches from the on-deck circle to select the slider as the pitch to hit. Alex told him to control the swing and the ball would fly.

The crowd was standing, too tired to clap in rhythm but too nervous to stay quiet. No one had left the ballpark. Suddenly the chant came from the standing-room crowd, a hundred feet beyond the center field fence: "Alex, Alex, Alex." Bruce stepped out and winked at Alex in the on-deck circle. Alex looked back to Mendoza in the hole and nodded that the parade was on. Bruce cracked the next pitch with a smooth swing and landed it in the Scarlet bullpen to make it 3-2. The crowd was breathless as "The Hammer" crossed the plate.

Alex nodded with both hands on his thirty-six-ounce weapon. He waited patiently as two fastballs were wasted outside, followed by an unhittable slider that caught the corner for a strike. Then another slider in the dirt made it a 3-1 count. Alex stepped out and noticed the giant ballpark clock heading toward midnight. He then looked at the third base coach giving the swing sign. The crowd was like an inconsolable child needing attention, crying for Alex to make things right. Alex looked at his bat and saw a little light. A firefly was resting on the trademark before its next takeoff. Alex held his bat horizontally, trying not to disturb the little creature as he reminded himself he was playing a kid's game. The firefly flapped its wings and cruised into the night, signaling it was time to go home.

Alex touched the plate with the bat, laid it on his shoulder for a moment, and extended his hands back as the pitch was delivered. A flattened-out slider stayed up as it crossed the plate. Alex powered his hands through the ball and sent it toward the fireflies in the outfield and then beyond the night toward the big light towers. For a moment, the crowd lost the baseball because it was so high. Finally they noticed it settling a hundred feet beyond the center field fence to the standing room only crowd, who were finally consoled from their yelling. Alex enjoyed every step around the bases. For the first time in a month, he allowed himself to smell the roses. He thought of the two dozen red roses he carried to the redheaded Patty O'Neil this morning and remembered their soothing scent. As he approached third base, he saw the crowd on their chairs jumping and screaming for joy. Finally, the entire team, except for one, was at the plate prematurely celebrating a record-breaking homerun before a victory.

The team was leaving that to Carlos Mendoza in the on-deck circle. The mass celebration finally made it to the dugout as St. Louis manager Mike Marshall went to the mound to help his pitcher get focused. It was a waste of time, as Carlos Mendoza hit a screamer on the first pitch down the left field line just fair and just over the fence to finish the magical month with a 4-3 win.

The dugout exploded toward the plate, hardly able to wait before Mendoza hit the plate. The group hug held on for several minutes, then opened up to the crowd as Mendoza, Hammersly, and Santucci led the team on a lap around the field, stopping to wave and shake a few hands. When they made it to center field, the record-setting, twenty-first-homerun-of-the-month and eighteenth-game-with-an-RBI, baseball came flying out of the standing room only crowd. Alex snagged it in his big right paw.

The Seven streaks had been completed, and the achievement would be written about for us long as humans remembered baseball or for eternity-whichever came first!

PART IV: THE DESTINY

Chapter 52

"**There** were millions of people across the country, who, stayed up for the entire four-hour and fifty-eight-minute game that ended at 12:03 a.m. on September 1 in our nation's capital. Most of them didn't care that Alex Santucci's record- setting homerun and subsequent RBI happened at eleven fifty-nine and fifteen seconds, with him finally crossing a crowded home plate at eleven fifty-nine and fifty-five seconds, giving him five extra seconds to spare in the month of August. For those of us who do care, Alex erased any doubt that his record-setting twenty-first homerun of the month did happen in one unbelievable August."

In Riley Preston's first minute of his report, shown throughout Saturday on *ESPN,* he summarized the joy that numerologists and statisticians in baseball had experienced the past month with "The Seven Streaks." He went on to report on each record that was broken in August and then finished his report.

"The Presidents, with a 77-53 record, and a twelve-game lead in NL East, are a certainty to be in the playoffs and a high probability to have the best record in the National League. Of course, the big question will be whether Alex Santucci will be sidelined more than the predicted two weeks from the laparoscopic procedure next Tuesday. Seeing the instant power from Hammersly, Santucci, Mendoza, and their back- to-back-to-back homerun explosion to win the game last night gives a preview of the fire-works to come in the playoffs, if Santucci can make it back to anything close to his August performance. One thing is for sure: for the first time since professional football has been played in Washington, baseball will not take a back seat in September and certainly not October."

• • •

The Presidents banged out two wins over the weekend to sweep the defending World Series champions. Alex's RBI streak had been snapped on Saturday, when he managed just an infield single in his four at bats. On Sunday, Travis Tyler won his twenty-first game after giving up a first-inning homerun to Carlos Ortega. Alex had two doubles and his forty-third homerun in a 10-2 rout of the Scarlets.

• • •

Off the field during the weekend, Alex's life was a blur, doing countless interviews at the ballpark and coming home to three women in total panic mode getting the wedding together by Labor Day evening. Sally's parents, her maid-of-honor, Claire, and her family, and Leah's kids and husband, Charles, were all in town. Luckily, they were all staying at the North Bethesda Marriott along with other family members from New Jersey and Philadelphia.

They all were invited to a dinner at the Pines of Rome on Sunday night. Alex had reserved the entire left side of the restaurant, which included two large connected rooms for the sixty-five guests. Marco and Pepe were excited to oversee the service. Each table was loaded with several appetizers and entrees, like a family meal. Plenty of wine and drink were flowing the whole night.

Alex and Sally spent the evening visiting the various tables and rarely sat to eat. He was under medical orders to limit his solid food content and alcohol with his planned surgery less than thirty-five hours away. Alex did not consider red wine as alcohol or that Italian bread was not really solid food.

Charlotte was thrilled to meet her three half-brothers

and two half-sisters for the first time. Laura personally invited Charlotte's mother, Margaret, to the wedding, hoping for the whole family to accept the past and bring Charlotte and Margaret into the family. Charlotte had arranged to bring Patty O'Neil to the dinner, a day after she was released from the hospital. Alex thought she could use the distraction.

Alex met his half-brother Paul and his half-sister Claudette along with their father Charles. They sat with their sister Nancy and Leah. Sally had made a point of having them sit with Charlotte, Margaret, and Patty. Alex became fast friends, with Charles talking about golf and the Florida beaches. Claudette, who was sitting next to her mother, had most of her mother's looks, according to Alex. At times he thought he was seeing twins. Finally, Alex found the time to squat between them at the table and take in their beauty from in close. Like her mom, Claudette was a talker with a magnetic personality. She asked Alex about baseball, Sally, Leah, and his political orientation, all in a five-minute conversation. Alex noticed in the middle of the conversation that Paul and Patty were quietly talking at the end of the table.

Claudette realized Alex being distracted and added, "I think Paul really likes redheads!" Alex smiled, knowing he had something in common with his half-brother!

The night and the dinner seemed to pass quickly. Sally and Alex walked out of the Pines of Rome restaurant at 12:03 a.m. The new day was just beginning, and it would be the greatest day in the lives of Alex and Sally. They tried not to think of the day to follow.

• • •

Sally and Alex decided to stay downtown at the Phoenix Park Hotel at 520 North Capitol Street on Capitol Hill. It would be a short ride to St. Dominic's and the

Presidents Park ballpark. Alex woke up at his normal five forty-five to enjoy some coffee and the morning paper. He then dressed and started a run east on Massachusetts Avenue, past the massive Union Station, and around the omnipresent US Capitol Building. He ran past the Roman-looking Supreme Court Building and in front of the Parisian-styled Library of Congress Building. Then Alex continued west down the hill of Independence Avenue, observing the glass-enclosed US Botanic Gardens and the curvilinear National Museum of the American Indian. He made it to the end of the National Mall, where he found a bench to watch the sunrise at 6:39 a.m. under the soaring Washington Monument. To the west were the majestic Lincoln Memorial and the newly rebuilt Reflecting Pool, now sharing the view with the World War II Memorial. The federal holiday provided for a quiet venue, with just a handful of runners, walkers, and sunrise watchers in attendance.

 Alex sat with a clear mind and quiet emotions. He seemed to have adjusted to the lack of pain medication since the B12 shots and serotonin supplement he had been on for almost two weeks. He wondered if his emotions were becoming normal or just too busy to become depressed. A sense of relief was his main outlook. He finally was getting to enjoy his wedding day and then face the surgery tomorrow morning. A beautiful, clear day accentuated the hints of daylight sneaking around the stately obelisk at the end of the mall.

 Alex was not receiving any special thoughts, feeling any insightful emotions, or envisioning any inspirational image as he looked east toward the US Capitol and waited for the first hints of the sun. It was a useful, quiet break in an upcoming eventful day. He enjoyed the next thirty minutes very quietly alone and without interruption as a single man. Then he slowly rose to his feet at 7:10 a.m. to head back to the hotel knowing that he would be married before the sun set at 7:35 p.m. He hoped that his life would then reach an equilibrium or a serenity that he could count on day to day. At the same time, he knew the past seven weeks had provided a lifetime of learning and a wide range of emotional experiences. He had discovered new feelings in old relationships, survived old fears in new relationships, achieved amazing professional success, and brought happiness to a whole community. He wondered if achieving greatness was about taking chances, like achieving the intimacy of being in love or surviving the tragedy of the loss of a loved one. If so, he thought, maybe reaching an equilibrium and serenity in life was overrated!

• • •

    The brightness of the sun was softened by thin slices of clouds above the field at the ballpark. As the Presidents took the field, the fans were hoping it was not the last time Alex Santucci would be in the starting lineup. Today he would give them more instant memories with some spectacular plays in the field and heroics at the plate. He spent an hour before the game signing autographs and continued giving autographs after each inning for fans, who, were waiting at the side rail of the dugout. It was against league rules but he was glad to pay the fine. The crowd was full of signs, wishing him well on his wedding day, and others offered prayers for his health. He showed his appreciation when he hit a two-run homerun in the third inning, followed by a diving grab of a line drive in the fifth inning. Then he hit another solo shot in the seventh inning and finally had a great catch of a pop-up for the last out in the ninth to ensure the 5-2 victory over Chicago. It gave the Presidents an 80-53 record, twelve games ahead of Atlanta, with twenty-nine games to go in the regular season.

    Alex would head to his wedding in the evening and then to his surgery on Tuesday with a .400 average, 45 Hrs, and 150 RBIs. As he walked in front of the Chicago dugout with the last out, the opposing team all came out, shook his hand, and patted him on the back. Alex then stood at home plate waving his cap to the fans, who gave him standing applause for five minutes. Finally, the crowd started to cheer what was on the video board in center field: "Get to the wedding! Get to the Wedding!" They wanted to make sure he would not sign autographs and leave Sally waiting for him at St. Dominic's.

"How thoughtful!" Alex said to himself as he headed to the dugout.

• • •

Alex, Phillip, Guy, Cousin Joe, and Alex's friend Erik Peters from the New York Icons walked into St. Dominic's while it was still light out at six-thirty. Phillip was the best man, and Guy, Joe, and Erik were the good-looking ushers. Erik had flown in from Tampa after their afternoon game, arriving at Reagan National at six-fifteen. He received special permission to leave the Icon game at three-thirty to catch a private jet provided by Frederick Meyers to make the wedding on time. The baseball commissioner and the Icon owner gave special permission to the future Hall-of-Fame player. The Icons won the game 7-2, with Peters going 3 for 3 with 3 RBIs in his three at bats.

They were all dressed in navy blue pin-striped suits with Presidents red ties as they faced four hundred guests in the impressive St. Dominic' sanctuary. The organ played one of Mendelssohn's Organ Sonatas as Alexis Tyler walked in with Erik Peters, followed by Cousins Cora and Joe, siblings Grace and Guy, and maid-of-honor Claire. The regal-looking bride, Sally-in her Jus-tin Alexander-designed, lace mermaid gown with a bateau neck-line-had her hair down, which was covered by a lovely headpiece and veil. Her father, Roger Keegan, walked her to the altar to join with her future husband, Alex Santucci. Father Higgins met the couple and oversaw their vows, then provided his blessing, which was followed by the offering, consecration, and Communion in a quickly performed Mass.

As the wedding party exited the church into the night, Sally and Alex were excited to have become husband and wife in the eyes of the church and state. Emotionally they had cemented their five-year courtship into an eternal relationship in front of friends and family. The wedding party greeted their guests as they left the church and headed to the Diamond Club at the ballpark for the wedding reception.

By nine o'clock, the party was in full motion with the whole ballpark at their service. The food, music, and dancing were inside the club, but many small groups were stationed in different sections enjoying the beautiful outside weather. After the toasts and cake cutting was done, Alex, Sally, and most of the remaining guests headed out to the covered pitching mound and camped out, telling stories about themselves. Some of the teammates talked about their wedding experiences, family members talked about relatives that had passed, and other friends were amazed to be there and kept asking ballplayers questions about playing on this field.

Alex rested with his head on Sally's lap, looking at his delicious bride, and listening to all the chatter. He felt so lucky being loved by such a beautiful, bright, and loyal woman. Sally kept playing with his hair, trying to enjoy the moment but was concerned about tomorrow.

As midnight approached, the friendly security at the ballpark reminded the party that they needed to return inside and end the evening. It was a gentle reminder that good-byes were in order. After they finished their role as wedding hosts and sent their guests home, Alex and Sally returned to their hotel room to settle in for their wedding night. They enjoyed every second together, ignoring that by late morning they would be in the different world of a hospital, and by noon in an operating room, before total exhaustion put them to sleep.

Chapter 53

Johns Hopkins is the largest employer in the state of Maryland. Combined, their Applied Physics Lab in Laurel, the university in Baltimore, and their hospital systems throughout Maryland employ over fifty thousand people. The surgical team that Dr. Walton put together for Alex's operation involved the two best teams from Hopkins and Georgetown. They were being paid special money to spend the whole morning practicing their procedure for any contingency. The media were camped out on the hospital's front lawn ready to broadcast from the beginning of the morning until the end of the day, when hopefully news would become available of Alex's condition and prognosis. *ESPN* was running an all-day history of reports highlighting the Santucci trade, the Presidents record-breaking August, the Labor Day game, and the big wedding. Starting at daybreak, hundreds of fans had gathered to light candles and say prayers for Alex. The crowd had grown to over a thousand by noon. Only immediate family was allowed in the private waiting area that had been secured by Dr. Walton. Sally, Phillip, Leah, Charlotte, and Laura were keeping each other company, waiting for updates from Dr. Henry Walton.

Alex had showed up for the procedure like it was an appearance on *The Late Show with David Letterman,* dressed in a suit and tie, signing autographs and talking with every staff member. He refused to show any concern to Sally when he was called in for the pre operation routine. She was a pillar of positivity with Alex and later with her now official in-laws.

After Alex received his IV and started on a low dose of diazepam, the surgical team came in to tell him about the procedure. Dr. Natalie Woodson from GU (Georgetown University) and Dr. Ross Chang from JHU (Johns Hopkins University) took the lead to educate Alex. They were not prepared for the physical specimen that Alex presented at age thirty-six or his attractiveness as a blond baseball superstar. Not since they had done surgical rounds in an emergency room did, they operate on an athlete so famous and back then it was a mediocre collegiate basketball player. Dr. Harold Howard from GU and Dr. Julius Jenner from JHU were the backup team and had trouble not engaging with the star baseball player. They finally got to tell Alex they were big fans after they were introduced. Natalie and Ross had worked together on various operations over the past five years and were now good friends as well as colleagues who kept in touch. The team had great anticipation in learning what made up the mass that was in Alex's stomach. They hoped they were ready for any contingency.

Working with the laparoscopic equipment was very much like taking batting practice every day against an All-Star pitcher with good stuff. Each procedure had its curves and sliders that led to swings and misses. At other times there were medium fastballs right down the middle of the plate that led to good hits and solid contacts. The real problems were the changeups, when things did not seem as they appeared and led to big misses and strikeouts. The early part of the operation was on course for a solid performance, with Natalie and Ross copiloting the journey to locate the mass intertwined between the adrenal gland and the pancreas.

The anesthesiologist had Alex on diazepam drugs to keep him out just enough to not feel any pain from any surgical cuts. Dr. Yolanda Escobar was ready with a host of knockout medications to put him out for hours if needed. She was referred to as the "long relief gal" who was always ready out of the bullpen to keep her team in the game. In reality she was more like the pitching coach, monitoring all the vital signs and the duration of all the medications being used to sedate the patient. She was also aware of the patient's size and his detailed medical background. Originally from Mexico, Dr. Escobar had grown up seeing the misuse of drugs in her neighborhood. When her father, an electrician, deemed it too dangerous to live there, they relocated in the United States. There she earned a scholarship to UCLA all the way through medical school. Now she was the top in her field, working with elite teams of surgeons on the East Coast. She was curious to find out if the adrenal gland was being "pinched" by the mass just recently by some further new growth or if the medication, Duloxetine, started a chain reaction of activity that led to the abdominal pain reported by the patient. She realized now that all of his organ tests in the past several years may have been influenced by the ongoing infection inside the mass. Ironically, she thought, this is why the Duloxetine was prescribed in the first place. What she did not see in the medical records were the unforeseen results: relief for an undiagnosed, mild depression and a possible jump-start of some adrenal activity, which certainly did not hurt Alex's athletic skills.

The backup surgical team was ready with the arthroscopic equipment in case they needed to help clean up any mess that could not be finished with the laparoscopic tool. Their intent was to avoid, under any circumstance, making a full surgical incision on the stomach, because it would end the season of baseball for Alex Santucci. Among the four surgeons, there was no division on the decision to avoid that incision!

The overhead television screens showed the progression of the operation through the little camera in the laparoscope. Dr. Henry Walton, dressed up in scrubs, was watching from a seat in the operating room. He wanted a front row seat as manager of this team of surgeons. It would be his decision to continue on to full surgery if necessary. He was not thrilled with what he saw as the tiny camera found its way into the abdominal cavity. Scar tissue was intertwined with the adrenal gland down to the pancreas. It had grown, covering what seemed to be an object or a mass of objects. This looked unlike any tumor or growth he had ever seen. Whatever it was, it seemed to be encased in a sealed web of mostly dead tissue.

Dr. Woodson started to lightly shave some of the tissues and vacuum it out. To the untrained eye, it seemed like going to a Greek deli and watching them carve lamb strips off of a turning rod for gyro sandwiches. So far, Dr. Walton could not see any sign of blood vessels that could lead to potential aneurisms. Finally, Dr. Woodson pulled away another piece of scar tissue and found a pool of liquid that included some small blood vessels. It appeared to be a contained infection, like an abscess, that may have been there for years. Ross told her to proceed while he vacuumed the area out.

She put the camera finally on the maze of objects that were dead center inside this mess. "Ross, do you see this? Or am I seeing things?"

Dr. Chang tried to get a closer look and could not make out the object.

"Natalie, can you clean up a part of it so I can see it?"

"Sure...but I can see it, Ross. I just don't know what it is or if I can start to take it out."

"Natalie, what do you think it is? I mean, I think I see it...Oh my God!"

"Yep, there it is. I thought so, Ross." Dr. Woodson lightly pulled out a piece from the maze. "I think it used to be a piece of wood!"

• • •

It was cold and misting as Alex stood on the sidelines. There were not any lights on the field, but somehow, he could see all the players. He had heard there was a game played on this field every night, but he never had the chance to come and join. He was always too busy, but tonight he was ready to enter the game. The light rain was slowing down the players some, but his team was moving down the field with great blocking, quick moves, and clutch catches. Finally, he felt the courage to run on the field during a time out. He was hoping to get in the huddle and see the faces of the players in this seven-man, rough-touch football game. He had heard about these games for years but never played in a league except every year at the Turkey Bowl on Thanksgiving morning. He felt the hood on his head as the mist blurred his vision. As he arrived at the huddle, he was in between Gene on his left and his grandfather Guy on the right. They were the two blocking backs having a lot of fun making their opponents miserable. The other four looked familiar, but he could not recognize them.

The two on each end were young and making fun of him. "That's just like Phillip to get a beautiful blonde pregnant. Your dad is one of kind, kid. I thought he would get here way before you."

The two middle guys were older, around his Uncle Anthony's age, but in great shape. "What are you doing here, Alex? You have a lot left to do before you play with us. We got enough guys. You know, the old ones get younger all the time, so they never quit. Oh yeah...Here he is-he finally made it!"

Alex looked over and saw a figure walking toward the huddle. It was hard to make out his face, but he had a good head of hair and some big forearms. Finally, up close, he saw him-it was Uncle Ernesto! "Hey, Alex, I got it, kid-but thanks for coming. I finally get to play with my son Joe. It's been forty-three years since I saw him last, Alex. Did you meet your great-grandfathers and Taylor over there?"

Alex felt flush with emotions. He could not keep his eyes open as they filled with tears. "Uncle Ernie...Why are you here?"

"It was time for me, Alex-but not for you."

Alex stepped out of the huddle. Ernesto stepped in and hugged his son Joe for the first time as the rest of the team held them together.

Cousin Joe and Taylor then stepped forward toward Alex, and he felt their touch on his right forearm. Joe said, "Listen, Alex. We were your dad's best friends. We know he's in a lot of pain. Tell him we miss him and everything will be all right!"

Alex felt their touch fade away as he saw darkness and tried to remember their faces.

• • •

Dr. Chang had given the order to the anesthesiologist to put the patient under for two to three hours. Dr. Escobar had quickly changed the IV bags and held Alex's right forearm to check the entry point. The backup team was directed to make the arthroscopic cuts to help extract the myriad of the soft fiber of splinters. It was a torturous two hours of extraction, like untying a string with massive knots. Dr. Walton was stunned by the discovery. He now realized why the MRI could not clarify what was in the mass. The amazing scanning machine was not programmed to identify cellulose wood fibers. The team was finally taking out was seemed to be the last piece that was somewhat intact. It looked to be about an inch long and half an inch wide. Dr. Howard grabbed it with his arthroscopic tool, pulled it all the way out, and dropped it in the tray. All four doctors hesitated for a moment while a nurse cleaned the piece of wood. She looked at it and tried to make out the engraved letters.

"What does it say, Nurse Logan?" Dr. Natalie Woodson asked.

"I think it has a L-O-U on it!"

"What the hell is that?" Dr. Howard asked, wondering what he had pulled out.

Dr. Henry Walton stood up, walked to the tray, picked up the piece of wood, and eyed it himself to really believe it. "It's from a Louisville Slugger!"

• • •

Sally, Phillip, Charlotte, Leah, and Laura were running out of things to do by 3:53 p.m. They were all watching *House Hunters International* on HGTV, waiting for the couple to make their final choice of a vacation house. There was great disagreement between Phillip, a licensed but semi-retired real estate agent, and the women on their predictions. He was ready for the spoiled yuppie couple to finish the show so they could watch the always-entertaining *Ellen* at 4:00 p.m.

• • •

Dr. Walton wanted to wait until the end of the procedure before giving the family the good news. His surgical teams had done an all-star job removing the growth in the stomach. They cleaned out everything and found the vascular system to be strong but swollen. They recommended a laparoscopic procedure after the season to make sure they did not miss anything and that everything healed properly. Otherwise, a couple of hospital days' worth of IV antibiotics and a week of soreness would be the only damage. Henry found the family and entered the suite with a smile on his face.

Everyone had a thousand questions for Dr. Walton, but Sally has one important one. "When can I see Alex?"

Chapter 54

Dr. Natalie Woodson's moment in the sun came at four-thirty, when she was tapped by Dr. Henry Walton to report on Alex's surgery and condition in front of the media. She was a Maryland-bred girl who went to Visitation Catholic girl's high school within the shadow of Georgetown University where she attended under-grad and medical school. She had been number one in all of her schools and had ascended to the top echelon in her profession as a surgeon. She was thirty-eight and shy but adorable, like the actress Kate Beckinsale with her English heritage. Her father was a British diplomat and her mother an Irish-Catholic product of the Washington Diocese Catholic schools. Her mother named her after actress Natalie Wood, after watching her in the movie *West Side Story* playing Maria.

Dr. Woodson was standing in front of the media with her perfectly tailored white doctor's coat. One thing going for her was that she was a closeted Presidents fan who, since 2005, had loved watching games until she fell asleep at night. Baseball fit her quiet competitiveness, which had been honed as a second baseman for the Visitation Preparatory School softball team and as a longtime competitive swimmer. Dr. Henry Walton introduced her to the media. She used no notes as she recalled by memory the total procedure for the reporters, giving her opinion on his prognosis and recovery time. The *CNN* medical reporter grilled her on the content of the foreign substance found in Alex's stomach. Natalie refused to speculate on what it was or how it got there, even though she knew exactly what is but had no idea of how it got there. Dr. Walton decided to let Alex to tell that story when he was ready.

She finished the press conference, having satisfied all questions with her knowledge and poise. Then she went down to Fell's Point in the city of Baltimore for some Bertha's mussels with the four other doctors on the team. When the dinner ended, the group of doctors took some time to walk the docks of historic Fell's Point, the original harbor founded in 1730 before the city of Baltimore existed. After the sunset at 7:35 p.m. on September 4, all the doctors headed home except Natalie, who headed back up Washington Street to Johns Hopkins hospital to see her famous patient.

Alex Santucci was sitting up in his hospital bed in his private suite when Dr. Woodson entered the room at 8:00 p.m. She was introduced to the entire family sitting around on couches and chairs in the large room. The all hugged her and made her feel at home even though she was there in a professional manner. Laura and Leah held her hand as she tried to read the patient's chart since the surgery. Charlotte wanted to know where she lived and if she was married. The reality was she lived alone in a large house off Huntington Parkway in Bethesda, a mile or so from the Santucci house, purchased during a failed marriage that ended over two years ago. She was currently looking for roommates. Within the next week, Charlotte would move in as a roommate, followed by Patty O'Neil and Bonnie Bramlett a couple of months later. The four of them would become best friends by Thanksgiving.

Sally was sitting with Alex as Natalie finally checked in with him. She did an abdominal assessment to check for any infection or swelling and a check of his entry wounds. He seemed comfortable and had the right pain medication to get him through the night. By tomorrow morning he would be up walking and released by the evening, but after his release he would continue to take oral antibiotics for ten days. Natalie gave Alex orders to not have any physical activity for ten days other than walking. Alex accepted the orders only if Natalie agreed to stay for an hour with the family and visit while they all watched the Presidents game. Immediately she felt a connection with Charlotte and was charmed by Alex and his inclusive behavior. It was a relief to be in the presence of a loving family, and besides it kept her from a lonely house for a couple more hours.

At eight-thirty that evening, Uncle Anthony came to visit with his forty-two-year-old son, Joe. Before greeting Alex, he pulled Phillip aside. "I'm afraid I have some bad news. Uncle Ernie had a stroke after they returned from the wedding around noon...and died this afternoon around two o'clock."

Phillip was visibly shaken, thinking immediately of Aunt Helen and his cousin Philly. "Oh my God, he looked so good at the wedding. Poor Aunt Helen, isn't this September fourth? It's been forty-three years to the day since Joe died. I completely forgot to call."

"I think they understand you have been very occupied yesterday and today. When do you want to tell Alex?"

"I think we should wait a bit...let him rest until the morning."

"Listen, the viewing is Thursday with the funeral on Friday."

"Wow, that's quick. I guess everybody they know is in Jersey!"

"Everybody except us in DC and the Angelucci's in Philadelphia."

"Do you know if Philly was there?"

"Actually, that's who I talked to. She said she couldn't reach you. She had just dropped them off and went to get some sandwiches from the Hoagie Hut. When she came back, he was not feeling well, so she took him to the hospital...where he went quickly. So she was with him the whole time."

Alex finally noticed his Uncle and Cousin talking to Phillip and called them over to say hi and meet Dr. Woodson. After pleasantries, Alex gathered everyone around to tell a story. "You know, I just remembered this dream I had during the operation. It must have been early on because I remember at one point I almost woke up, and I wanted to remember it more clearly." Alex looked around the room and saw everyone was quiet and glued to his every word. "I was on a football field; it was dark and rainy, but I could see the ball and the players. It was a rough touch game like they played on the field down the street on Sunday morning when I was pretty young. I ran into the huddle and saw Gene and Grand-pop Guy standing together, all wet but happy with smiles on their faces. It seemed weird because Guy looked so young and fierce without his glasses on." Alex paused as everyone chuckled imaging the situation. "They wanted to know what I was doing there, and I said I wanted to throw the ball. Then I saw two younger guys who said they were cousin Joe and Taylor, a friend of Phillip." Alex was reliving it as he spoke, trying to see the faces to remember the details. "They knew about Phillip and Leah. He said Dad, you are one-of-a-kind but that you are in pain and it would be okay." Alex had tears streaming down his face but wore a happy smile. He turned to his dad, held his hand and said, "They wanted me to tell you that they really missed you!" Alex recovered after squeezing Phillip's warm hand. "Then out of the blue, Uncle Ernie shows up with a football in his hands and wants to kick me out. He said it wasn't my time..." Alex paused, "Then Uncle Ernie looked at Joe, his son, and hugged him like drinking water from a desert oasis." He continued, "I think my great-grandfathers were in the huddle as well. They seemed pretty mean looking, you know: ready to play! I think they were happy to see Uncle Ernie. They were patting him on the back, calling him Ernesto and saying, *'Andiamo!'* It was fantastic and seemed so real, but pretty chilling now that I think about it!"

Phillip looked back at Anthony and his Nephew Joe, not having an answer for Alex except for a smile and firm grip of his hand.

Alex said, "You know, Dad, your Cousin Joe held my right fore-arm just like you're doing now!"

Natalie finally stepped forward after a few minutes of silence. "Alex, I think dreaming takes care of a lot of anxiety for us. That's pretty normal to see the people that you miss during this life-time. It probably happened when the anesthesiologist changed the medication to put you all the way under for the arthroscopic procedure. Surgeries can bring those memories up for all of us."

Phillip could not wait any longer. He stepped back from Alex to face everyone in the room. He explained what happened today with Uncle Ernie and the timing of his death. Sally burst into tears, and Laura and Leah took Alex by the hand. Natalie stepped back and sat next to Charlotte, looking for friendship.

Alex sat back trying to take in the information. He put his arm around Sally, who fell into his side for comfort. "We just saw him and Aunt Helen at the wedding. They were so happy. He was moving a little slow, but he looked great. I guess the travel was too much for him."

Natalie chimed in with relevant information. "It sounds like a brain aneurism, which was going to happen no matter what. I'm glad he got to see the wedding. It sounded wonderful!"

"Wow... so I saw everyone in Heaven. They get to play rough-touch football all day. No wonder Uncle Ernie looked so young and happy-he was seeing his son and getting to play sports all day. Now that is heaven!"

Alex hugged Phillip and kissed him on the cheek. "They said you were in a lot of pain-and they said it was going to be all right, Dad." Alex paused to study Phillip's face. "It's not just physical pain is it, Dad? You feel too much emotional pain from all the loss. I never realized it until today. It was so real to see your friend Taylor and your cousin Joe. They looked like great guys-so young and vibrant." He started to see Phillip in a different light as he stayed close to his face. "You were young and vibrant too. I still see that in you, Dad!" Phillip shook his head in silence trying to speak through the tears. "Son, I have everything I need in this world. You and Leah this past month have helped me understand my pain. God has blessed me with Grace and Guy, you and Carol, and now Sally and Charlotte. What else could a guy ask for!"

Alex motioned for his Cousin Joe to sit with him so he

could tell him about seeing his namesake, Joseph Angelucci, who died on September 4, 1969, in a car accident at age seventeen. His Cousin Joe knew that Phillip had lost his closest friend while in high school and that in 1989 another car accident took his next closest friend, Taylor. "You should have seen him. He looked so real and so handsome. I think you would make him proud."

Natalie and Charlotte supported each other while watching such emotion and love on display.

Dr. Natalie Woodson finally got the courage to break up the party. "I think Alex needs to get some rest tonight, but the good news is that he should be home by tomorrow night."

Everyone agreed, but Alex had one more question.

"When are the viewing and funeral service for Uncle Ernie?"

"Thursday night and Friday morning," said Phillip.

"Sally and I will be there!"

Chapter 55

The Branchburg Funeral Home on Route 202 just outside of Raritan was packed inside, with a waiting line out to the parking lot, for the viewing of Ernesto Angelucci. Nearly five hundred friends and family paid their respects during the four-hour marathon session. A five-minute prayer service was performed at the end of each hour for the World War II Navy veteran who spent eighteen months on U-boats in the Mediterranean dodging Nazi fire and securing important islands in the huge sea.

A limousine with a bed, IV, and nurse attending to Alex pulled up to the front door. Sally emerged first, wearing a navy-blue dress with white pearls and matching earrings. She politely asked people in the line if they could enter. Most of the people had no idea who she was but moved quickly to the side when Alex Santucci appeared from the limo. He was helped by his muscular cousin Joe and followed by Uncle Anthony and Aunt Flo, Phillip and Carol. The hundred or so crowd of people sitting in chairs in the large room turned with their jaws wide open when they saw the most famous baseball couple in the country work their way to the front to pay their respects to a fallen family member.

Alex was moving slowly, dressed in his navy-blue wedding suit with a matching tie. They went directly up to the family line of cousins and Aunt Helen. Seeing Alex in person two days after his surgery was a wonderful distraction for them.

Aunt Helen brightened up with a huge smile as she greeted Alex and Sally. "He was so proud of you. After you came to see him, it was all he could talk about. Every game he watched...he knew all the records...You were like a son to him. It gave him a lot of joy this past couple of months. Now he's with our son Joe in Heaven."

Alex took her hand and looked her in the eyes. "I know for a fact that is true, Aunt Helen. They are together in

Heaven playing football as we speak!"

• • •

The family stayed for a short visit paying their respects with the immediate family of Aunt Helen, Cousins Philly, Patrick, and Linda, and their spouses and grandchildren.

Patrick's son, Patrick Jr., refused to let Alex leave and spent every moment talking baseball or about his grandfather. He had a softball doubleheader starting at 7:00 p.m., which would be the first game in years that his grandfather would not be at. He asked Alex, Phillip, Anthony, and Joe to come and watch. Alex immediately accepted for them all and headed to the Bridgewater Marriott for an hour or two to rest and reload with his IV antibiotics.

It turned out that Patrick Jr.'s team was missing some players and could use a first baseman. Patrick Jr. called his Cousin Joe to see if he would play. They found a 4x- large jersey for him to go with his workout clothes for the morning. The players arrived early to take batting practice and soon discovered a buzz in the park about Alex Santucci being in the stands. Actually Alex was standing on the side of the backstop watching the players smashing the slow- pitched softball.

Twenty-seven-year-old Patrick Jr. had been a high school star baseball player who ended up playing Division II baseball at a Florida college for two years before returning home to graduate from Rutgers. He had been recruited for softball the summer after graduation and had been a star ever since, playing sometimes four games a week. He had a graceful line drive swing with occasional power to left field and a whiz in the infield with a strong accurate arm. His second cousin Joe had recently lost over fifty pounds to get down to 285 pounds. He was a powerful, one-man, wrecking crew of the softball when his timing was on. Alex took both of them to the side and gave them tips for both of their swings. With the light aluminum bat in his hand, he was tempted to take a couple swings, but he knew better and told them both he expected something special tonight for Uncle Ernesto!

• • •

Nat Sheridan had very few news items fall into his lap. He was prepared to let the Alex Santucci wedding and surgery story stay private. He had moved on to several mass shootings throughout the country that had provided wonderful headlines in the past few weeks. He was sure that the presidential race over the next two months would provide tons of salacious rumors. Nat had watched the press conference held in the hospital with that beautiful surgeon presenting good news about Alex. It made him happy even though it proved his headlines to be-once again-wrong! Nobody cared about that in his audience; they read his newspaper for the tease, not the ending. He was impressed by Dr. Natalie Woodson with her ability to answer questions quickly in plain English. She had a future on cable television, he thought. But more importantly, she was just his type: British looking and petite. She reminded him of one of the Spice Girls whose name he could not remember-the one that married the soccer star!

• • •

Charlotte and Natalie first thought of the idea, once they heard from Alex and Laura the whole story of what really happened when he was seven.

Alex had always thought the injury was his fault for standing too close to the batter. He was flabbergasted when he heard from his mom that the bat broke into a thousand pieces during a swing when he was catching. His stomach caught a major piece of the bat that cut open his stomach and caused plenty of splinters to enter into his abdominal cavity. The emergency room surgeon in 1983 thought that he had cleaned out the entire wound, but one piece with long fibers worked its way into the area in between his pancreas and adrenal gland. He was put on long-term antibiotics, which seemed to take care of the problem.

Laura came up with the alternate story that Alex was standing to close to the batter because her husband, Gene, was out of town, and her intent was to keep him from worrying about it and to stop Alex from playing catcher with those older boys. Alex ended up laughing when Laura finished the story because he knew the real reason for the alternate story. It was a classic passive-aggressive move by Laura because Gene was out of town and had acted distracted during that summer because of Charlotte, which she did not know about at the time. So she kept her doctor husband from knowing the medical details about Alex. Maybe she had thought, If he's around next time, he'll get to take care if it!

Leah and Sally then made Laura smile when they presented her with a glass jar holding the piece of wood with the "LOU" on it in. They told her they would have done the same thing. Laura gave the jar to Alex to keep for good luck.

Charlotte thought it would be a great story about Alex and would keep his fan base believing he was something special. No one would suspect her and Natalie of leaking it. Natalie was excited because she had never done something so devious before. They took several pictures of the piece of wood from a Louisville Slugger along with a page of surgical notes from Natalie's letterhead. They sent it anonymously to the *New York Post,* to the attention of Nat Sheridan.

• • •

Thursday afternoon Nat Sheridan received the FedEx letter with the items inside. He made some calls to Georgetown University Hospital and the media department with the Washington Presidents. Patty O'Neil had been told by Charlotte to give Nat her phone number. He reached Charlotte first, who was able to add the childhood batting accident details, which led to a confirmation without responsibility.

Nat sat at his desk late Thursday night with his next great story. Now he was getting some tweets about Alex Santucci at a softball game in New Jersey.

When it rains it pours, he thought, but now I can go home early. Hours before his deadline for the midnight website posting, he had tomorrow's headline:
Louisville Slugger Found in Santucci's Stomach! Childhood Accident Turns Alex into Real Slugger

Chapter 56

Patrick Joseph Angelucci Jr. sat in the front pew at Blessed Sacrament Church in the foothills of the Watchung Mountains waiting for his Aunt Linda to finish her eulogy for her father, Ernesto. She was the youngest sibling, the most elegant and impeccably dressed, and had acquired an acute fashion sense while working in Manhattan for fifteen years in advertising. Now fifty-three, she was living comfortably as a full-time mother in New Paltz, a small college town in upstate New York. Only ten years old when her brother died, speaking at her father's funeral completed a living mourning that had lasted forty-three years.

Patrick Jr. listened as Linda told the story of her father's life, a man without an education past ninth grade, who provided wonderfully for his family and was the most loved man in the Bridge-water-Raritan area. Patrick Jr. could only think of the hole left in his life now that his "Pappy" was gone. As Linda finished, Patrick Jr. looked at the program and wished his name was not there under "Eulogies."

He ambled his way up to the podium and turned to look at a packed church. He saw his family in the first few rows and spotted his big Cousin Joe, who hit a pair of titanic shots in the second game of the doubleheader last night to help them complete a sweep. In the row behind them was Alex Santucci, who stayed for both of his games last night, even though he looked dog-tired from the long day and signing every autograph request throughout the evening. Patrick Jr.'s eyes filled up with tears as he unraveled his speech. He wiped his eyes and noticed Alex again, who was pointing to his heart. Finally he saw who was sitting next to him: his favorite player for the Icons, Erik Peters. He nodded to Patrick Jr. and swung his hands, a signal to hit it out of the ball-park.

Patrick Jr. fought through the tears and told an enchanting story of a grandfather who was always there for him, came to every game he played, stopped each day at the

Hoagie Hut where Patrick and his father worked, and had been positive and supportive all of his life. He knew this was his time to carry on the torch of this family for the next generation. Like many men before him, they struggled with the challenge but ultimately prevailed.

•••

At the burial mausoleum double cousins Phillip and Philomena walked together to their seats to watch the final prayers over the flag-draped casket. Four United States Navy Seaman removed the flag elegantly and then in slow motion folded the flag into a neat triangle that every fifty-five and older American remembers watching in awe for the first time in November 1963. After the ceremony was over, the casket was put into its clean, air-conditioned spot above the ground down the hall.

The two Cousins waited in silence for the crowd to thin out, to do something they had not done together in forty- three years. The crowd had moved outside for the moment as Philly grabbed Phil-lip's hand and walked slowly down the hall to read the names and dates on the two-by-two marble-covered cubicles. They found her brother and his cousin, Joseph Thomas Angelucci, born May 25, 1953, died September 4, 1969. They had been together for three weeks in August for their last summer all together as cousins, being teenagers during the day and watching Joe at football practice in the afternoon. He was the starting quarterback his senior year at Bridgewater High School. The news came to Phillip a couple of hours after he went to sleep that Thursday night before the first Friday-night football game in school history.

The double-first Cousins stood in silence as they touched the chiseled dates on the marble face to trace their feelings with the hope of a memory or two. Slowly they retreated to a bench across the hall to sit. They could see from the bench that Ernesto was finally laid in peace next to his son. Philly started to shake and weep as she hid her eyes in Phillip's chest. He stroked her hair and wished they could have shared their pain forty-three year ago. They were separated then by an ocean. An inner calm came over him as he felt relief knowing the two earthly bodies were next to each other in peace and that Heaven would take care of the rest.

• • •

    Alex and Sally spent a restful weekend, their first one as a married couple, in their Johnson Avenue suite. They took long walks in the neighborhood and played some catch behind North Bethesda Middle School. It was soft tossing, but for Alex it felt good to stretch out some of the soreness slowly leaving his body. When they returned home on Sunday morning, they made some coffee and separated out the *Washington Daily* on the deck table. The Presidents had won again on Saturday night. The sports head-line screamed, "The Hammer Sizzles in September." It reported that Presidents star shortstop Bruce Hammersly had picked up where Alex Santucci had left off in August, leading the team to a 7-1 record in September. Alex studied the box scores and statistics for the first time in a week, trying to catch up on his teammate's play. He felt awkward being away from the team, but he knew that the time was needed to heal his injury and begin his married life with Sally.

    They had hundreds of cards and gifts that each needed a response. He was pondering a two-day honeymoon in New York City, which would be a surprise to Sally. By next Friday, September 14, he would be cleared to start his regular physical routine and was hoping to return to the lineup by the next Friday, the twenty-first, at home against Los Angeles. It would give him thirteen games left in the regular season to get back to speed before the playoffs started. The time off would allow him to focus on his threefold plan: to rehabilitate his body, to catch up on his emotional development, and to follow his heartfelt destiny to bring a championship to Washington.

• • •

The next two weeks for Alex and Sally was a preview of suburban life in the future, if that was ever possible. After a lazy Sunday and Monday, Alex surprised Sally with an Acela Express train ride to Manhattan in two hours and fifty-three minutes. He planned for them to be in Manhattan until Thursday or Friday morning, accepting an invitation to stay at Erik Peters's guest quarters in his penthouse. Erik's chef was available for meals in his dining room, and there was a butler to coordinate any questions about Manhattan. Erik was insistent at Ernesto's funeral that Alex use his place if he decided to take Sally to Manhattan this week. Erik was in Boston until late Thursday night trying to sweep Boston. New York continued to have the best record in baseball, ahead of Washington by one game. They had opened a ten-game lead in the American League East. The two good friends never mentioned playing each other in the World Series. As veterans, they knew talking about a matchup ahead of time would upset the gods of baseball.

On Tuesday night the famous couple accepted a dinner invitation from Cousin Philly to join her and Cousin Linda, who came in town with husband Peter. They had a comfortable time at a small Italian restaurant. Then they went to listen to some music in a small club and then back to Philly's apartment for dessert. They stayed up until 3:14 a.m. listening to stories about Phillip and Cousin Joe. Alex had never understood the depth of closeness they had with his father. Phillip had never shared much about his relationship with his Jersey Cousins other than fun and love for them.

Wednesday was a day of reading, eating, and naps.

Alex was still working on the novel *11/22/63* that he had started in Texas. He was starting to identify with the main character, who headed back in time through a portal in a diner in Maine. It plants him there in the late fifties, where he has to live for years to finally track down Lee Harvey Oswald starting in 1962. Alex sometimes wondered if he was a character in a novel sent back in time to track down a championship for DC. Fortunately he dropped that idea as soon as he would put the novel down.

In the evening, they took a cab to Citibank Field in Queens to see the Presidents take on the New York Firemen. It was the rubber game of a three-game series. Alex and Sally were introduced in the locker room at six-thirty and were greeted with a hero's welcome. Alex was forced to show his recently healed stomach wounds and his famous piece of wood recovered from his guts as reported in the *New York Post*. He carried around the famous one-inch piece of wood in a two-inch glass bottle to keep it safe. It was now his good luck charm!

In the morning they left for DC on the 10:12 a.m. Acela train from Penn Station to Union Station. Alex headed straight to the ballpark for a meeting with Dr. Walton and the training staff of the Presidents to decide on his rehabilitation for the next week. Sally took the cab home after dropping off Alex. She planned to see him at the game tonight.

After a thorough physical examination and several strength tests, Alex was cleared for full physical activity. He spent the next two hours doing some running, swimming, and yoga. He felt very strong, but his flexibility was not his normal, which was understandable. When teammate Perry Montgomery, who was on the disabled list showed up after four o'clock, he was thrilled to see Alex in his batting practice jersey. Perry threw some batting practice to Alex underneath the stands for some easy swings that made him feel like he was back at home. It was hard to believe it had been eleven days since he had last swung a bat.

The Presidents were starting a three-game series in Atlanta. Their magic number to clinch the National League East Division was eight. With nineteen games to go and a twelve-game division lead they needed a combination of the eight Presidents wins and Atlanta losses to clinch. They could get the number down to two with a sweep of the series.

• • •

On Saturday, September 15, Alex started his running routine with Charlotte, who had moved in up the street off Huntington Parkway. At 6:00 a.m., he enjoyed running in a new direction south toward downtown Bethesda. They found a nice back route through some neighborhoods to the light at Beech Avenue and Old Georgetown Road to cross over and meet Phillip at the Bethesda YMCA. They followed with thirty minutes of swimming and either yoga or weight work every other workout.

On Sunday, Tuesday, and Thursday, Alex took his workout pals down to Ayrlawn Field to work on his pitching. This time Alex had a bucket of fifty balls for himself to throw, a bat and helmet for Charlotte, and a catcher's mitt, mask and equipment for Phillip. By Tuesday Charlotte made contact with three balls; by Thursday it was up to ten, with her first line drive on ball number fifty. She never stopped talking about it the whole day!

Chapter 57

Alex returned to the active roster Friday night against the Milwaukee Millers. The Presidents had split the previous six games and needed a win and an Atlanta loss to clinch the division crown. Jerry Gonzalez moved from third base to second base to replace Chris Patek, allowing Alex back into the lineup at third base and batting third in the lineup. The locker room had trouble containing their excitement. The crowd was on the edge of their seat wondering how Alex would perform. Unfortunately, he looked very rusty at the plate and in the field, going hitless in four at bats while making two errors in the field. The Presidents looked listless, losing 4-1. They played the same way on Saturday night, getting shutout by a rookie pitcher, 6-0. Alex again went hitless in four at bats and had another throwing error from third base. The only good thing about Saturday night was Sunday morning! Atlanta lost an extra-inning rain-delayed game in Philadelphia, which ended at 12:47 a.m. on Sunday, September 23. That clinched a tie for the division for the Presidents. Later that afternoon, the Presidents would have a chance to celebrate their own division-clinching win.

• • •

Sunday morning Alex went to St. Dominic's alone, where Father Higgins was serving the Mass. Alex felt empowered by his sermon, which focused on second chances for those who are leaders. His major point was that leaders sometimes lose their way and expect things to fall back in place for them. He emphasized that to be a true leader you have to work harder than anybody else. He used the example of Christ taking three hard years of work to build his following. "Even on the night of his death, Jesus outworked the apostles, staying up all night, praying while they slept." The concept caught

Alex's attention. After the service, Alex stayed in the front pew pondering his thoughts while gazing at the beauty of the stained-glass windows hovering over the altar. He noticed in the program an hour of "reconciliation" or confession, starting in fifteen minutes. It gave him a curious feeling about wanting to try it. It had only been twenty-five years since his last confession!

Father Higgins found him in the pew and was thrilled to see him in good health and in person. He welcomed him back and asked about his bride, Sally, and his family. Alex filled him in on the last two weeks and then surprised the elderly man of the cloth by asking him if he was taking confessions.

"No, Father Servantes will be taking confessions in the church, but we can talk anytime in my office, if you like."

"Thank you, Father, for the offer, but I think I'll wait in line like everyone else. But I do have one question!" "Yes, my son, what is it?"

"Can you give me the sacrament for the sick after I go through confession?"

"You mean the 'Anointing of the Sick'. Yes, I would be glad to. Just come to my office after your confession."

Alex found the confessional line with six people ahead of him. None of them looked up to notice who he was. Most of them were older Hispanic women, under five-feet tall with scarves on their head. He stayed very quiet as he waited, wondering what he would say to Father Servantes. It was finally his turn to enter the small area of the confessional, where he took a seat across from the forty-something Father Servantes.

The priest was looking forward in a prayer trance of some kind. Alex decided to close his eyes and seek clarity in his soul. It was quiet for a minute, and he heard Father Servantes's comforting voice ask, "How can I help you with your confession?"

Alex became alert from his search and answered with religious preciseness. "Bless me, Father, for I have sinned. It has been twenty-five years since my last confession. I think I was eleven. It was soon after confirmation that I never felt the need to confess anymore."

"God is never in the past my son, he sees everything in the present. He knows your reasons why you stayed away and always accepts his children back if they ask for worthiness. Through the sacrament of confession, we find out if we are still worthy to receive the spirit of Jesus Christ through forgiveness."

Alex once again remembered his favorite parable about prodigal son, a son seeking forgiveness and acceptance from his father.

"Is there something that you need to confess, my son?"

Alex knew what was left in his emotional past that he never accepted.

"I never cried when my adopted father died when I was fifteen. All I did was play baseball all day-and for the rest of my life until now. Then about a month ago, I found out about a mistake he made which made me question my feelings about him. Then two weeks later, I cried about it after a stressful day and let go of my anger at him. So I went to see him the next day at his grave site and figured out something about my life-that I never really grieved about his death. Just last week I was at a funeral for my great-uncle and witnessed his grandson experience loss with courage."

"My son, I don't hear a sin there, but I do hear a very sad heart. May I help you with something?" Father Servantes waited through the silence and then saw a vision of a boy sitting with his father. "Alex, what was the last thing you did with your adopted dad?"

Alex immediately was sent back twenty-one years to the Johnson Avenue kitchen. It was late at night, and he was sitting with Gene, feeling hungry and eating everything in sight. He remembered they were talking about the Redskins and then Gene whispered something in his ear. He felt a tickle in his ear that brought tears to his eyes. Alex told Father Servantes, "We talked about sports after my baseball game that he came to see. I hit a game-winning homerun. He was very excited and was the happiest I'd ever seen him."

"What made him so happy, my son?"

He loved me... I mean, he loved seeing me...hit homeruns."

"Well, that sounds like two things he loved!"

"What's that, Father?"

"He loved you first and foremost, and he loved to watch you hit homeruns."

Alex quietly listened to the priest's words and then heard his words: "He loved me." He finally realized his soul felt that love unconditionally. He knew his dad's love was always deep inside his soul. He pondered the effect of the cleansing that his operation did to his body. With the growth and infection gone, maybe his feelings would be easier to recognize.

Father Servantes waited patiently as Alex returned his eyes to meet with his. "Well, Alex, I think your adoptive father has been a very happy man with your performance lately. Congratulations, my son. Would you like to receive a penance?"

Alex smiled at being recognized. The image of Gene and his friends in Heaven watching his games brought a smile to his face. "Yes, Father, I think that would help me focus."

"Very well, my son, how about two 'Our Fathers' and two 'Hail Marys',-and maybe...two homeruns!" Father Servantes smiled as he blessed Alex with the sign of the cross and the Prayer of Absolution.

Alex said his prayers at the altar railing with a smile still on his face. When he finished, he visited Father Higgins to receive his sacrament for the sick, making it a three-sacrament day and a four-sacrament month, including receiving the Eucharist and holy matrimony.

Experiencing these sacraments as an adult were very different experiences than when he was confirmed in the fifth grade. That experience turned him off to religion for twenty-five years. There were classes on Sunday and Wednesday nights where he had to memorize prayers to become of age in the church. It was a process that seemed to drain all of the Holy Spirit out of him that he gained from his first Communion experience, where he learned to take the Holy Eucharist after a proper confession. To Alex, the confirmation ordeal seemed like doing a lot of paperwork to get more spiritual, as opposed to taking the Holy Eucharist and confession, which were "of the moment" experiences. That reminded Alex that being in the batter's box and fielding a ground ball were "of the moment" experiences. He was looking forward to getting "of the moment" many times at the ballpark today!

• • •

Alex spent an hour in and out of the hot Jacuzzi and the cold tub before the game, hoping to create some shock waves to wake up his muscles. Playing two games had created some soreness, much like spring training when you play your first back-to-back games.

Manager Charley Jackson had no plans today to sit Alex or any of his other thoroughbreds. He knew it was just a matter of time before his horses were ready to ride, and he did not have an ounce of concern over the lackluster performance of his team during their first two-game losing streak in a month.

Ace Travis Tyler would be on the mound today hoping to ride his team to a division crown. Manager Jackson told him he would have one more start this season of no more than five innings after this key game. If today's goal was accomplished, he would have some extra days off before the playoffs started in two weeks. Tyler was a shoo-in for the Cy Young Award at the end of the season. His 24 and 4 record, low ERA, designation as NL strikeout leader, and a record sixty shutout innings in row would likely make the voting unanimous.

Tyler found Alex dressing in the locker room and sat next to him to thank him for being his friend and to see how his was feeling.

"I'm actually full of sacraments and ready to rock 'n' roll out there, but let's keep this between us..." Alex pulled Travis close to him." I think we should put on a show this afternoon. Let's set off some fireworks!"

"I'm actually full of sacraments and ready to rock 'n' roll out there, but let's keep this between us..." Alex pulled Travis close to him." I think we should put on a show this afternoon. Let's set off some fireworks!"

Travis sat back and looked at Alex, who seemed fairly serious. Travis was never one to boast, and he knew Alex was not a show-boat either, but they both had great confidence in their ability. "I'm with you, Alex. Let's bring some heat and brew these Millers!"

• • •

The autumnal equinox arrived on Saturday, September 22, at 10:49 p.m., making Sunday's contest the first baseball game of the fall. Clinching on Sunday would be the first step in getting to the Fall Classic. The challenge for the Presidents fans, at the sold-out ballpark, was to not be distracted by the Washington Potomacs football home opener less than ten miles east of the ballpark at FedEx Field. Number one draft choice, quarter-back Marcus McNeil III, better known as Big Mac III, had led the Potomacs to a 1 and 1 record in their first two games of the season, both on the road. Meanwhile owner Burton Parker had become a huge Alex Santucci and Presidents fan since the trade in July. He sent texts to Alex congratulating him on his record-setting hitting in August; he attended the wedding and many President home games as a guest of the Meyers family. Today he would show video updates of the Presidents game at FedEx Field to highlight their possible historic division-clinching win. Fortunately, it would be a great day for both teams!

Travis Tyler led the charge from the gate with a quick four-pitch, one-two-three inning to start the first. The Presidents stormed the batting box in the bottom of the first with a first-pitch single from Blake Hopson. Bruce Hammersly followed with ascorching double down the third base line, bringing up Alex Santucci. He had never faced the Millers pitcher Arturo Guerrero in a game. He threw a fastball and slider most of the time with an over-the-top delivery that hid the ball at times. Sometimes early in a game his fastball would stay up in the strike zone like the first two pitches to POTUS hitters. Alex was looking for that up-in-the-zone fastball and on a 1-1 count, he got it. He tomahawked a swing using his massive forearms, which lashed the ball, never reaching higher than twenty feet in the air, over the center field fence to give the Presidents an early 3-0 lead.

Tyler continued to be in command through the second and third innings, using only sixteen pitches combined to get six outs. Alex doubled in the third inning and scored on a Mendoza single to make it 4-0. The Millers were hopeless against Tyler in the fourth and fifth, striking out five times. Guerrero was sent to the showers in the fifth inning after Alex's triple drove in two runs to make it 6-0. Marty Morris added a homerun two batters later to make it 7-0.

●●●

Just before halftime at FedEx Field, Marcus McNeil III scored on a twenty-three-yard run to match the Presidents score at 7-0. The Potomacs crowd went wild when the Presidents highlights were shown on the massive end zone video screens. The Presidents fans followed suit, showing their excitement when the Potomacs halftime highlights were played on the video scoreboard high over the right-center field fence.

Travis Tyler lost the strike zone early in the sixth inning, walking the first two batters. The reining NL MVP from 2011, Brian Bowers, crushed a first-pitch, get-it-over fastball into the Milwaukee bullpen to cut the lead to 7-3. The Presidents responded quickly in the bottom of the sixth inning, starting off with a single by Hopson and a two-run homerun by Hammersly that made it 9-3.

Alex was up with two outs, needing a single to hit for the cycle. He thought about laying down a bunt with the third baseman playing way back or choking up and punching an outside pitch to right field, but then he thought about his penance. A deal is a deal, he thought. Wham! The ball shot toward the heavens. It looked like a high popup to the outfield; then a high gust of wind rushed off the river and pushed it toward the flower boxes just over the left field fence. It was his forty-seventh homerun to make the score 10-3 after six innings.

The game was moving along swiftly for the modern-era baseball game, and there was lots of scoring. At 2:47 p.m. it was threatening to be finished in less than two hours.

• • •

Big Mac III was guiding the Potomacs through the third quarter with a long ball control drive to match the earlier Cincinnati field goal to maintain a 10-3 lead. Burton Parker, for the first time ever, left his owner's suite before the fourth quarter. He went down to the field because he was full of nervous energy. Being a lifelong DC area resident, he was having major hometown anxiety about the Presidents and the Potomacs maintaining their leads.

He announced to everyone before he left the suite, "This could be one of the biggest days in DC sports history, and I have to get on the field to experience the players and the fans." He turned to his media director and said, "Make sure they keep up those baseball feeds every chance we get. I don't want to miss anything!"

The media director answered, "Yes sir, Mr. Parker!"

•••

    Tyler settled down in the seventh and eighth innings, allowing just one base runner. His confidence was in full command as he sat in the dugout waiting as the Presidents batted in their last inning as non-division winners. Beer sales were at an all-time high as last call in the seventh inning had just ended. The seasonal weather added to a comfortable party atmosphere. Bruce Hammersly added to the pending celebration as he continued to "Sizzle in September" with another two-run blast in the eighth inning to make the outcome certain with a 12-3 lead.

    Alex came to the plate mentally feeling as loose as he had ever been on a baseball diamond. He took his time drinking in the atmosphere and the crowd as they cheered, "We want a cycle!" They were referring of course to the most overrated baseball oddity of all time, hitting for the cycle: a single, double, triple, and homerun in one game. It was like getting three pair in a seven-card draw poker game; it looked good but did not always guarantee a win. Hitting for the cycle produced ten total bases and sounded sexy, but two homeruns and a triple or two homeruns, a double and a single both produced eleven total bases-but as a box score it did look as sexy. So far in this division-clinching game, Alex had thirteen total bases in four at bats. The record for total bases in a game was nineteen set by left-handed slugger Shawn Green in 1992, who hit four homeruns, a double and a single, going an amazing 6 for 6. No one in the history of baseball had achieved seventeen total bases in a game without hitting four homeruns in a game. Alex Santucci was about to become the first, producing his version of the cycle. It would be named by Ron Roswell, in his Monday morning article, as "The Santucci Cycle": three homeruns, a triple, a double, and 7 RBIs-like the number on his uniform.

Ex-Presidents pitcher Pedro Fernandez was cleaning up the mess for the Millers in the eighth inning, trying to get the last out before the inevitable loss after three outs in the top of the ninth inning. He threw a little harder than a slow-pitch softball pitcher these days but had great location with three different speeds-slow, slower and slowest. Ron Roswell, again from his morning article compared Pedro's approach, pitching to Alex Santucci in the eighth inning, to Yankee pitcher Mike Kekich in 19 71. Kekich had grooved a fastball to Frank Howard in his last at bat ever at RFK and who was rumored to have said after the game, "I wanted to see how far Frank could hit one!"

Pedro threw his normal first three off-speed pitches outside hoping to catch the plate for a strike. Even on a 3-0 count, Pedro never threw the ball down the middle of the plate. Later in the locker room, he would say to a reporter with a wide smile, "The pitch...It got away from me!"

Pedro fired his best eighty-three-mile-per-hour fastball about belt high, and Alex extended his thirty-six-ounce bat barrel, catching the fattest part of the ball. At the same time, 3:37 p.m., it would be noted, the Potomacs were kicking a forty-six-yard field goal to extend their lead to ten points with 2:16 left to go in the game. As the tumbling football headed toward the goal post at FedEx Field, the crowd at Presidents Park held their breath for a moment. They watched a tape-measure shot head for the rotating scoreboard above the Red Porch section, way deep in left-center field that was currently showing football scores. As the ball careened off the LED lighting of the scoreboard, it seemed to change the Potomacs score from 10-3 to 13-3. The bruised baseball rebounded down into the Milwaukee bullpen, a good eighty feet below. It was recovered by reliever Wayne Cauley, who had been traded by Seattle to Milwaukee after the Kansas City series before the All-Star break. He would enjoy saving it for his friend and opponent Alex, to give to him after the game. It was Alex's forty- eighth homerun of the year, tying the best year of homerun slugging by his hero Frank Howard.

    The Santucci Cycle was complete, making the score 13-3. The top of the ninth was pure joy for the 41,323 fans, who, were all standing, wishing that the moment of victory would continue forever. They hoped the Tyler fastballs would make the opponents' bats keep missing, the Santucci and Hammersly homeruns would keep jumping off the bats, the opponents' ground balls would keep finding the Presidents' mitts, and the air on the first full day of fall would keep this smell of triumph all the way to the World Series!

•••

    The 81,323 at FedEx Field were riveted to the end zone video screens after the Potomacs' 13-3 victory was final at 3:50 p.m. After shaking hands with the opponents, Big Mac III and Burton Parker stood together at the fifty-yard line surrounded by teammates in silence and watched Milwaukee's last hope against the determined Travis Tyler on the mound. They watched his last windup and delivery of the final unhittable fastball blister the mitt of Vito Valencia, which was recorded in history at 101 mph.

•••

    The final strike that secured the last out to clinch the NL East Division happened at 3:52 p.m. on September 23, 2012. Fireworks erupted immediately from beyond center field that could be seen ten miles away. They seemed to proclaim an end to eighty seasons without a postseason of baseball in Washington, DC. The crowd of 41,323 at Presidents Park would remember exactly the space they occupied when an ocean of craziness exploded in the stands and the field. People stood cheering in their seats, some put their heads in their hands and cried like babies, others ran down the aisles to get as close to the railings as possible. But most could not stay grounded as they jumped and screamed approval of their favorite team.

The collective roar coming from both stadiums could have sounded like two high-decibel rock concerts playing at the same time. The players mobbed Travis Tyler and Vito Valencia at the mound. Alex stood at the edge of the pile trying not to get molested as he looked into the stands to find Sally and Philip. They had made it to the railing of the dugout escorted by security. Alex slowly walked to the railing and hugged them both as he headed toward the dugout with the mayhem still on the field. He watched from there as the players slowly removed themselves from the massive pile in front of the mound and caught by local and national media for interviews. Alex collected himself, wiped his eyes, quietly thanked Fathers Higgins and Servantes for their timely sacraments, and headed back out to the field to enjoy the beautiful fall weather!

Chapter 58

The Presidents split their final ten games of the year, which gave them a 100 and 62 record, making them the best team in baseball after the regular season. As with most sports, once the playoffs start, best regular season records become irrelevant. But the stellar record did provide an extra home game per series, except for the World Series where home field advantage is determined by the winner of the All-Star game. If the Presidents made it that far, they would have Alex Santucci to thank for not having home field advantage. Manager Charley Jackson was able to rest his regulars for about half of the last ten games because of the expanded roster. Alex played most of the four home games and two games in Saint Louis, where thousands of Kansas City fans drove across the state to get autographs and see him play.

The team announced before the series that Alex would miss the Saturday night game, allowing Sally and Alex to spend an entire day in Kansas City to see her parents and friends from Park University and his Great-Grandfather Alex Skarstedt.

• • •

Leah traveled with Phillip to Kansas City to be there when Alex and Sally visited the elder Alex. They all wanted to tell him the story of how Alex became his great-grandson and how Phillip put the pieces of the puzzle together. It was quite an evening that left Alex Skarstedt speechless. He was too old to give Leah a lecture and too tired to do anything but enjoy Alex and Sally as they each held a hand of his.

Finally, he was able to wish them the best marriage possible and healthy children. "I know you will make it to the World Series and probably against that New York team. I remember we beat them in twenty-four but lost to them in thirty-three. I'll be hoping for the twenty-four result this time. I just wish I could be there, Alex!"

•••

    Alex completed the season going 5 for 22, his worst streak since the first half of the season-not that anybody cared to notice. All five of the hits though went for extra bases, including three homeruns, a triple, and a double. His final batting statistics were staggering: a .393 average, with 51 Hrs, 48 doubles, 12 triples and 162 RBIs. He ended up hitting an astounding .523 with 30 Hrs and 84 RBIs during his 155 at bats and 43 games in the National League. Overall, Alex ended up four hits from achieving the magical .400 batting average. His teammates became convinced that he purposely fell short of batting .400 because it would have taken too much attention away from the team's accomplishments, especially since the division was wrapped up. He did care about hitting fifty homeruns because it allowed him to join an elite group of sluggers in baseball history: only twenty-six players in all, including fifteen during the steroid era from 1995-2006 before testing was implemented.
    Alex would win the unofficial Professional League Triple crown but did not officially qualify for the batting, homerun or RBI titles in either league. The Commissioner's Office was overwhelmed with pressure to make an exception to the rules and award a special triple crown because of such an exceptional overall year. As the playoffs approached, Presidents fans were hoping that his great regular season of hitting would continue all the way to the World Series.

• • •

The National League Division Series started on Saturday, October 6, in Pittsburgh. The Commandeers had beaten Atlanta in the first one-game playoff of wild card teams. This was the first playoff appearance for Pittsburgh in twenty years, since the days of Barry Bonds. The city was excited about its young team led by superstar Armand McCullough, who officially won the NL batting crown with a .361 average. The Presidents strategy was to at least split the two games in Pittsburgh and then win the series at Presidents Park in front of the home fans.

Pittsburgh and Washington had met once before in post season during the 1925 World Series, when Washington was one game away from back-to-back championships, leading three games to one. Walter Johnson had won games one and four while on his way to winning game seven. With a 6-4 lead in the seventh inning, American League MVP shortstop Roger Peckinpaugh made two errors that led to four unearned runs. The seventh game had been canceled twice due to downpours and then played in wet conditions that became unplayable in the seventh inning during another downpour. Commissioner Judge Landis was about to call the game when Nationals owner Clark Griffith talked him out of it, saying that the championship would be forever tainted, though he feared for the safety of his team as well. Pittsburgh was the only team to come back from a 3-1 deficit in the World Series until the 1958 Yankees.

Travis Tyler was on the mound in the first game of the Divisional Series to lead the Presidents to a 5-1 win. Leo Lawrence gave up an early three-run homerun to Armond McCullough that held up in a 3-2 Pittsburgh win to even the series at 1-1. Baseball postseason returned to Washington, DC, after a 79-year absence when game three opened on Tuesday, October 9, to a wonderful 8-2 victory that put the

Presidents one game away from the League Championship Series. Veteran Pitcher Tony Johnson, the only pitcher on the President staff with playoff and World Series experience, pitched a beautiful five-hitter, shutting out Pittsburgh 4-0 to win the Divisional Series three games to one.

The National League Championship Series would start on Sunday, October 14, in Washington, DC, giving the players four days off-the most off days since the All-Star break.

• • •

Sally and Alex used the first day off to plan a honeymoon escapade to Italy for three weeks starting after the season finished, which they hoped would be after a World Series victory.

On Friday they traveled to Charlottesville, Virginia, to visit the area and see Guy Finelli and the Terps play against the University of Virginia (UVA) on Saturday. Grace and her boyfriend, Luke, made the trip from Raleigh to join them along with Phillip and Carol from Kensington. Cavalier alumnus, Bruce Hammersly, graciously opened his nearby estate to the Finelli-Santucci clan and secured a half dozen tough-to-find tickets as well. The young Terp team had started the season with a surprising 4 and 1 record but were two-touchdown underdogs to UVA.

Freshman Guy Finelli was starting to turn some heads running the defense from his free-safety spot. He already had four interceptions and four touchdowns scored: two on interception returns and one each on a punt and kickoff return. He also had six receptions, playing a limited number of plays on offense. This past week, he was also running the scout team offense in practice because the Terps' third-string quarterback (QB) was sidelined with an ankle injury. The Terps first two QBs were true freshmen, because the only veteran QB tore his ACL in an August practice.

The game at noon on Saturday, in front of a sold-out college football crowd, was a great distraction for Alex and his family. They were completely anonymous in this crowd, except for wearing red and white in a sea of blue and orange. He loved to watch football and saw several of Guy's high school football games last year. Today Guy was anchoring a defense against a tough Cavalier running game and solid receivers. Before the game, Guy told Phillip and Alex that he was not worried about the run because the new 3-4 defense was very tough against the run and that their QB was easy to read.

Right before halftime, the young QB for the Terps, Larry Mount, tried to score from inside the five-yard line but was drilled by a Cavalier linebacker at the one-yard line. He was helped off the field after suffering a concussion. The Terps punched it in to go ahead 14-12 at halftime. Four different times the young Terp defense had held a determined Cavalier running game inside the red zone to four field goals. Two other times Guy intercepted passes in the end zone to stop drives.

In the stands, the isolated Terp fans scattered throughout, gathered near the small Terp visitor section to "feel the love" of Terp Nation. Alex and Sally were recognized quickly, and all six of their gang, were welcomed to sit in the middle of the Terps section. At halftime, Alex signed Terp hats, shirts, and programs. The *ESPN* coverage of the game found him for an interview before the second half kickoff. This was when the nation was first introduced to the brother connection of baseball's superstar, Alex Santucci, and the future football superstar, Guy Finelli.

In the third quarter, the Cavaliers woke up the crowd, returning the opening kickoff for a touchdown. Then the Virginia defense intercepted a pass on the next Terp possession inside the twenty-yard line and scored on a draw-play up the middle. Then Guy Finelli shocked the college football world by scoring three straight touchdowns: two interception returns sandwiched around a punt return. Once he got his hands on the ball, Guy was almost indestructible at six-feet, five-inches, 234 pounds, with a

4.40 time in the forty-yard dash. Offenses were not prepared to tackle him, often throwing their bodies at him, hoping to knock him off his feet.

Virginia went back to the ground game after the fourth quarter started with a Terp fumble by second team QB Carson Bowe. They ate up eight minutes of the clock to score and added a two-point conversion to tie the score at 35-35 with five minutes left in the game.

Carson left the bench to enter the game after the kickoff and collapsed halfway to the huddle. Later in the hospital, they found a bruised kidney and an injured spleen, which led to a loss of blood pressure from some internal bleeding. He was carted off the field as number twenty-one started throwing passes on the sidelines.

Coach Hank Ford pulled Guy over and asked him what he was comfortable running on offense.

Coach Hank Ford pulled Guy over and asked him what he was comfortable running on offense.

Coach Ford looked at his prized freshman and somehow believed in what he said. "It's all yours, Mr. Finelli. Just be careful-I don't want to pull your brother from the stands to play quarterback!"

"Don't worry, sir. I got it covered. Just keep my wide-outs fresh."

Guy started from the twenty-yard line in the shotgun and ran for twenty-three yards on the first six plays. It looked like street football from the Red Grange days, but it seemed to be working. He threw three straight hook patterns to his wide-outs for another twenty yards. With two minutes left in the game, Guy ran the ball down to the twenty-five-yard line for another first down. Then he got under the center and handed off to the fullback twice to get to the twenty-yard line with fifty-five seconds left in the game. He called a time-out and stayed in the huddle, his team refusing to leave his eyes for Gatorade from the sidelines.

The Terp section was singing the Maryland fight song over and over, ending with, "M-A-R-Y-L-A-N-D. Maryland will win!" In the huddle, Guy called the play that he knew would win the game. He told his center that he would be standing in punter distance from him. The center nodded in approval. Then Guy told his right-outside wide receiver to run a five yard out at the first down marker. He wanted the right-inside slot receiver to clear out deep into the end zone, looking inside the whole way. Then he told the tight end to run a flag pattern, cutting at seven yards and aiming at the sidelines in the middle of the end zone. He told the left-side wide outs to go after the safety and to keep him left.

Before he broke the huddle Guy looked up at his team and said, "After we score, no celebrating, because we're going for two to end this thing. Don't forget!"

The team nodded and broke the huddle. Guy grabbed the full-back to tell him to forget about blocking and run a wide curl out of the backfield just in case he needed him.

Guy stood on the thirty-five-yard line calling signals. The *ESPN* announcers thought he was punting. The Cavalier safeties looked to the sidelines for instruction; the outside linebacker over the tight end moved to the outside to rush the QB. The ball was snapped, Guy read the left side, watching the free safety slide that way, and then he looked at his wide out short on the right side heading for the first down marker. The cornerback closed hard, wanting to prevent an easy first down. His fullback headed for the outside right flat, attracting the outside linebacker, keeping him from rushing the QB. Then the final read was the inside wide out taking the strong safety to the goal post. Then, as planned, the tight end was wide open heading for the end zone. Guy lofted a perfect spiral in that direction to the corner where the Terp fans were stuffed in the stands.

Phillip saw the perfect "split the difference" play open up in front of him and jumped up as it was thrown, yelling, "Touch-down! Terps Touchdown!"

Tight end Herman Fitzsimmons grabbed the ball like a pillow to hold during a good sleep and walked into the end zone untouched. Guy turned to the sidelines and waved off the extra-point team and pulled his team into the huddle without a celebration for the two-point conversion. He told his outside wide-out on the left side to come closer to the left tackle and for his inside wide-out to play wing back. He told the outside wide-out on the right side to go to the back of the end zone and come across the middle. Guy wanted the inside wide out to do a four-yard box out and the tight end to hook over the middle at four yards. He told the fullback to block and the left inside wide out to block for three counts and then delay into the end zone over the middle. He instructed the outside wide out to run a top-of-the-house to the left end zone's front flag. It was the extra point play Phillip taught him a dozen years ago.

Guy lined up on the eighteen-yard line and caught the snap. He looked to the right, reading the corner coming up on the box out, then the middle linebacker up on the tight end. He surveyed the back of the end zone opening up, but then the safety dropped back into the middle. Finally he checked the left inside wide out, who had just released his block and was heading to the middle. Guy fired the pass to the open receiver who then walked in for the two-point conversion.

The 43-35 victory would be the talk of the college week across the sports scene.

Alex, Sally, and the family met Guy after the game to congratulate him. Guy was trying to keep a low profile as he headed to the locker room. He received permission to travel home with his parents and family. On the way home they found a great restaurant in the Virginia country side to enjoy a great meal and rehash the game.

• • •

When Sally and Alex made it home at 7:34 p.m., they felt refreshed from the great game experience and time with the family. Watching Guy play and seeing Phillip and

Carol so elated from his success gave Alex an incredible joy that he did not know he could experience. It was an insight into the power of performance by someone who is close to you. It is like watching something in the mirror, except it is not the face you see, it is the energy of your tribe that you identify with your whole being. This energy can give one the confidence to succeed in their performance. Guy and Alex did not realize they were leapfrogging performances, now on national stages.

Starting with the Saint Louis series, Alex would set another standard for Guy to admire.

Chapter 59

Alex knew he was ready to start the series Sunday night, especially after going 1 for 16 in the Division Series. His bat was fortunately not needed in the series, as pitching and timely hitting were enough to hold off Pittsburgh. But against St. Louis, his run production would be needed, because St. Louis was the highest scoring team in the league. Travis Tyler would open up on the mound in game one at Presidents Park.

The baseball fans in the Washington area were in new territory cheering for baseball in the middle of October. What they did not know was that millions of fans throughout the country were becoming Presidents fans. Apparently in this election year, it did not matter if you were in a red state or a blue state; cheering for the Presidents was becoming a popular and patriotic thing to do.

The ownership had decided to erect bleachers behind the left field stands, which added three thousand seats for fans. These tickets were available on game day at 10:00 a.m., as well as five thousand standing room only tickets for fifty dollars each, which would bring capacity to almost fifty thousand for the home games. The 8:18 p.m. start would ensure a beer-infused crowd ready to cheer up the home team.

Leah, with her daughter, Nancy, and son, Paul, joined Phillip and Carol at the game. Patty O'Neil had taken care of getting tickets and made sure to visit Paul at his seat before the game. Charlotte and Natalie were guests of roommate Bonnie Bramlett, who was with the *ESPN* crew covering the game. There were plenty of male *ESPN* anchors willing to host the women during the game. Sally sat nearby with her friends, Alexis Tyler and Patty Peterson. Alexis was improving in learning how to handle the anxiety of Travis starting big games. She used her fellow wives for support instead of large amounts of alcohol.

∙ ∙ ∙

    Dr. Henry Walton had met with Alex Santucci after the Pittsburgh series to check on his abdomen and his level of emotion. His physical exam found everything working well. Blood tests taken the previous week found all organs working at normal levels, and his white blood count showed no signs of infections. It had been over a month since the doctor had adjusted his serotonin level and almost two months since he had taken Duloxetine. Alex's pain levels had been reasonable since the operation, he had been feeling some aches since the start of the Pittsburgh series. Dr. Walton gave him a B12 shot, increased his serotonin dosage, and started him on ibuprofen.

    Four days off and the new medication helped Alex feel more alive for the St. Louis series. He was starting to recognize that his mood disorder could mask the changes in his emotions and physical performance of his body. These changes could affect things like his eye acuity or his wrist soreness. Alex was back in charge of his body and was ready to get focused for the national stage.

∙ ∙ ∙

    Walter Johnson's granddaughter threw out the first pitch of the League Championship Series. Her father had passed away in August at the age of ninety-three, hopefully aware of the Presidents march to the postseason. The spirit of his family was felt by every member of the Presidents as Alex shared with his teammates the great history of Washington baseball. He compared Travis Tyler to the iconic Walter Johnson and Bruce Hammersly to the slugger Frank Howard, saying it was their time and moment to create a new generation of Washington heroes for the next century of baseball fans. But for now everyone on the team knew that Alex Santucci was their leader. They were going to follow him on a journey that would lead them into the World Series.

•••

First the offense exploded in Washington, continued in St. Louis with great pitching, and paused for some days off in DC to enjoy the series victory. Then it combined to great heights in New York to start the World Series and then started to finish the job in the nation's capital by going up three games to none.

Alex sat in the dugout in the bottom of the fifth inning of game four remembering the amazing seven-game streak. But it did not help him accept being embarrassed 15-0 at home in front of a crowd of fifty thousand that wanted to be at the ballpark when it happened. Nobody said it out loud yet, but maybe tomorrow with their ace back on the mound they would seal the World Series.

Everyone seemed to have a letdown today. To avoid a shutout, Manager Jackson sent up a pinch-hitter with one out and two on to hit for the fifth pitcher of the day. Unfortunately, Ren Rivera hit into a double play to end the inning. Paul Angelucci started the sixth inning and walked the bases loaded with nobody out. He had not pitched in ten days and was very rusty. Standing at the top of the steps, Charley Jackson knew that he was running out of pitchers and wanted his bullpen fresh to finish the series tomorrow. Travis Tyler would start game five, Lawrence was needed for game six back in New York if it went that far, and Danube Rivers had just pitched yesterday and would be needed for a game seven if necessary. Fields, Taylor, Williams, and Montgomery had already been used. He was hoping Angelucci would gut out the rest of this game, leaving Ramos, Peterson, and Counter fresh for tomorrow.

Unfortunately Angelucci had been nowhere near the plate with his twelve pitches so far and needed to settle down. His pitching coach had run out of things to say.

Alex joined Jackson at the mound. "Why don't you let Paul play third for a while, and I'll throw some strikes and get us out of this inning."

Charley Jackson looked at Alex for a moment, expecting to see a smile to go along with the joke.

Alex had led the Presidents to a four-game sweep of Saint Louis that was more like an ambush, outscoring the Scarlets 42-7. Alex was named NCLS MVP, hitting over .500 with 4 Hrs and 12 RBIs in the series. He had cooled off in the New York series, but Travis and Bruce had taken over in getting the first three wins in the series 3-0, 5-2, and 6-3. Today Tony Johnson was throwing batting practice to the Icons in the first inning, giving up eight runs before being replaced by Phillip Fields, who gave up another five runs by the end of the second.

Jackson noticed that Alex was serious about pitching. His bullpen coach, Wes Coats had mentioned that Alex was regularly throwing under the stands, hitting 99 mph on the radar gun he secretly used on one of his sessions.

After a stare-off with Alex ended, Jackson asked him, "Are you serious, Alex?"

With a matter off act demeanor of someone with extreme confidence who had played out this scenario in his mind already, Alex responded. "Paul's a good fielder and played third at Penn. I'm warmed up already, and I can throw strikes to get this inning over with. Maybe Paul will have success next inning!"

Jackson took the ball from Angelucci and said to himself, "What the hell!"

He looked up at Alex, handed him the ball, and said, "Well, it's worth a try!"

The distant cousins swapped positions, with the baseball world still watching at 10:35 p.m. on Sunday, October 28 and wondering what the hell was going on. The baseball messiah that had led his team to a record-breaking August and had the country following his wedding and his operation, his recovery in September, and a spectacular NCLS performance in October was now going to pitch!

Fox broadcaster Frank Quarters joked that Alex was trying to show up his brother's quarterback performance at Charlottesville two weeks ago.

Vito Valencia came out to check with Alex about signs after his eight warm-up pitches. Alex told him he threw two pitches, both fastballs: a two-seamer and a four-seamer, usually over the plate. The crowd at Presidents Park had been silenced by the rout but now sat up in their chairs to watch their baseball hero throw some pitches.

Alex stood on the mound, drowning out the noise and the tense situation. He focused by imagining playing catch with his dad, Phillip, behind the plate. He first faced left fielder Ty Smith, who took two quick strikes before fouling off a couple. Alex went with the four-seamer and struck him out swinging. Ritchie Urban, the catcher, took three straight pitches down the middle of the plate for strikes. It was the same for the pitcher, B. B. King, who was pitching a shutout and wanted to get out of the batting box and on the mound ASAP. The crowd rose for an ovation as Alex headed off the mound in a dugout that was a live with excitement.

The Presidents top of the lineup started the sixth inning by refusing to make an out. They got six straight hits off King, ending with a three-run homer by Abel Le Mont. King recovered to get the bottom of the order out, including Paul Angelucci, who Manager Jackson kept in, thinking he would get another chance on the mound in the seventh inning. Jackson pulled Alex a side to see how he was doing.

"This is the most fun I've had in years, Charley! Let me face Peters, Uribe, and Martinez. At fifteen to six, what do we have to lose?"

Charley Jackson shook his head and offered no argument. After the team left the dugout for the top of the seventh, he saw something sitting where Alex had been. It was one of those ancient mitts from a hundred years ago. He tried it on and punched it with his right hand. On the bottom it had some writing, which was hard to read. He pulled off his glasses because he was nearsighted and read the handwriting: "To Alex. From The Big Train... W. Johnson." Charley put on his glasses and laid the glove back down where he found it. He thought to himself, Oh my God. Alex is going to win this thing-tonight!"

Before he entered the batter's box, his close friend Erik Peters exchanged smiles with Alex before he got to the mound. Once Alex got on the rubber, it was all business. Erik took strike one and then chased a pitch outside for strike two. Then he attempted a bunt down the third base line that quickly went foul for a strikeout. With his head down and bat in hand, Erik headed to the dugout, smiling the whole way, jealous that his friend was having all the fun. Robby Uribe was a left-handed-hitting foul-off machine, as he sent ten pitches into the stands down the third base line before taking an inside pitch for strike three. He eyed the umpire veteran Hector Morales, who smiled back with pleasure, enjoying the mowing down of the great Icon lineup. Mario Martinez dug in the back of the batter's box, excited to face an "old school" pitcher from the previous century. Alex had an extended, out-of-date, windup before whipping the ball almost sidearm over the plate.

After the game, catcher Vito Valencia said, "It was moving all over the place like a kernel of popcorn on fire!"

Mario nailed the first pitch, lining it done the right field line, just to the right of the foul pole. Then he pulled the next pitch over third base, landing it just foul before it ended up as a souvenir in the stands. Then Alex fired a four-seamer high in the strike zone. Hector Morales turned and struck a pose for strike three! Mario dropped his bat and helmet in the box and headed out to his position at third base.

Hopson and Hammersly, soon to be known throughout the nation as H & H in the lineup, each singled to start the bottom of the seventh inning. Alex faced another ovation as he stepped in the batter's box against a tired B. B. King who was trying to sneak out one more inning to save his bullpen. Alex waited for a high fastball to drive and got one on the first pitch. It was his first World Series homerun and the first one to land in the temporary bleachers beyond left field over 450 feet away. King was done as Manager Chuck Grimaldo came to the mound to change pitchers.

Now the score was 15-9. Charley Jackson was quiet as the team headed out to the field to pitch the top of the eighth inning. It was clear they were going to finish the game-- win or lose-with Alex firing the baseball.

• • •

As the game headed to the eleven o'clock hour, local news across the country led with an update of game four of the World Series after seven innings. Most baseball fans had turned off the game at ten o'clock with New York leading 15-0 to watch a host of great shows on *HBO, Showtime, CBS,* or *NBC's Sunday Night Football.*

• • •

ESPN had Riley Preston reporting at the top of *SportsCenter* what he called, "an unprecedented pitching performance and comeback being led by Alex Santucci to cut the score to fifteen to nine. With this team and Santucci's heroics, anything can happen in two innings. If you are a sports fan, you should be glued to this game!"

The network ratings would show that viewership went from thirty-two million at nine o'clock to eight million at ten, and back to twenty-four million at eleven. Then it rose again to thirty-two million at eleven thirty when the *Sunday Night Football* game ended.

• • •

With nine days to go until the presidential election, even the White House had ceased operations for the night. The president had thrown out the first ball Saturday night at the first home World Series game in Washington, DC, since FDR. Teammates had forced Alex to catch the ball at home plate. When he returned the ball to the president, Alex was told, "It would be great for DC if you sweep these guys!"

Following orders from the commander-in-chief, Alex stood on the mound to start the eighth inning, trying to get his troops back on the offensive. His first objective was facing the three slugging left-handers in the New York batting order. Mike Rexatta, the Icon first baseman, had two homeruns already in the game and was looking for the hat trick. Alex ignored him and fired three four-seamers that made him look silly. Center fielder Allen Bradenton took a strike, then popped up a bunt and then swung at and missed a 98-mph fastball right down the middle of the plate. Rick Shooter, the right fielder, took two pitches for the first 2-0 count against Alex, who then walked off the mound to look at the crowd. They were all standing and cheering every pitch for a team down six runs in the eighth inning. It gave him some focus and an idea for a pitch. He dropped the ball down in his hand to try to throw a changeup and threw the ball over the back stop to make it 3-0.

Vito came out to the mound and reassured Alex. "Hey, no one can hit your two-seam fastball. Just throw it over- they'll foul it or miss it."

Alex reared back and let up on a fastball and caught the corner with an 85-mph pitch. Then he pitched another one on the corner at 85 mph to fill the count at 3-2. Then he let loose on his best fastball of the night at 100 mph causing a swing and a miss by Shooter!

Veteran Jerry Gonzalez started the bottom of the eight with a perfect bunt single down the third base line, catching Mario Martinez asleep. Valencia popped up for the first out, bringing Paul Angelucci to the plate.

Manager Charley Jackson was superstitious at this point about changing anything to the lineup. The *Fox* announcers were roasting him for not pinch-hitting for Angelucci. What they did not know was that Paul had been a great hitter at the University of Pennsylvania. Even though he struck out in his first at bat, Jackson was willing to roll the dice. It paid off when Paul lined a double down the right field line, bringing up the top of the order.

Blake Hopson tried to cut the score in half but struck out swinging, which brought Manager Grimaldi to the mound to order an intentional walk to Hammersly and to bring in the sidewinding right-hander Dutch Dailey to face Santucci. Grimaldi had done his homework and seen tape of Alex's troubles with sidewinders. This was his trump card in the right situation.

The *Fox* announcers were again going nuts about the strategy. "Why would you pitch to the hottest hitter in the universe with the bases loaded when you could avoid it?"

Alex was thinking the same thing. He had been practicing with the bullpen coach, hitting side-winders every day since the Icons won the AL pennant. He made two adjustments: he stood six inches farther away from home plate and prepared for a total vertical uppercut swing to get under the fastball. He measured himself in the batter's box and asked for time.

Umpire Morales, who was having a ball umpiring this game, thought to himself, this is too much fun watching this guy play like a kid on a playground.

Alex was ready as Dutch came to the set. It was easy to see the release point of the baseball as it came to the inside corner, like he imagined. Using his forearms and wrists, he launched his bat into a wicked downward motion and caught the ball perfectly on the way up. It headed to right-center, twisting toward the scoreboard and then the Presidents bullpen, and bounced off the back wall like a perfectly played cut shot in golf.

It rolled on the fake turf to reliever Clay "Bean" Counter, who was sitting on the bench wondering if this meant he might have to pitch the ninth. "Alex sure is trying to make this close," he said as he flipped the ball to fellow reliever Frank Peterson.

Peterson laughed and answered, "Are you surprised, Beans? Really! It's Alex for Christ's sake!"

Alex rounded the bases as tweets went off around the country announcing the 15-13 score. Manager Charley Jackson tried to take it in stride, as though hitting a grand slam and a three-run homer on back-to-back pitches while pitching three innings of scoreless relief was normal!

However, Jackson's nerves were tested when the Presidents loaded the bases with two outs. Jerry Gonzalez, who had started the inning with a bunt single, ran the count to 3-2 against Dutch Dailey. Finally, he got a pitch up in the strike zone, and Jerry hammered it to deep right-center, enough to clear the bases. Unfortunately, Allen Bradenton came out of nowhere and dove in a perfect horizontal pose to snatch it off the ground by two inches. The crowd fell backward into their seats and into that fear that it was never going to happen!

Manager Jackson dropped his head and took a seat on the dugout. A quietly religious man, he said a prayer to the Lord for more faith and patience.

Alex took off the WJ glove he was pounding with vigor during the flight of the Gonzalez liner and laid it back on the bench. He grabbed his mitt and yelled, "Let's go, guys, and shut them down!"

Charley Johnson said to himself, "Lord, is there any doubt!"

Alex felt an urgency standing on the mound at 11:42 p.m. In the back of his head, something was telling him that this thing had to get done before midnight. He remembered watching Phillip play slow-pitch softball on a sixty-five- minute time limit to get the last inning started. It felt like that tonight: after midnight might be too late to win. Maybe his luck would run out at the official end of the day. He knew that it had to be done without fanfare or notice. He thought about all those innings he pitched in Big Train's Backyard alone, playing each inning in his mind, striking out fifteen, then twenty. Every hour there seemed like a minute, trying to play without causing attention to him. One more time, he thought. Let's go one-two-three!

Alex worked quickly and without delay. In all he threw twelve pitches in the ninth inning, all strikes, only three foul balls and three strikeouts, setting a new record for consecutive strikeouts in a row of twelve. The record, when announced, was hardly noticed by the crowd who had been in a perpetual ovation on every pitch and every strikeout. They knew history was within their grasp, and they wanted to get their money's worth.

Alex had them in the dugout by 11:48 p.m. with time left for a rally. Manager Charley Jackson felt a sense of relief when Alex came in to the dugout. Now he could breathe again and finally make a change in the lineup. He told Henson Scott to get a bat and hit for Paul Angelucci to face Icon reliever Mentel Dressen, who had waited four games to shut down the Presidents in the ninth. Mentel had forty-two out of forty-two saves on the year with a 1.23 ERA. He had one pitch, a cut fastball that he had thrown for twelve seasons. This year he returned from a knee injury and looked twenty-eight instead of his current thirty-nine years.

Vito Valencia stepped up to start the ninth inning. Mentel always worked from the stretch and fired his first pitch toward the outside corner-he thought. It took a wicked turn and went right at Vito's right ankle. He popped up quickly and headed to first, glad to give up his body to get on base. Veteran catcher Henson Scott headed to the plate, one of a few major leaguers with a .300 average and three homeruns against Dressen.

Manager Jackson knew to save his last move of the bench for this moment. His inaction for four innings to bat for Paul Angelucci was because if they had to face Dressen to get a run or two, Henson Scott gave them a chance. The *Fox* announcers finally understood the strategy but made no apologies for their previous criticisms.

Henson headed to the plate with one thought in mind: no double-play grounder; stay away from anything starting out waist high or down because it would be unhittable. He prayed that a mistake pitch would be left up where he liked the baseball. He had been in the league for fourteen years, as long as Alex. The last three had been as a backup. This might be it for him. The first two pitches were down for balls. Dressen wanted no part of a walk to Scott, having to face H & H next at the top of the order. He started one outside to the left-hander, but it ended up over the plate. Henson noticed and instinctively drove it with all of his aging power into the Presidents bullpen.

The comeback stunned New York as they watched the score change to 15-15, still with nobody out. Montel took the new ball from Ritchie Urban and kicked at the rubber, trying not to think about blowing his first save of the year. He focused on the next hitter, Blake Hopson, who then struck out on three pitches. Bruce "The Hammer" Hammersly, who was ready to be the Presidents hero for a new generation, battled Dressen to a full count, fouling off five pitches. Then he got a pitch to drive, lining it to center field for a base hit. He rounded first and without hesitation went for second. The throw from Bradenton was perfect but so was the slide by Hammersly, coming in safely for a double. Grimaldi walked to the mound to see if Montel wanted to pitch to Santucci or Mendoza. He left with nodoubt: Santucci first, then Mendoza second, would see his best pitcher before midnight.

Alex Santucci walked to the plate feeling at peace with the clock at 11:55. He would have his chance to play and to finish what he started, to give the people of DC a holiday to remember on October 28. He was calm because he thought it would happen soon and then it would all be over. Before he stepped into the box, he closed his eyes and heard a prayer each from Leah, Laura, Rose, Philomena, and Theresa wishing him well. He felt the hard work and sweat from Phillip, Gene, Guy, Geraldo, Stephano, and the elder Alex ooze from his pores. He opened his eyes and felt the deafening sound from the crowd swirl around him like a baby's blanket.

He laid his bat on the plate, then on his right shoulder, and extended his hands. The pitch entered his world for a moment, and then he swung his bat and felt a union with the ball. When he looked up, he saw a two-hopper spinning toward shortstop Erik Peters. Hammersly had to watch from second base as Peters, playing deep, charged the ball. Like a grasshopper fleeting through the grasses, the baseball flew quickly and bounced off his chest and into his glove. Erik recovered and fired to first, missing the soaring Santucci by an eyelash.

Carlos Mendoza came to the plate two minutes before midnight ready to rumble. He rolled on the first pitch and hit a chopper toward third base, where Mario Martinez was playing even with bag, ready to start a double play. The baseball found a special spot in the grass for its second bounce on a concealed, tiny, protruding rock never to be found that gave the baseball freedom from the glove of Mario Martinez and launched over his head into left field. Bruce Hammersly, on his way to third base, changed his approach from a slide and started a wide turn toward home. Alex headed to second base, watching left fielder Ty Smith, who was standing nowhere near the baseball since he stopped, mistakenly thinking Martinez would easily field the routine double-play grounder.

Alex stood on second base watching fans jumping the rails, and heading toward the infield. The Presidents dugout exploded to mob Hammersly and Mendoza, all jumping and hugging in unison. Alex fell to one knee, holding his forehead in his hand, thanking the "Big Train," "Hondo," and his family for their help. He rose to his feet to join his teammates, and the fireworks exploded as the night ended at midnight and a new day of hope began!

Chapter 60

Thanksgiving morning started with a light mist of precipitation trying to mature into a nourishing rainfall, which was needed after a couple months of dry fall weather. The temperature was a wet thirty-eight degrees and expected to sneak up to forty-eight degrees by the afternoon. Alex had been up since 2:30 a.m. on this Thanksgiving holiday, Thursday, November 22, fighting jet lag from three weeks in Italy after the World Series win in late October. The festive parade held on Halloween went down Pennsylvania Avenue to the US Capitol building, where 777,000 people completed three days of hard celebration with teammates, family, friends, and fans.

Since he awoke, he had been bundled in a blanket in front of his new gas-fueled fire pit in the middle of his deck, under a moonless sky, reading the final chapters of the novel *11/22/63*. During his honeymoon in Italy, Alex's cousin Joe had put in the stone-encased heat source as a wedding present from all the Finelli's. It was a gift for a couple with everything and a welcomed surprise when they arrived back in town late Tuesday night.

He came to the final pages of the novel at six-thirty wondering how the character dealt with living in the past while knowing the future. He had experienced some of those feelings for last three months of the baseball season. Now with the season over and being with Sally, he felt settled with the past and had no concerns about the future. His immediate concern though, was waiting for the sunrise at 6:59 a.m. so he could go for his morning run.

Catching up on his e-mail messages yesterday, he noticed one sent from Phillip reminding the family and friends about the Thirty-Third Annual Turkey Bowl at Parkwood Elementary's field. As early as he could remember,

Alex would go with Gene to the Ayrlawn field to watch his adoptive father play touch football on Thanksgiving morning with some friends. Gene stopped playing in 1985, but Alex started the next year and then joined Phillip's game in 1992. This would be his twentieth Turkey Bowl with the Finelli's, having missed one due to a post-season baseball trip to Japan.

The Finelli game was special because it included everyone who wanted to play. It had special rules: an eighty-yard field with ten-yard end zones and first downs every sixteen yards. No kick-offs, and drives started on the sixteen-yard line.

Everyone was eligible to receive, and no rushing until the QB received the ball. All females and kids under twelve got a free down every time they caught a pass or ran with the ball. One-hand touch, except kids were allowed to be picked up and given a hug if they had the ball. This year with the weather being a deterrent, only the serious football players would be showing up.

Alex received a text from Charlotte at 7:00 a.m. saying she was leaving Natalie's house and was bringing a friend. They would meet halfway at the Bethesda Community Store at Greentree and Old Georgetown for coffee.

• • •

Alex arrived first at the tiny, old, two-room structure of hardly more than three-hundred square feet. All the patrons and store owners tried to act like they did not know who Alex was, but someone always had to recognize him and congratulate him on the World Series win.

"I hear you went to Italy for three weeks with Miss Sally. How was it? Did they know you over there?"

"Just got back Tuesday, it was wonderful seeing my family's hometown. And it was nice not to be noticed except by Presidents fans-who, by the way, are now everywhere!"

Everyone chuckled and wished him a happy

Thanksgiving.

Charlotte showed up with her friend right behind her. Patty O'Neil looked ready for some football with her lovely red hair in pig-tails over her Presidents parka. They both were dying for some coffee and joined Alex who was outside sitting at one of the tables sheltered from the light mist. They had both spent times recently with their families in Ohio but previously had taken two weeks to Aruba for some serious tanning. They both looked very healthy and beautiful.

They all headed out for the three or so miles to Parkwood field, each carrying small backpacks with cleats and an extra set of clothes. After the first mile, the three of them felt warmed up and enjoyed the cooler temperatures for the rest of the run. They came up the back way to the Parkwood field from Franklin Road past the basketball courts where the original homerun softball was discovered.

At eight o'clock, there were a group of young adult males in their twenties running on the field and throwing a football. Phillip and Joe had the field marked off and held a permit for eight to eleven o'clock. They stood on the side of the field trying to stay warm when Alex joined them with Charlotte and Patty. "All right, some fresh meat for the game!" Cousin Joe bear hugged Charlotte and Patty at the same time. "You guys are crazy to be out here. You must be Patty; I saw you at the wedding!"

Patty felt officially welcomed and grabbed a football to start throwing with Charlotte. Both women were tomboys who were very athletic and loved to play football.

"I think my dad and Guy are coming, but that might be it," Cousin Joe said.

Just then his father, Anthony, was heading down the hill from the front parking lot with Guy right behind him.

At the same time, one of the macho types on the field came over to talk to Phillip. "Hey, you old guys want to take us on? We'll give you a couple touchdowns if you want to play for a couple thousand bucks or so!"

Phillip looked at him without a smile. "How many guys

you got?'

"We got eight guys, and we'll play touch if you want, since you got a couple of girls!" Phillip responded with confidence, "I'll tell you what—we play seven-person, one-hand touch. No kickoffs. Rush when the QB catches the ball, and we'll give you two TDs for as much money as you want to give us!"

"Oh, man. You must be trippin', old man. You got a deal, two grand, all right!" The macho man headed back to his friends, laughing, already counting his money.

Phillip, caressing the football, walked out to the field along with everyone except Alex. He told the macho boys it would be forty-minute halves, running time, and the old men got the ball first. They stood near the goal line, huddling up. Guy and Joe silently smiled at each other as Phillip organized the huddle.

Uncle Anthony would play center because he could snap the ball back fifteen yards like a bullet. Cousin Joe would be a beast at the slot or tight end. Phillip appointed Charlotte and Patty at blocking backs, figuring they'd be able to delay out of the backfield, catch every ball, and always be open.

Knowing that Guy was uncoverable by these clowns, Phillip looked at him and asked what side he wanted to play flanker.

He answered, "Either side is fine, Dad. Just check with Alex."

Phillip looked up from the huddle a bit confused and asked, "Where the hell is Alex?"

On the sidelines, Alex had taken some time to tape his ankles and knees, just to be cautious because of the weather. Now he was finishing tying the laces on his cleats. He stood and put up his hood. Alex stayed on the sidelines a minute, feeling a Deja vu as he surveyed the situation. He looked on the field, not quite sure what was going on or who they were playing.

Finally, Phillip stepped out of the huddle and called him over with a wave. "Alex, we need you!"

Alex felt a tingle in his stomach and looked up to the sky

to see his dream. "I hope you guys are having as much fun as I am this morning."

As he trotted onto the field, one of the macho men recognized him and said a few cuss words to his friend who made the bet.

Alex joined the huddle and looked at everyone with a smile, seeing their eyes wanting to connect with him. A new friend, a found step-sister, a half-brother, a first cousin, an uncle and his father, all of them together, creating, a pure feeling of joy for him. He put his hand in the middle of the huddle for everyone to join together and said with the conviction of a truly happy man, "It doesn't get any better than this!"

CPSIA information can be obtained
at www.ICGtesting.com
Printed in the USA
BVHW041111040423
661730BV00001B/32

9 781088 127599